CHRISTOPHER A. SALVO

HENRY WILSON
and
AREA 51 SECRETS

20 Twenty
Literary Group

WARNING
MILITARY INSTALLATION
OFF LIMITS TO
UNAUTHORIZED PERSONNEL
AUTHORITY: Internal Security Act, 50
U.S.C. 797
PUNISHMENT: Up to one year imprisonment
and $5,000 fine

TABLE OF CONTENTS

CAST OF CHARACTERS

Mary Kent an office executive, heads the secret <u>**U.S. Department of Extraordinary Situations and Events**</u> (DESE)

Jack Henigson is semi-active agent with the Area 51 personnel with carte blanche on entry/exit of the **Area 51 facility.**

Mrazy Xilx is an alien body transitioned to a "Sean Connery type" and is the spaceship Admiral from the planet Ida.

Elizabeth Sam is copilot of the spaceship; **Black Lightning** is Elizabeth Sam before changing from Cat to Human Form.

Henry Wilson is the main character around whom adventures occur.

Seemore Manlein is a four-and-a-half-foot gnome from Norway, inducted into DESE.

Hepseva Manlein is the towering four-foot two-inch-tall wife of Seemore. They both love Southwest turquoise gems.

Wicca Dragon is one of the head witches who lives between a magically expanded wall partition at a local "Meetup Bar."

Seated One more than a witch. Comes from underground, arrives at witches' functions seated centered at "Meetup" fires.

Younger One is a witch who is totally solicitous for the comfort and host of the "**Seated One**".

Juday DuMealyworm is a very beautiful female witch who acts as a barmaid and who changes from Parakeet to a barmaid .

Miguel Barberry is the host of the "Merry Meet" where evil witches meet their master.

Maggot Caprae Miguel Barberry's associate

The Guest is the **Seated One**, the master of evil who sits on the chair of fire.

Matt Ovlas is a good friend of Henry Wilson with whom magical events, both incredulous and frightening, occur.

Wyatt is the converted name of **Eddy Erp** and a good friend of Matt Ovlas. They have several "spell attacked" adventures.

Frank German is a hero veteran and DESE volunteer, sought out by Mary Kent because of his military qualifications.

Wispy Whisperers are almost transparent, other worldly spirits who influence thoughts from bad to good.

Peganni is the offspring of the fabled Unicorn and flying Pegasus who travels at the "**Speed of Spirit**" and *invisible* in flight.

Larry Carl is another enlisted veteran in fighting off the assault on our country.

H. Brad Gaunt or HB Gaunt, is of military background who, after meeting Mary Kent, becomes an agent of DESE.

Members of Reference Groups: Glenn Kohen, Kathy Lewiesle Scott,

Peter Swain, Hercules Canue, Brad Barker

CHAPTER ONE
HENRY WILSON

It was a dark and stormy night.

This is the way so many stories start, or at least the way the spooky ones are supposed to start. Does that mean that this story is to be spooky? We will see.

Very few do start that way because the phrase is so much of a cliché. In this case, the opposite is true. It was instead a bright sunny day with very few clouds and almost no chance of rain. It had not rained for several weeks now, and the massive estate lawns were starting to show tinges of yellow from the drying grass. The temperature/humidity index was 105. People and animals were suffering and some already perished. Henry approached the Victorian house that was near the end of his paper route.

The atmosphere was virtually suffocating and the plantings around the house were starting to wilt, and their leaves were beginning to droop towards the dry earth. Several leaves had already made their journey and lay there, yellowing even further and approaching the dark, brownish color of wrinkled and curled up dead leaves. Fortunately, there were only a few plantings and shrubs. The house was only sparsely planted and many of the basement windows were easily visible from the outside as a result.

The front of the house had a raised porch, and several steps were needed to reach it. It had an elaborate gingerbread trimmed set of balusters joined by a top and bottom railing. The floor of the porch also showed areas where the painted surface showed aged layers of paint, most recently covered was its' newest layer.

The house is situated on a hill and quite a bit away from several more recently built houses on the old estate grounds. The house was an old Victorian building with that fancy gingerbread type of molding trimming the roof lines at the front and rear gables. The house was recently painted to make it more in tune with the newer houses in the area. The color was an attempt at modernizing the building with the body of the building being a light to a Wedgewood blue with the gingerbread a medium forest green color. This was probably a common choice for old Victorians when the feeble, ineffective attempt at modernizing fails.

The "widow's walk" at the top of the building was a different color. Its vertical balusters were of gray coloring on one surface and alternating with the green on next. The top railing covered ages of old chipped paint with a covering of a gaudy, bright gold paint, but not gold leaf. The walk further set the building apart from the newer houses because none of them were that high and none had a widow's walk. The balusters and railing matched the coloring of those at the porch level.

It did not work. The color combinations were of no help. The house still looked old and the attempt to change its appearance to a modern look totally failed its goal. The windows were very long. They approached the ten-foot height mark and supplemented the twelve-foot ceilings inside.

The approach to the house was a wandering, multi-colored flagstone walk, with multi-colored and varied perennial flower plantings on either side. This could have been attractive if the weather had not been so dry. Even here, the flowers were wilting, and some had already dried up badly because of the lack of rain or even watering by the house's occupants, if there were any. Even the Wisteria Vines had wasted away and some still withering flowers and leaves were trying to hang on.

As you approached the front door you saw that the top half was glassed, and the lower half was of paneled wood with a modern type brass mail slot about twelve inches long. Most houses of that vintage were full glass matching the long windows and never with a mail slot. Mail slots were much later so it is most likely that the door was a replacement and certainly much newer than the rest of the building exterior. None of the glassed areas were thermo-paned, or even double glassed, a departure from the wiser building techniques of today. There were no double-paned insulating windows and "E" glass was not there at all , even as an afterthought. The interior of the house was then drafty in the fall and winter and hot and steamy in the summer. Today was very thick, hot, and very steamy. The phrase "you could cut the air with a knife" applies.

The street on which the house was located was totally deserted. Not a person, bird, dog, cat or even butterflies or other bugs could be seen. Nothing. It was as though there was no one or any living thing on the entire length of this plain and otherwise uninteresting street. It was ominous.

Henry had been a paperboy for a several years now. He started after his thirteenth birthday. It was a challenge at first, but now has almost completely changed into a comfortable routine which meant that the trial and test phase of the new job had passed and now he hardly had to think about what had to be done to be a success. His route included the apartments on Richbell Road in Larchmont but also included the Veterans of Foreign Wars building on the Boston Post Road and individual houses on the streets on the other side of the Post Road.

He sometimes would roll the newspaper up tight and bind it with a rubber band. Rubber bands had to be bought and that meant he would need to spend money he really did not have. Soon he learned how to roll up the paper, fold the ends, throw it twenty-five feet onto a porch, walk or sometimes he would even place it into a mailbox or mail slot. Occasionally, he'd miss though, and the paper would wind up in a bush or hedge, but rarely now, since he'd been practicing with a two foot diameter trash can in his back yard. He still sometimes used rubber bands in certain situations, but rarely if at all.

Six Wisteria Lane was different though, especially since the installation of a new mail slot. Although his paper tossing had improved to near perfection, he was not so good that he would have been able to toss the paper directly into a mail slot from the street. Jack Henigson insisted that his paper is to be delivered directly into the building. They did not want it left outdoors exposed to the weather. Part of the reason was that since Jack Henigson became confined to his wheelchair, it was difficult for him to brave the elements.

It was not part of the regular routine to deliver directly to a patron's house, but Jack Henigson rewarded him well at each Thursday collection. He did not mind, and the extra money was very nice. The Henigsons never stood him up on collection day, unlike some of his customers. Some would suspiciously not answer the door and their curtains would move almost imperceptibly. The disappointed Henry would then need to leave the Thursday paper and try to collect each delivery day thereafter. Eventually he would catch them at home and get paid, most often without any tip at all. Sometimes it would be several weeks before he could catch the wayward clients.

The Saturday after collection Thursday was accounting day. He would need to go the main paperboy office and turn over his collection monies to the Mamaroneck "Daily Times" delivery managers and whatever was left out of his "bill" was his. Therefore, he would need to carry the non-payers until they paid. Then it would be all "profit". It was always a mixed blessing. He felt badly about his dishonest customers but then he felt good that their late payment was all his since he already paid his paper bill. He would owe nothing on their accounts.

Today was somehow different. The empty streets and no visible life signs seemed threatening in some unfathomable way. Jack Henigson himself received the paper from Henry this time. This was highly unusual indeed. Henigson never before did this, although he would meet Henry at the door on some Thursdays when he would tip him handsomely besides paying his bill in full. Meeting Henry directly on the porch on a Thursday was a rare event but never on other days so what was the occasion for this unusual event? Henry asked himself. However, there were no answers coming. He would need to wait.

Mr. Henigson reached up and opened the door from his wheelchair and cheerfully said "Hello there Henry! How have you been? I have not seen you for a whole month. Is everything all right with you?"

Henry was surprised at the unusually friendly inquiry but replied "Yes Mr. Henigson, everything is great. I will be restarting school right after the summer vacation, but I will continue with my paper route so I'll be seeing you now and then."

Henry then handed Mr. Henigson his daily paper and they gave each other a big smile. Henigson paid Henry for the week's paper bill and added an amount that was equal to the bill as a tip. Henry was awestruck. Jack Henigson then took the paper in his right hand. He undid the rubber band, which kept it rolled up, with his left. He unfurled the roll and opened to the front page. There it was.

The 'DAILY TIMES" headlines read: "HEAT WAVE KILLS 3" Three people, Moses Tarkington, 78, of Riverside, Peter Sherrington, 90, of Brewster and Mary Kent, 56, of Larchmont succumbed to either heat exhaustion sometimes followed by a stroke, or both, and died as result of their inability to cope as excessive heat indexes approached 108. The article followed with details of their lives, surviving relations and funeral arrangements. It then told of the number of people who had to have emergency treatment for heat stroke and exhaustion, some of whom had to be hospitalized and re-hydrated. The paper issued warnings that young children and older adults should take steps to protect themselves from the heat wave by drinking plenty of fluids, especially water and staying out of the heat, preferably in an air-conditioned place. The paper also commented on caring for pets as well.

Of particular interest was the death of Mary Kent who had worked in the Department of Extraordinary Situations and Events. She was the youngest of recent heat related deaths and not really in the range of the debilitated elderly who were most likely to succumb. Her death was outside the norm but not viewed as suspicious. Her department was a clandestine government organization, not unlike the CIA, which dealt with events ranging from extraterrestrials to possessed persons and all unexplainable events. Whatever could not be explained, scientifically or otherwise was in the realm of the DESE, and no other department.

DESE dealt with events deemed damaging to public safety, especially when such occurrences would damage sensitive and vital US interests. DESE did not deal with miracles or unexplainable events that were beneficial but only those that were destructive. DESE reported directly only to the president and did not need to share reports with the FBI or the CIA despite the new regulations for interdepartmental cooperation post 9-11.

DESE was outside the Department of Defense, the Department of Homeland Security, the Department of the Interior, and the Environmental Protection Agency (EPA). DESE was a department important enough to have its own offices and autonomy. It was subject only to presidential control and approval. President Kennedy who acknowledged the existence of Area 51 created DESE. It was later supported by President Johnson after the events of clandestine Area 51 became public knowledge. However, that this department even existed was less known than the CIA.

The length of the heat wave was extraordinary. Heat waves were not unusual because they occurred every now and then. This one had the added characteristic, along with high heat, of extraordinarily high humidity, but over an extended period. The duality of extra high heat with extra high humidity did the trick and produced the tragedies of death, physical personal disablement, and disruption of all types of utilities and other public services.

He first saw the headlines, drifted a fast survey of the front page and his eyes stopped for a long instant and focused on the lower left hand corner of the paper. His attention shifted to a small paragraph on the front page where a small, boxed directory of what is contained inside the paper along with a synopsis of the weather. It was then that Jack Henigson did a double take.

Henry saw that Henigson appeared disturbed and asked "Mr. Henigson, are you all right? Is there something I can do?"

Henigson saw Henry's concern and smiled a big smile at Henry. He then quickly shook his head saying "no" and added a vocal "No, Henry. It is just that I am troubled that this heat wave has lasted so long and caused so many people so much misery. I am sure that it cannot last much longer and will break soon.

Thank you for delivering my paper. I am happy that I will now be seeing you weekly on your collection days. I will be around and looking forward to tomorrow's news.

Goodbye. See you later."

Henry was relieved. Henigson appeared shocked and surprised at the same time, but Henry thought that he might have fallen ill, especially since he apparently was not in the best of health, being confined to a wheelchair, but was happy that he was all right.

Henry said "goodbye" and the door closed. Henry turned and continued his paper route.

CHAPTER TWO
ELSEWHERE

The full moon shined brightly on this warm May 23rd night in an isolated section of the Smokey Mountains located between Tennessee and North Carolina. It was so bright that one could easily read a newspaper. In an open meadow ringed with great evergreen trees, so that it almost appeared as a private banquet hall, were several hooded people. They stood around a moderately flaming campfire, not big, but quite pleasant. There was a faint chanting and some almost monotonous, low toned singing. It really was not heard beyond a distance of one hundred-fifty feet away.

In the middle of the fire was a small black cauldron that contained about three gallons of liquid. There was a bubbly liquid in it which was greenish gray in color and quasi syrupy, but it was not maple syrup.

The witches were preparing for the summer solstice when the earth's new life comes into full flower. At the same time, they were discussing preparations for the fall Samhain Celebration that was handed down from the Pagan Celts. This was a celebration of the Wicca. The witches knew that their fellow witches were carrying out this Sabbat in other parts of the United States, but in this part of the USA, the witches were in great enough numbers to have developed a nicely sized coven. In other parts of the country, covens were harder to grow because there were just not that many witches in those areas.

Head witches, Rick Mantiny and Dioti Covingten are very proud of their roles in life. They are proud to be in harmony with nature and at peace with the forces of nature and mother earth. Along with them were Amber Nightraven, Morgan Ravenwood, Silver Moonstone and Krystal Morrigan.

As though the cauldron and its fire were not enough for them to cast their spells, they lit five candles at the five points of a star, or the symbolic pentagram which they held as a significant Pagan Earth symbol.

Dioti and Rick were deep in concentration and thought regarding their spell when Dioti said to Rick, "I wish we had more of our coven here so that our spell would have even more spiritual power. You know the saying: "Many hands make little work". It also applies here in a sense. The more members we have in our coven, the greater the power of our spell. Its power is in direct proportion to the number of Wicca we have in our coven practicing our Craft and following the Rede."

The witches now each drank from their cups the strange brew that boiled before them, but now down to a simmer. They laughed and happily said to each other "Merry Meet" and then prepared solemnly to recite the Witches' Creed or the Rede of the Wiccae, which creation is generally credited to its author, Doreen Valiente.

Dioti Covingten and Rick Mantiny put down their cups and crossed their arms over their breasts and then started reciting the words of the Rede, softly at first and then as if a choir, or an ensemble, the rest of the witches closed a circle and joined in. As they did, they were illuminated by a fire, which grew eerily brighter with each additional sentence said, but neither larger nor higher. They recited the words of the <u>Rede:</u>

"Hear now the word of the Witches, the
secrets we hid in the night,
When dark was our destiny's pathway,
That now we bring forth in the light.

Mysterious Water and Fire, The Earth
and the wide-ranging Air,
By hidden Quintessence we know Them,
and we will keep silent and dare.

The birth and rebirth of all Nature, the

passing of Winter and Spring,
We share with the life Universal, rejoice
in the Magical Ring

Four times in the year the Great Sabbat,
returns, and the Witches are seen,
At Lammas and Candelas dancing, on
May Eve and old Halloween

When daytime and nighttime are equal,
when sun is at greatest and least,
The four lesser Sabbats are summoned,
again Witches gather in feast.

Thirteen silver moons in a year are,
thirteen is the Covens array,
Thirteen times at Esbat make merry, for
each golden year and a day.

The power has passed down the ages,
each time between woman and man
Each century unto the other, ere times
and the ages began.

When drawn is the Magickal circle, by
sword or athame of power,
Its compass between two worlds lies, in
the land of shades of that hour.

Our world has no right to know it, and
the world beyond will tell naught,
The oldest of Gods are invoked there,
and the great work of Magic is wrought.

For two are the mystical pillars, that
stand at the gate of the shrine,

And two are the powers of Nature, the
forms and the forces divine.

And do what thou wilt be the challenge,
so be it in love that harms none,
For this is the only commandment, By
Magick of old be it done.

Eight words the Witches Rede fulfill:
If it Harms none, Do what Thou Will!"

After recitation, they merrily and happily socialized and drained the cauldron's brew that gave them enough power virtually to make them not only happy, but also almost glowing in the moonlight. Faces and clothing both cast an iridescent eerie light green glow. And so the night went on until near sunrise. Fellow Wiccam said goodnight to each other before the sun had a chance to cast its light on their bodies. For some reason their celebration is traditionally always to end in darkness so that their desires would be successful. So it was that Amber Nightraven, Thirsty Ravenwolf, Morgan Ravenwold, Krystal Morrigan, and Silver Moonstone said "goodnight" to Dioti and Rick both of which set a spell to close down the fire and wipe all evidence of their celebration away at the single stroke of a hand wave. A wand is not necessary for such mundane, basically household types of spells, they both agreed. Two witches with the same goal and a hand wave at the same moment had more than just enough power to accomplish the task.

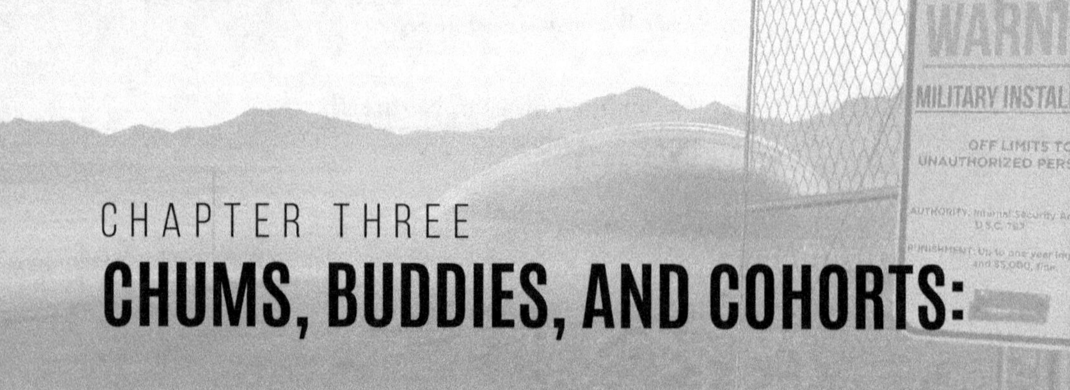

CHAPTER THREE

CHUMS, BUDDIES, AND COHORTS:

Henry left Jack Henigson's gate and continued on his way. Henry was virtually the end of his paper route. As he exited the street, where Jack lived and continued on his way home. He met his best pals, Joe King, Vic and Gordon Velardi. They were all fellow classmates at the Barry Avenue School and they "chilled out" together. In translated terms, "chilled out" means that they were in each other's company, which they greatly enjoyed and were just being themselves without fear of criticism or correction.

Their lives were carefree, and they were quite a happy lot, running, laughing and playing. They especially liked to play catch and would get together on an afternoon either when the weekend began or, if during the week, then after school, weather and homework permitting. Things always changed when Harold Murrow's sister, Maggie, joined the group. She was always the catalyst for change. The boys always behaved when she was present.

The boys also liked to play "stickball" on Hall Street. This is a street that has a minimal amount of vehicular traffic. That was no problem. Stickball playing was very nice. The bases were at the front door of Laverty's house, the start of the driveway at the Camarella's house and the corner of the street. Home plate was a beat up, flat garbage can cover laying in the middle of the street which would clang both when the batter left it for first base and when he arrived coming in from third base, completing a home run.

Henry and Joe both had a common interest: homing pigeons. Joe had about twenty and so did Henry. The pigeons were very interesting. They would produce a small egg, about the size of a robin's in a small square box, several of which lined the walls of Henry's pigeon coop. The pigeons that had an egg in the nest would always find their way back to the coop, no matter how far away Henry would take them.

These pigeons were homing pigeons, and they would always find their way back to their nest. The egg, or newly hatched chick along with mom and dad, was now a family. It was not necessary for the egg to have hatched. Its very existence testified that the pigeons mated. The mated pair is true to each other for life. Each took turns sitting on the yet un-hatched eggs. They would have several chicks a year.

The interbreeding of pigeons led to so many different varieties. The "Isabellas" are very pretty and have a light pink/orange/brown color with darker barred wings of the same color. They are delicate birds. The "King" pigeons are the opposite. They are much larger than the "Isabellas" and exhibit a solid white color. Henry periodically would check the nests to make certain that no eggs cracked and were fouling up the nest. At the same time, he would make sure that none of the babies had died or were injured. These things almost never happened.

However, one late afternoon, as Henry and Joe were looking at and checking one of the King pigeon's nests, he would have sworn that its eyes glowed an intense, projected red-orange which seemed to radiate and brighten the darkened pigeon coop. The pigeon stared directly into Henry's eyes where he sent the beamed light ray. Henry did a double take and guessed that the event was a result of the sun's glare into the coop. Joe was with him at the time and both boys turned to each other in both shock and amazement.

Joe said, "Did you see what I saw? It was weird! What was that?"

Henry answered, "I did. I guess it was the sun's reflection in the bird's eyes. What else could it have been?" He continued, "Strange! I've never ever seen anything like it before though."

The boys both shrugged off the incident as unexplainable and let it go into the ethereal wilderness of wandering youthful thought.

CHAPTER FOUR
MARY KENT

Mary Kent was nearing the age of retirement, but her abilities and extracurricular mystic and abnormal psychology studies super qualified her for her office. She lived alone in a rather ordinary 2500 square foot newly built house on a 100 by 75 foot nicely landscaped lot. Her welcome home friend was her hilarious cat, which both entertained and companioned her. The cat was almost so human that Mary would swear it probably could tell jokes.

Mary Kent's deciphering abilities included everything from voodoo, witchcraft, demons, warlocks, elves, fairies, werewolves, vampires, mythical creatures, extra-terrestrials et cetera. Mary was spending too many extra hours in her office and laboratory working on a hard push encompassing twelve or more hours a day to develop an explanation for the strange weather phenomenon if not to discover a solution. Why was this heat wave not breaking?

Were the sun's perpendicular beams not hitting the earth as close to the equatorial line as it should be? Was it closer to the Tropic of Cancer line? Was the seasonal tilting of the earth itself affected? Was the earth drifting closer to the sun? Could it be due to a change in air mass flow? What could possibly be the reason for such a departure from normal weather patterns? How powerful a force could create such a massive physical event? Could the cause be something other than one of a physical nature? What could have changed?

There were so many questions and each question presented with a multitude of variables so that the paths, which required investigation, were almost impossibly increased. Still Mary carried on. She knew that the earth and all living things thereon were endangered. Although her department did not need to report to, or coordinate with, other government agencies she was always able to access, both unilaterally and secretly, their data and facilities. Her department was considered as being so important that, by revealing her accession to data, she could endanger her research projects. Just as important was her access to those agencies' ties with other international services all around the world, wherever civilization and such data might exist.

She first explored the NOAA. The National Oceanographic and Atmospheric

Administration's database is usually rich with atmospheric and oceanic data. Their historical and daily charts revealed the directions of winds, highs and lows, precipitation or the lack of it, temperature changes as well as their adherence or departure from the norm. The world's ocean currents were also charted. The Atlantic Gulf Stream and the Pacific Kuro Siwoo currents were included as were those of the Indian Ocean. Virtually all the air and water currents around the world were available at the flick of a computerized button.

All this data was overkill for Mary because the excessive heat only involved the North American hemisphere and especially the United States. The puzzler was that the rest of the world was "normal". Things were curiouser and curiouser as Alice in Wonderland would say. It appeared that nothing was happening in the rest of the world except the usual weather patterns. So why was the Northern Western Hemisphere solely affected?

Mary's investigation into air mass drifting and circulation revealed that there was almost no movement or change across the entire country over the entire period. The exception was that those areas in which rain would normally be expected, according to weather standards, did not get that rain. So not only was the country hot but it was also too dry. Large, forested areas in the West and especially in California were hit with more than the usual number of fires. California was struggling to keep multiple housing developments that had encroached into forested areas from being destroyed by fires. This was most true in the Los Angeles area including Temecula, Palmdale, and areas west of LA., and many other places. Not all these areas had trees. Some were just grass and scrub fires, but they endangered houses anyway. Areas in Wyoming around Jackson Hole, Utah and Idaho were also being toasted and roasted by the greater than normal fires. Then there were also the fires in Southern Georgia and Northern Florida and its Everglades.

Mary was still at a dead end. Her invested efforts and time revealed that there was no physical reason for the lack of change in the continent's weather. She started to consider other possibilities, but the question was where to begin.

She started to investigate the mystical side of the problem. She decided to explore from the outside in. That is to say from outside the North American Continent from extraterrestrial influence to voodoo.

She felt she had to investigate in detail the events prior to and those around Area 31 as well as the U.S. space program including the rash of UFOs. Investigation started with research in all the more "common" newspapers such as the "Enquirer" and "Star" and even as far out as the Asheville "Mountain News" and many other papers numbering in the hundreds.

Mary reasoned that the news reported by members of the public was more likely not to be tainted by official maneuvers to hide the truth. She did realize that there was probably some influence among UFO enthusiasts, which could embellish the truth. The general truth had to be contained in the many newspapers from varied places around the country and Canada.

She then searched the files from the Air Force and the Army, which were supposedly melded into files at the Department of Defense. What she found was quite interesting because reports of the same incident had different slants. The public's version held nothing back and even showed original photographs and videos of UFOs and had many eyewitnesses from field workers to doctors and police officers. The military version was much more reserved. They showed reluctance to endorse any of the reports, even though some commercial pilots with earlier military experience also concurred with the public reports. It appeared that the US Government was hiding something. What could it be?

The government reports usually stated that what people saw was a weather balloon or thermal layer reflections of light. The many photographs of disc-like flying saucers and those of multiple lights spread over a wide area, reports from police, experienced commercial pilots were all denied and inadequately explained away and ignored by federal and DOD officials. They fully denied that Area 51 had seen anything more than a dropped weather balloon. There was no UFO and there were no extraterrestrial bodies to be seen, examined or collected at least in the initial reports. Later news reporters and television documentaries in area 51 stated differently for decades. The matter was never acceptably closed and remains open to speculation to this day. Area 51 remains mysterious.

Mary also investigated foreign reports regarding UFOs. She achieved both the same information and misinformation from all the foreign government agency positions as in her own USA. She was not discouraged. This section of her probe was complete. She was reluctantly satisfied that there were no influences outside of this world but remained dissatisfied with official government reports.

CHAPTER FIVE
DELIVERY

It was a sunny summer day with temperatures in the seventies. The "heat wave" had not yet developed and the weather could not have been any nicer. It had rained the night before and that rain stimulated vegetation growth and spurred the blooming of bunches of flowers.

Henry went to the top floor via elevator in the red-bricked Richbell Road Apartment complex to continue his newspaper deliveries. It was sort of fun for him and easy delivery. He'd take all his papers in his newspaper delivery bag, and because he was inside a building, it was not necessary for him to need to roll up or rubber band his papers. All he had to do was go to the top floor and exit the elevator. Then he would take the stairs, which were immediately adjacent to the elevators, and toss the papers as they matched the numbers on the apartment doors.

There were four apartment doors on each floor and there were eight floors. That meant thirty-two apartments but not all of them received newspapers. He would need to put some effort into knowing which apartment received a newspaper and which did not. He would still be able to deliver all his customer's papers in each building in between ten and fifteen minutes' time. He would be much delayed on collection Thursdays because he would need to ring the doorbell, wait for an answer and if the door opened, he would need to find the responsible payer. If the door never opened Henry would have wasted at least two to three minutes at each unopened door. Multiple unopened doors added up to a lot of wasted time. Sometimes he would need to make change. He would need to do that for at least a fourth of his customers. The apartment people accounted for most of those needing change. He rarely received a tip and at least ten to fifteen percent of his customers either weren't home or didn't want to open the door to pay him.

His paper route included two of the seven buildings in the complex, so it took him between twenty minutes to a half hour to complete his apartment house chore. It easily took him twice as long on collection Thursdays.

He would then leave the apartment complex and continue his paper route, cut across to the VFW building via its parking lot and delivered a paper there. Then he crossed the Post Road to the street adjacent and parallel to the Post Road and behind the Lazy Boy building.

This was the road where Mary Kent had her house.

Henry had at least a dozen houses slated for paper deliveries on this street. All the houses were about the same age, having been built as part of a housing development. Fortunately, they were made from different plans so that they all didn't look alike. That made it a little easier for Henry to tell them apart. Of course, the numbers on the houses helped. Thank God that the post office department had some smarts, or was it the city fathers? Not all the houses received paper deliveries although at least eight of them did. The remaining four would receive an occasional free paper to entice future subscription.

Henry enjoyed the change from the apartments where the same delivery to similar doors and similar floors in similar buildings with similar elevators became monotonous after a while. Here he was in the fresh air and sunshine. The pleasant temperature and low humidity made it even more pleasurable. Henry enjoyed these elements.

As he approached Mary's house he was looking forward to her smiling, pleasant and rather attractive face, and cheerful personality. It was evident that no one was at home. Mary's car was not in her driveway. Her black cat was rustling the window curtains to say hello and probably looking forward to Mary's return from her regular workday as well as a quick feeding. Cats are always very active and very social when they are hungry and seeking something to eat. Mary's extended hours were a thing of the future. The future crisis had not yet started. It was slated to increase her time away from home.

The cat's head quickly parted the white sheer curtains at the multi-paned window and peered out at Henry. Ultimately, its entire black body was on the window side of the curtains. It was not a large cat, but it was so black that where there was a shadow caused by the curtain folds, the cat's outline disappeared to being virtually invisible.

When it talked to Henry through the windowpane, it would wink its bright yellow eyes, which appeared as hanging in the blackness of space. The eyes appeared as glowing coals in a charcoal fire. Their brightness against the black body made it seem as though they were lit from somewhere inside the cat. They shined out brightly in a void field of black nothingness. They appeared and disappeared like magic as its black eyelids closed over them in a blinking action. First, you saw the bright yellow glow and then nothing. It was the blackest cat Henry had ever seen.

Then the strangest thing happened. The black cat stood up on its rear legs. It peered straight out at Henry just as a laser beam might. Henry had to shut his eyes because he would have sworn that a light flashed out of the cat's eyes and into his. He felt strange for an instant and then thought he was going blind. He closed his eyes and then he put both hands up to his eyes and rubbed gently. He felt as though the event had changed him somehow and that there was a communication channel opened between this animal and himself. The sensation in his eyes waned quickly and he was back to normal in an instant.

Henry remembered his pigeon coop experience and found the current happening awesome.

He looked back at the window and the cat was still standing. Henry was further surprised when he saw the cat smiling and waving at Henry. Henry did not believe that anything happened and put it out of his mind immediately. He thought, "It's impossible for cats to smile; they just are not built that way. The "waving" was probably that it was chasing a fly or something in the window."

As Henry watched the cat's smile waned and it fell back onto all four legs. Its tail was straight up like an antenna as it jumped down onto the floor and disappeared as quickly as it appeared.

Henry thought, "A black cat moving that fast is like lightning, black lightning for sure!"

Henry noted that the hour was still relatively early in the afternoon and Mary was most likely still at work so pussycat had a little bit more of a wait before dinner. Henry tossed his folded paper onto the porch and continued on his route. He was probably as disappointed as was the cat at not seeing Mary. It was always very pleasant to see her and visit with her on collection Thursdays. She always gave him a tip, which though small was always welcomed by Henry as a validation and appreciation of his services.

Henry completed his route on Mary's street and turned onto Wisteria Lane. Here he would deliver to another twelve houses. Wisteria Lane's houses were varied in design and age. The landscaping went from almost negligible to fancy. The house was not extremely expensive nor was the neighborhood exclusive. Today Wisteria Lane was extra pretty. The houses with nice landscaping displayed flowers at their maximum bloom. The varied colors reminded one of a Kincaid painting with bright pinks, oranges, red and whites all over the place. It was almost fairytale pretty.

Jack Henigson's house was at the far end of the block. It stood out because of its Victorian architecture. Jack was a unique individual. Although Henry rarely saw him, it was always an adventure to speak with him. Henry remembers the one time they had an extended visit.

Such visits with Jack were rare even though he was in his wheelchair. One would think that there was not much in the way of duties a wheelchair bound person had to do, but Jack was always busy doing something. Today was special because Jack and Henry took some time to become more acquainted on a personal level. Jack learned about Henry and Henry learned a lot about Jack.

It turned out that Jack was a very highly educated man. He had all kinds of degrees and had attended many kinds of colleges and universities.

In his early college years, he attended the University of Connecticut at Storrs where he majored in Sociology and Psychology where he gained a dual bachelor's degree. After graduation, his studies were in law at Columbia University in New York City and finally he felt a patriotic call and entered West Point. He graduated as a Second Lieutenant.

Jack saw Henry approaching and shouted out "Hey there Henry! Come on in. I have something to show you. You're going to find this very interesting and maybe even exciting."

As Henry approached, he noticed that Jack was talking to something lower than the hedges, which served as a barrier between the street and Jack's yard. Henry came closer and he could see that Jack had a dog on a short leash. It was not just any dog. This dog had six legs, a short snout and seemed to smile at Henry.

"Hey Henry, did you ever see such a dog?" Jack said.

Henry noted that the dog was very unusual beyond its six legs. Its coloring was unlike that of any other dog he had ever seen. It was multicolored with red, blue, and purple spots, which seemed to glow at times, reflect sunlight at other times and even change their positions. Henry was not only surprised; he was both shocked and amazed at the same time.

Henry was full of questions. "Where did such a creature come from and what was it and why did Jack have it and why is Jack showing this dog to me?"

All these questions were soon to be answered in Jack's own time. Henry would just need to wait.

Henry replied "Never. Where did he come from? He looks like he came from another world, or at least another continent. I've never seen anything like it!"

Jack said "Henry, I'm telling this to you in secret. You must promise me that you'll never reveal to anyone what I'm going to tell you now."

"Agreed." Henry answered.

Jack replied, "I want you to meet Mr. Xlix." The dog bent its two front and two middle legs in a type of bowing down at this introduction. It seemed that the animal knew he was being introduced and maintained a cordial protocol. "Cordial protocol" is strange for a dog. Somehow, it weirdly applied in this instance. Henry felt that this was more than just a dog, because it acted like a person instead. Henry simply chalked his feelings up to his lively imagination. Like the cat earlier, Henry would have sworn that this dog winked at him too! He again shrugged it off and attributed the idea as a figment of his imagination,

Jack continued "Henry, I realize that I've only known you for only a short time, but I've looked into your background and history, and I feel that you are the one person I can trust to help me with this matter."

Jack did not tell Henry how he qualified him for what he had in mind, but he had sources beyond the ordinary. Jack was more than confident that Henry, although only fifteen- and one-half years old, was his "man". Jack knew that Henry was the special person for him and his goals without any doubt or reservation.

Henry said, "I don't know Mr. Henigson. I guess it depends on what the problem is. You know that I must be home eventually and not too late. Then there's school and homework and all that stuff and then there's my paper route too". Henry continued, "You know that I have responsibilities".

"I know all there is to know about you Henry. I know what you like for breakfast, lunch and supper. I know what time you turn off the lights each night and what time you get up, including weekends. I know how you tie your shoes. I know what your favorite color is. I know all your likes and dislikes. I know almost everything about you. There is very little I don't know. I know that you are honest, an intelligent thinker. That you love your country and town. I know that you are an excellent law-abiding citizen.

Whatever is still unknown is negligible. I know everything that is important for our relationship and for what I have in mind for you." Jack replied.

Henry was shocked at these revelations and he really wasn't sure how to respond. His mouth opened, but nothing came out. His eyes widened and his eyebrows rose. He stepped back a bit and started to speak.

"Why Mr. Henigson I am totally stunned. Why in the world would you have any interest in my personal life anyway? I am just a kid. I'm still in school; my education is still ahead of me." Henry replied. "I still am even too young to drive!"

Jack Henigson was not surprised by Henry's reaction. He had expected it. It was characteristic of Henry to act this way. Henry was not angry at this intrusion into his personal life, but his curiosity was triggered. He just wanted to know why. He wanted to know the facts and the reasons that Jack Henigson had investigated him, a young kid, so deeply. While it was true that Henry was "just a kid", he also had a mature and sober side to his intellectual mind. It was not all just fun, games, and using a Walkman or Ipods or MP3 players and the crazy, funky music common to his age group. No. Henry also had an inquisitive, scientific side to his personality which was not obvious even to those who were close to him.

Jack started to explain his situation to Henry. He detailed what he does during the day. There was a great mystery in Jack's eyes. His brow furrowed and knitted together. His eyes narrowed. His expression changed from smiling and cheerfulness to very deep seriousness. His smile was wiped away. He then motioned for Henry to come into his house. As they entered the house Jack checked the outside one last time, looking from side to side apparently to see if there was anyone outside viewing both the exchange and the entry into the house. Jack apparently required privacy for a meeting that appeared very serious in Jack's mind.

Jack started "First, Henry I have been aware of you and the special abilities you possess. Even though you come by our street on a regular basis, and you are going to school, I have been asked by our government to enroll you, although under age, into a secret service of the government. Your country needs you and your special talents in a very special and very important way. I need to know that you will not tell anyone who is not authorized to know the information I reveal to you because this matter is vital to the very survival of the United States and the Northern Hemisphere. In short, you must solemnly swear that whatever secrets I tell you on behalf of our government never gets told to anyone, not even your mother or father or brothers or sisters. This is very special, very secret, and very important and I need your commitment now. What do you say Henry?"

Up to this point Henry respected Jack very much. He always was a straight shooter, honest, generous, friendly, and cheery and so forth. Never-the-less Henry was shocked and did not know if Jack was really a child molester or some other kind of weirdo. It took Henry a few minutes to know his mind and to gather his thoughts. He shifted a little closer to the front door, looked down and then, just as quickly looked up at Jack. The motion took only a second.

Then Henry replied "I don't know what you are talking about. You sound very strange. Are you O.K.? Has the heat gotten to you? Do you want a glass of water? Is there anyone else around the house that can help you?"

Jack replied with a very serious look on his face. Jack replied, "No Henry, I am quite all right. I am not out of my mind. But before I tell you anymore, I need to know if I have your word to secrecy and commitment to your country despite your youth." He went on "I certainly hope that you realize that even this conversation is private and is to be kept secret, and just between the two of us. You can take your time to think about it though. While the matter is urgent, there is no hurry for you to make your decision. That's an oxymoron if I ever heard one." Jack chuckled.

Henry replied "Gee whiz Mr. Henigson, I must be honest. You have surprised me, shocked me and scared me. I'll need to give it some time and I will get back to you, quickly but in no hurry."

Hey!" Jack said, "That's another oxymoron!" They both laughed together.

They each then said "goodbye for now" and Henry left Jack warily. As he opened the front gate, his thoughts hung for a minute on Mr. Xlix. "Strange." He thought. Then just as quickly, thoughts about Mr. Xlix left his mind as an egret flew overhead and distracted him.

As Henry left Jack's front gate and turned into the street, he kicked a stone, whistled and shuffled his way down the street to home. Henry didn't realize it, but he spent more time in Jack's house than he would have believed, but it was now sunset and going into dusk. His parents would be worried if he didn't get home soon. It was late, but hopefully not too late for dinner.

CHAPTER SIX
JACK HENIGSON

We have all kinds of heroes in our day. Some are police officers, firemen, ambulance personnel and other emergency workers. Others are soldiers, sailors, and marines. Still others are the people we meet every day, especially mom and dad. These last two were the heroes in Henry's life, not to minimize the importance of the others.

Henry's mother was a schoolteacher. His father was a Fairfield, Connecticut dentist. They were both educated professionals and hard workers in Henry's eyes. Mom would make three lunches at night before going to bed and then in the morning all had a quick breakfast and dispersed into their different directions.

Henry in serious and deep thought, would say things like "Mom, if the sun is the center of the universe, what are all those stars out there? Are those other "big bangs" too? Are there planets revolving around them too, just as where we are?" Cyndy, his mother, was a science teacher, and her specialty was astronomy and she loved physics too. She always spoke to Henry about the size of space and that it was continuing to expand and had been doing so for billions of years. She spoke to Henry of the "Big Bang" theory of the universe and the formation of the planets and their moons.

Then Henry floored his mother when he added, "Mom, I learned that the Universe is expanding. Is that true? If so, where is it all going? Is there an end to space? Is it related to time? How are space and time related, if at all?"

Mom just looked at Henry and smiled "Henry, if I knew the answers to all those questions on a factual basis, I would probably be working on the space program with scientists who know a lot more than I. Dreaming is a wonderful thing. The world is full of wonder, and I want you to grow up to know all about it. To study the mystery and to learn more and more each day is probably the biggest wonder of them all. So, my son, go on and take up all the mystery in the world and beyond. You will love it!"

Jack Henigson was a hero too. He was a hero in battles first in Korea and then Viet Nam. He won all sorts of Medals of Honor and a Purple Heart. Henry suspected the Purple Heart medal helped him to gain the wheel chair. Jack was not a cripple all of his life. He began using a wheelchair only after the wars.

Jack wasn't going to sit American progress out on his wheelchair. No sir, he had a lot more gumption than that. Jack also had an engineering degree in "Engineering and Applied Sciences" from the University of Rochester in New York. His education included chemical engineering, physics, astronomy, computer science and biomechanical engineering. If that were not enough, he also had studies in psychology with concentration in the para normal.

Jack felt he was too young to sit and stew. He wanted to be part of progress and science. He would never allow himself simply to retire. His mind was too active, sometimes keeping him awake at night even though he felt that his body was bone tired.

When he recovered from his injuries and, after being discharged from the service, he applied for, and was offered, a government job in the DESE. His credentials were magnificent, and he was welcomed with open arms.

He commuted to work two ways. One was in his converted-for-the-handicapped Ford Crown Victoria and the second was via computer, namely tele-commuting. He bought the Crown Vic at a surplus police sale at a good price, most likely because of the mileage on it. But he liked it and the fact that it still had a spotlight on the driver's side and strobe flashers as well. He thought that was fancy and cute and could even be of benefit in an emergency. He bought his computer new (but the government paid for it even though it was his choice). It was the latest with a 400-gigabyte hard drive and 3500-megahertz processor which needed special refrigerant and a fan driven cooling assembly just to keep it from frying itself. It was very fast.

Though it might have appeared to those outside his house that he never left, he really was at work every day, sometimes for as much as ten hours. Just about no one knew this fact, except those in his office. He was able to access all the databases just as Mary Kent was able to do. He had no limitations or reins on what he wanted or needed to do or investigate.

Jack liked his work. In the DESE, all his knowledge came together. He could never have hoped for a job like this outside the DESE. They just didn't exist unless he'd work for a foreign government. He had to wonder and doubted that any foreign government would have such a surreptitious and way-out department as part of officialdom. Working for a foreign government would never happen in Jack's lifetime. He was one hundred percent American. He would be loyal to his country to the end. Jack was a real patriot in the order of John Hancock, Patrick Henry and even George Washington!

Jack had always had an interest in not only the occult and weird magical phenomenon, but he was also very open minded. The possibility that Area 51 basically was the "Stargate" to the universe was very real to him. He doubted that it was anything like the TV program of that name, but that evidence pointed to the realistic occurrence of actual alien visitation.

He coupled that with other evidence of UFO sightings all over the world. In Stockholms-Tidiangen on January 20, 1959, it was reported that eight reliable people witnessed a flying saucer over Stigsjoe, Sweden. It was only 300 meters over Lake Leangsjoen. Unlike most reports, this UFO moved slowly, and the people had a chance to have a good look at it and described it as being as much as eight meters wide with a two-meter luminous ring around it. They had a three-minute study of the object.

On the evening of March 12, 1959, five UFOs were spotted over Storesund, Norway near Bergen by Birger Storesund and several of his neighbors. All five moved overhead in silence, separated both in time and distance from each other, but eventually all were visible at the same time but in different parts of the sky.

Involved in all of this were the CIA, the FBI, and FOIA in the USA only. There were sightings in the Argentine Antarctic as well as in the USA and many other places around the world. All the people who witnessed the UFOs were respected, experienced and reliable citizens from varied walks of life. They were doctors, police officers, priests and airline pilots who were formerly military fighter and transport pilots and from many different parts of the world. How could they all be wrong? Obviously, they couldn't. There were too many of them and there was no connection between them. Each incident was different and separate from the other. The distances between people and UFO experiences were thousands of miles apart. Each incident stood on its own merit.

Jack reminisced and thought about the past. He recalled how his encounter while at Area 51 had him meet up with Mr. Xilx, a very unusual creature for sure. How many six-legged dogs are there anyway? And with varied coloring which changed as did the "horse of many colors" in the "Wizard of Oz" while you were looking at it.

Jack was working for the CIA at the time and investigated the happenings at Roswell, NM. He was in the field going over the area where the earlier reported UFO was to have crashed, but this was the actual site and not the one shown to the public and newspaper reporters after community pressure forced the admission of some responsible persons in the public interest. That area was only a few miles away and the public was limited in their access. The military created a ditch and the false appearance of deeply embedded scrape marks on and in the ground that simulated a crash site. It was all a fake. The public never ever had a clue to the deception. It was bought one hundred percent. The last thing the government wanted was to have souvenir hunters and the curious coming around Area 51 perimeter on a constant basis.

That crash incident happened several weeks earlier. The base personnel, scientists and the military had all completed their investigatory studies of the site involved and wrote reports reflecting their conclusions. They left the area and were finished with it. It appears that, as far as they were concerned, despite all the fear and concern it generated, and the alarm in the 51 facility, that the "official" investigation just put the literal earth-shaking event to sleep as just a larger than usual meteor hitting the earth and shaking up the entire 51 facility. Jack did not buy it and his unique self was sure that there was more to it than the initial investigation reported.

Jack's inquisitive mind was not satisfied and decided to do a little additional search of the actual site himself. One early morning, just as the sun came over the horizon, Jack started out. He liked the crisp dryness of the early western desert air. It stimulated him, his thought processes, and his imagination. He became creative at this hour and in this climate. He loved it and he loved his work.

Dealing with the mysterious and the newness of an unsolved, unexplainable situation was right up his alley. The weirder, the more peculiar and off the normal path of his day a problem was, the greater was his inquisitiveness and his imagination. These qualities were both highly interactive this morning. He just had to satisfy his curiosity. He felt that before the day was over, he would have done just that.

He brought a Geiger counter, a six-inch wide, long handled garden cultivator with six-inch tines on it, a narrow-pointed shovel, a camera, and a small tape recorder for making notes. Then he picked himself out of the four wheeling SUV he used at work and walked a remaining hundred yards to the crash site. All the earlier investigators parked their vehicles in the newly established driveway and the established walking path to avoid the three-inch spiked cacti, snakes, scorpions and whatever. One investigator followed the other and this continued as they walked about the crash site.

Jack, however, was not of the same breed. Jack always stood out and he was an individualist. Jack established his own "driveway" in the desert and his own walking path. It was not in the same direction or path as that of the earlier investigators. The most the other investigators took to the site was only a pencil and pad of paper. Some had cameras, but that was it.

Jack was upset that the investigation was so nonchalantly done. It was as though his fellow scientists did not really feel it was of high importance despite the emergency alarm and all the fear this unknown object engendered. Their general consensus was that the object, despite its speedy entry, was just a large meteorite or something similar.

Jack was not so certain and was very upset at what he felt was a careless investigation lacking thoroughness. An extraordinary event which elicited Area 51 personnel fear of losing their lives and the base as well needed a more intense investigation.

Jack had a nagging feeling that there was more to the fearsome meteor and was not at all a meteor. It was just a sixth sense nagging suspicion. He decided to check out the site on his own. He recalled, when he was with the investigational group that the object had to have crashed creating a straight-line pathway resulting in a grooved trench of varying depths. The earth still showed signs of being scorched, Jack thought, by heat, but he did not rule out radiation damage. The length of the trench was about five to six hundred feet long. It was not that wide, being about twenty-five to thirty feet across. The width of the trench was consistent, but the depth varied by as much as ten feet in spots. Jack unloaded his Geiger counter and noted that there was minimal to no radiation. He first checked the perimeter of the site and daringly jumped into the shallowest grooved trench. He used his cultivator and with a hoe like scraping action he began to dig deeper. He repeated this at each area where the trench was shallow. He went to where the trench terminated. That was where the object has to be, he thought.

Jack did not find much after working for several hours. The coolness of the early morning desert was starting to grow into noonday heat and Jack was not happy about his beginning sweat. He was ready to call it a morning and he was going to leave. He had only one more area in the groove to check, much further ahead and near the most distant area of the crash furrows. He thought, "It won't be a completed trench search unless I check that also. I might as well finish it up right." He went to the distant grooved area and resigned to the task before him. He began to work.

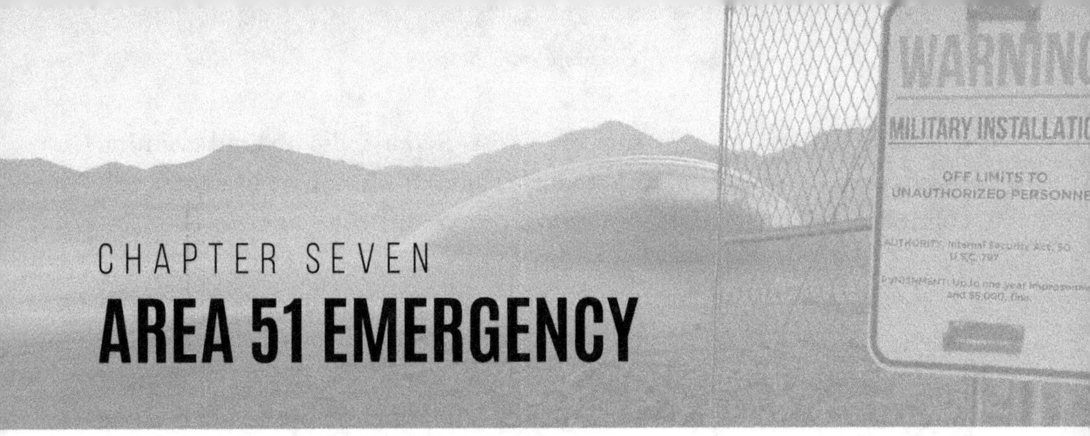

CHAPTER SEVEN
AREA 51 EMERGENCY

Upon tracking the UFO, it became obvious that it was headed for Area 51. That triggered a warning. All technicians, agents and workers at the Area 51 facility heard the sudden alarm. The workers at Edwards Airforce Base surprisingly found themselves terrified. They never had to deal with anything like this. They never expected an attack from any country or any kind of group, military or civil. Little did they know that this was not an attack. There was no radio contact, just silent advancement of this item towards the earth, right over Groom Lake and the Base with no communication of any kind. Just radio silence.

For those aboard the aircraft, the speed at which they were moving did not permit, with a shortage of staff, any attempt at communication from the spaceship. It was more important to try to gain control instead of conversation.

The aeronautical engineers at Area 51 and Skunkworks have been quite happy about their U2 spy plane and the stealth bomber. They had the distinction of incredible creation. The "black" night hawk stealth fighter 117 was quite an encouraging achievement.

The U2 plane flown by Francis Gary Powers was flying at 70,000 feet. It was believed that, flying over the Soviet Union, radar detection did not have that range. Unfortunately, it did, and the plane was shot down. Now, about five or so years ago, they developed another aircraft which could fly at Mach 3.5 or 2700 miles per hour. That is faster than a rifle bullet. The ceiling on that new aircraft, as it was reported at that time, several years ago, as 90,000 feet. It is unimaginable to consider incredulous improvements at this date. One can be very sure they exist. Reports also abound claiming speeds over 5,000 mph on rocket assisted aircraft which have been remotely controlled, but such control sometimes proved difficult.

Despite all the sophisticated developed projects the Area 51 Groom Lake, N.M. facility could produce, it never expected any threats from the sky, yet there it was. The object was moving close to the speed of light which meant, according to Einstein, it would soon disappear and become pure energy. No one knows what happens after that speed is reached. If it slows down for some reason, will it return to its original matter of self or not? No one knows or has the courage to experiment, yet!

The strange, unexplainable, silent, and mysterious object contained living, intelligent creatures. While on earth they were crying "Emergency! Emergency!", those aboard the fast-approaching craft were doing the same thing.

"Emergency! Emergency!" the spacecraft automatic warning system screamed. Managing the craft were two aeronauts working feverishly to slow and redirect the craft. The Admiral, who is the head aeronaut, was managing to slow the craft by redirecting it, but unfortunately only slightly. Slowing it down he had to fight the inertial pull of the earth's gravity and against the speed at which they were traveling. It was an impossible task.

He, in reserved acidic cheer, reported to his second in command pilot with consternation, "I have been able to slow and redirect, but gravitational pull is too great. We are out of control and our systems are not able to succeed in avoiding hitting the planet. Announce the crash warning for whomever is left of our crew."

All those aboard put on their crash gear and protective apparel, including the Admiral.

He then added, with faint hope in frustration, "I will try to minimize impact by using our full reverse thrusters and try to avoid a head on impact by easing our attitude. That will be as if we were making a voluntary landing, which we are not!"

Still, although in despairing hope, especially for those aboard, he added, "The new mineral, Haydenium, in our metal shell material will prevent us from being crushed to death in a metallic sandwich as that metal is extremely strong. Its strength was tested against fracture by thrusting heavy explosive projectiles at it."

Scrambled aircraft, meant to protect the base, could not match its speed. Those trying to minimize its collision damage here on earth by blowing it up realized that the strange craft was travelling at a speed which neither cannon fire nor our fastest missiles could reach it. Shooting it apart was not going to happen.

The three members of the space vessel, still surviving the recent plague they experienced, quietly put on their gear and space suits, buckled themselves in and assumed "crash" position. There was only one staff member left who overcame the unwelcome infection.

Traveling at even their slightly reduced speed made avoidance of an impact impossible.

As the earth was rapidly closing in the aeronauts assumed crash position. There was no hope or time to do anything else.

It seemed like hours, but there it was: impact which created a loud boom and a local shaking of the earth including Area 51. Both those on the base and on spacecraft watched as the two, earth and space vessel, met. It seemed like forever. Then the diving object struck the earth, fortunately not on the nearby base.

It skidded several hundred feet across the earth's surface and finally buried itself in the sand and stopped. As its depth increased, the inertial pull of gravity, now fading and not a factor, eventually stopped, and the spaceship ceased being buried deeper. The sand being loose, and further loosened up by the impact, covered the vessel over and it disappeared. Only a dimple in the free flowing, covering sand was evidence that anything had happened and barely noticeable to the cursory viewer.

After letting a bit of time pass, several security personnel exited their building in radiation and secure clothing to investigate. As it was nearing nightfall, visibility was not efficient. The investigators reported that there was nothing to see. The spaceship was fully buried in covering sand.

Jack Henigson was part of the investigating team. He was not satisfied with the report and thought he could see the otherwise unexplainable dimple on the otherwise flat surface of sand.

He would investigate the "earth dimple" he saw the next day when all the excitement was non-existent, on his own. He was cautious and did not want to let the other members of the facility know. "They had their chance, their opportunity. Now this is my time to investigate as I know how."

CHAPTER EIGHT
MR. XILX

Jack scraped and continued to scrape and hoe. He noted a shiny object about two feet from where he was working and went towards it. As he approached, he noted another shiny object in the same area. He began to uncover one shiny area but found it was attached to the other by a soft material. His curiosity was now getting the better of him and he worked faster and feverishly. The soft material continued and spread to another shiny spot and then another and another. Jack continued in this manner until he found what looked like a leg. He kept being prodded by excitement and saw that the leg, soft material and spots were all attached to what looked like a bulk of some kind.

When Jack completed his excavation, he saw what looked like a spotted dog, but with shining spots and six legs. This dog was unlike any he had ever seen before. Jack thought that the dog was a variant of a coyote affected by radiation around Area 51 and its experiments. It was the size of a Collie type of dog, but its name certainly could not be Lassie! The poor animal probably was in the way of the crashed UFO but the softness of the desert sand in this area most likely prevented it from being crushed. This animal had to be dead, Jack thought, and picked it up in a blanket he had retrieved from his car.

Jack brought the animal to his car. The day was beginning to heat up. He recovered his tools and put them in the back of his SUV. Fortunately, the SUV was air conditioned. Jack always had a great appreciation for the inventor of air conditioning, especially on a day like today. He got into his vehicle and began the trip back to his base.

Jack was driving for about twenty minutes. The AC was working very efficiently, and the SUV was moving along. The "roads" were really expanded trails through the desert. They were not paved and they were not smooth. Jack could barely make thirty miles per hour without jostling all about the vehicle. Then there was his unexpected passenger lying on the floor of the adjacent seat. He did not want to create any more damage to its body by bouncing it around anymore than he had to.

The AC had brought the temperature inside his SUV to about seventy-five degrees, which in air-conditioned comfort would provide almost a chill. Jack relished it. The desert heat brought the heat up to as high as one hundred twenty degrees almost constantly. He was listening to a Sinatra special on radio host Sidney Mark's program. Jack loved Sinatra. He found his style and tones very comforting.

Then it happened. The radio frequency started to drift, which was unusual because the radio station's signal was very strong in this area. It was fading in and out and then changed to static. Jack became annoyed and gave up. He turned down the radio and was intent on listening to the car engine and rumbling road noise.

Jack now became more attentive to the strangeness of road and vehicle noises. The sounds of his vehicle running over this terrain were well known to him. The squeaking, grinding and humming of his engine were like home for Jack's ears. He then started to hear yet a new, unfamiliar, and unfathomable sound. Jack slowed down to see if the sound would decrease. He really did not need to be stuck in the afternoon desert heat out here with a dead dog.

Jack did not hear the sound diminish but instead it started to increase, even though it was still not very loud. It was a humming sound; almost reflective off his engine but it was not that of, or from, his engine. Jack thought of stopping, but the thought of the desert heat and the consideration that he might not be able to restart his engine made him give that thought up. Instead, he decided to continue driving slowly and hoped that he would be able to make it back to the base without breaking down.

The sound did not abate. It definitely was not coming from his engine. Jack was alarmed when he finally realized that the humming sound was coming from the animal to his right. The hairs on the back of Jack's neck stood on end. The hairs on his arms even stood up. Jack was having a very fast "fright, flight or fight" reaction. He did not know if this animal was docile, vicious, rabid or what. He grabbed the tire wrench he had in his back seat and was making himself ready for anything. He slowed the car down even further and put it in "park".

Jack gingerly leaned over the dog with tire wrench in hand, ready to give it a clout should it prove dangerous, and slowly peeled back a corner of the blanket the dog was wrapped in. To his amazement, the dog had its eyes opened. The animal was still humming but also there was more than just that. Strangely enough it also seemed to be smiling at Jack. Jack was so shocked that he dropped the blanket's corner and backed away.

Jack realized that the humming sound the dog was making was the same sound that was coming over his radio. The dog was mimicking the last Frank Sinatra tune! Jack realized that this was not an ordinary dog. Jack had to wonder if this dog was even a dog at all!

Jack could not continue driving until he was sure he was safe from his extraordinary passenger. The SUV motor was still running as was the AC. When Jack determined that the vehicle seemed to be safe and OK, he turned back to the dog. He again leaned over with wrench in hand and was once again ready to clobber the animal if necessary. He began with the same corner and saw the same eyes and the same smiling animal. This time he pulled the blanket half covering the animal off so that he could see the entire animal. The animal did not seem to be injured, at least on this side. The extra legs and the shiny spots puzzled him.

As Jack was pondering what to do next the animal began to stir. Jack started. He moved away from the animal a bit and unlocked his door in case he had to run. To his amazement, the animal began to upright itself. How could an animal be hit by a UFO and lying under the earth in the desert heat for so long even be alive? Much less, how could such a creature have the strength to get up?

Unless the earth covering protected the animal from the hot desert and minimized water loss, the animal would be dead. Apparently, this was not the case. The creature was alive. Further, the coolness of the air conditioning, the motion of the SUV and the ability to breathe air without impediment all reinforced each other to arouse the animal.

The creature jumped onto the seat next to Jack. Jack turned white, froze and just stared at the being. He was amazed that it appeared uninjured. He was happy that the animal did not seem aggressive and hostile against him. Rather, it appeared docile and even friendly. It was still smiling! Jack realized that the smile was real!

Jack said with hesitation and trepidation "Nice doggy, nice doggy. Just sit there and soon we'll be in a nice spot, safe and sound." The dog did not move. It just sat there smiling. What was strange was that the animal did not pant like a dog usually does in hot weather. "Why is that?" Jack wondered to himself.

There still was more. The spots had gained fluorescence and shined even more. Jack offered the animal water in a shallow pan he had in the SUV. The animal quickly slurped the water just like any dog would. It had to be very thirsty indeed. Its experience had to be harrowing. The animal somehow survived miraculously.

Jack soon realized that the animal was not a threat, at least at this time. The biggest surprise was still to come. After the dog had its fill of water, Jack reached over in an attempt to test if the animal was indeed friendly. The attempt to pet it failed. Jack realized that the animal could be hostile. The animal quickly withdrew and lowered itself on its six legs. It did not growl at all. Instead, much to Jack's surprise and additional shock the animal spoke to Jack in a Cockney British accent.

"Sorry about that." the dog said.

Jack's mouth fell open. His eyes opened wide. And he jumped back even further, if that was possible at all. It was. He was all ears and eyes. What was next?

The dog continued, "I am not from your planet. I am from a planet in the area you people call Sirius, the dog star! Appropriately enough." He continued; my name is Mrazy Xilx. You can call me Mr. Xilx. That is what my friends call me! I want you to be a friend to me. You saved my life and I am grateful. Please call me Mr. Xilx and be my friend."

Jack's open mouth opened further, although it appeared as though that would have been impossible because it appeared fully opened already. The same thing happened with his eyes. Even they opened wider. He was beyond shock and although he was pale, he became even paler. He looked as if he were close to passing out from shock.

Jack did not say a word. He was one hundred percent wordless. There were no words which exist that would suffice in a situation such as this. He closed his eyes, took several deep breaths closed his mouth and after a few minutes he was composed. Then slowly Jack opened his eyes, still not believing what had happened to him.

Jack opened his mouth to speak except that no words came out. He stuttered and stammered for a full minute by the clock. Then Jack said "What are you? Who are you? How can you speak? You are a dog and dogs cannot speak. In addition, even if you could speak, how is it that you know my language and that I wouldn't hurt you?

Mr. Xilx replied, "First questions answered first. Last questions answered last." Xilx continued, "I am citizen of the planet Ida which is part of a solar system that circles our sun, Sirius, in a distant tenth orbit from it. The distance is about four hundred thousand earth miles from Sirius. We have found that your earth's climate and atmosphere compares almost identically to ours on planet Ida.

While it appears to you that I have the body of an earth dog, I am not a dog as you have on earth. Nothing could be further from the truth than the thought that I am an earth dog. Us Idaians are more advanced intellectually than you earthlings. Despite our unfortunate crash landing here at planet earth, we were able to make the trip that covered multiple light years. Your people are not even prepared to make a space journey of even one light year!"

"So as far as you're concerned, I am an intelligent being with a self, as well as a thinking and feeling individual with a personality and tremendous capabilities. I am omnivorous, I have likes and dislikes, needs and I am a producer of services. While we are not human, we are a group of Perseids that have evolved on our planet."

Xilx continued, "I have the capability of speech, as you can hear. I can speak many languages from many worlds. Your language, American English, is easily learned over the airwaves and signals from your planet. We have noted that one Al Gore is credited with the creation of what you call the Internet, and we thank him for it because it made our job of understanding your planet easier. All we had to do was "log" into it. Once we did that, we easily accomplished our task. Of course, the development of Bill Gates' word processing set up and certain so-called web sites, such as Alta Vista, created to do translations, made our learning task very easy. The initial problem was to separate one language from another because we would get all your world's radio signals at one time. We first were not sure if it was only electromagnetic and atomic particle noise, but we soon deciphered it into your many languages. Nevertheless, I prefer the British cockney accent. It's so melodic, has personality and not as crude as some of your American accents. So that's how I choose to speak."

'We found your planet and its inhabitants very interesting, especially those who look like us but have never evolved beyond a bark and a wagging tail! Of course, we also have six legs instead of just four!"

Jack was still flabbergasted. He was thinking of what to do next.

It was the weekend and there was not the usual amount of security around his department. Jack became concerned about the safety of this unique creature. He feared that if he took the animal to the laboratory,

It would be imprisoned, poked at and possibly have tissue samples taken from its body. Although testing, scientific, and "medical" examination was necessary along with quarantine, Jack was very hesitant to bring the animal to the lab. It was apparent to Jack that his companion was probably of little threat, although he was concerned about disease transmission and the like.

Jack finally decided to follow through as a scientist should, he brought the creature to the laboratory, and had it quarantined under Xilx's protest. Jack told Xilx not to speak when he was under quarantine. Xilx was not obtuse. He understood that he looked like a common earth animal, only with six legs instead of four. Xilx recognized that if he started speaking, the interests of the laboratory personnel would be increased and the investigation as to who and what he was would become greatly complicated. He did not need nor want that.

The laboratory scientists were very interested in the dog, especially its "coat of many colors", the variations of which were somehow controlled by the animal itself and tended to be demure and not active the way they were when Jack first picked up the animal. This lack of activity led the lab scientists to concentrate more on the six legs of the creature which they concluded most likely was because the animal had been subject to the atomic test sites and was probably a mutation. That is all. It was an earth dog born in the wrong place, subject to radiation and genetic change. They did not notice that the dog never panted. After ten days of quarantine, the "dog" was to be released to the Humane Society but Jack intervened and asked if he could have the "dog" as a pet. They gave Mr. Xilx to Jack with their blessing while laughing heartily. They could not fathom who would ever want a six-legged dog as a pet. "A freak of nature that probably would have been euthanized at the pound otherwise," they thought. Jack took him home.

Xilx became very comfortable in his new earth-bound home. He settled in and said to himself "this will do for the time being" he thought.

Jack thought otherwise.

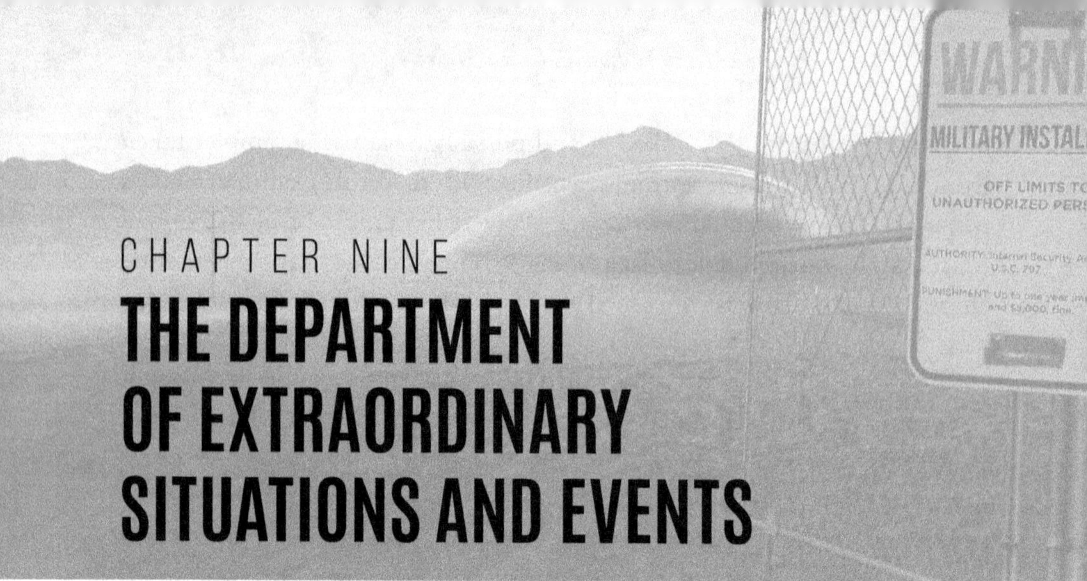

CHAPTER NINE

THE DEPARTMENT OF EXTRAORDINARY SITUATIONS AND EVENTS

Mary Kent was a key figure in this clandestine government agency. Her investigatory talents were always put to the test and on a regular basis. There was always something new every week. There was never a dull moment.

Recently she received news from London, England that someone was flying a strange vehicle like the car in the "Flubber" Disney movie, near the Houses of Parliament and the "London Eye" on the Thames River was going north and east of Kings Cross Station. It was a short sighting and not many people saw it. Those who made the report were not the sort one would call reliable. However, the report was made and Scotland Yard put out the news in their "Strange Events" publication that was also picked up by DESE. Perhaps this was just a fictitious story, but it did grab one's attention.

While this news was not out of the ordinary for Mary's department, it was notable and her department kept watch to see if anything similar occurred over New York City or Washington, DC. The FBI and Scotland Yard were constantly sharing information and that was where Mary accessed it.

Mary's main current concern was the present excessive heat wave and why it seemed to center on the Northern part of the Western Hemisphere. Mary thought, "Why was this heat wave present for so long. Why was the jet stream so far north and why were weather patterns not changing as they normally did?"

The weather was blamed on so-called "global warming" which was causing the melting of glaciers and the warming of oceans. The static nature of the heat wave and its centering over the hemisphere that was home to her was an extremely unusual occurrence and never happened before in written history.

Scientifically, Mary decided that it was not just a physical event. She started to investigate other reasons. She investigated the paranormal. She investigated the occult. She investigated the netherworld influences on the world.

She found that there were solar magnets and solar heat containing vessels in places around the western half of the northern hemisphere. These vessels collected solar heat, and each was called an actuarius solaris. Mary learned of these devices from her investigations into the occult. Mary said while thinking aloud "These were placed by the Veneficum Decurium, a secret order of witches which is as secret in sorcerer circles as is the DESE in the United States." Mary continued to speak aloud while thinking to herself "The U.S., Canada and Mexico could have no winter this year. This summer is onerous and oppressive enough." She repeated "really bad enough indeed."

Mary noted to herself that the newspapers reported that even the Great Lakes were drying up. Glaciers were melting. Greenhouse gases and carbon dioxide from human activity were blamed as was the hole in the ozone layer. Mary realized after her scientific investigation that none of these were the problem.

The situation became more serious every day. It was getting so severe that President GW Bush had called the DESE and spoke with Mary about the problem.

GW said "Mary please make an extra effort to give us a finding as to what the cause of this problem could be. I have been in touch with the CIA, NOAA and the FBI but they don't seem to have even the slightest idea of what is going on. I'd really like to avoid a third catastrophe in my two terms as president, but this seems to be one in the making. I'd really like to avoid it and spare the country of another disaster. The World Trade Center and hurricane Katrina were enough." George went on, "Mary I don't think there ever was a president of the USA who was ever afflicted with so many catastrophes. Imagine a major catastrophe near the beginning of each term. Please see if you can come up with anything that could give us a heads up on what's going on."

Mary responded "Mr. President I understand. We are doing our best and I feel that our department may be on to something. I'll report as soon as I have something definite."

GW said, "Mary, I know you are doing your best and I'm glad to hear that you may be making headway because the FBI, NOAA and the CIA are at a dead end."

They said their goodbyes and hung up. Mary realized how serious the problem had become. Although it was not the first time, she'd received a presidential telephone call she knew that when they did come that probably most of the government's agencies were really without an answer.

Mary checked with agents in different parts of the world on a constant basis. If there were any unusual occurrences in the areas monitored by the agent, they were to call immediately and inform headquarters. Mary had enrolled the strangest of creatures in her organization. Since she didn't get any urgent calls from any of her agents on the heat problem, she decided to call them instead.

She first called Seemore in Fairbanks, Alaska. Appropriately, Seemore was a real Gnome and the fact that he read the "Nome Nugget" was no accident. She continued to check along the northern limits of the western hemisphere. Next, she called her agent in the Eastern half of Canada. She next called Labby who lived in Happy Valley, Goose Bay, Labrador. You might say that Labby was a real Labrador Native, because Labby was a real, talking Black Lab with four legs and a tail. He lived with his co-agent Lamont Craggor, who was only a two-legged human and they helped and covered for each other on research projects. She then would go to other regions and speak with her agents in Cos Cob, Connecticut, Miami Beach, Florida and then centrally in the USA to Fort Wayne, Indiana westerly to Cicero, Chicago via Hinsdale, Illinois via Ann Arbor, Michigan and then to Salt Lake City, Utah, Phoenix, Arizona, and Roseville, California and its branch at Huntington Beach.

Her agents were not of the usual kind. They were not always human, but they were of this world and usually not from outer space. However, this was not always the fact. Many of their locations were not in the center of big cities but tended to be on either the outskirts or some distance away from big city centers.

CHAPTER TEN
DECISION MADE:

The cause was supernatural. All her science told her that this heat wave was nothing natural. She also had evidence that there was nothing extraterrestrial in this heat wave. NOAA reports that the temperature was cooler over the Atlantic and Pacific Oceans than over the intervening land masses. It additionally reported that normal weather patterns continued over both oceans with rain showers and wind jets at sea level and aloft. The commercial pilots were reporting these conditions in their PIREPS NOAA further reported that the "jet stream" which guided storms and air masses were still working well in all these ocean regions. Therefore, at least by the process of elimination the heat wave was not a natural event. Since her research also told her, despite the Roswell, New Mexico reports, that it was not at all from beyond this world either. The conclusion had to be that there was some earthly force, which was not of nature's cupboard, that was causing the problem. Therefore, it had to be supernatural and that opened all kinds of weird doors.

Mary said aloud while speaking to herself and anyone else who was around "This heat wave was created by beings who could invoke the supernatural, the most likely the Evil Witches' Group, the Veneficum, with perhaps an axe to grind in revenge for the persecution of their order for the several hundreds of years before." Mary wondered, "Was there more? There had to be. Witches were burnt at the stake in Europe as well as in Boston. However, their part of the world was not affected. I wonder what the reason was."

Mary's many sources reported that the solar vessels were placed in Saskatoon, Saskatchewan, in the Hudson Bay area and in the Labrador

Peninsula as well as Bangor, Maine near the statue of Paul Bunyan and the blue ox, Babe. Then she checked with her southern sources in Wrightsville Beach, North Carolina and an agent stationed in the mountains of Asheville, N.C. near Chunns Cove Road on Piney Mountain Road. He discovered a Vessel near exit six on Interstate Route 240 high up under the overpass where some homeless travelers would sleep and pass the night away. However, some of these persons were apparently more than just travelers.

Mary's agents also discovered solar Vessels in different parts of the United States and Canada. The California agent headed by Frankie German found a containing vessel near the Pollo Loco restaurant near his station in Fallbrook, California. Frank also discovered one closer to Temecula and in distant places as dispersed as Flagstaff, Arizona. In the East, one was uncovered north of West Palm Beach, Florida on Singer Island, which is a part of Riviera Beach, by the military liaison agent, H. Bud Gaunt who had very considerable experience in matters of surveillance. That vessel was specifically found on Ocean Drive near the Martini Condominium.

Of course, because the Northeast has major hubs of human activity in Boston, New York and in between it was mandated by the Veneficum that they have their own special collection of vessels hidden somewhere in the maze of newly constructed roads and EZ Pass towers which were designed to make travel easier. The "Big Dig" and its underground passages would be an ideal place for mayhem especially tunnel collapses and falling ceilings. This is what they planned, created, and caused.

Boston was special because that is where members of their order were burned at the stake and dunked in lakes to drown. Mary continued speaking aloud to herself "the Veneficum would most certainly have a great interest in Boston. Indeed, what with their cruel history of torturing witches!" Mary chuckled to herself at this thought.

New York City would be involved especially after the activity of Al Qaeda and the Trade Center attacks. As a world-renowned center of finance, international politics, and its density of population involving so many different peoples from all countries on earth, New York City would be ideal to use as an example to the rest of the world. Al Qaeda thought so and there is no question that there will be other misguided, belligerent groups that would involve New York in any kind of disaster they could develop. There could be no doubt about that. Any attack would involve a major population base to drive home the pointed reason for their attack. New York City will always be a prime target. The Veneficum would make use of this city.

Although few would believe that any foreign or domestic group of people caused the heat wave. Anything beyond nature would be very difficult for agents and persons outside DESE to believe and much harder for them to comprehend. There could be no doubt that Rudy Guiliani would be able to gain an immediate grasp on the problems and deal with it. Now that Guiliani's term has expired, it will be just another task for Mayor Blumberg to deal with, as if he did not have enough problems.

When the real facts ever became known to the Homeland Security team and the government allied CIA and FBI, such as they were currently organized, that the heat wave was extraterrestrial or supernatural the matter would be out of Blumberg's hands and in the hands of the Federal government and mostly in the hands of DESE. This meant that it would be Mary Kent's problem.

CHAPTER ELEVEN
SEEMORE

A very interesting individual is Seemore Manlein. His very existence is unique, especially in the United States. People like Seemore are not native to the USA but are of Scandinavian origin having migrated to Europe and the Eurasian region about three thousand years ago. However, gnomes are not new to normal human life. They are very widely dispersed and are known in many different parts of the world. They are not rare, but they are secretive. They like living in Germany, Switzerland, Sweden, Denmark, and Norway. They also exist in secrecy in Brittany, Finland, and Iceland. They are inhabitants of Poland, Bulgaria, and Albania. If these countries are not enough, it is additionally known that they also are inhabitants of Hungary, Yugoslavia, and Czechoslovakia, Holland, Belgium, Luxembourg, Siberia, and western Russia. They are "little men" in size, but their powers are immense.

Unlike large gnomes, smaller gnomes have a less nasty demeanor than their Siberian relatives. They reportedly have found joy in revenge, so it is always best to stay on their good side. They are short people, between two and four feet tall, usually of fair complexion with rosy cheeks. The males usually wear long grey beards. The beards are grey even at a young age. They are many times stronger than a human and can run at speeds between thirty and forty miles per hour. If humans can make five miles an hour they are running very fast. Gnomes have better vision than a hawk.

Gnomes avert cats of all kinds, but they are generally very protective of all animals, including cats. They are especially protective of animals that are sick or mistreated by man. There is a mutual friendship between them and the animals. Sometimes the animals, especially wild creatures, are willing to help gnomes at any time. Gnomes like to live in peace and away from man and populated areas.

Their enemies are mainly Trolls, and other beings who would try to destroy them or their homes. Otherwise, they are mostly peaceful beings and never worry. The one weakness gnomes have is that they enjoy playing practical jokes on mankind and they have a love in the possession and the creation of gems and jewelry. They are vegetarians and love berries and nuts of all kinds. They love mushrooms, applesauce, potatoes, beans, and peas. Give them a drink of fermented honey mead or fermented raspberry mead along with spiced up wine or Glugg, especially as a nightcap.

Mary Kent discovered Seemore many years ago and quite early in her career. She became very interested in the unusual. Seemore was without a doubt very unusual. She discovered Seemore during a hike through the Kjolene mountain chain between Sweden and Norway.

Seemore found her curious and Mary certainly felt the same way about him. Seemore seemed more like a pet rather than a person. He was more than a yardstick high and looked comical with his red hat and long, gray beard. Gnomes like red hats. His rosy cheeks seemed to glow with light, and one could see that he had a cheery smile as well. There seemed to be little to fear and Mary was comfortable with him. She sensed that Seemore was also comfortable with her as well.

After some hesitancy to communicate, Mary sat on a rock outcropping and did not appear as any threat to Seemore. Seemore found another rock within speaking distance near Mary and a conversation started with Mary ending the silence first.

"Go Dag," said Mary.

The gnome replied, "Go Dag". Surprisingly he quickly added in British English "you don't need to struggle with Swedish. I understand English very well because I spent some time in Northern Britain. I left it because I missed my mountain home. You interest me because of that cane you use to help you hike. The carving and the imbedded polished gemstones you have inlaid on the handle are very nice." Seemore continued, "I really like it. Is it possible for me to examine it?"

Mary replied "Of course, if you promise not to run away with it!"

The gnome replied, "I am not a thief, but I like gems. I have a collection of my own at home." Then Seemore pointed to a particular stone on the cane and asked "What kind of stone is this?

Mary looked over and said, "Oh that's a turquoise from Arizona." Mary continued "That's in the western United States. The Indians use them with silver and make all kinds of jewelry."

Seemore's mouth dropped open, although it was a little hard to see that with that heavy beard. Seemore could only say "Really?"

Mary answered "Really".

Seemore continued, "I love turquoise." He continued with great interest "Where can I get some of this gem?"

Mary answered, "It occurs in many parts of the world, but some of the best is in the Southwest USA."

Their conversations continued and Mary learned that Seemore lived near the hiking trail with his wife, Hepseva. They lived at the base of a large tree with additional quarters in two other trees in the area all connected by underground passageways.

Seemore took a liking to Mary and a friendship evolved. He took Mary back to his tree home, which was a very unusual thing for a Gnome to do, being secretive and all. Seemore introduced Mary to his wife Hepseva who was very shocked at the intrusion of this human being into the privacy of her home. Hepseva became very angry with Seemore and started throwing pots and pans at him. Of course, Seemore ducked. It was very unlike Gnomes to display a temper like this because not only did they seldom worry, but they seldom argue as well.

Mary, of course, was also shocked to see this small woman of a bit taller than three feet carrying on like any wronged human woman. Mary said to Hepseva "I'm very sorry. I did not mean to cause any problem for you."

Hepseva stopped attacking Seemore and looked at Mary in sudden surprise. She did not expect a word from this intruder. Hepseva's hesitation made her rethink what she was doing. She looked directly at Mary and said to her "I apologize. I didn't expect to make a scene with a perfect stranger present. I probably should have waited for you to leave before I crowned Seemore. "You see" she continued, "I wasn't dressed well enough to receive company. Especially one from the other world…………" Hepseva's voice trailed off as she hesitated while her eyes fell upon the silver-turquoise covered cane handle. Her mouth fell open as well. She said to Mary "What kind of gem is that? Mary responded "Turquoise, from southwestern U.S.A., Arizona, specifically." Hepseva said "Ohhhh, I love turquoise." It turned out that Hepseva was the boss in this household, as it seems to be all over the world. Women run the show.

Hepseva continued, "Where did you say that these gems came from?" Quickly, without waiting for an answer she added, speaking very earnestly to Seemore, "Seemore, I'd like to visit this Arizona and collect as many of these pretty stones as I can. I have just fallen in love with this color and this type of carving." She saw that Seemore was not eager to accommodate this desire. He did not like to travel far from his familiar surroundings. He was very comfortable right where he was, thank you. Hepseva was fast to add "We can come back after we've collected enough to satisfy both our likings."

Seemore raised his hands in the air to protest, but when they came down all he could say was, "My dear Hepseva perhaps a change would be good, but on a temporary basis only. We may try it only for a short time." He loved Hepseva dearly and would do almost anything to keep her happy.

Therefore, it came to pass that Seemore and Hepseva came to the United States' Arizona State. Actually, Hepseva liked it so much that she did not want to return to the Norway-Sweden mountains. Seemore liked the area in Northern Arizona and settled for the time being on Mount Humphreys' over 12,500-foot elevation. Seemore and Hepseva settled in the woodsy part of the mountain where there were nut trees and berries and where vegetables could grow nicely. They were quite comfortable there for several years. They traveled to the desert areas of Arizona and amassed quite a collection of Turquoise. Everything in their house was decorated with aquamarine-blue-green turquoise. They both were delighted with their turquoise decorations. The floor of their home was decorated in turquoise as well. The doors even had turquoise inlays as well in the door handles.

Eventually, the Manleins had their fill of the Southwest and of turquoise, although they still liked it. It was just that there was so much of it that they feared that they might need to either move out of their house or build a new one just to accommodate the gem. They knew that transporting it back to the home country would be totally impossible.

Although it was many years intervening, Mary Kent and the Manleins kept in touch. Since the humanity of the Manleins was questionable, they basically kept out of public view. Making and keeping in touch with them was easily solved when Mary attained her position at DESE. She provided the Manleins with the latest in technical communications and visited them regularly. Their relationship was very special, and Mary was always welcomed in the Manlein home.

In one of their recent conversations, Seemore voiced that he would like a cooler climate. He had had enough of the Arizona heat, although he lived high on the northern side of Mount Humphrey. It was high enough to be cool and comfortable but there was more. It was one of those circumstances when one knows that he had just about enough of something. In this case it was Arizona. He also let it be known that he had enough turquoise to last him his lifespan of five hundred years or so. He wanted a change. Mary offered to come to Arizona to meet with the Manleins and talk any change over. Mary felt responsible for the Manlein welfare, and her interest was more than just humanitarian. Her offer was accepted, and Mary arrived the next day.

Seemore and Hepseva greeted Mary at the entrance to their tree home. It was only moderately difficult for Mary to locate the house, although all trees look alike, especially in a wooded mountain, but the directions Seemore gave Mary rekindled her memory. She had been there before when the Manleins moved to Arizona many years before. She had to rent a Jeep to make it up the mountain logging trails to the Manlein home, but she was there and it was good to see her friends again.

Mary bent over and gave them both a hug and there were tears of happiness in the Manlein eyes. Mary was not far behind. The reunion was quite emotional.

"Mary", Seemore started, "We are so happy to see you once again. The spring is almost over and we're just about ready for summer." Seemore continued, "While we are very comfortable here, we really are not looking forward to another summer in Arizona."

Hepseva chimed in "That's right, Mary. We miss our old country although we don't think we'd like to return to the Kjolen Mountains. We would like to try some place else. This part of Arizona is getting too populated for us. Too many people are around here. We want more security and more privacy. The wild animals are fewer every year. They are our friends, and we are less able to help them and to meet with them."

Seemore said, "Mary, is there another place that you know of that is less populated and less busy? Arizona has changed a lot in the past seven seasons. Can you help us?"

Mary was beginning to understand their plight. Gnomes do not care to be near "normal" humans. Humans kill animals, sometimes for food and sometimes for sport. Gnomes see no sport in killing at all, and they do not eat meat. They are vegetarians. Civilization's shopping centers, housing developments and All-Terrain Vehicles were coming dangerously close to their home and the Manleins did not like that at all.

"Well," Mary began, "We could explore the more northern states. Those states would get you away from Arizona heat and they are more isolated, although there is human population there. It is more sparsely populated than Arizona. You would not be totally in isolation. One such state might be Montana. Another could be the mountain areas of Washington State. There you'd find it probably more like home in the Kjolen Mountains. If those are not to your liking, there is our State of Alaska also known as Seward's Folly."

Seemore asked, "Mary, our homeland was a snowy place in the winter. We also were bound by the sea at the perimeters of our Scandinavian peninsula. We liked the sea. We visited it regularly. We miss seeing it so very much. We miss the smell of salty air and the sight of sea grasses. Are these places anywhere near the sea? Is there a coastline anywhere in these places?"

Mary responded, "No Seemore. The State of Montana is landlocked. The State of Washington has a seacoast, but you wouldn't like it there. The temperatures are mild and rainy most of the winter months. They even have a northern rain forest, which is unusual because the climate is not always warm. The part of the State of Washington you'd like would be more inland and away from the sea."

Seemore was crestfallen. He was depressed. Hepseva was his mirror image. Both were in despair.

Mary then said elatedly, "There is a place I know of where you could probably have all of what you want without going to Maine and it's probably either equidistant or closer than Maine. It is Alaska, one of the most recent states to enter the Union. I know of a place that our department maintains in Fairbanks, Alaska. It is a seafaring town, and the mountains are to the North. Its climate would probably be ideal for you and it's all set up."

Seemore and Hepseva did not jump for joy at this. Their life style was to live in , or on, or under one to three trees at once. It would not be easy for them to adapt to a real human way of life. They were not sure of this at all, and they let Mary know about it. They held nothing back. They were naturalists and their lifestyle was somewhere between that of a human and a caveman, animal-like. A bathroom would be a big shock to them.

"Mary, but Mary", Seemore pleaded, "we cannot live in a human house. It is not our way. How can we go from living in the forest to living in a house? A human house at that! Ha!"

Mary replied, "Seemore and Hepseva, I understand your fear and your plight but it's not as bad as it seems. You see, the house is not in the center of town, but in the wooded outskirts way outside Fairbanks. It has all the modern conveniences and more. Our government maintains and protects it. You will have virtually no interference or interaction with humans at all!

The telephone and television I gave you earlier will be nothing compared to how this house is equipped. You can find out what is going on any place on earth, including the Kjolen Mountains in the old country!

Besides, you would be doing me a very big favor. Right now, there is no one assigned to that outpost. It is a voluntary office. Most Americans do not care to be so isolated from city and family. Most have rejected that assignment. As a matter of fact, recently all of them have. What is monitored there is vital to the welfare of all of earth's creatures, including your friends, the animals. It is also vital to world peace and the free world's security."

Once again Seemore and Hepseva didn't know what to say. This torrent of words coming from Mary was very unexpected and they did not have an immediate response. It all made sense, but in a strange way, to both. They needed a little time to talk this new idea out. Hepseva and Seemore went into a huddle barely five feet in front of Mary. They whispered back and forth to each other with an occasional louder burst of still whispered speech. There definitely was fire and excitement in their discussion. Suddenly the whispering and the gesturing stopped, and the huddle was broken.

They both presented themselves before Mary with their arms folded. Mary thought "Now that's a defiant body language pose if I ever saw one. Now what?" Mary braced herself for what she thought would be a severe tongue lashing from both of the defiant gnomes. Short though they were, their voices could boom like thunder and Mary would have liked to avoid that!

Seemore took the lead and started talking. "Mary," he said, "we have talked it over and mulled over the possibilities. The climate and number of humans around here has increased too much. We both have decided that a move would do us good. We trust you Mary and we know that you would do nothing to hurt us but only to help us. We will go to Alaska and give it a try."

Now Mary's mouth dropped open in surprise. She studied body language in her human behavior courses and knew when the observed body signs would be defiant or not. These Gnomes betrayed her knowledge and were agreeable instead! She just could not believe it. Mary replied, "Seemore, you are so very right. However, there is one catch.

Seemore said "I knew it. I knew it was too good to be true. I just knew it." Then he put on his crestfallen face once again.

Mary came to the rescue and replied "Seemore it's not as bad as you think. The only thing you must do is to take good care of the house. I have no doubt that you will do that. "

Seemore beamed. He shouted, "Hezabezala!" He shouted. "If that's all the catch is we'll have no problem." He shouted and cheered again with Hepseva joining in, "Hezabezala!" There was happiness in the Manlein household once again.

Mary continued "You'll need to keep a lookout on the environment and periodically I'll call you for a report. It will be no problem. Your love of nature and natural things would put this right up your alley!"

Seemore screwed up his right eye and looked askance at Mary and said "What kind of report Mary? What do you mean by that?" Hepseva looked suspicious as well, not knowing and being concerned as to what Mary meant.

"Well, the government has this house there for a reason. It is an environmental station and is part of the department I work for." explained Mary.

Seemore was still expressing a screwed-up face and asked, "What department might that be, Mary?"

Mary replied, "The DESE."

Seemore did not change his posture and asked, "What in the world of man is the DESE anyway? It sounds like some kind of disease or sickness. What is a DESE?"

Mary clarified her statement and said, "DESE stands for the "Department of Extraordinary Situations and Events". It borders on the scientific, the natural, the psychic, the magical and the supernatural regarding global happenings that are not easily explained by ordinary means. Therefore, the word "Extraordinary" is in its name."

Hepseva now opened with "Do you mean that there are magical and supernatural things going on in Fairbanks, Alaska? Do you mean that there is a science up there which is involved with psychic mind things and in and out of nature? Is it spooky up there? Whatever do you mean anyway?"

Seemore added "You know that Gnomes don't work in the human sense. You do know that don't you? We do not want to be held down to a "job" the way humans are imprisoned in a "job". We need to be free. We need to roam the woods and explore nature. We need to mingle with the wild animals. We need to be free."

Mary could see that the Manleins were very concerned over losing their "Gnomedom". She quickly interjected "No, no Seemore, it is nothing like that at all. All you must do is remember what you see and what happens around you. Then periodically I will call you to make sure you are both all right, perhaps once a week and then you can tell me all about it."

"Don't worry," she said assuredly. "You will enjoy it. I guarantee it!"

Both Gnomes yelled together "A guarantee! A guarantee! You can't beat that!" They both shouted "Hezabezala!" in unison. Then they danced a jig in a small circle on the living room floor and as they did so they latched onto Mary and included her in their circle. Mary was delighted. It was done. Mary established an agent in the remote Fairbanks, Alaska wilderness. Everyone was happy, but none more than the Manleins. They would be going back to a wilderness environment like their Kjolen Mountains in Sweden but in human style. They would have a house with indoor plumbing. No more did they need to make cold outdoor trips to the Outhouse. They'd be very happy about that. Toilet tissue would be a surprise for them too. No longer would they need to worry about mistakenly using Poison Ivy leaves! They would now be introduced to toilet tissues instead. It would be a major improvement in their daily "duty", but one to which they would need to become accustomed.

CHAPTER TWELVE
H. BUD GAUNT

Mary was very happy with the installation of the Manleins in the Northwest. That was not the end of her project. She needed to establish personnel in key places in the U.S.A. so that the country would be properly monitored. She needed someone in the Northwest, Northeast, Southeast and Southwest at least. Intermediate posts would be filled ad libitum, only as filling those positions casually occurred. It was not an emergency as long as four corners of the nation are monitored.

She was looking for someone in the Southeast that she could count on, not necessarily human though. The Manleins were Gnomes and not just human. Anything similar or better in the Southeast would be great. She recalled that on a trip to a military establishment at Rockport, Illinois she made the acquaintance of a former Merchant seaman who dabbled in military supply. She found him to be an interesting individual with all the quirks of a seaman who had seen a bit of the world. She recalled that he liked to be addressed as "HB". So be it, she thought. "HB" it is.

Mary looked back into her business card file to locate "HB" It was necessary for her to go through her records of five years ago to find the card. She had recalled that during a conversation with "HB" that he said he had had enough of the Northern cold weather and established himself in the Palm Beach, Florida area. "That would be an ideal spot for my second agent." Mary thought to herself. Mary gave "HB" a telephone call and he himself answered after five rings.

"Hello! Hello "HB" answered in a gruff, impatient voice. "Who is this and what do you want?" he said, still gruff.

Mary was almost afraid to answer but she knew what her goal was and that it was something she had to do. Mary took a deep breath and ventured into the unknown "Hello "HB", this is Mary Kent. "I met you about five years ago at a military meeting in Rockport, Illinois. We had a conversation during which you handed me your business card."

HB responded, "Oh yes, oh yes, I do remember. You were working for a government agency at the time. I don't recall the name of it because you said that it was a secret. Very strange department, I thought." He continued, "But it's nice to hear from you. To what do I owe this pleasure?" said "HB," anticipating an interesting response from Mary.

The silence was oppressive. Mary started to speak but was not able to get her words out in a sensible, coherent manner. Nevertheless, being the head of a very important department, she knew she had to talk and quickly before "HB" became tired of waiting and hung up.

Mary responded "Mr. Gaunt I need to talk with you about a special government mission. We need your help with a certain project that I cannot reveal on the telephone. Would it be all right if I came down to your place for a special meeting on the matter?"

"HB" was silent and thinking for a moment and then answered. "Mary Kent, after all these years! I have not heard from you or my other "friends" in the government and now you call me for some mysterious meeting. I'm not sure that I am interested anyway, but I thank you for your call."

He was about to hang up on Mary but did not after he could hear her yelling into her telephone begging him to not hang up.

"HB" said curtly, "Well, what is it anyway?"

"It's very important and vital to the security of the U.S.A. It is also a very special situation for the right person with the right qualification. I think that you could be that person. I need to speak with you in person. The telephone is too public and what I have for you is too important." Mary replied.

"HB" responded, "You know Mary, I've done many things for my country. Some have been less than intelligent while others were not only highly intelligent but noble to boot."

Mary took this reply as acceptance and ventured to ask, "When can I come down?"

"How about coming over this coming weekend? I have basically retired, but I'm still interested in a good jaunt for my Uncle Sam" answered H. B.

HB continued "You arrange it and I'll pick you up at Palm Beach International Airport."

It was agreed. Mary would make her trip from LaGuardia Airport to PBI. When she met with "HB" she would make her pitch. It would be very good. It had to be because "HB" was a highly educated engineer with a military background and more. When she reviewed his curriculum vitae, she knew that he would be a prize, a reliable and a hard worker for her department. She would need to divulge more information to "HB" than she ever would need to explain to the Manleins. It would most certainly be worth it. "HB" would be an ideal agent in an ideal location. She needed that and if she could, she would achieve it!

CHAPTER THIRTEEN
FRANCESCO (FRANKIE) GERMAN

Mary's brain was a milling dynamo. She couldn't stop thinking about what she had to do. She tried to put the selection of agents aside, but the need to accomplish what she conceived as her necessary sphere of watchful agents around the country would not let her stop. She even woke up in the wee hours of the morning thinking and thinking about where and who a needed agent would be, could be.

She had the Northwest covered and if needed, she and her local New York City area personnel could cover the Northeast, but four corners of the United States had to be monitored and she still had need of Northeast and Southwest agencies and people she could count on under any circumstances.

Once again, she reviewed her trusty business card file. Unfortunately, she was not able to access anyone in the Southwest quarter of the U.S. She went through the department's files, the FBI files, the CIA files, the newly created HSA (Home Security Agency) files and whatever political files she could access, and there were many. Probably too many!

Mary pursued this project for almost a month and then she decided to review old newspapers and magazines. She went as far back as the Roswell Incident in 1947. She pursued articles on outer space, aliens, space travel, black holes, the expanding universe, current satellite imaging, California earthquakes, mudslides, topography, and California geography. There was not much that missed her eye. She read about current and not so current events, especially in California. "That's the ideal place for the Southwestern outpost and agent" she thought out loud speaking only to herself.

She came across an article in the "North County Times" newspaper from the San Diego, CA area. It told of about an older man who came from a small Sicilian town, Sant'Agata Militello, and emigrated to the United States about the late 1920's. He had made his home in Eastern United States but being tired of the cold northeastern winters decided to move to the warmer climate of California.

What piqued her interest was not only was this man not highly schooled in his childhood, because he was in his twenties when he came over, but because he continued his education on his own. Although he was a carpenter-cabinet maker by trade, he went to night school and became a licensed real estate agent. He was basically a very intelligent man and made a very good fortune in California real estate.

His friends knew him as "Frank" and that was the Americanized version of his given name. Frank is the name he went by. Close friends called him "Frankie". He did not respond any longer to the name of "Francesco". He was American and his name had to be American too.

There was still more. Frank had an interest in sciences of all kinds. He was interested in Physics, Astronomy, Chemistry and Biology and to some degree Agriculture. This last trait was probably an inherited green thumb from the "old country" he left behind in his youth. He probably would have become a doctor or some type of scientist if he were born in the United States. This was the kind of innate brilliance this man had.

Frank was one of the people who reported seeing a UFO over the hills east of Fallbrook where he lived. In 1947, the time of the Roswell Incident, Frank and several other reliable citizens of Fallbrook made the report, which was demeaned by the authorities, although one of the reports came from a State Policeman. Frank followed the incident and reports thereof faithfully. In his newspaper interview, Frank revealed how disappointed he was not only at the disbelief of the Authorities, but also how severely they tried to quash the reports.

Mary thought, "This man sounds interesting and is certainly as good as anyone I've discovered in California for reliability, common sense, and responsibility.

Mary located Frank's address and telephone number and called him. It was easy for a government agent to discover this information although the telephone was unlisted. It was much more difficult for Mary to introduce herself to a perfect stranger who knew nothing about her, her history, her place in society or her job much less her interest in him. She toiled with a manner of introduction but came up blank. She was really at a loss to know what to say was her reason for contacting him.

The more she thought about it, the greater the number of ideas popped into her head. She thought, "I'm a woman. I should not be at a loss for words or imagination. This should be no problem." That is what she thought but it was a problem for her. The myriad ideas that popped up also fizzled out and almost as quickly. Ultimately, she realized that the UFO incident was an ideal reason for her to make contact and ask for a meeting. This is what she did.

"Hello Mr. German?" she said when he answered. Once again, she heard nothing on the other end as she had with "HB". She thought, "Is it me or them? Is this what the mindset of the kind of agent I seek is? She realized that it was. These people were thinking and analyzing beings. They were also independent and did not have any desire or need to converse with people outside their circle of acquaintances. They did not want to rush into acknowledging a stranger or into simple-minded conversation. So, he said nothing.

Mary said "Hello, hello. Is anyone there?"

Frank replied "Yes this is Mr. German. What can I do for you?" Then he followed up with a curt "I hope this is not a sales call. I am on the "Do Not Call" list, you know". Frank was a fighter from way back. Whatever he had or possessed he worked hard for, and he was wary of strangers' calls. Cold sales calls really ticked him off. He had no problem or hesitation in letting the caller know that just about right at the start of the call.

Mary answered, "No Mr. German this is not as simple as a sales call. It is a call from a U.S. Government department, and I would like to discuss the Roswell incident. I want to discuss what you reported at length. I have notes here about a report you made regarding this event."

Frank was stunned and again remained silent but this time in shock. It had been decades ago that the Roswell incident occurred. Frank thought the entire event was dead, gone and buried. The Authorities, meaning those who created the officially announced version of the Roswell incident, had virtually if not completely, destroyed any factual reality on the matter. Frank had put the whole affair in his head years ago even though it was still very much alive in his mind as though it had just happened. He had not thought about it for at least the past ten years.

The voice at the other end of the phone inquired "Hello, are you there? Hello?" Mary was fearful that her choice agent prospect had hung up because of the cemetery-like silence at the other end and was happily surprised when Frank responded, "Yes, I'm still here. I am very shocked at hearing from you about this. This occurred in 1947, a very long time ago. Why are you interested in it now? That was almost fifty years ago! I cannot believe that you are from the U.S. government! The government was the reason Roswell was denied as being true. They came up with all sorts of reasons why the incident was not credible."

"You will need to prove to me that you are an official government agent. I can't believe it. Are you a newspaper reporter? Are you from the "SUN", "ENQUIRER", or "STAR" newspapers? Are you looking for a sensational revitalization story such as the one that was run about the baby who was born with a gold tooth in his mouth? Is that what you are doing?" Frank countered.

Mary had to protest being put into the category of a sub-rosa reporter. She also was not sure how she could convince Frank that she was a government agent since her department was so secret. She did carry credentials though and if she could get Frank to a meeting, she would be able to present them to him. She was sure that that would do the trick and gain Frank's confidence.

However, gaining Frank's confidence would only be the beginning. It would be necessary for Frank to agree to secrecy as well because Mary's department had to be protected. That would be the next hurdle, but Mary felt that once the two had met and Frank had knowledge of what Mary had in mind that he would readily agree. The secrecy question would then become minor, and the task Mary would assign to Frank would be major. The task would be right up Frank's alley. Frank had great interest in extraordinary situations and events. Mary's department would be to Frank's delight. The more she thought about it, the more she knew that Frank was her man!

Mary said "Frank, I'd be very happy to prove my identity to you, but it must be in person and in a one-on-one meeting between us only. When can we arrange it?

Frank was once again surprised that this "reporter" may not be a reporter after all but exactly who she claimed she was. He was and was not playing a bluffing game all at the same time. Therefore, he was a little flustered when he answered. "Well, er, well, umm, I don't know. I am sort of retired so I guess that any time it's convenient for you would be convenient for me. "

Mary was delighted. She was looking for that answer. She responded Mary took this reply as an acceptance and ventured to ask, "When can I come down?"

Frank was always open for a good fight and a good adventure as well, and although he was suspicious of the person at the other end of the telephone, he decided that a meeting could be a very good idea. "How about this coming weekend?" Frank replied. It was set.

Frank continued, "You arrange it and I'll pick you up at San Diego Airport." This sounded familiar to Mary, and she realized that the same words were virtually spoken by HB in Palm Beach. In fact, it was another weekend trip for Mary. This was no accident. Mary tended to be free at weekends so most, if not all, her trips away from work would be on weekends.

It was agreed. Mary would make her trip from LAG to SAN International Airport this weekend.

"Just let me know when and what airlines and which flight." Said Frank. When she met with Frank, she would make her position known along with all the proof he needed. There would be no doubt left in Frank's mind about who she was and what her position was and what her office was when she had been finished with him. The only catch was that before she could reveal much of anything she would need to swear Frank to secrecy and have him agree to reveal nothing to anyone, especially not even the existence of DESE under penalty of law!

Mary thought that after she had met with all these prospective enrolled agents that all which was left was to create an agency in the Northeast. She was not hurried about this because her local people could fill in at a moment's notice.

It was now her job to deal with the problems facing DESE at present. There were not many. The last event was the change in the circulation of water as it went down a drain. In the Northern Hemisphere water would swirl clockwise and reverse in the Southern Hemisphere. They were suddenly switched for some strange reason. In other words, the Northern Hemisphere water would swirl counterclockwise and reverse in the Southern Hemisphere. It was Mary's job to find out why and even to correct it if possible. Could it be that the earth suddenly rotated in the opposite direction from normal and without anyone noticing the sudden change? Certainly not. The puzzle was that the earth kept its proper rotation as from its beginning.

Mary never did get to know why that phenomenon occurred. It corrected itself with the same lack of fanfare as it had shown when it first started: none! It was suspected that subterranean forces such as volcanic pressures and shifting subterranean tectonic plates were most likely the cause. There was an increase in earthly tremors and earthquakes in that same period. When these forces subsided, the drainage circulation patterns readjusted themselves to what was considered normal.

It might seem an unimportant issue, but such changes could adversely affect the weather and tremendously change weather patterns. This seemed like a job for one of the Greek gods of mythology and not one for a mere mortal. She wondered back then "How could a single, simple human being make such a correction affecting the planetary functioning of our home planet, the earth?" She was once again speaking out loud to herself hoping in vain to hear an answer from some place, any place. Then she said to herself "I need be able to have someone to talk to who has a similar background as I do. I just need to have input and discussion on what ails the country, and me." She added the "and me" as a quick afterthought. She knew she was right about this. It was necessary for her to have an equal for intelligent discussion and conversation with another intelligent and rational human being.

The task before her was just too much for one person, male or female. Sure, she thought, it really is very lonely at the top. All the responsibilities and sometimes all the work are yours alone. It is said that an executive must delegate duties because it is impossible for just one individual to handle major tasks. Mary realized the full truth of this. She also realized that also she could talk over her problems with the President.

That, however, would not be a conversation of equals. The President was her superior, her boss, and although it was all right, it was not what she needed. She needed another person as an equal with whom she could have a give and take without fear of judgment and repercussion.

CHAPTER FOURTEEN

BLUE CLAW, HORSESHOE CRABS AND WARM WEATHER

Henry's close young friends, Joseph "Joe" King, Mickey Tedesco, and Samantha Perkins enjoyed the salt air and the marshy shore of the Long Island Sound community where they lived. They would accompany Henry during his excursions to the West Basin of Harbor Island Park at the end of Rushmore Avenue and the Post Road. It was especially nice because the weather was warming up. Henry enjoyed the warm summer sunshine. Henry and his friends would explore their environment just as many normally curious young people do. They were all too young to drive and although they had bicycles, they did most of their exploring on foot.

Since he lived near the salt waters of Long Island Sound, he liked to explore the waterfront. The many little creatures he could see on the muddy banks below the seawall at low tide fascinated him. There were a great many Horseshoe Crabs, which came out in the late summer months, probably to mate. They were large, dark chestnut brown color with the body and head as one unit which took the form of a medieval helmet with many legs and a spiked tail.

There were hundreds of entertaining black Fiddler Crabs. They would be romping around on the mud but immediately, if they saw your shadow or if you stomped upon the earth they traversed, they would run into their holes in the mud leaving their one big, oversized claw to enter their burrow hole last. This was most likely for defense. Then most of them would stay at the beginning of their hole and would not go in deeper unless further threatened.

Of course, when one stomped on the earth of the mud flat, the piss clams would shoot up a spike of water indicating where they were hiding. If Henry dug at that spot, he would find a clam under the mud.

The tall sea grasses mixed with cattails and the myriad types of seaweed intrigued him. It really seems as though he had a naturalist bent. What really held his interest was the time of year when the season would start to change, and the air became a little chilly even though the sun was warm. This was the time when the Blue Claw Crabs would ride in on the high tide and warm themselves on the seawall of the West Basin. The sun would have warmed the stones in the seawall and attracted the cold-blooded crabs to its hearth. Henry would then arrive with a bushel and a crab net. He would carefully look down over the seawall and check the existence of a hedonistic crab. Then slowly, without casting his shadow in the water, he would lower his crab net and simply but carefully guide his net in a slow approach to that unfortunate crab and in the last instant, he would quickly move the net into attack mode and scoop up his prey. In a half hour he would fill up his bushel basket and go home to feast with his family on Blue Claw Crabs.

It was a delight he would remember all his life. Later in life he always wondered why his parents never asked him where or how he obtained the crabs. It was a puzzle. He would wonder about this well into his old age.

The Blue Claws were delicious. They tasted like lobster especially when drawn butter was included. He only had time to engage in this sport on the summer weekends. The best time was the months of August and September.

He would also borrow a friend's rowboat and row about the West Basin out to Long Island Sound around Orienta Point. He liked the slightly choppy waters but only if they were not too choppy. He would like to fish with his bamboo pole, earthworms and red and white bobber for small blue fish called "snappers". He had not yet heard of sandworms which would have been better fish bait. The fish would be too small to eat, but fun to catch and throw back into the water, only to catch again. Henry and his male friends enjoyed fishing together even though they rarely brought any fish home.

Henry always had interest in his natural environment. This interest would make him valuable to Jack Henigson. Henry Wilson would eventually have an interesting future that would be almost immediately intense.

The rest of his summer months, he would occasionally occupy his time helping in his father's Fairfield dental office. He would take a short train ride up to his dad's office or else he would go to the office accompanying his father for a day's effort. He could hardly call it work because he had no pressures on him, and he could take a break anytime he wanted to and window shop at he Brick Walk Market complex at this leisure. His dad was happy just to have his companionship and interest. He would help his father in his office by doing minor secretarial things like filing charts, mailing, and creating statements and dumping out the garbage during the rest of the week, and not on a full-time basis. It was a rather haphazard now and then thing. His services at his dad's office were not required but something he would do when the whim hit him or if he needed a little extra pocket money.

His father was a hard worker, arriving at his office at least one-half hour before his first patient and leaving a half hour or more after the last patient left. Sometimes it would be necessary for his dad to return to the office to complete some laboratory work that was left over from the day's efforts. His dad would come home exhausted from his day's work whether it was or was not a full day's work. His stress level and his labors were that intense.

CHAPTER FIFTEEN
FLIGHTS IN DARKNESS

The creation of engineering marvels and the development of new products with a scientific approach to entering the unknown was "HB's" source of adventure, excitement, and personal satisfaction. Even though he was retired, he kept his mental acuity by improving on current technological marvels and delving into new ideas that he would put into functioning reality.

"HB" was a type of pioneer. His interests in optics and imaging kept him from vegetating in his retirement. His former company "RELANZ OPTICS" was still his love and it was difficult for him totally to forget what he knew and to build on his accomplishments and knowledge. His interests in the military application for his products and ideas were the result of his early education while in the Air Force and later at the Air Force Military Academy. We have all heard that it's hard to keep a good man down, well "HB" was a good man and it was impossible to keep him down.

He dealt very deeply and intensely in optics, LCD monitor type displays and electrical engineering, but his optics interests crossed over into laser manufacture and the relationships of light, energy, electricity, and heat.

His curiosity in the optics field led to experimentation and theory that ultimately produced highly accurate night vision scopes that had no equal. A pilot could fly at high speeds and low altitudes with just about the same security and safety as in daytime over enemy territory. Such high-speed flights in total darkness, combined with intelligence gathering, permitted our air force to the successful completion of combat missions in different parts of the world without fear.

In some ways one could say that the development of such ancillary visual aids counterbalanced the effectiveness of radar, although not completely. Radar could be of minimal use when aircraft were on top of their targets. Radar would only be effective for detection of enemy aircraft when they were at a distant point in their flight to their targets. However, should the enemy aircraft fly below the radar beam then an attack would be a total surprise. It would be like the hand of God striking out of the darkness and smiting an enemy. Death and destruction came out of nowhere and with no warning whatsoever. This would create an extremely fearful event in the lives of the victims of such an attack, but just another day's work for the military pilots who had to engage in such a mission.

"HB", although he had a military background, was more interested in the development of such exotic adjunctive, mostly defensive, weaponry. He knew the military applications and implications of all that he was very capable of developing. His interest was in the creation of such helps to our country's services and science turned to the practical matter of winning a war. He was not a fighter, but a lover instead. He loves his family of four children and his wife Ann very much. It must be said that he also was a lover of his work as well and he had to split his time between them both. Eventually, he started doing some of his research at home, so that he could be with his wife and his family. That put him in Seventh Heaven because he had the best of both worlds: his family and his work, which was really his hobby, in the same place. These days it is mostly "HB" and his wife, Ann, who occupy their home together as his children have grown, left, and have established their own lives and households elsewhere although close by.

Becoming involved with the Government one more time in these late years could be just what the doctor ordered for "HB". Although his interests were still intense, the lack of practical application was beginning to get him down a bit. He was looking forward to meeting this rather mysterious person who was coming into his life at this time. He had no idea what it was about or even if the visit was a joke, or a hoax played on him by former associates in his earlier government contacts. He did not even care at this point in his life. He thought, "I can get a good laugh out of it even if it's totally phony". The time for the visit from this mysterious stranger was very soon to be at hand and "HB" would be ready for whatever came his way.

He always had a bent for adventure and looked forward to meeting this Mary Kent person no matter what. "HB" liked entering the unknown and Mary Kent was not only part of the unknown, but apparently so was her government position. "HB" was completely intrigued and becoming very eager for their private meeting. The privacy part made the whole pending get-together even more mysterious and "HB" could not wait for it to happen.

CHAPTER SIXTEEN
SAN DIEGO

San Diego is a place on the Pacific Ocean like no other. It is home to the aircraft carrier the USS Midway which set new standards of naval aviation in the last half of the 20th century. The USS Midway blazed new trails of sub-Arctic air operations off the coast of Greenland. A captured German V-2 rocket was launched off the Midway in 1946. It was the dawn of naval missile warfare. It was the first carrier home ported in a foreign country, calling Yokosuka, Japan home for almost 20 years. The USS Midway remained on active duty spanning the surrender of Japan in WWII, the Cold War, Vietnam, the era of détente with Russia and Desert Storm.

The moored Midway now is at the San Diego Aircraft Carrier Museum located at 910 N. Harbor Drive, alongside Navy Pier. Frank always had a military interest tucked away somewhere in his brain. This is one of the attractions in the area where Frank German lived a bit north and nearer the junctions of routes 15 and 76 which is more inland and away from the ocean itself. San Diego is loaded with activities, parks, museums and more. Although Frank would pick up Mary Kent at SAN airport, she would not visit Frank's home. Although Fallbrook is near San Diego, the distance from the airport is too far.

Mary would prefer to stay at a closer hotel to the airport. She picked the Best Western Inn in Miramar because that would be a much shorter drive from the airport off Interstate 15. Mary would complete her business with Frank in short order, spend the night in San Diego and return to LGA the next day. If she had time, she would visit the famous San Diego Zoo in the morning. She said to herself "It does not need to be all work, does it?"

Her answer was "No it does not and there would need to be a fun time as well. After all, it was the weekend.

She would arrive on US Airways flight 6929 with two stops and depart on US Airways flight 6930 with three stops the following day. She said to herself "This is the way air travel in the USA is today: a struggle!" Mary was not happy with the prospect of getting into a full airplane or the fact that somewhere enroute one of the connections would be late and that the time of her suffering would be greater than it already was.

She probably could have taken a US government plane to San Diego but preferred to keep a low-key profile. Besides, what would Frank think if he had to pick her up at an unfamiliar military airbase? "Easy, he would think I work for the government! I do!" she laughed to herself only partially out loud for a change.

The time had come, and her five plus hour flight was ending, and the landing was near. She was very thankful for that. Now the only thing she needed was a safe landing and everything would be all right! She hoped that Frank would not stand her up and that she would recognize him from his photographs in the government files.

The plane made its landing on the three double wheels it had all at once. The landing was so gentle that the airplane landing at two hundred miles per hour was "painted on" so smoothly that it was not even noticed that the landed aircraft was no longer airborne. There was not even a side-to-side sway. Mary sat in the rear of the airplane near the emergency exit doors. That was always her preference, just in case. It took a short while for the passengers ahead of her to gather their belongings and start the procession out of the airplane's front door.

The pilot and the flight attendants were at the front door of the airplane and helped to usher the passengers out. Mary said her goodbyes with pleasure and started her walk down the exit tunnel to the terminal.

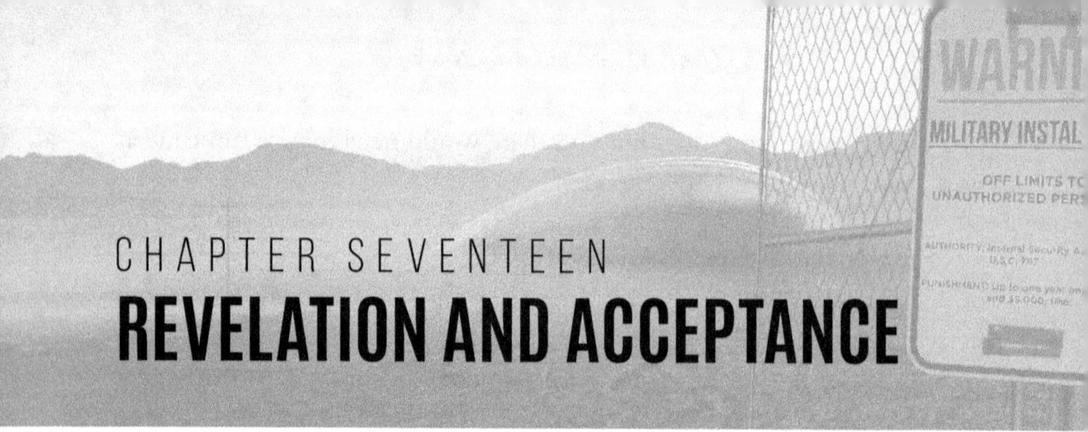

C H A P T E R S E V E N T E E N

REVELATION AND ACCEPTANCE

It was not until she entered the public area that she saw someone holding up a sign who was wearing the cap of a taxi driver. The sign said "Mary Kent". She knew that this was her connection to ground transportation, but she was not certain of who the cab driver was. Sure enough as she came closer she recognized that it was Frank German himself, posing as a limo driver! Mary was amused and could not help but smile a little at the comedy.

Mary approached the sign bearer and said "Hello. I am looking for a taxicab. Are you renting your taxi?"

Frank was once again stuck in a wordless condition. The woman he was looking at was a trim, attractive woman in her fifties with graying hair mixed with colors of reddish brown. She was dressed in a conservative business suit. Frank thought that it must have been a difficult flight for a passenger who was dressed so formally. He was right.

Frank responded, "No, I am not a taxi driver. I am waiting for a special person as named in my sign. Can you read it? This last statement was not kindly spoken but stated with a bit of disdain and impatience because the person he was talking to obviously had no common sense or was from a foreign world where placards held by drivers for their prospective passengers was unknown.

Mary was acting a little coy and then said, "What would you do if your passenger did not show up? Then would you be able to provide me with transportation?"

Frank was getting a little annoyed at the persistence of this stranger. He thought to himself, "Why in the world would this stranger pick on him when there were obvious cab drivers all around him who would just love a fare-paying passenger? When all the passengers left the plane and the immediate driver reception area was now vacant, Frank was left alone with no one to pick up. He began to think for an instant that the person who was pestering him may very well be his passenger. There could be no other reason, but why the wise shenanigans?", he wondered? Frank realized that this person had to be his passenger and that she had put him through a tolerance and patience test.

Frank asked, "Don't tell me; I'll bet that you are Mary Kent! Am I right?"

Mary developed a broad grin and said, "You better believe that I am. I know who you are from your photographs on our files. So where are we going and when?

Frank was not surprised. It seemed to him that he was very right. This Mary person could be a "buster". She was apparently very intelligent and very smart. Sometimes the two do not go together. In this case they did. It was a patience, tolerance and an intelligence test. Only an ignorant clod would have shown impatience and intolerance to another human being who was completely unknown to him. Frank knew that since he displayed all the positive traits that he passed her gauntlet of a test with excellence. Any other "cab driver" would have been quickly "ticked off" and told Ms. Mary to go somewhere in an unkind, and possibly loud, fashion.

Frank replied, "We can go back to my place in Fallbrook at Grace Place, or we can stay in the immediate area. Whichever would you prefer?"

Mary had already researched the area before she left home and knew that Fallbrook would be too far for her after a five-hour plus flight. She elected to stay in the immediate area instead because she did not need to be involved in additional transport time just for a conversation to win over Frank German.

I have heard good things about the Gaslamp Quarter. There is a highly rated place there called the Gaslamp Plaza Suites on E Street. We can go there and have a private consultation. The airport is too public and a little too noisy. I understand that it is also very close by, say about five miles. That would be ideal.

So off they went. Frank did not have a limousine however, but only an older model Rolls Royce with heated seats. Mary was impressed. She felt a little like royalty. Frank put on his cab driver's hat and had Mary sit in the back. She felt like she really was in a chauffeured driven limo, although she smirked that it was just a Rolls Royce. Certainly, it was not a limo, but it was close enough and Mary liked it.

When they arrived at the Gaslamp Plaza Suites, they let a valet park the Rolls and entered the coolness of the hotel. They found themselves in a quiet and private corner location and sat quietly for a moment to gather their thoughts and to recover from all the decisions they had to make regarding where to go, how to park and other minor goals. After they both caught their breath, Frank broke the silence.

Frank said, "Mary, somehow you look familiar, but I know that I have never met you before. Perhaps it is the way you approach this meeting or something. Nevertheless, I find it hard to consider you a stranger, although you are."

Mary replied, "This is true. What I really think is that because we probably have a similar mindset and are of a particular mental acuity that all seems familiar although it all comes down to the facts, at least for me, of your dossier at the office."

At this Frank's eyebrows raised and he realized that some of what Mary was saying might be true, but not all of it. Frank had no information regarding Mary beyond that, which she revealed to him during their earlier telephone conversation and now their airport greeting. Frank also realized that here was a woman who dealt with the facts and was all serious business. Even though she had a smirk on her face, Frank could tell that laughter was a limited commodity in Mary's life.

Mary continued, "Frank I am the head of a secret United States government agency that is much more secret than the CIA. Because of this, all secrecy must be continued. Before I give you any details, it is necessary that you swear under oath to keep secret all that I am going to tell you at this meeting. Is it a deal?"

Frank, of course, was flabbergasted. He did not know what to say right away. Ultimately, he decided that after all this trouble, there was no point in fighting the inevitable and he said, "Yes, I surely will agree to secrecy providing that such secrecy will be in the best interest of my country. Will that be the fact? Will that be so?"

"Yes," Mary answered. Mary then began her conversation with Frank thusly, "Frank I want you to repeat after me the following words." Upon saying that she removed a small digital recorder from her purse not bigger than an old fashioned, ink flowing fountain pen. She instructed Frank to speak into the fountain pen recorder the following words: "I, Frank German, hereby agree under solemn oath to keep secret all the information to be revealed to me at this time by Mary Kent, the head of DESE, a secret United States government agency. Any future secrets I may obtain for the rest of my life, providing that all is in the interest of national security of the United States of America shall be kept secret from all unauthorized persons."

Frank was surprised that a fountain pen could hold all that he had said, but he was impressed that in fact this was the truth. He slowly, carefully, and contemplatively restated the words that Mary spoke, one or two words at a time. Finally, it was all stated and recorded.

Mary said jokingly, "Now that's all part of the record, literally. And now we can get down to business." She continued, "Frank your country needs you and your talents. Not in the military sense which usually follows that phrase, but rather in a much more serious situation than just military. It involves intelligence, but not spying. It involves being aware of environmental and societal behavioral changes and reporting changes to my department weekly. "

Frank inquired, "Your department? You haven't told me anything. What department is that?"

Mary answered, "My department's name will give you an idea of what we are up against and the nature of the business. My department's name is the "DEPARTMENT OF EXTRAORDINARY SITUATIONS AND EVENTS" otherwise abbreviated as "DESE"."

Frank said, "That cannot be a real government department! It sounds too much like Halloween to be real!"

Mary explained further, "Frank, you recall the events at Roswell, New Mexico, do you not? That was an extraordinary event. You recall all the sightings of UFO's some twenty or thirty years ago? According to the newspapers and government reports, you had a great, almost insatiable interest in that happening, didn't you not? That interest of yours made me interested in you."

Mary continued, "Those were extraordinary events also. So were the strange, gigantic patterns in wheat fields and pastures. It was then that the government established the DESE. The authorities did not want to alarm the public so the whole creation of that department was hush-hush, with the consent of the security committees in congress who are also sworn to the deepest secrecy. However, DESE does exist and we are and have been investigating all the strange events of our time."

Frank's mouth was open in amazement. He sat there and said nothing.

Mary continued, "Frank, here are my credentials. I am a bonafide government agent with police and military powers and more. I am regularly in direct communication with the President of the United States."

Mary spread out her credentials that included identification cards and badge in front of Frank. He was finally convinced that she was who she said she was and in the reality of his situation with her. He became quite interested in what was going on and what his part would be insofar as Mary's recruiting went.

"Frank", she continued, "I need to know if I have your commitment to this very secret and very special service to your country. In short, I need to know now if I can count on you. There is no battle involved with guns and the like, but mostly science and the application of science to natural, not-so-natural, and perhaps extraterrestrial events affecting our country."

Mary paused, "Do I have it. Do I have your commitment?" Mary went on, "I need to know now that I can count on you with your knowing the additional few facts I have just stated. This is a very serious business and not science fiction. I may sound like science fiction, but I assure you that the facts are all very real and that what may seem like a Hollywood movie scenario is reality instead. It is a reality that your government has managed to keep under wraps in order not to panic the public."

Mary pointedly asked and insisted that Frank had to either make a commitment or deny that commitment. It was now very necessary for Frank to either commit or get out of the pot. The ball was in Frank's court, and it was time. There could be no more evasion.

All this information was milling around in his mind and Frank was almost spinning mentally. Frank began to speak, "Mary, I am still young enough to go on a new adventure even though I am retired I have good health, good spirits and I am very ready and anxious for action. Mary, bring it on! I'm more than just a match for what comes my way, especially after Roswell!"

"Very well", Mary continued. "DESE has agents at the four corners of the United States at present. Others will eventually be brought in to fill in the central parts of our country, but it is not an emergency. Our department deals with much more than just what happened at Roswell. That was extraterrestrial. We also deal with the occult, the mysterious, and the supernatural. While the events at Roswell border on the physically natural, although foreign to our world, the occult and supernatural are more difficult to deal with." Mary paused, mostly to catch her breath and reorganize her thoughts.

Frank was now eager to hear more. He impatiently said, "Go on, go on Mary. I want to know all there is to know. Tell me more!"

This was a big change from the reticent Frank with whom she began her connection. He was so eager that Mary was beginning to be concerned that she had not triggered a five-hundred-pound gorilla that would be difficult to reign in!

"Our department needs environmental researchers and observers who simply need to have an awareness of what is going on around them. This does not mean only your house, street, or neighborhood, but the entire area of the country where you live and actually state by state." Mary continued. "We shall supply you with monitoring devices and gadgets which would keep any technocrat interested and occupied. These devices are various secret government items and sophisticated equipment that must be kept secret. They border on the paranormal and somewhat mystical, as well as scientific devices. Every time I say this I can't believe what I am saying because it seems so unscientific, but that's where we are and that's the nature of our business and surveillance". Mary said almost in exasperation.

Frank was more intrigued than ever. Fascination was beyond fascination. He could not believe what he was hearing, but it was for real. Our government was dealing with the mysterious occult! This was way beyond his Roswell, NM experiences and way beyond his expectations. He became more and more eager to take part in whatever this undertaking was to be. In the back of his mind, Frank still had some idea that somehow Roswell would become involved in this environmental monitoring.

After this longish disclosure by Mary of her department and the requirements, which Frank must adhere to, Frank replied, "Mary, you have yourself a devoted recruit. I couldn't think of anything more incredible than to be a part of your organization. When do I start? When do you need me to begin? Where do I start? More importantly, HOW do I start as your recruit? Basically, it's a who, where and when.

Mary responded, "Frank, of course I am aware of all the questions you may ask. This is not the first time I have interviewed a recruit and it most likely won't be the last either. All I need now is your signature on this document which states in writing all you have agreed to. Compensation for your services will be most adequate because there are not many people in the USA who would qualify, as you do, for this position. It is very special as are you.'

Frank was satisfied and said, "Mary, now that all this is settled, let's go to dinner and afterwards, I'll drive you to your hotel. We can carry on any additional discussion over dinner, and this is the ideal place to have it unless you'd like to go elsewhere?"

Mary answered, "No this place is quite all right. It has very good reviews and we have already settled in. We can have an early dinner and you can show me some of the sights. It would be kind of you to drop me off later at Best Western in Miramar. I'll handle your confirmation with my office sometime in the next twenty-four hours and I'll be leaving to get back East to get back to work."

Frank said, "I'll be very happy to oblige. It will be my pleasure to be of service."

Mary's face became very serious. She continued her administrative conversation with, "Frank, after I get back to my office, I will send you details of what we need from you as our agent. Once you understand what we need to do, I will additionally send you the hardware and monitoring equipment you will need, probably along with a DESE employee to instruct you on how the machines are used and where and how they are to be placed. You will hear from James Barrett of the GSA. James Barrett is a CPA originally from Cos Cob, Connecticut who is intimately involved with the detailed workings and needs of our department. I have known James Barrett for several decades and he is as honest and reliable a person as can ever be found anywhere. James knows that all our needs are very special and unlike those ordinarily provided to any government agency. All those needs and all our supplies are highly technical and super-secret. James Barrett will see to it that all our secrets are kept and that you will obtain security clearance for the items you will be possessing.

Frank was now over just being simply impressed and became very serious about what was going on with Mary. He was all eyes and ears and his mouth stayed shut. Frank gave his full attention to Mary's words.

Now, in Frank's eyes, Mary changed from being an unknown female from Washington, or wherever she came from, to being the official head of a very serious and clandestine government office. She became as serious as one expected Henry Kissinger to be serious. Frank now knew that his mission would be highly important and that the lives of Americans and the security of the United States was dependent on what he would be doing, at least to the extent that he would be called upon to perform his duties.

Frank was no less eager to serve, but the sudden display of a more sober personality change in attitude also impressed Mary. She now knew in her gut that Frank would be the ideal agent for the work before him, whatever it might turn out to be. Mary had an idea, but she kept it to herself. She was satisfied. They were impressed with each other and the seriousness of whatever project that may present itself before them.

If the Roswell incident was any indication of how serious our government felt this entire topic could be. If it was important enough for our government to create a secretive government department, then it was perhaps very serious. The nature of the projects before them, both known and unknown, had to be of no little matter at all. It had to be of great importance. The security of the United States and perhaps of the entire world may depend on what they plan and what is done both in the present and in the future. There is no one who knows about the next day. The future is unknown, at least that is the common belief held by all of mankind. Even the Bible says that we should worry about today because there are enough troubles in the here and now. We are worried about tomorrow when tomorrow comes.

Mary returned to her Southeastern New York home via Washington, DC where she met with the powers above her, namely the President of the United States because the nature of her department. In a manner of speaking, her position was a secretive "cabinet" position because her department head was the President. This "cabinet" position was never meant to be made public. Congress secretly created this cabinet position to deal with supersensitive matters including alien space visits, both to and from alien planets, the supernatural, and the scientifically unexplainable.

The very sensitive nature of the operatives' toil and the result of their work is so highly sensitive that even the Public Information Act would never get anything from them. This department would continue as a secretive part of the Act as created by Congress and not publicly known.

There is no higher office than that of the President. The Vice President was also privy to the DESE information so that he could carry on in the absence of a vacuum which might be created if something happened where the President could not function. Mary's office is considered important to USA security by the Executive and Legislative branches of Government.

Mary wasted no time after returning from her meeting in Washington. The President was very happy with the progress Mary was making in her department and approved of all her efforts. She was not home long before her thoughts were trained on achieving the enlistment of "HB". She checked her schedule and knew that her trip to PBI would steal another weekend for her to clear "HB" and once more prove her office and her department's existence. Mary unpacked, made herself comfortable, and because it was still in the early afternoon, she sat down and made her call to "HB".

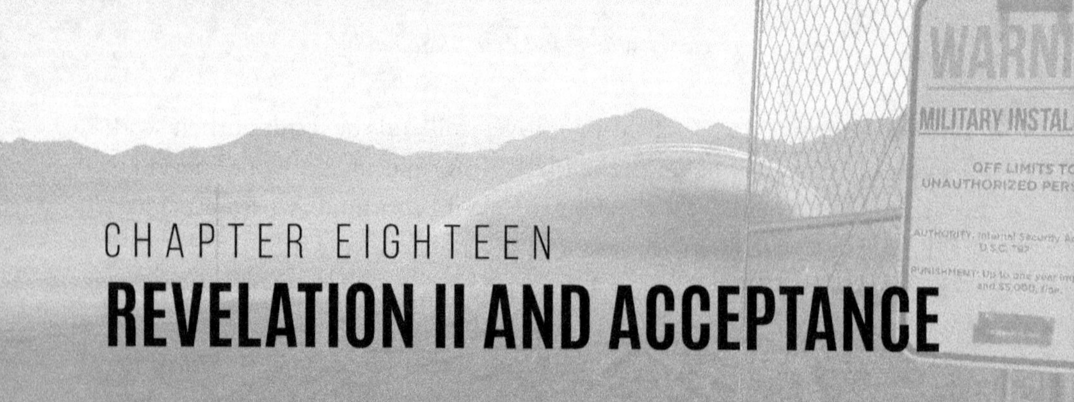

CHAPTER EIGHTEEN

REVELATION II AND ACCEPTANCE

Mary made herself a cup of tea to which she always added a little sweetener and milk, but almost never lemon, and she started to dial 1-561-555-5555 and waited and waited for "HB" to answer the call. The phone rang and rang and rang. She thought to herself, "Isn't that the way it always is. No answer, not even an answering machine." She realized that it was another sunny afternoon in the Florida Paradise and anyone who could be out enjoying the weather unlike the dismal New England's gray sky climate.

She was about to hang up with the telephone halfway gone to its cradle when she heard someone on the other end shouting.

"Hello, hello, hello" in the similar gruff voice "HB" had answered the first time she called. She knew she had the wizard himself. There was no time to waste. Mary knew that she had to respond very quickly, or he would hang up and probably not answer a second call from her, at least not right away. The telephone was only halfway to her mouth when she responded in haste, "Hello "HB". How nice it is to hear your voice one more time. This is Mary Kent. You recall that we had to set up a meeting date and time?"

"HB" grunted, "Uh huh, uh huh, so we did. Is that what we are going to do now?"

Mary answered, "Yes sir. That's right. Now is the time. I am very eager to meet you and arrive at PBI on a nice sunny day like today."

"HB" grunted again and said, "Well you don't want it to be like today. It's raining for a change. It does this when the front comes through or in the afternoon when the day has been hot. It was hot today. Here's the rain."

"Oh", Mary said. Then she added apologetically, "I'm so sorry."

"HB" mellowed a little bit and was not so gruff this time. He said, "It's quite all right. It usually doesn't last long and then the sky clears and it's beautiful again. Besides we can always use the rain."

Mary was relieved that "HB" was less gruff. She was fearful that the "gruffness" could affect their relationship and "HB's ability to act as a reliable agent. "Usually", she thought to herself, "the gruffness relates to a lack of tolerance and patience. However as before, the gruffness only lasted a short while before the familiar "camaraderie" rang in. Mary thought, "This guy must get one heck of a lot of telephone solicitation calls for him to be so gruffly defensive at the very start of each call. She was sure that "HB" probably started all his telephone calls this way. She felt it was a defensive quirk of "HB's and that it would not interfere with their business. "HB" would be very reliable as an agent of DESE. This was her final evaluation.

So, the idle talk continued for a short while when "HB" asked, "Well, when are you coming anyway? I've been waiting for your call a bit too long if you ask me. As a matter of fact, I still think you took too long to call me even if you don't ask me!"

Mary laughed. She then said, "You're quite right. I apologize, but I had additional interviews to do. I will explain everything when we meet. Would next weekend be all right?"

"HB" coughed a fake cough and said, "Well I don't know. I must consult my social calendar. Just one moment please."

There was a distant shuffling of pages some place away from the telephone and then "HB" returned. "Well Mary, you're in luck. I have this weekend free. When will you be arriving? Mary suspected that the paper rustling was phony, but she went along.

Now it was her turn to "rustle" papers. After letting "HB" cool his heels a bit, Mary came to the phone and reported, "I am to leave JFK on Jet Blue Flight 41 very early in the morning and arrive at PBI at 9:45 AM." She added in a teasing voice, "Is that too early for you?

"HB" now laughed, "Don't you worry about that. This old bird will have already jogged five miles, had breakfast, showered, shaved, and dressed up at least a full hour before you arrive. I'm very eager to meet you and I'll be there to pick you up."

Mary recalled how Frank met her and asked, "How will I know you?"

"HB" replied, "don't worry, I'll be wearing my General's Uniform, and you can't miss me. I'll be wearing a red rose in my left-hand pocket, and I'll be at the passenger exit gate. Can't wait meet you."

Mary said, "Then it's settled. I'll meet you then."

They both said their semi formal goodbyes and hung up. There was nothing to do but work the full week and then board the airplane for Florida. This was not really a bad deal. Mary liked Florida somewhat and had a cousin there who lived on Canterbury Drive North in West Palm Beach. She would like to see her cousin Larry Carl again because she hadn't seen him for quite a while. That would be her next telephone call, but not right away. The telephone gauntlet with "HB" was enough for at least a short while.

Her cousin Larry Carl lived further inland than did "HB". "HB" was Oceanside on a barrier island called Singer Island, originally owned in whole by the Singer sewing machine magnate. The main road going to Singer Island is Blue Heron Boulevard and connects past Interstate 95 to Military Trail. Larry Carl lived off Military Trail and was slightly closer to PBI Airport than was Singer Island, so it was a better place for Mary to spend a day or two. She wanted to renew her "cousinship" with Larry Carl as she had not seen him for several years.

Mary once again dialed the 561-area code and the rest of the telephone number and Larry Carl promptly and cheerfully answered. "Hello, can I help you?" he said.

Mary answered, "You most certainly can. Do you have any idea who this is?"

Larry Carl replied right away, "Of course I do. This is my long-missed cousin Mary Kent from New England where the sun rarely shines, sand the weather is gray just about all winter long!"

Mary was very impressed. She also happily and cheerfully responded, "Why yes! I am surprised that you recognized my voice so quickly. How nice it is to hear your voice again at long last."

"Well, Mary, you recognized my voice immediately too did you not? Why should you be any more amazed that I recognized yours as it is that you recognized mine?" retorted Larry Carl?

Mary said, "Perhaps I had an edge. I know I was calling you, but you could not know who was on the other end of the telephone, therefore your memory of my voice is what is remarkable. I am flattered and take my hat off to you and your memory."

Larry Carl thought for a short moment and said, "You know, you are very right! I <u>AM</u> very good indeed."

Larry Carl and Mary reconsidered old times and talked about the people they both knew as well as relatives they each had not seen for a long while. The conversation eventually came around to what Mary was doing these days. Mary was evasive, because her department is to be kept secret, and even a cousin would not rank a share in the knowledge of its existence.

Mary squirmed only a little and said, "You know that I am a government employee. I still work from 9:00 AM to 5:00 PM five days a week and sometimes I have additional duties for our Uncle Sam."

Larry Carl said, "Uh huh" (which means "yes" for those of you who don't understand grunting), "Go on, tell me more."

And Mary did. She told him that she had a meeting with a prospective government enlistee in his neighborhood for her department which Mary kept unnamed and nebulous. She told Larry Carl that the appointment was very special and that it would occur this coming weekend. She then asked, "Larry, could I stay at your house? That way we can get up to date on everything that is going on in our lives. I would be a great opportunity and I'll spring for dinner each night that I am there. How's that?"

Larry Carl jumped at the chance. He said with only a slight touch of sarcasm, "How do you like that? Mary, I've been wondering if I could get dinner someplace this weekend. I've just been starving myself almost to death and I have been waiting for just this opportunity, or one like it, to come my way. Why Mary, it would be my pleasure to take advantage of your "cooking" even if it's out at a restaurant."

Mary caught the sarcasm but ignored it. "She said then it's settled. I'll be dropped off at your house by the person with whom I have my appointment."

She added, "I'd like to see what changes they've made to the Sailfish Marina on Singer Island. I understand they have redone the place. I always liked it there. Is that still a good place to go for dinner?"

Larry Carl replied, "It has just been redone. I think that you would like it there. If not, there is always the Seaspray. It is located right on the ocean. We will take a drive around the Palm Beach Shores part of the Island and drive by the Ocean Palms Motel toward the fountain there on Park Avenue and just generally check out the changes that have occurred since you were last here. It was almost ten years ago, was it not?"

Mary replied, "It is hard to believe that so much time has passed, but you are very right. It has been exactly ten years! You know, you are remarkable. Do you have all this written down and immediately at hand? How do you do that?"

Larry Carl said, "I just remember. It just came to me. Perhaps I am on a different time track than most people. I could not really explain the why of it. It's just the way it is!"

Larry Carl continued, "When you get here, we'll renew old memories, and you can check out the new developments and shopping centers. You do like to shop, as I recall, do you not?"

Mary answered, "What woman doesn't? I enjoy shopping very much. I can't wait to see you and be there."

Larry Carl added, "Then it's settled. I'll see you on this weekend and that is that."

Mary and Larry Carl said goodbye to each other and hung up. Her trip was settled. All she had to do now was go on it!

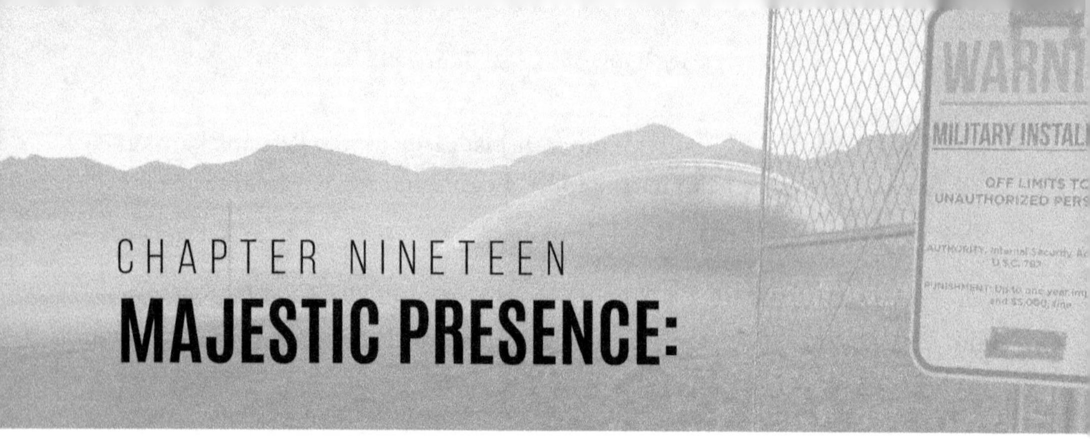

CHAPTER NINETEEN
MAJESTIC PRESENCE:

Mary boarded her flight to PBI. It was only fifteen minutes late on taking off, which is the same thing as being on time, the way the airlines work today. She was very happy. She finally was on her way to see the perhaps grumpy "HB" for their first face-to-face meeting.

The weather was clear all the way down the Eastern Seaboard. The sky was a deep clear and crisp looking blue. There were marshmallow clouds across from, above and below the airplane. They were few though and there was a good distance between them. The clouds added accent to the beautiful blue sky. Below she could clearly see the layouts of farms, fields, highways, streams and various buildings as though she were some deity surveying her domain. There was almost no haze anywhere and the earth's surface was clearly visible in detail. Mary liked that.

In about two and one-half hours' time she heard the announcement to prepare for landing and she could feel the airplane banking and turning.

The stewards cranked out the order, "Put your seat backs straight up, close your tray tables and click your seat belts. Turn off all electronic gadgets and place your portable luggage under your seats or in an overhead compartment."

This was followed up by a quick stewards' patrol up and down the aisle to make certain that the passengers complied with orders and had their seat belts fastened as well.

Then there was quiet, only broken by the whirring of wing flaps being extended and landing gear being lowered. It would only be a minute or two longer before they would have landed and disembarked. Mary always became a little tense at this point in the landing. She knew that there were two most dangerous times in an airplane's flight: landing and takeoff. She was landing. She "white knuckled" it all the way down. She could feel herself helping the pilot first turning this way and then that way, although the pilot never knew it. Mary knew she helped him and that is all that mattered. She helped him in her mind's eye.

Mary always had a window seat near the rear of the airplane. It is her preference. She waited patiently as the passengers ahead of her retrieved portable luggage from the overhead compartments or under their seats or both and filed out single file and one by one.

Mary finally arrived at the exit door where she met the smiling and cordial faces of the flight attendants as well as the pilot as they said their thank-you and farewells. Mary acknowledged them and said, "It was a very nice flight and a very nice landing. Thank you." Then she gave them a very happy smile and stepped out onto the gangway tunnel. When she arrived at the other end, she sought out the face of "HB" who promised to pick her up. Mary did have her government's edge because she had earlier reviewed all information on "HB" and his military history. It was easy for her to locate a photograph. She knew what "HB" looked like although she would need to allow for changes in appearance because of the passage of time.

Mary had to walk towards the baggage claim area and past the security gates before she would even have a chance at seeing "HB". However, the minute she exited there he was. He wore a sea captain's hat, a rumpled air force jacket with the official air force wing emblems on the sleeves and several military decorations under his left jacket pocket. There was no general's uniform but there was a red rose in his pocket as he had promised.

Mary realized that she once again had the advantage, which is as she preferred it. None of her prospective candidates knew what she looked like and as a result, none of them could approach her first. Unfairly, she knew what each of them looked like and she could choose her manner of approach. She did.

She went up to "HB" and said, "Excuse me. Is that a sailor's uniform or an air force uniform? Are you a sailor or an aviator? What is the rose is for? Are you selling roses or are you a taxicab driver? I need a cab."

Mary wondered if "HB" would react as Frank did in her earlier "taxicab driver" approach.

This forward and insulting woman took "HB" aback. He was not pleased. "HB" stood there silently and just about refused to acknowledge the presence of this person.

"HB" reverted to his gruff grumpiness. He turned his head back to face this woman and said, "I am not a taxicab driver! I am just a man waiting for a woman who was to be on this flight. I expect that she would be a gentle woman who is dignified and respectable. I truly doubt that anyone who is as forward and as insulting as you could be that woman." "HB" gave her a "Harumpp!" looked away and continued to ignore her.

"HB" waited and waited, still ignoring this woman who just stood there waiting and had since become silent. Much to "HB's" chagrin, the exit line from that flight had diminished to nothing. There were no more passengers exiting. "HB" slowly came to the suspicion that perhaps, and unfortunately, this brazen woman, who was still present, was the person he was waiting for. He did not know how he could face her after the things he said.

Slowly and sheepishly, he turned to her and asked, "Could you be Ms. Kent?"

Mary said, "Why yes, I am. I was wondering how long it would take you to realize the error of your ways and make a correction. My first name is Mary just in case you have any additional doubts about my identification."

"HB" turned as red as a very red radish. He then started to apologize without end. He was very embarrassed and sorry. His apologies would not stop. Mary had to intervene to cease his self-flagellation.

Mary said, "Please stop. It is all right. My approach to you was a part of a test of sorts. While you must admit you failed the initial part, the second part brought you out of the depths and into success." She went on, "What do you say we get out of here now and go someplace cool and quiet. We have a lot to talk about and I have some very sensitive papers to show you and to have you acknowledge."

"HB" was relieved. He did not expect to be excused so easily.

"HB" was not one to labor intensely in the past, so he quickly took the cue and said "We can go to the Breakers Hotel in Palm Beach and have a nice quiet and relaxing lunch there. It is not that far, and it is very pretty and comfortable. You will like it."

Mary had heard about the Breakers for a long time but had never been there. She liked the idea very much and readily agreed. Since she only had a carry-on piece of luggage for her short weekend stay, she did not need much. She told "HB", "Let's go. I have my luggage with me, so I do not need to go to the luggage pickup. However, please drive slowly. I haven't been here for several years, and I would like to soak in the atmosphere and the changes which have occurred over that time."

"HB" quickly agreed. He was thankful for being let out of the doghouse as rapidly as he was and would do almost anything to get away from the area that might encourage Mary to bring it back up.

They went to his Jaguar, and they were on their way. The sky was almost cloudless. The sun was bright, and the air temperature was not quite eighty degrees. They took the main approach to Palm Beach via an extension of State Road 98 and across the bridge over the inland waterway. They then went north on A1A and had passed the Breakers because Mary wanted to see more of the area.

Soon they were heading west on the very Royal Poinciana Way esplanade. They then turned around because this road would have led them off the island and then they headed back to the Breakers Hotel.

After perusing the various restaurants and dining areas they both decided to enter the Flagler Steakhouse which is in the Breakers Golf and Tennis Clubhouse. Their lunch was first. For some reason Mary was famished and it was lunchtime. It is a traditional American steakhouse specializing in first grade beef. The door bulletin read, "Open for dinner nightly, casual dining for lunch daily". Well, this was to be a casual lunch and the surroundings were excellent.

There were not many people around and the couple could take a private corner of the club house dining room, which they requested.

Mary had her briefcase with her and although Mary did not drink this early in the day, she was definitely up for a Vodka Martini, shaken, not stirred, and with two olives for color and taste. Ever since she saw the Double 07 movies, she decided that this was the way she wanted to order her Martinis except not with gin and with two olives instead of one. She found that gin made her ill. Mary liked the olives too.

When the drinks had been served, their orders were taken for lunch. The staff at the Breakers were very efficient. Mary's apprehension regarding "HB" melted away with the help of the Martini and she started to get down to business.

"HB" was impressed. It appeared that Mary was all business and beyond their short tour on the way to the Breakers and the Vodka Martini, that was it. Now it was down to business and no fooling.

Mary grabbed her briefcase and placed it on the table. She opened the briefcase and pulled out several papers. She looked "HB" closely in both of his eyes at once and said in a semi-hush husky voice, "HB", first I want to present my credentials to you so that you know who I am. I report to no one except the President of the United States. I do that regularly and more often should there be a national emergency of any kind. Here is my I.D. card and my Badge. I do hope you are impressed!" she said with a smile.

"HB" silently nodded and smiled back.

"I need you to sign an agreement of secrecy, which simply states that under penalty of law you will not reveal any secret information I intend to divulge to you regarding our meeting at this time. This agreement will be signed and sworn to by you right now. Do you agree?"

"HB" nodded "yes" in silent agreement. Mary moved the papers over to him over the table's surface and he immediately signed without reading.

"My department deals with extraordinary events and situations. It is called "DESE": The Department of Extraordinary Situations and Events" and is a secret part of our government even more secret than the FBI and the CIA. It is to be kept that way. The public and the newspapers are never to ever get a guess that it exists. You need to understand that should information about our functions and unnatural happenings that we may uncover and investigate could produce a national panic that could be disastrous, similar to the "War of the Worlds" broadcast in the 1930s. We do not need that, do we?"

Mary continued, "HB", I have read about your background and about your interests in work. Your Uncle needs you, not as an active military person, but as an alert private citizen, working as it were, "undercover", although there is no element of subterfuge or cloak and dagger type of involvement. No.

What my department is interested in is what goes on every day in our country, both environmentally and about our public's social conduct and mental well-being, as a society and not necessarily individually. When one pursues the "individual" eccentricities and activities, there can be all kinds of aberrations. What our department is involved in are the "quirks" of all kinds of people in our population as a group. In short, we involve ourselves with every citizen."

"However, that is not enough. What we are mostly interested in is the "Why?" Why do people in general do the things they do, not as individuals, but as a group or as a local society. Even going beyond that, we ask why the grass is green and why is the sky blue! I am sure that you've heard of this before. It is an old term, an old saying. We ask the "why" of happenings from the tides to the weather, to the moon rise to the sunrise. We ask about all things. What we look for are aberrations from the so-called "norm". Those changes must be quite profound and wide reaching. We may ignore a small change in a confined local area unless that same change occurs in multiple places around our country within a short time and affects a great percentage of our population." Mary went on.

Continuing, she added, "We are a "watchdog" agency. What we need you to do is just to be aware of your immediate area and the general area, with the greater awareness being extended to the entire southeastern part of the U.S. We will supply you with all kinds of scientific monitoring equipment mostly dealing with our environment because that is the major area which universally affects man and the creatures on our earth. Your scientific interest in optics and visually surveying your local environment, as your optic investigations are having you do, probably is right in line with the functions we have in mind for you. That of observation and reporting what you see and what the instruments we will send you tells you. You will analyze, compile and report what you see to DESE on a regular basis."

"HB" was quiet throughout this sort of "lecture" and thought very little. It was mostly "information assimilation". It was all before him. The only matter that he was not sure of was exactly what he would be monitoring and why he would be monitoring anything at all. Had something grossly unusual occurred? Was our country or our world in trouble? Was there danger on the horizon? What could cause a national panic anyway? It was all a big mystery to him, but he felt the urgency in the companion now sitting across the table from him. Nevertheless, he could not wait to devour the gorgeous one-inch thick, 16-ounce steak just placed before him. It appeared that his companion, Mary had the same ravenous appetite he did because the conversation immediately quieted down to almost a hush, all materials were put aside and gave way to a very nice, fancy steak knife and a fork!

While they were busy putting away their medium cooked, red center steak, the baked sweet potato, and the sweet yellow corn on the cob, they spoke only minimally. However, they did continue their conversation to a diminished degree. They continued, even with their mouths semi-full!

"HB" was more adept at speaking with this oral impairment, and he struggled to say, "Mary, I signed your paper in good faith. I have full confidence in you because of your I.D. and your papers as well as your dissertation. I will be happy to help, but "how" is somewhat of a mystery to me. What is this all about? Has something happened? Is there something going on that I, as part of the public, do not know? I would appreciate your letting me in on a little information about current happenings and exactly what kind of a department you are running. How is it organized and what does it really do and what is its real function?"

Mary had to stop the enjoyment of her meal to reply. "HB" I can understand that there is concern and confusion about your involvement in my department, which only a few moments ago, you never heard of. Your trust and belief in my department and me is welcomed. We started in "business" at about 1947 after the Roswell incident. It is hard to believe that it is that long ago, but facts are facts. Our government was forced to recognize that we earthlings are not alone in this universe. We have company arriving on a regular basis. These arrivals are never announced. This company comes from other worlds, not from earth. Just about all of them are beneficial to our world, but there are always the one or two rotten apples that make things bad for the rest. They blend in with our population and sometimes it is possible that their goals will not be to our benefit but instead to our detriment. That is a chance our government is not going to take. This is the basis for our department's existence and formation. We continue to monitor the environment with these and other factors in mind."

"All we need from you is a minimal amount of watching and analyzing. Even there, all you must do is fill out a weekly report on a routine basis. It is a simple type of questionnaire that will barely take you five minutes to complete. Remote analysis will always be finally performed and checked at our headquarters where we are more fully equipped."

"HB" mumbled, "I see."

Mary completed her thoughts by saying, "Of course, "HB", if you have something very unusual or suspicious to report, it is not necessary for you to wait for the end of the week to file your report. You should call it in the minute you realize its nature or its unique characteristics. This is most assuredly so when you note what could be detrimental to us all as a people. You should never wait." Mary placed heavy emphasis on this last sentence. She was very serious, and "HB" could see it. He was entering this very serious business. It was obviously part of the mysterious "unknown" which we sometime hear about. This was it.

Their entrance to the Breakers was regal. Although "HB" was a sort of a disheveled sailor/airman in his mixed-up uniform, their entry to the Breakers was "majestic" in a way. He was her older escort, and she was a trim woman who appeared to be quite the prim and properly dressed royalty. They made an impressive pair. Nevertheless, "HB's" heart belonged to this wife Ann who was at home. This was a pure business association and that was exactly what it had to be for it to be a successful working relationship.

"HB" said to Mary, "I have always had a sneaking suspicion that the rumors of Roswell could not have been one hundred percent fiction. I also believe that the average American thinks the same way. The very existence of a government agency like yours would certainly prove it, is that not so?" Then "HB" quickly added, "A rhetorical question needing no answer. I now have a much-improved idea of your organization's function and I will be very happy to be of service. It really is a more real "secret" service than the Secret Service itself, is it not? That is another rhetorical question. Where do we go from here?"

Mary looked at "HB" and replied, "I will forward all the materials and equipment you'll need within the week. The materials and equipment are super-secret and you have agreed to keep that secret and maintain security. James Barrett from the GSA will be in touch with you and probably will accompany the equipment when it is shipped to you. He will be happy to answer any of your questions and instruct you in the placement and use of the equipment you will receive. Do you have any questions?"

Mary stared into a somewhat of a poker faced "HB". There was no display of emotion or any type of readable response. "HB" simply said, "I understand it all well and any questions I may have will certainly be answered as time goes on and the same for any questions which may develop in my mind. Right now, I have no questions at all. I thank you for the opportunity to serve once again."

Mary responded, "Great! You asked where do we go from here? My answer to you is that you can go back home and carry on with your business as though nothing is different in your life. I would appreciate it if you could drop me off at my cousin's residence in West Palm Beach as he is waiting for me. I have not seen him for a number of years, and I can't wait to see him again!"

The glow came back into Mary's face and her serious side dissipated into a very normal person. "HB" was relieved to see the change because he became more concerned with the seriousness of his new position in direct proportion to the grim look on Mary's face during her dissertation at lunch. Now they could both go back to being "normal" whatever that means.

"HB" said, "Of course I would be delighted to take you to your cousin's house. That is no problem whatsoever."

Mary replied, "Wonderful. I will call him on my cell phone and let him know that I am on my way."

They went to the valet and retrieved the Jaguar and piled in. They then tooled their way back over the waterway bridges to the mainland and crossed Interstate 95 and went northward on Military Trail to Canterbury Drive North. "HB" followed Mary's instructions and the pair soon arrived at the front door of Cousin Larry's home.

Larry saw the car pull up and came out the door to greet his long-lost cousin and carry in any baggage. Except for her carry-on and her briefcase there was nothing for Larry to cart. Mary had learned to be quite self-sufficient over the years and her traveling experience taught her what she needed and what to leave at home.

Larry walked up to the car as it pulled into his driveway and opened the passenger door. Mary stepped out and he greeted her with a hug and a kiss, which was eagerly returned.

"Why Mary, how you have grown!" Larry said in fun and with a chuckle, knowing that this phrase applied mostly to growing children and not adults.

Mary laughed, "I see that you have grown yourself and fortunately it is mostly vertical and not horizontal!"

They both laughed at that comment. Mary then went on to introduce Larry to "HB" who had come out of the car and over towards the greeting pair.

Mary said, "Larry, I want you to meet my associate here in Florida. This is "HB" Gaunt who lives in the area and with whom I've just had a very nice business meeting." She looked over to "HB" and smiled.

"HB" smiled at the two of them and shook Larry's hand. He said, "Larry I am very pleased to meet you."

Larry replied, "I am also happy to meet you. Anyone who is associated with Mary must be an excellent human being. I thank you for bringing her over to me. I have not seen her in years, and it is always a pleasure to be in her company. Thank you again."

"HB" answered, "It is no problem. I agree with you about Mary. She is indeed quite a human being. I am happy to know her."

"HB" then added speaking to Larry, "It is a pleasure to have met you. I expect that we will be seeing each other again. I will be going now since it is apparent that you two have a lot to catch up on, as I understand from Mary. So long."

With that, he wheeled around like an older Zorro on his heels, went to his car and hopped over the open convertible's door and into the driver's seat just as though it was his horse! It was an amazing instant to witness. Mary and Larry turned their heads, said nothing, and just looked at each other as if to say, "Are we in the Old West or what?" "HB" left quite an impression on Larry and additionally impressed Mary who never would have thought that this "old bird" had that much agility.

Larry Carl and cousin Mary entered the house. They settled in and Mary was given the front left bedroom with an adjacent bath, separate from the master bedroom that had its own "private" bathroom.

They sat out on the rear patio and Larry said, "Mary, I am going to get us a nice tall glass of iced tea, we will sit down and relax, get reacquainted and talk over old times. I'll be right back!" Larry scooted off into the adjacent kitchen and in no time, there were two glasses as well as a pitcher of iced tea on the serving table next to the two chairs.

Mary started the conversation, "Larry I see that you have made some very nice changes in your house. I like them very much. How are things and what are you up to these days?"

Larry replied, "Well I have made a few changes, haven't I? I put in a new kitchen and moved some partitions around to give the place a more open feeling. Not too shabby, don't you think so?"

Mary nodded in agreement, "Yes, it is very nice. I remember that when we were much younger that we used to play on those palm trees in front, fooling ourselves into thinking that we would be able to climb them and retrieve the coconuts. You almost made it as I recall. That is until you fell out of the tree near the top!" Mary snickered.

Larry said, "I almost had my hands on those coconuts too! I just missed them by a hair!" He looked at Mary somewhat sheepishly and grinning! Then I lost my hold on the tree and fell! It was not funny!" Larry protested. Then they both laughed at the memory.

They conversed and went over old memories and family photographs for the better part of two hours. This was a very fond moment for them both and they recalled the things they cherished which lay in the heap of times past like a hill of old laundry waiting to be sorted into darks and lights before washing.

Larry showed Mary around his house and his gardens. The gardens were full of all kinds of colors crotons, roses and almost every variety of Florida plant with any color or sweet smell filled the eyes and the nostrils. Mary sniffed all the flowers, and they all had a sweet perfume odor. It was delightful and Mary enjoyed it immensely.

It was now late in the afternoon, approaching five pm and time for dinner. Mary asks Larry, "Larry, it is time for the Sailfish Center dinner I promised you. Let's get the show on the road and go to Singer Island for the early bird special!"

Larry laughed and answered, "You have got a deal. Remember that it's your treat! Anyway, I am not sure the Sailfish Center has "early bird" specials at all. However, they might, and it is worth a try. Let us get spruced up and go off to dinner."

Mary agreed and they went off in different directions to freshen up and prepare themselves for dinner. Mary was ready ahead of Larry and met him in the house's foyer. They jumped into Larry's BMW convertible and made their way via Blue Heron Boulevard, over the inland waterway bridge and past the Phil Foster Memorial Park and onto Riviera Beach's Singer Island. They made the first right turn and soon found themselves in front of the Sailfish Marina.

Mary had many fond memories of this place. She had dined there many times with her parents and cousins. It had changed a bit since those days. It was not as fully open as it had been in the past. Mary thought that it still had its charm and attraction. It was still charming and a delightful place on the Island.

The dinner onslaught did not yet begin. They took a table overlooking the marina and the yachts moored at the docks. The sun had not even approached the thought of setting, and since it was still early in the summer, it would be several hours before the sun would set.

It was a beautiful Florida day. The sky was royal blue at its zenith and light blue at the horizon with almost no clouds. The inland waterway was smooth and displayed its beautiful aquamarine teal green-blue color. Pelicans guarded almost each dock-supporting pier with one stationed atop each upright pillar. The seagulls made their usual screeching sounds as they communicated that mealtime was at hand and called out to their fellows.

Mary thought to herself, "This is not a bad life. Turf for Lunch and Surf for Dinner! Furthermore, she was at each of her most favorite places." She was quite pleased with herself. She was slated to fly back to JFK the next day, but she wanted to make the most of her time here.

The dinner menu was intriguing. She ordered Bahamian Conch Chowder as an appetizer. Larry ordered the Mate's Platter consisting of two Conch Fritters, two Pistachio Scallops, two Coconut Shrimp, and Crusty Calamari. The entree for Mary was a Sesame Seared Fillet of Tuna and for Larry was the Snapper Vera Cruz. The salads were a Spinach and Watercress Salad for Mary and a Grilled Scallop Salad for Larry.

The Florida air and atmosphere just whetted their appetites greatly and they both dug in heartily and before they knew it, there was nothing left on their plates. The busboy cleaned up and the waitress was there asking if they wanted desert. Mary replied, "Without a doubt! How about getting me a slice of Key Lime pie and a cup of coffee?" The waitress made her notes. Larry, in turn, said, "I'll have the same, thank you!" Dinner was now complete.

They ate their dessert and enjoyed their cups of coffee, taking their leisure time and they would extend their time there as much as they could.

They knew that they would leave the Sailfish Marina after they finished, and they were in no hurry to do so. It was enjoyable just being there.

They left the Marina and went south to Inlet Way, made a left turn at the end and then traveled north on South Ocean Drive, past Riviera Beach's beach. They then continued north on East Blue Heron Blvd to where it turned in to North Ocean Drive, also known as A1A or Florida 703, and past the luxurious ocean front condominiums, once again over the inland waterway to connect with US1 going southbound back to Larry's house.

It was a good, fast tour that Mary wanted so that she could fondly renew her old, cherished memories of when her parents lived there. She missed them very much.

They finally arrived back at Larry's home and went into the house. Larry offered Mary a night cap and Mary accepted.

Larry said, "I'm going to make us a couple of Rusty Nails, can I get you to join me? Then we can sit out on the patio until the sunlight totally fades."

Mary replied, "But of course! A Rusty Nail is perfect way to end the day. Tomorrow, I need to get back to JFK and continue working."

Larry answered, "All work and no play makes Jane a dull girl! You certainly can't spend all your time working, can you?

Mary said, "I most certainly can, but if I don't watch it, I'll be working almost all the time. It is not a prospect I seek nor is it one that I will permit. However, I do need to get my work done no matter what. Don't you worry; I'll make time here and there for fun now and then. It won't be all work, believe me!"

Larry replied, "Good, I'm glad to hear that. It has been too long since you have been coming down here to visit us. I certainly hope that it won't be that long before you return this time."

Mary assured Larry, "It most certainly will not be. Time goes by too fast, and if we don't watch it there won't be any left at all. Tomorrow morning you can take me to Palm Beach International Airport, and I will be back home in short order. I hope to return at least once every two months from here on out. "HB" is going to need my help in getting his work done, although he is highly capable. So let us see what the future holds."

Larry said, "I'm game. Let's see if your return actually comes to pass." He gave Mary a wink and a quick smile, almost appearing sarcastic, but then he laughed and so did Mary.

"Well, Larry, it's been fun. Now I am going to turn in and get ready for my flight tomorrow morning. I can use a good night's rest after all of today's running around and mixing business with pleasure." This time Mary placed emphasis on the last part: "business with pleasure" and emphasized the last word. She gave Larry a poke and pointed out that it was not all work and that this "Jane" was not going to become "dull".

CHAPTER TWENTY
RETURN AND REORGANIZATION:

Mary returned to her home in the New York area. She picked up the weekend's papers collected on her front porch and then simply sacked out on the sofa while her telephone messages played back. She dropped her carry-on in the foyer and bee-lined it for the sofa where she laid down for a few moments to catch a new breath of wind. Her constant companion, Guinness, her black cat, immediately greeted her with heavy purring and leg rubbing. Guinness was so happy to have her back home although he was not hungry, what with the tower feeders' cats need today and automatic scoop potty boxes. He was as comfortable as a cat could be.

Guinness was lonely, however. Although most people might think of cats as being aloof, this one was quite affectionate, curious, and almost human. One would think that he could probably even speak if the situation and opportunity were right. Guinness was assumed to be a descendant of one of the cats found near the Roswell wreck that were thought to be feral and not associated with the event at all. The older cats are captured and put under watch at the Area 51 laboratories. When it was determined that they were no threat to humanity they were then sent to shelters, but some were kept at the laboratory to keep the mice population to a minimum. When Mary, in the course of her duties, visited Area 51, she fell in love with this strange black cat. She swore that it smiled at her and winked its right eye. Of course, everyone knows that cats cannot smile, and it is farfetched to think that they can "wink" one eye at will. Sometimes Mary would swear that the cat was a human person judging by its personality and actions.

Guinness proved to be not the usual sort of cat. Mary had a feeling that the cat had mystical powers and would always keep an eye on it when she was home. She never would leave Guinness alone on any Halloween night, just in case. Mary laughed as she ran over that thought. Nevertheless, she assigned it all to silliness and put it out of her mind. Occasionally, Mary thought she saw the cat "reading" the papers, she felt that it was something like when a cat looks into a mirror and becomes enthralled with the other "good looking" cat on the other side and nothing more.

Mary had a hard day saying goodbye to Larry and then traveling from PBI to JFK. She was tired. She went to her desk and emptied out her briefcase of its papers, including all those that detailed her agent contacts and agent development accomplishments. She decided to take a short nap and then prepare herself for the morrow later that afternoon or early evening.

She had a very comfortable bed and an even more comfortable pillow. Mary fell right off to slumberland and did not awaken until almost two hours later. She was a little groggy but not too groggy to be re-energized into action when she saw that Guinness had been playing with the papers she put on her desk, and that they were all spilled and spread out all over the floor. Mary awakened out of her drowsiness and went to Guinness and scolded, "Naughty cat! Shame on you! Don't you ever do anything like this again!"

Guinness did not scurry away as "normal" cats would but instead simply stood his ground and gave Mary an affectionate, "Meow" and rubbed against her legs and purred loudly. Mary said, "Oh Guinness! I can't be angry with you. I've left you alone and gone so far away so many times. I know that you need company. Perhaps another cat, but no. Then I'd be leaving both of you alone and that would be even worse." Mary put the paper-spilling event out of her mind and totally gave up on the second cat idea as being a poor thought.

Mary started to re-sort her papers into different agent folders. She was thankful that at least all the papers spilled out in a right side up orientation and still somewhat in page order so that it was not necessary to flip them over first and to check them before any resorting was needed. That saved her much time and extra work.

Mary did not need to get approval from Washington regarding her choice of agents and their supplies. Whatever she thought she needed was right and certainly all right with the President. She had "carte blanche". Whenever she had a need for a second opinion or a question, her prime consultant was the President of the United States. She had to account to no one else. However, she would need to keep him informed as to details regarding her agents and their supplies.

James Barrett, CPA from the government GSA provides and checks with the DESE to see to it that all necessary supplies are presented to agents. When she went into her office on Monday, she would consider what each agent required. Her list would not be short, but it would not be a mile long either. Her liaison with the US General Services Administration federal supply service was James Barrett a former CPA she knew some time earlier who hailed from Connecticut. James Barrett was directly enlisted by the President and sworn to keep and fill all DESE orders and its needs a highly classified secret. Her orders had to be secretive because of her highly privileged and clandestine agency, both invisible and unknown. It had to stay that way to avoid worldwide panic, at least that was the consensus of higher echelon thinking.

She started to sort out the different agents and made some notes as to what their supply needs should be, based on their education and their abilities, although no agent she selected would ever be considered a "slouch". Not all her requested supplies would come from conventional sources. The unconventional sources would need to be directly purchased in person by one of her departmental agents and in secret because those supplies would be bought in Magickal supply houses. The supplies purchased there are not at all conventional but rather of the supernatural and paranormal variety.

Supplies for Seemore would be different than those given to the more technically educated agents. Seemore would have equipment such as the

"Extrasensory Perceptor" which came in the configuration of a satellite conical television antenna as well as a one-foot-long wand-like rod with a sensor at the end called a

"Percipio-accipio".

Each of these items basically did the same thing except that one would be easily portable. Both items are voice trained and triggered by the command "Percepio"

And he would be given a

"Premonition-Mood-Emotion" conducting and deducting device. This device would be able to report in digitally coded numbers and in the English language the feelings and direction the emotions of the area and the public were headed. "Cor-Cordis" It was in the shape of an amulet which is to be worn as a pendant medal around the neck.

Also a

"Thought Reader and Inducer" which could generally read the thoughts of those Seemore thought were persons of interest and even to induce pre-coded thoughts into their minds. This came in the form of a fountain pen. "Cogito-Lector". This item would be vocally triggered by the owner's voice frequency and the command "cogito" to induce thoughts and "lecto" to read thoughts;

And a

"Confugio" device that would permit him almost to magically transport himself from place to place. It would have special safety settings that would avoid transportation into a wall, under a lake or inside a tree et cetera. All the devices are voice commanded. The command for this item is "fugit".

An Environmental reader called the

"<u>Dissernat-Clarus</u>" which would report on the various factions of the environment, but beyond that of usual weather report. The command for this piece of equipment is "clarus".

Then there are the Enchantment Divisions.

These divisions obtain their supplies from the stores, which deal in the Magickal Wiccam Supply, namely the witches' super shopping centers. The most famous of which, among witches and those interested in the occult, "World Mart" super centers. There one could buy all types of Crucibles, Wax Dolls, Spirit Jars, Soul Jars, Anima Jars, Essence Gift, Solar Jar, the Seeming, the Tasting, Anima Warp and Black Candles.

Seemore would receive a small sampling of each of these. An agent skilled in enchantments would instruct Seemore as to the applications of enchantments and spells. Seemore probably would be more easily acquainted with enchantments and spells than any of the other agents. As a gnome, he had more interaction with faeries and elves and other little people who have survived over the ages by using their skills and any spells or other magic they might come across to help them. Seemore would need less instruction because of earlier "on the job" experience and would be given a more generous supply of this type of equipment.

Frank German would also receive the above supplies, but in addition he is to be admitted to an instructional tour of Area 51 and he would be informed, in detail, regarding what happened there and what the findings were. Frank should jump at this chance, after all these years! The only catch is he would need to adhere to his pledge of secrecy under the severest penalties. In any case, his suspicions, curiosity and his beliefs would be reinforced, and he would never again need to wonder what exactly happened at Roswell.

Brad Gaunt is also to be admitted to Area 51. This admittance would be like a supplementary education on a higher academic level, namely a postgraduate course indeed. It is based on all the actual findings and scientific facts insofar as the government knows it. Information on extraterrestrials would be included. It is called introduction to DESE 101. Brad, because of his education, scientific and business background as well as military experience, would readily grasp the nature and purpose of the equipment he would be receiving.

Both Frank German and Brad Gaunt will also be instructed in the use of the Enchantment Division supplies. Frank German would probably not be at all surprised by the devices and their functions because of his belief in the extraterrestrial Roswell experience and his tour. Brad Gaunt, however, was a well-educated military academic graduate and would most likely be shocked that the US Government ever used such supernatural and paranormal devices.

Both Brad and Frank would be introduced to and instructed in the uses of all devices both instrumental and supernatural. Both men would readily accept the nature of their equipment once they completed their tour of Area 51. There would be no doubt in their minds regarding the valid use and employment of their new and strange equipment. There should be no surprise, that these accomplished and scientifically curious men would become extremely eager to employ their new devices as soon as they possibly could. They would be like children with a new toy. Make no mistake, however, these were not toys and each device had a serious application and meant business.

Brad and Frank were destined to receive a more generous supply of technical equipment than the more mystical, paranormal devices.

Mary wasted no time in contacting James Barrett and getting him to secretly obtain and ship the needed supplies to her agents.

She next contacted her instructing agent, the highly scientific Eddy Erp, who is also skilled in the use of paranormal and mystical devices. Ed has been with DESE since its beginning. He has a broad scientific background with PhD degrees in Physics and Engineering as well as a master's degree in the Sinister, Oscuro and Mystical Arts.

He is referred to commonly as "Eddy Erp" and as "Wyatt" because of his last name and its association to "Wyatt Earp" of Western fame. "Wyatt" is the name Mary prefers to call Edward Erp because it is simpler to say. It is a pseudonym and minimizes outside connection with her department. This is just as well because Erp was better known by his associates as "Wyatt" anyway. Wyatt would either accompany the supply shipments or he would arrive the next day to impart his knowledge and experiences with the gear soon to be in each agent's possession.

CHAPTER TWENTY-ONE
SUPPLIES FOR SEEMORE:

Seemore is in heaven at his home in Fairbanks, Alaska. His life was not boring because there was much contact with the outside world. He would sit at home with a new or old issue of the "Nome Nugget" and keep up with the news. In addition, Mary had supplied him with a special connection to a satellite telephone system and satellite television, which pulled in stations from all over the world.

It was early in the summer when Wyatt visited Seemore. Alaska was just warming up and trees and flowers were budding. Wyatt presented his credentials to Seemore and Seemore was satisfied, especially since Mary had informed him of Wyatt's coming and described him.

Although Wyatt had been told that Seemore was a Gnome, he was not prepared for the meeting. Wyatt was totally surprised, almost to the point of shock that Seemore was so short, standing only slightly taller than the average run of Gnomes at about four foot and three inches tall.

Seemore was almost equally surprised at meeting Wyatt. Wyatt was slightly taller than six foot two inches tall. It was harder on Seemore to look up from his short stature to the face of a man who was taller than Seemore was used to. It hurt his neck and he would complain after a while, grab and massage his neck so that he could continue a conversation while looking his visitor in the eye.

Wyatt, on the other hand, had to look down on Seemore. All he saw mostly was either the top of his head or the top of his cone-like hat.

In any case, Wyatt was almost equally uncomfortable looking down as Seemore was looking up.

They reached an unspoken working compromise. If they stood about four to six feet apart, the disparity in their heights would not be too big a factor in their communication. Their angles of viewing each other would not be so severe and thus more comfortable.

The other half of it was that Wyatt could not easily ignore Seemore's bulb-like red nose. While it was not bright red, it was certainly very outstanding and almost a bright red. The redness of Seemore's cheeks tended to reduce the prominence of the facial centerpiece, his nose. Nevertheless, Wyatt would have sworn that it glowed! Rudolph the Red-nosed Reindeer had nothing on Seemore, that was certain.

Wyatt began conversing with Seemore once the preliminaries were completed. He said, "Seemore, I am certainly glad that I found you. Your place is a bit out of town and the roads here are not the finest. Of course, I did know where it was. Finding it is something different."

Seemore replied, "Surely, we are not in the center of town, but it's close enough for me! I have enough equipment to know what's going on in the world, thanks to Mary. I just love my forest friends, especially Peganni. I have other friends as well and they all keep me company. However, my best companion, Hepseva, is always with me."

Wyatt asked, "Who is that? And who is Peganni?"

Peganni is a friend of mine who is as pure as the driven, newly fallen snow. He has a soul that is so pure that he can counter gigantic evil. He can heal hurts of any kind, physical, mental, or emotional. Peganni is part Unicorn and part Pegasus. He has both the Unicorn horn from his father and the wings of Pegasus from his mother. He has the dual powers of each of his parents. He is their offspring and has the best of both, including their deepest love. He has the magical powers of the Unicorn and the power of Pegasus as well as the ability of flight. Peganni is very special indeed.

Then Seemore introduced Wyatt to Hepseva, his wife. "Wyatt, this is my beloved wife, Hepseva who came out here with me from the old country. I don't know what I'd do without her. We both share the same thoughts and the same interests, and all at the same time too!"

Wyatt thought to himself, "Yes and the same height too!" Wyatt smiled, tipped his head in a short bow and said out loud, "I am very, very pleased to meet you. I am sure that Seemore is sharing his assignments with you, and I hope that you find them interesting."

Hepseva replied, "I most certainly do. You might say that I am his own very private agent," and then she paused a second, looked askance at Seemore and then down at the floor and giggled an embarrassed giggle and turned a little rosier red, if such a thing were possible because her complexion was always ruddy.

Regaining her composure, Hepseva said to Wyatt, "I share all Seemore's thoughts and there are no secrets between us. His interests are my interests. I love all the animals of the forest and they are all our friends. We are both eager to be of service to our adopted country. When can we really get started? So far, all the reports are very routine and there has been nothing unusual to report."

Wyatt replied, "Nothing unusual is a good thing. We want there to be nothing to report that is out of the ordinary. The routine and ordinary are what we want. It means that there are no problems, and no problems are a good thing, not a bad thing."

Wyatt continued, "We know that this post may not have a lot of excitement in it. We hope to have no excitement. Unfortunately, trouble comes with excitement and that is something we neither need nor want."

Seemore answered, "Hepseva and I are in agreement with you. Peace and quiet are a good norm. We both appreciate it. I think that what Hepseva is interested in are all the additional gadgets and devices you have brought with you as well as those which arrived yesterday. That's how we knew you were coming, especially since the note attached to the shipment said so."

Wyatt smiled and said, "Oh, eager beavers hey? Well, it is now time to instruct and demonstrate the uses and applications of all these devices."

Wyatt continued, "The first item, the "Extrasensory Perceptor", gives the operator the ability to see and feel things not apparent to the unequiped person. It will allow the user to feel what another person, or a group of persons, actually "sense". It is a wide-ranging device and may cover several square miles or so of space. Its accompanying wand the "Percipio-accipio" allows the user to isolate a particular group's feelings and emotions. Its range is more specific and even adjustable to examine the condition of just one person, if the operator so desires. Seemore, you need to train these devices to respond to your voice. The sound frequencies of your voice become programmed into these devices as well as the others. For this device you must press this reset button and hold it down while you say, in the same tone of voice the command, "Percipio" twenty times. Then you must lock down the reset button so that it stays programmed to your voice command. You can program the "Extrasensory Perceptor" and the "Percipio-accipio" at the same time by using the correct word. The procedure is the same for each as is the command. The word "Percipio" said once in your voice will then start the device operating."

The "Premonition-Mood-Emotion" device digitizes all language and feelings and emotions. Emotions such as happiness, fear and grief are read and deciphered. There are no secrets from this gadget. Its accompanying smaller form is the "Cor-Cordis" which reads the very same emotions and the emotions of the heart, especially those of love and grief. It is easily portable since it can be worn as a necklace charm or amulet. This is also voice commanded. The trigger word is "Cordis". All these devices are voice commanded and the programming procedure is the same. To turn each item on you just say the triggering word. You do the same to turn it off.

The fountain pen, the "Cogito-Lector," can both read and induce thoughts into another person. This device is useful when a situation, such as a riot, needs to be controlled. Thoughts are induced to a crowd to produce peace and the avoidance of violent conflict. This item is vocally triggered by the owner's voice frequency and the command "Cogito" to induce thoughts and "Lecto" to read thoughts;

Wyatt demonstrated the use of these devices using Hepseva as a guinea pig in order to show Seemore how they worked. In reverse, he also used Seemore as a guinea pig as well in order to demonstrate to Hepseva the nature, depth and operation of each item. He went down the line explaining and demonstrating the function and use of each piece of equipment until the Gnomes were well satisfied and fully acquainted with their use.

Wyatt also showed the Gnomes where to position their devices as well as how to use them. After a dinner of forest-grown berries, nuts, and mushrooms, it was time for Wyatt to leave and to get to instruct and demonstrate these devices to the next agent.

Wyatt wanted to leave before dark so that he would not get lost in the hinterlands of Fairbanks and get to the airport. Since the hinterlands were almost barren, it would have been hard for him to lose his way. They all said their goodbyes. Both Hepseva and Seemore enjoyed his company, despite his height, and were sorry to see him go. They realized that his services were needed elsewhere and reluctantly returned their goodbyes to Wyatt. It was agreed that they would meet on a regular basis.

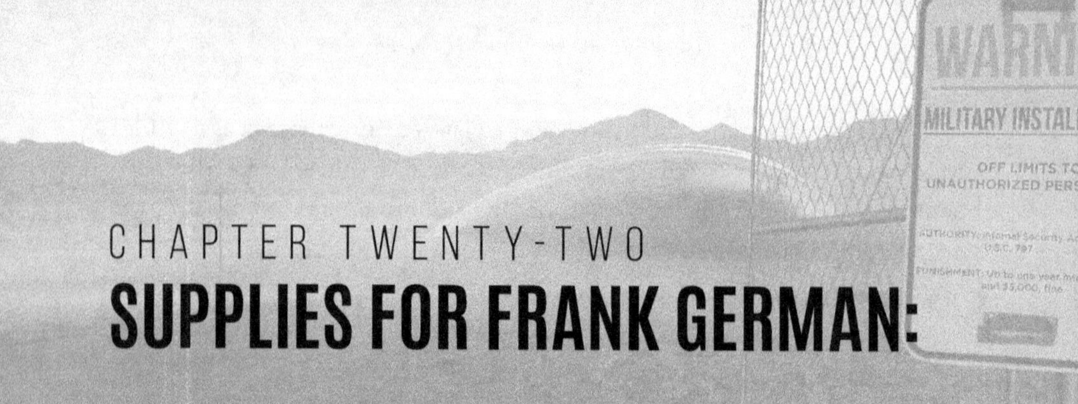

CHAPTER TWENTY-TWO
SUPPLIES FOR FRANK GERMAN:

Wyatt's trip to San Diego to meet with Frank German was uneventful. There were no delays on any of his connecting flights. Wyatt went directly from Alaska to San Diego. The trip was full of gorgeous scenery with mountainous panoramas all the way. His seat was on the port side of the airplane, and it was his favorite: a window seat. As Wyatt's airplane approached the landing, he wondered about Frank and what type of person he was. The first agent Wyatt met was something out of a fairy tale or Snow White and the Seven Dwarfs. A Gnome! Wyatt only hoped that this next agent was a bit more normal. The description and particulars he gleaned from Mary and his department's files pointed out that Frank was normal and perhaps even super normal. Wyatt was eager to meet him and would do so a few minutes after landing.

Supplies for Seemore would be different than those given to the more technically educated agents. Frank German and Brad Gaunt were given possession, instruction and demonstration of the "Extrasensory Perceptor" which came in the configuration of a satellite conical television antenna as well as a one foot long wand-like rod with a sensor at the end called a "Percipio-accipio". Each of these items would be voice trained and simply triggered by the command "Percepio" "Percipio-accipio".

They both were given the "Premonition-Mood-Emotion" conducting and deducting device. The trigger word would be the same for all agents, in this case the word to turn the device on and off, as with Seemore, is "Cordis".

Frank German and Brad Gaunt were also given the fountain pen, the "Cogito-Lector", which can both read and induce thoughts into another person. This device is useful when a situation, such as a riot, needs to be controlled. Thoughts can be induced to an individual or a crowd according to the operator's wishes.

Frank and Brad were given the "Confugio" device. This piece of equipment will permit the operator to transport himself magically from place to place instantly. It has special safety settings that would avoid transportation into a wall of under a lake or inside a tree et cetera. As with the other agents, the voice command would need to be programmed and the word "Fugio" would start it. It was equipped with a classified government issued and manufactured GPS system. All the operator had to say was the address of the place he wanted to arrive at and he would be transported to that location immediately. It took a little discipline to be careful of what he said because he could find himself there, especially if he failed to say the triggering word "Fugit" to turn it off.

An Environmental reader called the "<u>Disserenat-Clarus</u>", abbreviated "DC", which reported the various actions of the environment and much more than of a usual weather report. The "DC" is a stationary piece of equipment that reports daily to the DESE central offices and only needed placement and occasional monitoring. It is not voice commanded but simply placed in a strategic location and turned on via a key lock or a remote electronic signal.

The Enchantment Divisions contained a multitude of supernatural supplies. The Enchantment Division especially dealt in witchcraft and its implementation as well as real magic and not just simple card tricks.

The stores in which the Enchantment Division bought its supplies were mostly from the Magickal Wiccam Supply. There were all types of Crucibles stores which dealt in the Magickal Wiccam Supply. There were all types of Crucibles, Wax Dolls, Spirit Jars, Soul Jars, Anima Jars, Essence Gifts, Solar Jars, the Seeming, the Tasting, Anima Warp. and Black Candles. None of these supplies were vocally commanded. Seemore, being closer to the strangeness of magic, elves, faeries, and the like, received a full supply of each. An agent skilled in enchantments would instruct Seemore as to the applications of enchantments and spells.

Seemore probably would be more easily acquainted with enchantments and spells. As a Gnome, he had more interaction with faeries and elves and other little people who have survived over the ages using their skills and any spells or other magic they might come across to help them. Seemore would need less instruction because of earlier "on the job" life experiences and would be given a more generous supply of this type of equipment than would either Brad or Frank.

It happened exactly as the DESE administrators expected. Both Frank and Brad were more resistant to the use of Enchantment Division supplies than was Seemore. Brad was more resistant than Frank because of his higher technical educational level. Brad said, "Tried and true and scientifically proven facts and equipment developed from those facts is what we need, not Voodoo mumbo jumbo." In contrast, however, Frank was eager to learn the uses and interpretations of the Enchantment Division equipment and actually made a better student than the more scientifically inclined Brad Gaunt. It was expected. It is expected that Brad would eventually comply and use the equipment as necessary and as instructed. Brad did eventually comply and used the more "spiritually" oriented devices eagerly. Brad would never acknowledge that there could ever be anything scientific about Enchantment Division equipment. To him it is Voodoo and nothing more. The fact of the matter is that Voodoo is a part of his equipment, but he had not yet reached that far into his instruction. Wyatt would have his hands full when that moment indeed arrived!

CHAPTER TWENTY-THREE
SUPPLIES FOR HB GAUNT:

Wyatt left San Diego and flew on a government transport directly to Palm Beach. His precious and secret supplies were offloaded and placed in a separate, secured area. Military personnel that had clearance to guard classified equipment were on hand. In the meanwhile, Wyatt looked for HB Gaunt in the waiting area, which in the government section of the airport was not very big. Since HB had been in the military, the matters of security were not new to him. The now common procedure of electromagnetic examination, x-ray inspection and nitrate sniffers were already known to him.

HB and Wyatt finally did meet, but not in the waiting area. HB was just inside the entrance door, once again wearing his quasi-military Air Force and Navy combinations of uniforms. Wyatt was the only person there in stiff civilian suit, tie and polished loafers. All the others around him were dressed in some other type of military dress since this was a military government area. It was easy for HB to spot Wyatt. HB was just as easily spotted by Wyatt because of his irregular outfit. Wyatt heard that HB was perhaps somewhat eccentric.

HB went over to Wyatt and said, "Hello there. I'm HB Gaunt. Are you looking for me?" HB was not really one hundred percent certain that this person was the Man from Washington, but he felt that it was a good guess since there were only four persons entering the room from that arriving airplane. Wyatt stood out like a red flare.

Wyatt replied, "I'm looking for a very serious, intelligent man, mature in years and manners. I'm not sure you are him."

HB's pride took a shock. He felt the put-down and returned the statement with, "I'm looking for a serious, intelligent man also, but one with manners and respect for other human beings. I'm not sure you're him either."

They both stopped and stared into each other's eyes for a short, frozen moment and then they both burst out in laughter. It was impossible to hold back, although each of them tried choking back their laughing, only to fail in an explosive rupture of laughter.

"Well,", Wyatt began, "Now that we've got that over with. It's nice to meet you anyway."

HB returned with, "The feeling is mutual." They both shook hands and Wyatt's visit was now underway and he had finally met the reputable HB Gaunt. HB continued, "Let's go over to my place so you can show me what all this is about."

Wyatt replied, "I would like to do that. Is your car large enough to carry all this equipment?" Wyatt waved his hand towards the packages guarded by military personnel. There were several dozen packages in the group. The packages were mostly small ones. Mixed in with them were at least five larger parcels.

HB took a quick survey of the size of the delivery and said, "I think we can do it all in one trip. I have the Lincoln Navigator with me and there should be no problem at all.'

Wyatt answered, "Great. The less confusion and the fewer trips the better. Why don't you pull up at the loading area and let's get going." With that statement Wyatt motioned to the two guards to gather up all the packages and move them out to the loading platform, while HB left for his vehicle. Wyatt added to the guards, "But still stand guard over them while we're waiting for HB to arrive with his SUV."

Wyatt saw the white SUV pull up and realized that there would absolutely be no problem at all in doing the loading in one trip. The vehicle was large enough to carry twice the equipment he had brought with him, or even more. Wyatt was relieved because after his three-hour flight, the last thing he needed was even more stress in dealing with simple loading and unloading. His instructing HB would be tough enough.

They arrived at HB's place, high above the ground on the twenty-third floor. From this location on the ocean front, one could see for miles and miles, since Florida is so flat.

HB helped carry the packages up to his apartment using a cart. It was not necessary to make more than one trip.

Wyatt went through instructions on the "Extrasensory Perceptor", explained its use. He demonstrated on Wyatt using the wand alone, tuned into HB's feelings alone. Wyatt said, "HB, I can sense what you're feeling, and you are wrong. This is not so much hogwash. While your feelings are yours, they become mine to examine. How else can you explain what I am getting reported to me regarding your skepticism?"

HB was shocked. He thought that his feelings were his alone to read, control and understand. He now knew better. Wyatt actually and accurately read his thoughts and feelings!

HB said, "Wow, that is not believable. I cannot believe it." He then added quite eagerly, "What other goodies do you have for me?"

Wyatt did a double take. HB was interested in what he had to offer in the realm of the non-scientific. Wyatt went on, "Actually, I have something which I think would be of great interest to you. It is the "Cogito-Lector". I will demonstrate. Wyatt spoke the command: "Cogito" and programmed the device to produce the emotion of fear and aimed it at HB Immediately HB shrank in place. He became frightened and fearful. Then, not wishing to have HB experience a heart attack, Wyatt changed the setting, in the next minute, to the peaceful and pleasant and non-threatening setting. HB once again experienced immediate change of emotion to one of pleasant peace. HB began to smile like a fool. Then Wyatt turned the device off.

Wyatt asked, "Well, what do you think now? Do you still feel that these instruments are voodoo as I have heard from you? Or what."

HB very quickly responded with resounding emphasis, "Absolutely not! I am amazed. I would never have believed that such instruments existed, much less ever invented!" HB went on, "Where in the world did you get this equipment anyway? How in the world did you ever get this stuff?"

Wyatt went on to explain, "Actually, this "stuff" is not so much invented as it was discovered."

"Discovered?" HB asked.

"Yes, discovered. Since you have security clearance, I can tell you. Do you remember the incident at Roswell, New Mexico some years ago?" Wyatt asked.

HB answered, "But of course. Who doesn't? If they are old enough, one cannot ignore or forget the entire hullabaloo which followed those reports."

Wyatt went on, "Well, these instruments, as they are right now completed, and their basic engineering and design, came off the spaceship which crash landed there. It is a national secret, and you are never to reveal any part of this information to anyone who is not equally security cleared as you are. Any level below your clearance level is never to know of these facts. Do you understand?" Wyatt added quite sternly.

H. B. responded, "Definitely. I feel that I am privileged that you have shared this with me. It puts the entire voodoo attitude I had in an entirely different light. What we've found is a new division or a type of science yet to be discovered and experienced in our world!"

Wyatt went on. "Well, there is more. This is just the start of these devices. The other half of the "Cogito-Lector", that is the "Cogito" half tells us what you are thinking. The "Confugio" apparatus will transport you from place to place at the blink of an eye. The other devices have equally surprising functions. These devices will most certainly be an important part of your armamentarium."

"However," Wyatt kept on speaking, "There are the serious "Enchantment Division" devices such as the Spirit Jars and the Solar Jars which are most interesting. These are contrivances, which will enable an individual to store the namesake spirit or spirits inside the jars and release them at will. The technique, which we use to save and store as well as releasing either the "spirit" or the "solar" energy, is well known and I shall help you to both effectively and efficiently use them.

HB was very much impressed by this time. The spiritual devices were beginning to interest him, and he could see no reason that he had to have a closed mind about their use. He kept saying to himself, "Keep an open mind. Keep an open mind."

Wyatt went on to say, "The Spirit Jars work two ways. The first is to harbor the spirit of an individual and the second is to release that spirit. Sometimes the spirit is beneficent and sometimes it's malicious. It all depends on how you dial the top lid and where you point at the lid's arrow. These spirits will then either directly affect the immediate environment or the individual you direct it to. It works something like a bow and arrow or a slingshot. It also works very fast."

"The Solar Jars are a new apparatus. They will store both sunlight in one section of the jar as well as the sun's heat of the day or days. It can build up to a very hot level. However, when the heat is released, it can affect a very wide and distant area. It does not affect only one city block, but the whole city! Several of these could devastate vegetation everywhere. Lack of water to help vegetation to withstand such heat could convert an area into a desert or a quasi-desert. It is also possible to change the climate of an area with this device. Once again, depending on how you dial the top lid, and where the lid is pointed." Wyatt continued.

"The Anima Warp can change the direction a person is taking, from good to evil and also the reverse." "All these devices work very well and great care must be used in their employment", Wyatt added ominously.

HB was quite impressed and interested in all that Wyatt had to demonstrate. It went like that all afternoon. Wyatt went from one item to another and then another and another. "HB would be no problem," he thought to himself. "He's just like a kid with a new toy!"

It was late in the afternoon when they were finished. HB looked at Wyatt and said, "Oh my gosh, oh my gosh, I would never have believed that such things as you've shown me here tonight ever existed. I have most certainly been missing something very special in my education. I am looking forward to working with DESE and I hope to be a valuable contributor for the department. I want to do whatever I can that the department needs. I thank you so much Wyatt." With that HB shook Wyatt's hand so diligently that it reminded one of the old-fashioned well pump's action. HB was so completely taken with what Wyatt had demonstrated to him that he was totally sold on the project, whatever it might be.

CHAPTER TWENTY-FOUR
REPORTS FROM SEEMORE

Mary Kent was sitting quietly and relaxing in her study, reading up on current events, when her telephone rudely intruded upon her peaceful concentration.

Mary shrugged off her mesmerized mental concentration and tried to find the ringing telephone. She located it after a few frantic moments of shuffling papers and searching through shed clothing, sweaters, and such.

"Hello!" she frantically shouted into the telephone. There was no answer. She once again yelled into the telephone, "Hello, is anyone there?"

"Hello, is this Mary Kent? came a timid reply in almost a tremulous and quasi falsetto.

"Yes, this IS Mary", she replied in a lower and more civilized tone. "Who is this and how can I help you?"

"Mary, Mary, do you not recognize my voice?" said the stranger anxiously on the other end. This time the mysterious voice was a little less timid.

Mary thought she recognized the voice because it was now in a more normal tone but was not completely certain. "Seemore, is that you on the other end?", she asked. "Seemore, is everything all right? Are you all-right? Is there a problem?"

Mary was very concerned because the outer territory agents were not to contact her unless there was a real emergency or a serious problem or abnormality of any kind. Therefore, something very serious must have happened.

The voice on the other end became more certain of itself and this time, quite a bit more firmly, said, "It is I, Seemore, reporting from Fairbanks, Alaska." Seemore almost sounded pompous this time.

"Seemore, I thought it was you, but I was not quite certain!" Mary said. Then her thoughts developed the realization that this could not be a social call because the agents were not to call for anything but very serious events. Anything beyond their normal weekday reports as scheduled, and those reports were to be held to a very short group of statements and in a prescribed and ordered format.

Mary knew that she would never receive a call from any agent on a weekend so there had to be something very serious going on, at least in Seemore's mind. The question had to be asked, "What happened, Seemore? Is everything all right? Is there an emergency?" Mary asked in deep concern.

Seemore noticed the change in Mary's voice and sensed her anxiety. He replied, "Well, Mary, I am not certain that there is a major problem. There is just an unusual type of event and you asked that we report any such event immediately. That is what I am doing now."

Mary said, "Well, what is it?"

Seemore then asked, "Mary are you all right? Is everything there o.k.?"

Mary, now at the edge of her seat, said, "Yes, yes, yes. Please tell me what is happening up there in Fairbanks. I am very anxious to know, not that I am unhappy to hear from you personally. I always am happy to talk with you, but this call is completely unexpected, and something must have happened. Or are you both lonesome up there?"

Seemore replied, "Well, now that you ask, we are both all right and not lonesome. I am in my element here and love the area and its wildlife. We've made quite a few friends up here including a tribe of faeries and a group of elves who have come down here from the North Pole to warm up."

Mary, with baited breath said, "Yes, yes, yes, yes! Please go on."

"Mary, it is very unusual for me to see what I am seeing. All the instruments I have up here reveal nothing different or strange, but this is very strange to me and I felt that I had to share it with you right away, although it has been happening for several days now." Seemore went on, "I'm not sure that it is important, but it is definitely unusual."

"What is it, Seemore? What in the world is it that you are talking about? Please get to the point!" Mary answered even more on edge than before.

Seemore did just that. He replied, "You know about the Northern Lights?"

Mary answered, "Yes, go on."

"The strange happening is that they are not Northern at this time." Seemore said.

Mary asked, "What do you mean?"

"I mean that they are now South of us and not North." Seemore incredulously answered. "The blessed things are now South of us. Can you believe it?"

Mary replied, "No I cannot believe it." She went on. "How could that be?". She continued, "Better yet, WHY would that be anyway? It does not make any sense, but there must be a reasonable explanation."

Seemore responded, "Perhaps, but I do not know what it could be. Did the earth shift on its axis? Did the magnetic North Pole change its position? If so, how could that be possible anyway?"

Mary answered, "This opens the door to so many questions and so few answers. I will need to call my scientific group together and see what they come up with." She continued, "It does not make any sense and I am glad that you called. This is a major event and one that I cannot take lightly. We must know why this happened and what caused it. You say that this first occurred several days ago?"

Seemore said, "Yes, several days ago. I wanted to be sure that it was not a fluke, a strange twist of nature, a momentary thing. It was not because it is still here and is still happening." Seemore went on, "Are we in danger? Should we be concerned? What do you think of this?"

Mary answered cautiously, "I really could not tell you. However, I cannot understand why a shift in position of the Northern Lights should really be of any great concern. As far as I know, the Northern lights occur because of solar radiation striking the terminal ends of the earth's magnetic field."

"Yes, does that mean that the terminal ends of the magnetic field have shifted or what?", Seemore added. "Tell me more."

Mary replied, "It seems that the "solar wind" strikes the earth's magnetic field and can develop up to one million megawatts of electricity. A proton flare from the sun can create a spectacular display and you, Seemore, are in the right place at the right time for the best show."

She continued, "In the past, the Northern Lights are expected in late August. Your neighbors to the North and East, the Innuits around Hudson Bay, thought that the sky was a huge dome with cracks in it that let in light from outside its shell. They believed that the spirits of those who passed on would go through these cracks and get to heaven via a narrow heavenly bound bridge. Those spirits that went before them and were already in heaven lit torches to guide those who were now arriving. It is those torches that are called the Northern Lights.

In the Middle Ages, it was believed that the lights were reflections of heavenly warriors doing battle in the skies.

In the recent past, it was thought that the lights were an omen warning of illness, death, and plague. If the lights were of a red color, it was believed that it meant that a war was about to break out.

These days, the awesome power of an event provides respect and need for physics research and intellectual investigation on a scientific basis. Nevertheless, there are those who still are fearful and do not wish to test the powers that be by any form or degree of defiance against the phenomenon.

You at Fairbanks, Alaska have a great spectator's seat. Your position, Fairbanks, Alaska at 64.8 N Lat, 147o 45" W Longitude and the corrected geomagnetic latitude of 64o 49' N Latitude, are ideally situated there for a great showing" Mary said in conclusion.

Seemore responded, "I really don't understand. In Sweden, the Northern Lights were always to the North and never in the South. Why would it be different here, on the other side of the earth from my home country? This is still the Northern Hemisphere. It does not make any sense."

Mary replied, "I can understand your concern. I will consult our environmental division tomorrow at work. I promise that I will get back to you first thing. I would not worry though. You said that this phenomenon has happened over the last few days so I wouldn't think that it could be very harmful, although it is interesting." Then she quickly added in afterthought, "Nothing has happened to you or anywhere around you, or has it?"

Seemore said, "No, no, no. We are quite all right although we are very concerned because it seems to us that the earth has been tipped upside down. That which is to be North is now South, and we need some help to get us to solve our confusion. This is just not normal!" In another afterthought, he added quizzically, "Or is it?"

Seemore went on, "All the devices and measuring instruments we placed have not demonstrated or recorded anything abnormal. As a matter of fact, everything is super normal. Everything except the Northern Lights!"

Seemore was flushed and chagrined. His face was redder than usual, and he was only a slightly bit more jittery than usual. Nevertheless, he could not stop talking. "All my forest friends have visited us. You should know that these friends are my personal reporters regarding any disturbing events, and they have not given me any evidence of anything going wrong. Even my dear friend, Peganni, who flies around has not reported anything unusual from up in the air. He visits us at least once a week. He is just about due for a return any day now."

Mary interjected, "If that's so, then he has not really witnessed the Upside-down Northern Lights, has he? Since this is the fourth day or night of the event as you told me, Peganni would only be able to tell you about it on his next visit. I would be very interested in knowing what he reports to you."

Seemore said, "So would I. I cannot wait to see him. I will call you immediately after my visit with Peganni."

Mary asked, "What airline does Mr. Peganni pilot for? I do not think that there are many airlines to Fairbanks, AK. In fact, I know that to get to Fairbanks, you probably must use one of the "puddle jumper" airplanes. Is Mr. Peganni a bush pilot or what?

Seemore kept silent for a short minute and then suddenly was no longer able to hold his laughter. Seemore laughingly responded after an explosive session of raucous laughter, "No, Mary, Peganni is not a pilot at all. He is not even human. Peganni is a very special creature of good against evil. Hold your seat, Mary; as a matter of fact, you should probably sit down for this."

Mary was very intrigued. She said, "O.K. I am sitting. What's the mystery about anyway?"

"Peganni is a combination of the best spirits in the world. Peganni is part Unicorn and part Pegasus and has the powers of both. I have known him all my short three hundred years of life." Seemore informed Mary.

Mary was happy she was sitting. If she were not sitting when she first heard what Seemore had to tell her, she realized that she probably would be sitting on the floor instead of a chair. She knew that Seemore had contacts with mythological creatures of the world of all sorts. She never expected that combination creations such as a Pegasus and a Unicorn could ever really exist. She was both shocked and surprised at the very same moment. It was a double whammy! Sitting was a very good place to be when Seemore broke this news to her.

Mary could only say, "Wow!" and then was speechless.

Seemore broke into the silence at the other end and quickly informed Mary that he had already given this information to Wyatt when they first met. He guessed that Wyatt probably did not believe him; otherwise, he should have reported such a creature to Mary. That most likely was the explanation. Wyatt probably felt that the story was a bit of fiction and that Seemore was pulling his leg. Wyatt never saw Peganni at all and did not believe in such creatures, even though the person standing in front of him, Seemore himself, was such a creature.

Mary went on, "You are telling me that you and Peganni actually communicate in some way. Is it verbal, mental telepathy or what? It certainly is not writing. How exactly do you communicate with this creature of wonder?"

"It's very easy," Seemore said. "We simply get together and we talk, just like you and I, right now!"

"You mean that your ability to communicate is just as we're doing now? Is that what you're saying?" said Mary. "Are you saying that you understand each other too?"

Seemore responded, "But of course. That is the way we like it. We just talk, horse to man, or in my case, horse to Gnome. I will get a firsthand, or rather "first hoof", report on what the mal-positioned Northern Lights are doing south of me instead of being north where they should be!"

"Very interesting. I did not know that you were so talented, but it is not an unreasonable ability for you", answered Mary. "Please let me know whatever you find out, no matter how unimportant or slight you may think it is. Even the smallest clue will be of some help. The Northern Light shift is probably not as disturbing as it is curious. We shall find the reason for it. I will get my staff on it first thing in the morning," replied a still somewhat concerned. Mary.

"Great!" said Seemore. "I'll call you as soon as I get more information or learn something more."

Then they both went through the usual "goodbye" ceremonies. They both agreed to keep in close contact and immediately inform the other of any revelations which develop.

CHAPTER TWENTY-FIVE

REPORTS FROM HB

Mary was very happy that she was able to get a good night's sleep, especially after hearing the virtually "out of this world" report from Seemore. She rose and shook off her early morning drowsiness, then hopped into the shower. That helped destroy any remnant of sleep and stimulated a state of mental awareness devoid of the residual influence of Morpheus.

She dressed leisurely. All the while, in her fully awakened state of mind, she thought of Seemore's report. Mary was eager to get to her offices and communicate Seemore's report to her staff members to get them started on researching the strange events at Fairbanks, AK.

First, however, she felt that a good breakfast was in order, starting with a good cup of Java from Columbia. She mused over the contradictions that coffee was called "Java" although the best came from Columbia, S.A. and not Java, Indonesia! She acknowledged that the world was full of strange things including Peganni! Indeed, she thought, a double mythological occurrence. Wow! Unbelievable! It is no wonder Wyatt did not report it. It was a good thing for him that he did not because he would have had to take some vacation time to get over the "breakdown" his office would be sure to assign to him!

She spread "I Can't Believe It's Not Butter" and Concord Grape Preserve on her multigrain toast and dug into her bacon and eggs breakfast. While sipping on her second cup of coffee, the telephone intruded on her peaceful solitude.

Her Caller I.D. told her that the call was from HB from Florida! Mary almost fell off her chair. She thought, "This is the second call inside twenty-four hours! I wonder what this could be about, nothing mythological or "other worldly" she hoped. She additionally realized that the name of her department was becoming more and more appropriate regarding the report from Seemore and who knows what HB had to offer!

"Hello, hello, hello!" bellowed the voice at the other end of the telephone. This voice is very different from that of Seemore whose call started out in a squeaky tone. It had obvious urgency and demand for response.

Mary hesitantly responded in a fearful tone as to what the content of the upcoming conversation could be. "Hello yourself" Mary managed to say with only mild force, not wanting to offend HB at the other end of the line.

"Mary is that you?" the voice, toned down somewhat, inquired hopefully.

"Yes, it is Mary. Is that you HB?"

"It certainly is. There have been strange happenings down here and I feel that you need to know what is going on. We must talk." HB replied in a very serious tone.

"Well, tell me what is going on. Do not just talk about it. Just give me the details", said Mary.

HB started, "The other day I was down at South Beach on Lincoln Road. This is the Florida summer, yet there was this band, the Old-World Symphony, playing Christmas music on the esplanade while I was having dinner with my very good friend, Larry Carl, and some other friends. We all looked at each other with very blank stares not knowing what to think.

Suddenly, from somewhere in the sky we all heard Jingle Bells but there was nothing to see. It was seventy-four degrees, and we were dressed in shorts and short-sleeved sport shirts. The sky was clear. You could see the stars shining brightly and it was quite balmy. It was very difficult for us to understand the situation. Then suddenly, within a matter of seconds, the temperature dropped to about thirty degrees, and we were freezing."

Mary was astounded. What in the world was HB relating anyway? Her head was spinning because she tied this world inversion to each other: first the southern placement of the Northern Lights and now a sudden shift in a tropical climate from seventy-four degrees to below freezing. It did not make any sense whatsoever. It was especially puzzling because the meteorological event was accompanied by a human performance, the Old-World Symphony.

Mary asked, with eyes wide open in amazement and anticipation, "What happened next? Did it snow or something?

HB replied, "No, it did not snow, although we wouldn't have been surprised if it had. We were so very cold to the point of tooth chattering. We could only stay outside five minutes or so and we had to run into one of the boutiques bordering the outdoor restaurant seating area to warm up or else we felt that we would freeze. The Bel Glade area west of Palm Beach had a temperature of thirty-two degrees this morning. The entire event was bizarre! Fortunately, the freezing cold only lasted for about twenty minutes, but it was enough to get and keep our attention. What in the world is going on! HB continued, "Mary, do you have any information about this? Can you shed any intelligence our way? It certainly was a freak happening but the combination of the orchestra, its choice of out-of-season music, suddenly extremely cold weather and the sound of Jingle Bells from the sky where nothing could be seen is just too weird. It must be much more than just coincidence!"

Mary regained her composure to some degree. She asked with some trepidation, "Is there anything else I should know about? How are those instruments you have panning out? Have they given you any indication or prediction of strange events or actual happenings?"

"No, Mary, I have not been able to check them all. I would like to have my friend, Larry Carl, help me out. Would you check him out for security clearance? I have not yet approached him, but I am certain that he would be an asset and a great help to me. Of course, if you feel that you do not want another agent here as my auxiliary, I will understand and abide by your opinion."

"Well, well. HB you have given me several things to think about, haven't you? First the nature of your report and now you are making a request for an auxiliary agent!" Mary paused and then continued, "HB, if you really feel that there is need for help, I will permit it. There is no argument from me there. Most importantly, before anything at all is revealed to him, you must be aware that it is necessary that he have security clearance first."

Mary did not let HB know of her relationship with "Mr. Larry Carl" and the fact that she already knew all there was to know about Mr. Carl. Mary felt that the fact that Larry was her cousin was nobody's business but hers. She also felt that it was fortuitous that HB even knew Larry. It would make the entire business of investigations easier. Unfortunately, it also meant that Larry would need to become aware of what his cousin, Mary, did for a living. That did not thrill Mary very much, but she would make the serious officialdom speech to Larry and keep him in line that way. In this business there is no fooling around. This business is very serious. Lives, property, and national security could be in jeopardy.

HB responded, "Of course, Mary, there is no question about it. That was my first request to you, and I am very happy to comply. I am up there in the Palm Beach area and this event happened in Miami!"

"I know that your area is large, especially when you add the whole Southeastern United States. Your equipment will monitor the entire area, but you probably could use some help in the reading, collecting, and analyzing all the data you obtain." Mary replied. She went on, "You will need to instruct Mr. Carl in the use of the equipment you have. Do you feel comfortable doing that? Will it be necessary to send Wyatt down there one more time to instruct him personally? I would have no problem in doing that at all.

"I feel that I have become familiar enough with all the materials I have, including those which deal in the so-called "supernatural" realm. You realize that I first must ask him to join me in this "venture" beforehand. I feel sure that he would be very interested in helping me out. He visits Miami often and travels all over the Southeast. He would be an ideal assistant for me. All you must do is to let me know when he has full clearance, and I will start him off immediately."

"I will do that. I have several matters to research today, including your report, but I'll have my office check out our Mr. Larry Carl today. If there are any problems, I will call you right away. If there aren't any you can assume by the day's end that he is cleared. I will make investigation into his record a priority, especially under the circumstances." Mary replied.

HB was grateful. He answered, "Thank you, Mary. I appreciate all of that. I am very intrigued in what is happening and your department, especially after my episode on South Beach's Lincoln Road.'

Mary said, "I agree. Keep in touch, especially if you witness any more events like that one."

HB agreed. They both said their goodbyes and hung up. Mary was quite mystified and was very eager to get to her offices so that investigations could start and so that she could find the underlying cause of these mysteries.

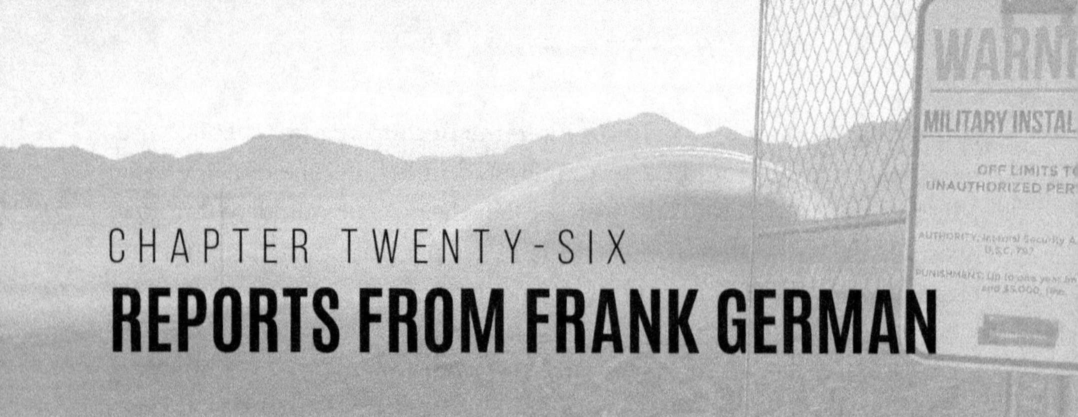

CHAPTER TWENTY-SIX

REPORTS FROM FRANK GERMAN

Eventually, Mary finally made it to the secret offices of DESE. The reports of the past forty-eight hours were very heavy on her mind. Such events were exactly what her department was created to deal with. Her only question is where to start. For her the answer is obvious, as it would be to any clear-thinking individual. She would start with the scientific facts. Then she would need to follow that up with the not-so-scientific devices she had become accustomed to using and working with.

Mary thought, "I haven't heard from our San Diego agent Frank German. Perhaps I should call him before he calls me." Mary subconsciously realized that Frank was due to call her. As a matter of fact, his call was overdue. If agents in different corners of the country had events to report, what could possibly keep Frank out of touch with her office? There could be no doubt that Frank would be calling and very soon too. Nevertheless, Mary went about her business. She had plenty to do and much to consider. If Frank does not call, it could mean that there is nothing for him to report and that there is nothing out of the ordinary in his part of the country.

Mary started in the computer room and delegated parts of the problems and strange events to various personnel, including Wyatt who was back at the central office. She began with her department's meteorological division and then to the NOAA. The matter was also turned over to the Department of Homeland Security as well as the National Security Agency.

All the departments and referred agencies reported that they all had confirmation of the happenings but could not give any reason or any explanation for the extraordinary events.

Mary even consulted with the experimental division of her department. They had a working prototype of a global magnetometer. They were the first to come up with some reasonable explanation. Namely, they discovered that the earth's North-South Pole readings had shifted but their equipment only reported the facts and not the reason those facts occurred. In short, although they could confirm the change, they were not able to tell why the change happened or what caused the change.

Mary realized the scope of this change. Fortunately, since the advent of GPS and earthbound receivers, any disaster could be averted. She thought of all the ships and airplanes that used the earth's magnetic readings to guide them on the earth's surface. These conveyances were all in danger and those on board could lose their lives because of lost directions and inability to know where they are and where they are going. Fortunately, GPS readings are not affected by the earth's magnetic field and so they remained accurate. However, not all the earth's vehicles have such exotic GPS systems at this time and there were reports of both ships and airplanes arriving at the wrong airfields or ports. Fortunately, there were no reports of accidents or deaths.

The day was almost over when it happened. The telephone call that Mary had wanted to happen, did. It was Frank German from San Diego. Frank was running on in his speech. Mumbles and jumbles with incessant sentences that did not follow the previous thought. Frank seemed to be in a panic.

"Frank, Frank. Hold on a minute. I cannot understand a word you are saying. Let me go into my office to take this call in private and away from both noise and prying ears" said Mary to Frank.

She went into her office and quietly closed the door, gently but quite securely, being careful not to draw any more of the Staff's attention than necessary. "Now, now Frank, try to calm down and try to make some sense while you slow down your speech."

Apparently, Frank was very excited over something. He was so excited that his speech came out in jumbles and made very little sense.

"Frank, sit down a minute if you're standing, and take several deep breaths. Did you do it?" asked Mary.

Frank whispered, "Yes I did." His response was breathless and very soft.

Mary said, "Good. Now do it again."

Mary could hear Frank comply. She could hear his deep breathing and exhalations. "Now", Mary said, "Tell me what is going on. What has happened?"

Frank replied, "Thank you. I did not realize that I was that excited, but I couldn't help it."

Mary, now becoming anxious to know the "why" of Frank's panic call said impatiently, "Well, what is the problem? What do you need to tell me? What in the world has happened that you can barely speak?"

Frank began, "Well," Frank hesitated and continued, "it has never happened here before, as far as I know. Our temperature has dropped to below freezing, and in the matter of minutes." He continued, "You know that this area produces much in the way of vegetables and fruits. We have a very ideal climate, that is, until today. The area will be ruined!"

Mary said, "I understand your shock, but the sub-freezing temperatures won't last very long, and…"

Frank quickly interrupted Mary with, "But you don't understand. That is not all. There's more Mary."

Mary answered, "More? Such as what?"

"Mary, we have snow! There are six inches of snow on the ground! It was not even forecasted! It is a surprise even to the weatherman! There has never been any snow in San Diego, as far as I know. It is going to kill all my plants. My fig tree, my oranges, my vegetables, and all that will die. Mary, what is going on? What is happening? Has the world turned upside down or what?"

Mary told Frank, "Look Frank, you have equipment and testing devices. Do they tell you anything? Have you run any tests at all? What do the instruments reveal to you?"

Frank was silent for a short minute and then replied thoughtfully, "You know, I didn't think to look at them! I was so shocked at what was happening that all thinking ceased. All of us San Diegoans could do is to react as best we could to prevent crop damage and crop freezing as well as trying to keep from freezing ourselves!"

Mary replied, "Frank, you must check your equipment, and I mean all the instruments, those which are scientific and those which are "cultural", O.K.? Frank, are you there? Frank, Frank" Mary repeated, almost frantically.

Frank answered, "Mary, I am so sorry that I failed to think about it. I will do that right away and call you back within a few minutes. It's just that it is so shocking."

Frank continued, "Mary, I could use a little help. My wife, Leslie, has a scientific bent. Would you permit me to use her help in solving this puzzle? I really need an assistant."

Mary thought a bit and then said, "All right. This is almost a crisis, but she has to swear to all the secrecy and promise not to reveal anything she ever learns with us to anyone. I would suppose that she probably is aware of your dilemma anyway, by this time. Is that not so?

Frank said, "Most likely. It is almost impossible to keep things from a wife. They have a sixth sense about things. I trust her with my life. I trust her completely. What do you say, Mary?"

Mary, now a little upset at being pressured into an immediate response said in a desperate exhalation, "Yes, of course. Now let us get on with it. Let us solve the problem. Get going, Frank."

Frank said, "Right away. Thank you. I will train her myself. It's just that all that is happening is so shocking" Frank repeated.

Mary said, "Of course it is. That is what those instruments are for: to deal with shocking and surprising unforeseen events. This is certainly extraordinary is it not?"

Frank answered the rhetorical question anyway with a "Yes it most certainly is and that's what's in your department's name as well. This is up your departments' alley. Since I was elected to serve in your office, I guess I will be getting on with my job and getting you the information you need. Do not get me wrong. I like this job. I like what I am doing. I really, really do. Seriously, Mary, I really do mean it" Frank repeated almost apologetically.

"I can see that our country needs the services of your department very desperately, especially with what is going on here in "sunny" San Diego! Up to now, I had my doubts, but snow in San Diego in the summer is just not a usual and customary event! I am going to get on the stick and get that info to you right away! So goodbye for now", Frank said eagerly.

Mary responded, "Goodbye for now. Make sure you get back to me as soon as possible. This is a very serious and a very important matter. I expect that you will do well for us. I am counting on you, Frank."

Frank answered, with a gulp in his throat being hard to swallow, "You bet. Bye." Frank hung up firmly. Now the show was his parade. He had to get the information the government needed to develop a reason for the unseasonable events.

Frank ran out of his house and checked Peripio-Accipio. He took out the wand and commanded, "Percepio!"

The wand shook on its own and started to glow red. Frank thought that he would be burnt, but the red was only a color and not associated with heat. Then the wand, still being held by Frank's right hand, started to turn around and made Frank turn with it. It then pointed in one direction and moved back and forth in a short arc then it came to rest in the middle of the arc that it was tracing. Then it stopped. The glowing decreased to yellow and then turned itself off, emitting a loud "beep", signifying that the direction where it pointed was where Frank had to investigate.

Frank was quite hesitant to do so, but duty called, and Frank yielded. The wand looked like a conductor's baton and so it did not attract much attention when Frank entered the business section of his town. He thought that the wand would direct him to the mall, but it was not so. It directed him past the almost empty mall towards a slightly wooded area about fifteen hundred feet behind it. The Cor-Cordis amulet about his neck started to vibrate. That was the signal that told Frank to turn it on. Frank uttered the trigger word, "Cordis" and immediately he began to sense what was going on in that wooded area.

He understood that there were "witches" in that glen with a very small fire in their midst. The witches were milling about the central fire, uttering words that Frank did not understand. He understood all this but never saw them, except in his mind's eye. He could envision their faces and even what they were wearing down to the color and patterns and fabric weave on their clothing as well as any pins and the pentagram emblems or jewelry they were wearing. Although his eyes could not see through the berm between them, his mind's eye saw them all, in vivid detail, as projected images in the sky above them. He could see them and every detail just as though he were only ten feet before them!

However, the fountain pen in his pocket also started to vibrate. Frank uttered the command, "Cogito", to read the witches' thoughts. What he learned scared the Bajezzus out of him. He learned that the witches were angry about the treatment they had been getting from the American people, going as far back as the sixteen hundreds and the burning, and dunking of witches. They only loved the earth and its creatures. They developed potions and magic to preserve their environment and conserve the goodness of the earth. Yet they were constantly portrayed as wickedly evil, bad, and even demonic. They were angry about this because recently one of their brethren was viciously attacked and maltreated by people in a certain section of Western North Carolina. They decided to even the score by performing black magic and upsetting the economy and peoples' lives. Frank thought, "They most certainly are doing that, and I am not happy."

Frank learned that these witches caused the six inches of San Diego snow. "What to do? What to do?" Frank felt that he had a dilemma. Then it occurred to him to use the other half of the Cogito-Lector and commanded it with "Lecto". Frank was not exactly certain how to use this device, but he remembered Wyatt's instructions to concentrate deeply on what projected thoughts he wanted people to think. He took the pen out of his pocket and pointed it at the glen. He thought, "Let these people know that what they are doing is wrong. That the solution to their problems did not lie in the destruction of livelihoods and property, but in the achieving of understanding with the present-day public." He expressed his thoughts repeatedly. He concentrated so hard that it hurt. He felt that his head would burst. He continued, despite his conceived agony, for about ten minutes. He noticed that something was happening.

The Cogito device revealed to him that the witches' thoughts and direction of vengeance had changed into one of benevolence. An added dividend was that the snow, which had covered the canopies around the shopping mall, started to melt. The best event was that the sun started to show itself and began to emit the usual San Diego blue, cloudless sky and the sun's heat was being restored.

Frank was overjoyed. He decided to leave the area before they discovered the stranger in their proximate "midst". He scampered back to his apartment, unloaded the devices he had been carrying and wearing and immediately called Mary.

Mary was apparently awaiting his call. The telephone barely rang once, and Mary was on it. "Well, Frank." she answered. "Did you learn anything, anything at all?"

Frank responded in delight. "I most certainly did. I learned how to use the devices Wyatt brought me. They worked terrifically."

Mary was now quite excited. "Well, tell me. What happened? What did you learn?"

Frank, delighted in the fact that he now had Mary almost begging, took his time in answering. Eventually he did yield the answer to Mary.

"Mary, I got the snow to melt, the sun to come out and warm San Diego, but more importantly, I learned why we had the snow at all."

"You must tell me right away. Do not keep me waiting. It is a matter of national security that you tell me right now!" Mary's tone had changed from one of begging to that of an authority figure that demanded, not begged, for the answers.

Frank noted the change and decided to get serious. "Apparently, the snow and cold was caused by a witches' spell. It seems that they exist all around our country and they want fairer treatment and that old word, "respect". I used the Percipio-accipio, the Cor-Cordis and the Cogito-Lector to learn where the source of the problem came from. I learned what their thoughts were and concentrated on changing their minds." Frank was the one who was quite excited now. "Mary, they work! The devices work like a charm! I had absolutely no problem with using them. What a delight they were to work with. Thank you so much, Mary. I am in your debt." Frank said humbly.

Mary replied, "No, Frank. You have it backwards. Your country owes you. We are all in your debt, not the other way around. You have done our country a great service." Mary continued, "I must go now. I will be in touch soon. Keep checking the devices for at least forty-eight hours from now to make certain that the witches do not change their minds."

"Roger", Frank said. "I will call right away if I notice any changes or anything else which is off the norm."

They each signed off and said their goodbyes in a more friendly than formal tone. Each was quite satisfied with the report and Frank's chest puffed up with pride. He knew he did an excellent job.

CHAPTER TWENTY-SEVEN
SHORTFALL IN COVERAGE

Mary was very pleased with Frank's report. It was time for her to share the report with her less known and least present and surreptitious cohort, Jack Henigson. Jack, while a member of Mary's department, was also deeply involved in the National Security Agency as well and acted as liaison between the two departments. He coordinated data and reports between the two. However, the NSA was never aware of the existence of DESE. Jack's interests lay more with DESE than the NSA. Although he did efficient work for each, the NSA never would know of Jack's secret affiliation with DESE.

Jack kept a low profile at each agency. It was not generally known that he even worked for the government, so secret was his affiliation with DESE. The more familiar a figure he became at each location, the better the chances that his cover would be blown in any clandestine operation which required his participation.

Any future undercover or secret work he might need to do, as an agent of DESE, would be more difficult and compromised under circumstances of popularity and friendship with the agents in each department. He would be known wherever he went. It had to be most important to avoid having everyone know where he went. That is to be avoided. His missions are always kept secret. That is the rule, and the only way Jack could operate safely. Causes and forces unknown and being or bordering on the supernatural and foreign to our world, could never know of Jack's mission whatever it might be. Jack had special powers that went beyond those granted by the government alone. These gifts would manifest themselves in very mysterious ways. Jack did not realize his full potential. His gifts would reveal themselves according to the occasion and need of the moment. It would be only then that Jack would become aware of his "gifts". Other than that momentary revelation, Jack really could not know the limits of his abilities at all.

Mary conferred with Wyatt on the coincidence between the San Diego and the South Florida freezing events and asked him to investigate the existence of a possible relationship between the two. "Wyatt", she asked, "I had this strange call from Agent Frank in San Diego, and I need to have you delve into it."

Wyatt asked, "What kind of "strange" report are you talking about?"

Mary then gave Wyatt all the details to which he responded, "Wow! That is not our usual sphere of work, but it most certainly is an "extraordinary situation and event", isn't it?"

Mary understood that such was the name of her department. Wyatt was one hundred percent correct. This San Diego report was the kind of event that was completely the responsibility of her department and its reason for existence. It had serious economic and even national security implications that had to be assessed. The power to control weather conditions over such a wide area showed grave national liability and needed to be fully understood and dealt with.

Wyatt continued, "I'll get right on it." Then they ended their conversation with a mutual "We'll be in touch." Then each continued to do their respective jobs.

She needed time to digest Frank's report and his revelations. She recalled Seemore's report and noted that these events had both occurred on the Western Coastline of the North American continent and wondered at the correlation. She felt that having Wyatt dig deeper into the matter was what needed to be done.

Mary made one of her infrequent calls to Jack several hours after her conversation with Frank. She seldom called Jack because of Jack's furtive interdepartmental status. Minimal contact meant increased security for Jack.

She dialed the secure number to Jack's telephone. Jack answered after several rings with a cheerful, "Hello! This is the Seymour Krants Funeral Home, a place of happy "Pick-Me-Ups" and "Lay-Me-Downs". We are friends to mankind. We are the first to pick you up and the last to let you down. May I help you?"

Mary was shocked. She thought she had dialed the wrong number and was embarrassed that she had dialed a funeral home. She became flustered and apologized to the person at the other end of the line. "I'm sorry", she said somewhat disconcerted. "I have the wrong number. Goodbye."

"No, no", Jack said, recognizing Mary's voice. "You have the right number, Mary."

This spooked Mary even more. Not only did she call a funeral home, but also the person at the other end knew her name! This was something that did not make her happy at all! It made her want to end the conversation even more quickly than she usually would. Her telephone was on its way to the cradle when she detected a continued but louder speech at the other end of the line and hesitated.

Jack quickly said, "Mary, don't hang up. This is Jack. You have the right number. I was only kidding!"

Mary was quite relieved. She did not think she had made any reservations at a funeral home and did not care to be popular at any such establishment at this time or at any time in the immediate future. "Jack", she said scolding, "how could you answer the phone that way? You scared the Bajezzus out of me!"

Jack said apologetically, "I'm sorry, Mary. I just recognized your number on my caller I.D., and I was just playing around. I did not know that you were so easily frightened. I only answer that way with friends and sales calls!"

Mary said, "Apology accepted." She went on, "Jack, there have been strange occurrences which I know you will find quite interesting. They are not only interesting, but they probably mean that I have some work for you to do. I am very concerned, beyond just being curious, about the National Security inferences to be drawn from what has happened." Mary's voice was quite serious.

Jack's interest peaked and he answered, "Mary, you have my full attention. The words "National Security" are up my alley. What exactly do you mean? What has happened?" Jack's voice had now taken a turn towards the somber and serious. Whatever could affect the security of his country was certainly very grave for him.

Mary went on to relate the happenings on the West Coast in detail. Jack responded to each report with a "Yes, yes, go on; go on." and "Is there more?"

"Yes", she said, there is more. Mary recalled the report, which she almost forgot, from HB in Florida about the sudden severe cold snap experienced in the Palm Beach area. She also related this to Jack.

Jack was now fully awake and almost in a hyperactive state. He became quite agitated at these reports. Not only are the events highly unusual, but he felt that they called out for him to get seriously involved. He responded to Mary, "Why did you not tell of these things sooner?"

Mary answered, "Jack, they just now all came together. One report could have been a fluke. Two reports could have been a coincidence, but three reports are no longer just a coincidence, but smell of conspiracy! That is when I call Jack!"

"I understand" Jack said.

"Jack, I'd like you to try to find out what is going on. I will contact Seemore in Alaska and ask him to investigate further as well. In fact, I am going to ask all agents who have reported strange goings-on to do their full investigation as well. It is certain that these events are no fluke. We all must get to the bottom of this as soon as possible or we might not have any control of the final outcome. I do not like to have matters in the purvey of my department get out of hand."

Jack replied, "It is important that a detailed explanation be found. If there is a connection between events, we need to be aware of it."

Mary said, "I agree. It must be done right away. I have the feeling that we are already late on the matter. Who knows how long these occurrences have been planned and by whom. We need to know right away!"

"I'll get on it and I'll be in contact with you as soon as I know something," said Jack as he hung up the telephone. Then he began to think out his plans.

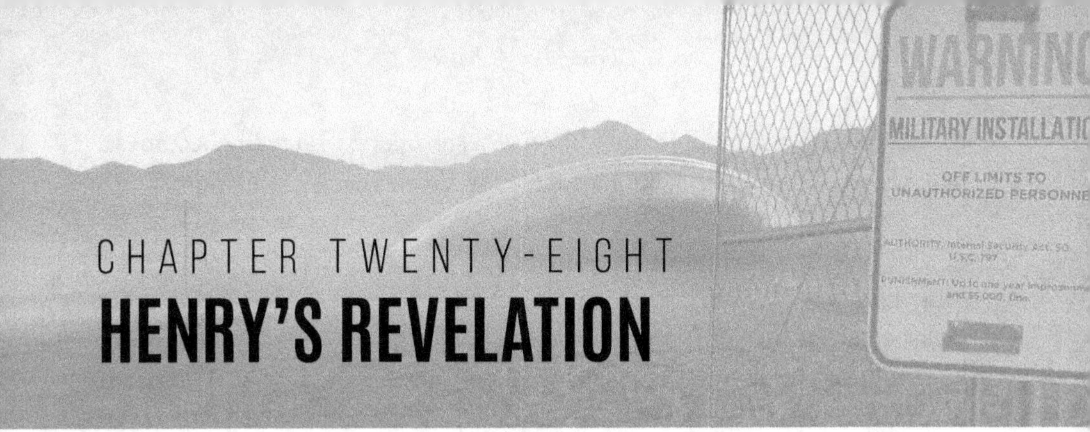

CHAPTER TWENTY-EIGHT
HENRY'S REVELATION

No sooner did Jack get off the telephone with Mary than the doorbell rang. Jack jumped in the suddenness of both events and went to the door. Jack was pleased to see his paperboy, Henry, doing his weekly collection. Jack had just been thinking about his plans and he felt that Henry should and would be a part of it.

Jack had already recognized that Henry was no ordinary young man. Jack's intuition told him that, as with most human beings, only some of Henry's abilities were in the forefront and used in daily life. Although Henry was not aware of the extent of his powers, Jack knew that the characteristics Henry possessed supplemented his own.

Jack's extraordinary powers were manifested "on the spot" and "as the moment dictated need". Jack's mind told him that Henry had powers which complemented his own and that Henry was not even slightly aware of the existence of such traits in himself. He had not even the slightest inkling that such an attribute existed in anyone, much less himself! Henry was in for a shocking revelation!

He knew himself only as a kid and with the game-playing mind of a kid. Henry knew himself to be the son of a dentist and a friend to his fellows as well as a newspaper boy and nothing more. He felt that he was his own man and not extraordinary in any way. He was just an average young man on his way to high school! He had shown traits of maturity beyond his years, but he still was just an innocent kid, unaware of the wiles of the world. What could there possibly be beyond that at his age!

Jack Henigson recruits Henry Wilson as a sub agent who really becomes a major asset. Henry gets personally introduced to Black Lightning

Jack was very pleased at the timely opportunity Henry's presence gave him. This was the perfect moment in Jack's life to present Henry with what Jack perceived as Henry's new role in life. The question is would Henry be ready for the same or not? Jack had to find out right now. The needs of DESE and his country required it now. Jack did not have the luxury of waiting for Henry to mature further. The time was now here to present Henry with his new role in life and a jump into maturity and one for which Henry might not be ready.

Jack was his usual happy, smiling, and jovial self as he eagerly opened the door and invited Henry in.

"Henry!" exclaimed Jack loudly. "It is so nice to see you!" Jack said as a spider to a fly. "Come in. Come in. Sit and visit with me a while."

While Jack was always cordial, friendly, and smiling happily, Henry sensed that this was not a usual visit. "Jack has something on his mind", Henry thought and went along for the time being. The fly went into the house and was enticed into the web, so said the spider.

Henry, sit down and join me, Jack repeated. Have some iced tea. It is freshly brewed, and it is the delicious Southern type of sweet tea. We love it here and I am certain that you will love it too.

Henry did not say a word, but sat down in a comfortable armchair, which almost swallowed him up, and reached out for an offered cold glass of sweet tea. The room was an oldish paneled type of room with long drapes over the windows and not very bright, but adequate for most tasks. The lack of bright light was compensated for by Jack's smile and cheerfulness.

Jack spoke to the attentive and curious Henry. "Henry", Jack said, "Do you belong to any organizations like the Boy Scouts, Explorer Scouts or anything like that?"

Henry said, "No, I don't. When I was much younger, I was a Cub Scout, but now that I am grown, I haven't joined any of the organizations." Henry then added as a curious afterthought, "Why do you ask that?"

Jack fidgeted somewhat in the chair opposite Henry's. He looked about, to the right and left, up and down at the ceiling and lastly the floor. Jack said with hesitation, "Henry, sometimes we are called upon to perform duties which are unexpected. You are quite young but mature for your age."

Jack paused and looked Henry boldly in both eyes at once! Henry shrank from the stare only a little bit, and rapidly recomposed himself. Henry returned the stare.

Jack continued, "Henry, have you ever thought of government service? Do you have any thoughts on it? What are your deepest, heartfelt feelings about service to Uncle Sam?"

Jack stopped and waited for the so-called "Pregnant Pause". The silence was quiet loud. Not even the curtains felt the summer breeze. They did not even move. Henry would have sworn that the ticking of the mantle clock even stopped. There was no sound, only the pause that did not refresh, unlike soda pop.

Henry gulped and swallowed a "pregnant" swallow and said, "Well, I never really ever thought about it, to tell you the truth. I still have several years before I could even think of enlisting in the service. Why in the world would you ever ask that question of a paperboy anyway?" Henry gave an earnest quizzical look at Jack and expected an answer.

This put Jack on the spot. He knew what he had to do. He knew things about Henry that Henry did not know about himself. Jack struggled to put his words together in an understandable response. It would need to be an answer so phrased that it would not frighten

Henry away, but rather one which would rather arouse his interest and curiosity. Such was the kind of answer Jack was searching for in his heart and mind. It had to be a response that would inspire Henry towards government service, not in the future, but right now.

Jack realized that Henry is a minor and not legally able to enter into a contract to which he could be held accountable. However, Jack also knew that youthful inspiration and eagerness could ensure that Henry's interest and curiosity would bind him to the government even more strongly than any contract or agreement. Jack was eager and Henry was game.

Jack continued, "Henry, there is a very serious and important need our government has of you. This need is top secret, and you must swear that you will not repeat what I am about to tell you to anyone, not even your mother or father. Do you understand? Should I go on, or should I stop right here and now?"

Henry sat in curious silence.

Jack continued, "Henry, do you agree to these limitations on your free speech about which I just informed you?"

Henry was silent for a short, but measurable, moment. He stirred and shuffled his feet, but remained seated where he was. He looked directly at Jack in an unblinking, steady stare for several long seconds before he responded.

His eyes revealed a maturity beyond his years and then said, "Jack, I have known you for several years now. I have been observant, and I have noticed the strangest things about you. The strangest of all is the fact that publicly you present yourself as a wheelchair confined cripple instead of the athletic person you really are. You have hinted in the past, at some of our encounters, that there is more to you than meets the eye. You have also inferred that there is more to me than meets the eye. I must admit that is the hard one. I have known myself all my life and, as far as I can tell, there is nothing special about me at all. I am just a regular kid. I fit in very well with my friends and vice-versa."

Henry paused, giving Jack time to think, which he most certainly had been doing during Henry's discourse. This gave Jack time to develop the expected response and explanation. Finally, Jack said, "Henry you know that I am quite fond of you and that I would do nothing to hurt you or put you in any kind of danger."

"Yes.", Henry nodded in agreement and Jack continued.

"I would not be talking to you except that there are serious matters happening right now which can affect all Americans. Our country's resources are not developed in the field where "special" services are needed." Jack paused.

"Special services?" Henry asked in increased curiosity. "What kind of "special services"? It sounds like a social service function or even a military one. Certainly, our government has all these bases covered. Are they not?"

"They do not. Not these services." Jack answered peremptorily. He continued, "For your wise-guy information, "special services" with Uncle Sam does not mean anything social. It means something military if anything."

Henry acted as though he had a defensive chip on his shoulder, realizing that his earlier remark was out of place, "So? Tell me more. You must explain."

Jack responded, "So yourself. In this case the "special services" means using special talent. A talent that not many people have or talents which this world will acknowledge. As a matter of fact, sometimes people with such talents attempt to forget them or even deny, to themselves, that they even have them."

"Really?" Henry asked almost sarcastically.

"Yes, really" Jack answered. "Sometimes it is possible to determine that a person has this mysterious talent even before they really know of it themselves." Jack stared Henry in both eyes once again, but this time he flung himself as in flight and stopped within eight inches of Henry's face. This made Henry pay quick but uneasy attention. Henry's eyes opened wide as he unwittingly jumped slightly in a reflex action to Jack's sudden and unwarned proximity.

Henry said defensively, "Okay, Okay. You've made your point, but what exactly are you talking about anyway?"

Jack moved away from Henry in a sudden reverse flair, the opposite of that which brought their faces within a sudden eight inches of each other. Now, a flashy ten feet away from Henry, Jack said, "Henry, I am talking about you!"

"About me?" Henry questioned in both shock and surprise. "About me?" he repeated incredulously. Henry was short of additional words. His head was running so fast his mouth could not catch up. He flustered trying to speak and then just stopped trying just like that!

Jack decided the time to speak was when Henry could not. Henry was out of words. His mind had so many words to say that they all got stuck in his throat and did not come out of his mouth. Not even one word. Jack continued with his explanations to Henry. He may not have such an opportunity again.

"Henry, my boy", Jack said knowing that this phrase was probably overused in our society, but he went on anyway, "Henry, there are mysterious things happening all over this world. They happen every day and we hardly ever hear of them. Even more mysterious are people of power. Power in the form of superior intellect and a mind which can produce telekinesis, the ability to read and change minds. The ability to transform shapes and bodies from one to another. These people even have the ability of teleportation. They can be here one instant and there the next, even though the "there" may be several thousand miles away.

These powers depend only on what that individual can imagine. They achieve what they can conceive. They have a blank check to change things, events, and matter to suit their own concepts. They do this by using their own willpower and intense mental strength. Furthermore, they do not need to expend any great effort towards achieving the results they desire. They get what they need and want with minimal effort."

Henry was now alertly attentive to Jack. He was awe struck and he followed Jack's every word. "Henry, there is a real kicker in the whole thing. It is a kicker that will astound and surprise you very, very much."

Henry warily asked, "What is that? What is the kicker?"

Jack answered, "The kicker Henry is that they never know they have such strengths or powers. They sometimes live their whole lives without ever using even the slightest of their talents only because the need to use those gifts never arose. And so these gifts lay dormant and unknown to their possessor."

Henry said, "You must be kidding. I cannot believe it. If I had such strengths and powers, I most certainly would know it!" Henry paused in thought and then asked "Jack, how is it that you know all these things? How could one ever know? Most importantly, how could you know? "

Jack responded, "It is simple, although some only realize what they have only after an emergency of some sort develops a need requiring some superhuman feat. Then, and only then, do they begin to have an inkling of their powers."

Henry said, "What do you mean?"

Jack said, "In example, the most common type of superhuman feat comes about when a life is in danger. It is not completely uncommon in news reports to sometimes hear that in a moment, when a person is under a fallen tree or a fallen car, that a fellow human being called upon himself to raise that tree or car off the distressed victim. You hear of this almost all the time. The newspapers are full of such events. The real question is: Where did those powers and strengths come from? Why do they even exist?"

Jack paused, as though for effect and then went on, "While such events are unique and occasionally common, there are events which never make the news and which you never hear about that are just as powerful, and even sometimes more powerful."

Henry's curiosity became fully engaged at this point and asked, "Like what? Tell me more!"

"Well,", Jack went on, "let us say that a vase or something like that was going to fall off a shelf. You noticed it and did not want to allow gravity to have a pull on it. You wanted the vase back on the shelf it originally occupied. Then suddenly, just by your thinking about it, the vase gets put back on that shelf. You never touched it. It was only your thought processes that produced the effect you desired and nothing more."

Henry was amazed. He wondered even more why Jack was even telling him all this. He had to ask Jack, "I understand what you are saying. That is all well and good, but why in the world are you telling these things to me? Why at all?"

Jack once again whirled back to within a few inches of Henry's face and dropped a gigantic bomb with a severe and almost audible thud, although it was purely mental.

"Henry, it is because you have all the powers I speak of. You do not know it yet and the only reason I am telling you is because our government needs your help. We cannot wait for you to find out about yourself on your own. There is no telling how long it would take you to discover the secrets within you. Your Uncle needs you right now! There is no more time!"

Henry almost fell out of his chair. This was too much. Henry could not believe what Jack was telling him. He responded, "Jack this is not believable. I have never had the extraordinary powers you describe. I have never done anything beyond the usual and customary things a boy my age would ever do. I have had a fairly dull life."

Henry went on, almost apologetically, "I play with my friends. I visit my dad's office. I deliver my papers. I play and observe the shoreline creatures that make their home between the high and low tide line as well as those that come in with the high tide in the early fall. That's just about all that I do and have done. Where do you get the notion that I have the powers about which you are telling me? If I did have those powers, what is there about you that can see that this is a fact anyway? Tell me that!"

Henry stopped, awaiting a response from Jack, which did not come rapidly. After a few moments' silent pause Jack answered Henry's query. "Henry", he said, "your gifts are simply not developed. You never had the need to use them. When those gifts are fully developed, you will also be able to tell your fellows from the ordinary folk which are not so endowed. In short, you will be able to discern your "own" kind."

Henry could not believe his ears. Jack was implying that he had the very same gifts he had described to Henry just a few moments before and even more! There was no way Henry could determine just how Jack's gifts were developed and to what level. Henry was dumbfounded. He had no words except his body language. One moment he would be forward in his chair and the next, he would be back in the chair's recesses. These movements would take place at least once every fifteen seconds. It appears as though he had Attention Deficit Disorder, but nothing could be further from the truth. Henry was quite attentive. The reason for his movements was that what he was being told made him quite uneasy and upset.

Henry finally gained control over his emotions and his mouth began to utter words. They were somewhat silent words at first but eventually developed with ever-increasing volume. Henry said, "Jack, is that why you have always been so kind to me? Is that why when I come to visit with you it is almost like coming home? Is that why I have always been comfortable here? Are you and I the "same" kind? What in the world could you mean by that?" Henry said in a perturbed and disturbed vocal tone.

"Henry, I have known of your abilities ever since the very first day I saw you in your mother's arms. You emanated an aura of radiant power, mental, physical, and psychological strengths at that young age which you could never know about. You were not even toilet trained! How could a babe in arms know much of anything?" Jack said.

Jack continued, "You and I, and others, are blessed with certain strengths that most human beings do not have. I say blessed, however that may be a mixed blessing because with those strengths and powers come an almost superhuman sense of right and wrong, of responsibility and of the most dire and basic needs of humanity as well as a duty to make things better for all of us." Jack went on speaking while Henry remained motionless in silent attention.

"I do not know if our abilities are a result of a mutation or an evolutionary advancement for man, but I do know that it exists because I exist, you exist, others exist all of whom have the ability to communicate all types of feelings, emotions and words without saying anything and over vast distances. Sometimes those distances could be thousands of miles, all depending on the severity of the problem. It is almost a type of mental telepathy, but even more than that because actual feelings and emotions are transmitted as well." Jack continued.

Henry was beginning to understand. This conversation with Jack turned on a switch in Henry's head. Suddenly Henry not only understood what Jack was saying, but he knew what Jack was going to say before he said it! There was no need for Jack to say anything more. Henry understood completely. There was more. It was as though static electricity had entered Henry's head. He did know of Jack's thoughts and feelings but there was also a noise in the "background" of his mind, which he found disturbing. It was almost like a ringing in his ears. Henry broke into Jack's monologue, "Jack, I don't think that it is necessary for you to continue. Your words have triggered a mental reaction in my head. I am suddenly aware of all you are thinking and what you are telling me. I understand completely, even before you say it."

Jack responded with a sigh of relief, "Whew! I am very glad to hear that! I was beginning to think that I was dealing with a very stubborn person. I am happy to know that this is not so." Jack went on, "I'm beginning to get some feedback from your mind now and it tells me that you are becoming aware of your abilities. It's about time!"

Henry communicated to Jack, without the benefit of words, that he was disturbed by the "static" ringing in his ears to which Jack responded verbally, "Henry, you eventually will be able to turn down and adjust that "ringing" in your ears to a point where you will not find it disturbing. What you are hearing are the thoughts of those persons who are like us but whose thoughts are not directed to us."

"You recall that I did say there are more of "our kind" in the world. That is what makes the "tinnitus" sound you are hearing. It is all of our gifted "kinds'" thoughts coming together, in your head all at once. They are all our friends. Do not let it disturb you. Eventually you will not even notice it. Should there be a major event, you will be able to "tune in" to whoever is sending you the message. It is sort of like turning the tuning dial on a radio, but better because it is your own very personal "radio" on the world!" Jack explained.

Henry was relieved that he was not developing some type of inner ear disease and that he would not need to live with a disturbing problem for the rest of his life. He was completely awed at his newfound abilities. He had suspected that there was something strange in his life, but he could not determine exactly what it could have been. He first noticed that when, as a much younger boy, he went onto the mudflat on the West Basin of the Mamaroneck waterfront, that his curiosity about the fiddler crabs, that lived buried there, seemed to draw them out of there little "tunnels" just by his thinking about them. They would not stay out very long, and they would not stray far from their entrances, but it was as though they were "summoned" and hundreds would appear at once. Henry only thought about them, and their strange, oversized fiddler clawed arms, and they would appear. Henry felt this was only a "curiosity" and had no idea that their sudden appearance could ever have been thought related. Now he knew.

"Jack", Henry said, "I do not know what to say. I came into your house a much different human being than I will be when I leave it. What is the reason this has happened to me? And who is this "Uncle" you keep referring to anyway? What does he need to do with me anyway?"

CHAPTER TWENTY-NINE
HENRY'S GIFTS

Henry waited for Jack's answer to his questions. He found the entire afternoon with Jack very tiring, physically, mentally, and emotionally. Henry realized that after the revelations of this afternoon that he would never be the same innocent little high schoolboy he was before his entrance into Jack's house. He knew that he suddenly "aged" and matured quite a bit in a half hours' time. No wonder he was tired, and he was entitled to his tiredness. Rest and peace of mind was not to be, at least not yet.

Jack looked Henry square in the eyes and said with great earnest, "This has not just now happened to you. This is the real you. Why it happens to us is probably a matter of inheritance, evolution but who really knows? We are here and we are different, but we are all the same. I feel that we are an advancement on the nature of man. Perhaps it is evolutionary. Who really knows? It makes no difference. We have a very special place in the human sphere of things. It is a responsible and exciting sphere as well. You will find it quite rewarding. Henry, welcome to your new world and your new life! Congratulations!"

Henry was not certain as to the full meaning of Jack's words but being congratulated almost always seems a good thing, no matter why. That was Henry's feeling anyway. It made him feel that he is a good and worthwhile human being as well. Henry now felt more at ease with Jack's congratulations.

However, there were the phrases, New World and New Life, which concerned Henry. What exactly did Jack mean by those words?

Henry asked, "New world and new life? Jack, am I going away? What is new about my life? How has my world and my life changed anyway?" Henry was completely puzzled.

Jack sensed what Henry was feeling before he said anything. Jack began to answer Henry's questions before the last words were uttered. "Henry, the powers you have just become aware of were always there. Your world will become richer and full of wonder as each day passes. You will learn new things and see new places. You will experience what few men have experienced. Your sphere is no longer just the earth. Your dominion is now the universe!"

Henry became more filled with wonder at each word Jack spoke. Jack went on, "Henry, the other question you had in your mind was "who is this Uncle". Your Uncle is exactly why I had to bring you to the realization of your abilities and not wait until you discovered them yourself over some extended time."

Jack continued, "You recall that when I spoke of "gifts" I also spoke of the responsibilities that go with those gifts."

Henry said, "Yes, yes, yes. What do I need to do now?" Henry asked. He was very concerned and fearful as to what might be expected of him now.

Jack responded, "Actually, you do not need to worry too much. Your Uncle is the Uncle of all Americans. It is your Uncle Sam."

Henry became even more apprehensive. "Do you mean that I am going into the military? The Army? The Navy? The Air Force? The Marines? I'm too young, Henry protested."

Jack laughed a short, but powerful laugh, and said, 'No, no Henry. It's nothing like that. You will never be involved in anything military, ever. Your gifts have earned you an exemption. You will serve Uncle Sam differently. That is the reason you are here. That is the reason I have led you to your self-revelation. It is time for you to "grow up" in a sense."

Jack continued, "I want to introduce you to a very personal friend of mine. I want you to keep what you learn next an absolute secret from everyone, including your parents. No one is ever to know what you will learn next. I am asking for your agreement and solemn promise for this to remain secret. Do you agree?"

Henry was spending his entire afternoon apparently being constantly dumbfounded. There was one secret after the other coming upon him. He said, "Of course I agree. If you have been through the afternoon I've been through, what's one more secret?" Henry laughed.

"My friend is around the corner of the next room." Jack stated. "Mr. Xilx, please come out and meet my very good friend, Henry!"

When Jack finished saying that, the draped doorway's curtains rustled and out came the strangest creature Henry ever saw. It was a six-legged cat, or was it a dog? What exactly was it anyway? Henry added one more curiosity to his afternoon's delight. Jack said, "Henry, I want you to meet Mr. Xilx." And then he turned to Mr. Xilx and said, "Mr. Xilx, I want you to meet Henry Wilson. We call him Henry only. It's much simpler."

Henry made a medieval bow towards Mr. Xilx and said, "I'm very pleased to meet you."

To Henry's surprise, Mr. Xilx also bowed as a dog with six legs could ever bow. The bowing down was not the only surprise. The major surprise was when the dog spoke in near perfect Cockney English, "I am also quite pleased to make your acquaintance also."

Henry was so shocked that he fell back into the depths of his chair. He looked at Jack and laughed aloud for an extended time. He said, "Jack that was the funniest thing I ever heard or saw. How did you do that? An exercise in ventriloquism or what? How did you do that anyway? After this afternoon, I certainly am able to use this very humorous comic relief. Thank you. How ever did you make this puppet do that?"

Jack looked at Henry very seriously. Jack was not joining in the fun.

Henry's laugh faded like a cloud covering the sun. His face lost its radiant smile. He returned Jack's serious look. "Jack, you mean this is all real ? This is not a puppet. What am I seeing? What is going on anyway?"

Henry's laughter reddened face began to grow pale and he put himself even deeper into the recesses of his chair. He waited for what he hoped would be an affirmation of puppetry and ventriloquism from Jack, but none came.

Jack explained, "Mr. Xilx is a real person. He is his own "man" with his own soul. He is an intelligent, thinking being who has the welfare of the universe in his spirit. Mr. Xilx is a Starship Admiral from a distant planet. I happened upon Mr. Xilx during one of my quasi-military assignments at a secret location. I found him unconscious, stranded and injured. He has been with me ever since. I have learned much from him and vice-versa."

Henry thought, "I have spent this entire afternoon being amazed and shocked at what really is in fact a strange new world."

"You are very right, Henry", said Jack upon hearing Henry's thoughts. "It is a strange new world for you. This is not a dream, but stark reality. We live not only in our world, but also in our universe. Space is constantly expanding. Our knowledge of it increases every day in so many ways. We are only just now going into its exploration in our own primitive fashion."

"It is true. Your world is just now beginning to make child-like strides into the environment beyond your earth. There are not many worlds like earth that can sustain intelligent, creative life," said Mr. Xilx in his Cockney English voice. When Mr. Xilx spoke, Henry noticed that the spots on his coat changed color, which was only slightly distracting. Somehow, as Xilx spoke, the colors supplemented the subject and tone of his speech. It was as though the colors were also speaking, but in a visual sense, they reinforced his words as he spoke in quite a pleasant fashion. Apparently, Henry thought, audible speech was not the only means of personal communication in Mr. Xilx's world, wherever that might be.

Xilx responded, "That is quite right Henry. In my world, on the planet Ida, we do not always need to use sound to communicate. We do not even require the use of the changing colors you see on my coat. We also communicate as you and I just did, via mental telepathy. Here on earth, I imagine it would wreck the Bajezzus out of the telephone companies' incomes, but so be it. Even long-distance telephone calls are at risk because, depending on the urgency of a situation, our telepathy can reach several thousands of miles, without much effort."

Henry was now quite afraid even to think. Both Jack and Xilx could read his thoughts instantly. The color of his face had only slightly returned to normal from the initial surprise. He was shocked beyond belief. Nowhere in his wildest imagination could he have ever conceived of the present situation as a reality.

Mr. Xilx felt Henry's shock and sought to help his recovery. Although the weather was warm outside, Mr. Xilx summoned a cup of warm, not hot, chocolate milk, which was shaken, not stirred, into a foamy top surface that Henry found quite pleasant. The summoned cup of chocolate milk came to Henry floating in a breeze into the parlor and presented itself before Henry at face level. Henry gladly took it and took an immediate swallow. Mr. Xilx said, "Henry, I hope this will help you to recover from your shock. I understand what you are going through. Xilx then privately confided to Henry, "I went through about the same thing when I saw Jack, the human being, and realized that he was an intelligent creature with the power of speech."

"Wow!" Henry exclaimed. "That sip of chocolate milk helped quite a bit, Mr. Xilx. Thank you." He then exhaled a "whoosh" and said, "I need some time to gather my senses, my thoughts, my life. This is just a bit more than I can handle, and I am not even sure that I can handle it at all! I mean, what do I do? Where do I go from here? What is the story of my future? How does this current realization, this new knowledge of who I am, integrate into my life, past, present, and future? What about my mother and father? What about them? Right now, I need a little time alone to think things out and to reclaim my own head!"

Jack responded, "It's true that you need some time to think. Contrarily it is not true that you need to be alone at least, not at this moment. Right now, you need Mr. Xilx and I more than you know. We alone know your plight and we alone know the answers to your questions. We alone can help. You have joined us in a new reality for you, but an old one for us. We shall help you and guide you over the "bumps" as you fully reach your potential. Ultimately, you will turn all that you have learned here this afternoon over in your mind and in your leisure moments, all will become clear, and you will be at ease."

"Believe it or not, you will also be very, very happy. "Believe me, Henry, you will be happier than you could ever imagine. The world will be at your feet and your fondest wishes and dreams could be yours." Xilx said with a twinkle in his eye.

Henry did not reply to either of his companions. Instead, he slipped further back into the comfortable cocoon-like easy chair and fell asleep. Xilx and Jack looked at each other and communicated the common thought, "We'll let him rest an hour or two and then we will awaken him. He needs some respite from our announcement to him of his previously unknown and unaware abilities." They understood that the boy needed some escape from what had to have been a stressful series of revelations, even if it came in the form of sleep. They both then left the boy in peaceful slumber and as they left the room the door partially closed itself behind them.

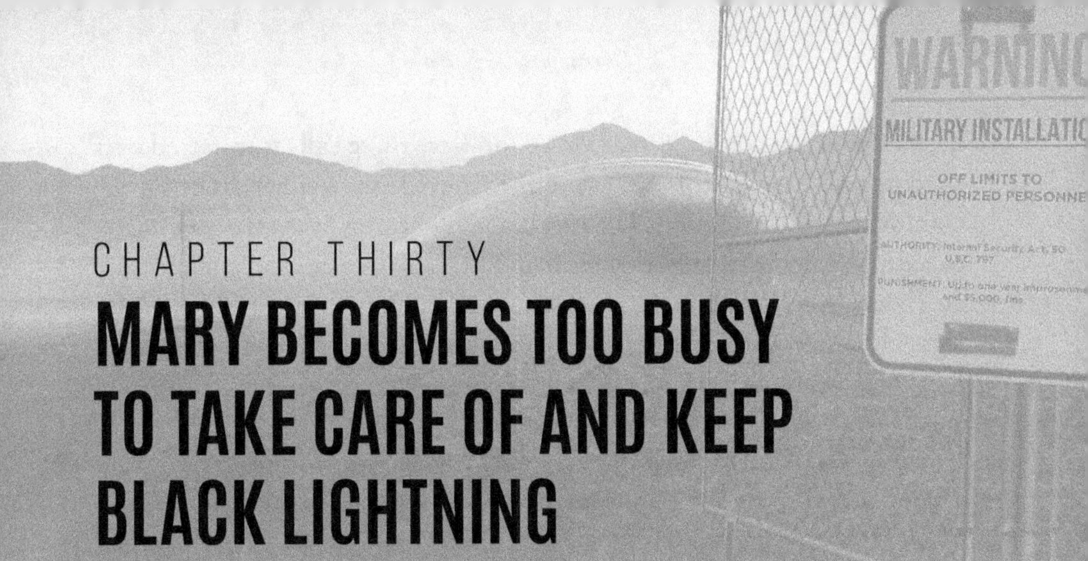

CHAPTER THIRTY

MARY BECOMES TOO BUSY TO TAKE CARE OF AND KEEP BLACK LIGHTNING

Mary was now busier than ever. There was so much research to do relating to the widely varied and distantly located environmental disasters. She found that she had to spend more hours than she expected at work. It seemed that the time this project demanded of her increased a little each day, to the point where there was almost no reason to drive home at all.

She had reports from Seemore, HB and most recently, Frank German. They were all quite varied in the events reported, but Mary felt that there was a common thread between them all, although she was not able to make a connection.

Each of her agents were to return additional follow-up reports to her. Mary was on edge and uneasy. She had to wait it out. Those reports should have come in within forty-eight hours of the initial intelligence. She could not conceive of the need for additional time for a more recent report from any of her agents. There was always the possibility of unforeseen complications that could delay her hearing from her agents. That made her uneasy, but she did her best to cope with her anxieties. She had no choice.

Mary found herself beginning to lose her energy. She was considering sleeping by the telephone in her office so that she would not miss any of her agents' calls. Fortunately, she did have access to secure telephony and decided that she could sleep at home and have these calls transferred over a secure line. She did this and was quite relieved. She left her office for the comfort of her own home. The cat, Black Lightning, was also very happy to see his owner back at home. He demonstrated his affection and pleasure at having Mary back home via licking and rubbing against his mistress' legs. He also found that this would always bring forth a savory canned meal of fish or other equally delightful meal.

"This cat is no fool", Mary thought to herself. "He knows how to get around me with ease. It is almost as if he were human." With that thought, Black Lightning began to lick her leg gently, but the tongue's rough surface did not feel soft and got Mary's attention immediately. She recognized it as a begging attempt for her to open a can of meaty cat food and serve it to Black Lightning on a virtual silver platter. She did this and Black Lightning immediately ceased its leg rubbing and licking.

"I guess you have what you wanted," she thought to herself as the cat attacked the cat food. Considering that the cat was alone all day and with some days requiring Mary to be at work even overnight, she contemplated, "That poor, lonesome cat. It has been so patient with me and still loving. I sometimes feel that is not fair for me to leave it all alone for so long. I guess that I should do something about that." Mary felt guilty and sorry for the cat.

Mary finally entered her boudoir and thought, "Now I can have some peace." Mary thought as she went to her bedroom. Her peace was short lived however, because her mind was still on the yet-to-be received reports from her special agents and their auxiliaries. She made an attempt at resting and sleeping, but it would be uneasy until she received the anticipated intelligence she needed.

Somehow, she did manage to get some needed shuteye and sleeping was not as uneasy as she expected it would be. She attributed her deep sleep to exhaustion she felt before lying down on her super tufted, pillow-top mattressed bed.

She was awakened quite early by a telephone ringing. It was not even dawn yet. Perhaps this is one of the calls I have been waiting for. She shook the sleepy cobwebs out of her head and grappled for the phone.

"Hello", she said drearily, "Who is this? It's five forty-five a.m.!"

"Well, thank you for the time check, Ma'am. However, that is not the reason for this early morning wake-up at an odd-hour call!" the caller answered.

"Well, what in the world is the reason? Please explain!", Mary responded.

"HB and I have been scouring our instruments and the area with the sophisticated instruments you let us use. We have found some very interesting…….", said the caller.

Mary interrupted the sentence with, "Who in the world are you? Whom am I speaking with?"

"Mary," the voice said. Do you not know who this is? This is your very special cousin Larry from West Palm Beach, Florida! You saw me only recently! Have you forgotten me already?", said Larry.

"Oh, Larry, Cousin Larry!" Mary responded, now being quite awake. "How nice it is to hear from you. Why are you calling me at this ungodly hour anyway? What happened? What earth-shattering news do you need to tell me at this hour? What could it be?"

"It is very strange that you are using such words Mary, because that is exactly what this call is about: Earth-shattering tremors where none have ever been felt before! We think that this one originates from the Indiantown Burt Reynold's Ranch area. We have these readings on the tremorscope, and we thought that they came from that region. So, we investigated late last night." Larry answered.

"Florida earth tremors must be very rare and very frightening. Florida is just about all coral rock. Did you discover anything?" Mary asked, now fully awake and very interested.

"Yes, we most certainly did! What we learned will probably put chills in your bloodstream because it most definitely affected HB and me that way and very much so," Responded Larry.

"Well, Larry, get to the quick and cut to the chase, will you? This suspense is too much! What did you learn? Tell me now!" Mary demanded.

"Well, yourself, Mary. We got up near the Reynolds Ranch and using the Disserenat-Clarus device, we found that the source of tremors developed off a high ground area in the middle of a marsh. When we came closer to the source, we used the Cor-Cordis instrument and discovered the existence of malevolent beings ahead of us and hidden behind bushes in that marsh. The Cogito-Lector let us know that in the marsh highland there were a group of witches with extremely evil thoughts. They are part of a group whose goal it is to undermine United States government security nationwide and to create all sorts of havoc and destruction across the USA.

There were about a dozen witches and warlocks all bent on such demolition and destruction. They were all singing, dancing, and chanting around a central low fire and drinking an inebriating cocktail of scorpion, palmetto, and stinkbug juices which they use to increase their power and strength of the spells their evil chanting induced on our country and, more specifically, this region in Florida" reported Larry.

"Wow," said Mary. "Bug juice indeed! Yeeeech! Is there more?"

"Yes," answered Larry. "Guess what this is all about, Mary. Guess what their gripe is." said Larry.

"What could it ever have been?" Mary asked, quite puzzled.

"They feel that they, as a group and entity in the USA, they have been maligned since the Salem witchcraft trials, burnings and lake dunkings in the 1600's. They feel that they have had enough in a land where religious freedom is supposed to reign and they consider it unfair that they are despised, feared, and frowned upon in our society. They have mixed feelings about Halloween though. In some ways, they feel proud that children run around in witches' costumes one night a year. However, they are not happy that all witches are portrayed as evil, scary, and coercive in order to get "tricks or treats"! Talk about mixed emotions! They want to be recognized and respected as doers of good and protectors of the environment instead! Can you imagine this?" Larry asked.

Mary did not know what to say. She was stunned into silence, which, for Mary, was a rare occurrence. After a moment's contemplation, she said, "It is most difficult to imagine any of this. Are you sure that this report is for real? Larry, dear cousin Larry, are you pulling my leg?"

Larry answered, somewhat offended, "Mary, I am nowhere near your leg! I am in Florida. Your leg certainly is not that long!" Larry said humorously. He then added, "What I have reported to you is as I was instructed to do so by my good friend, HB. Mary, this is much too serious. They were really hoping to develop major flooding and Tsunami-like waves in the area. That would not be funny at all. They had memories of their creating that short cold snap in Southern Florida only a few days earlier as a trial run. Mary, this is very serious indeed!"

Mary apologetically responded, "You are right Larry. I apologize. Please have HB give me a call as soon as he can. I need to talk with him too."

Larry then answered, "Of course, Mary. I am not offended that you need to double check your cousin's report with a complete stranger. Not at all. I'll be happy to give him the message."

Mary said, "Oh Larry, don't be silly. HB is the main agent and his report is needed to make the whole report official. I have no doubts about your report at all. Anyway, there are all kinds of matters I need to discuss with HB"

"As I said earlier, of course Mary, I will give HB the message. I'm sure that he needs to talk with you in any case. We are both concerned about these goings on and the power these witches can exert. Imagine, how can there possibly be freezing in South Beach and earth tremors in the Palm Beaches! We are on a bed of coral rock that makes up most of the peninsula. We are built upon layers of a subterranean coral base called

Florida. It is not granite. It is not the result of upheaval of the earth as it is in other parts of the world. That takes some very powerful magic! They're fighting mother nature, that's for sure." Then Larry added his au revoir, "Ciao Mary. We must keep in touch, especially now, in light of what has happened. I'm going to pass on this message to HB and I'll definitely be in contact again with my dear cousin. 'Bye for now!"

Mary answered, "Ciao. We'll definitely keep in touch." With that, they both hung up their respective telephones.

Mary thought quietly to herself, "I've yet to hear from Seemore and Frank. I also really must get HB's official report as well. I cannot wait!"

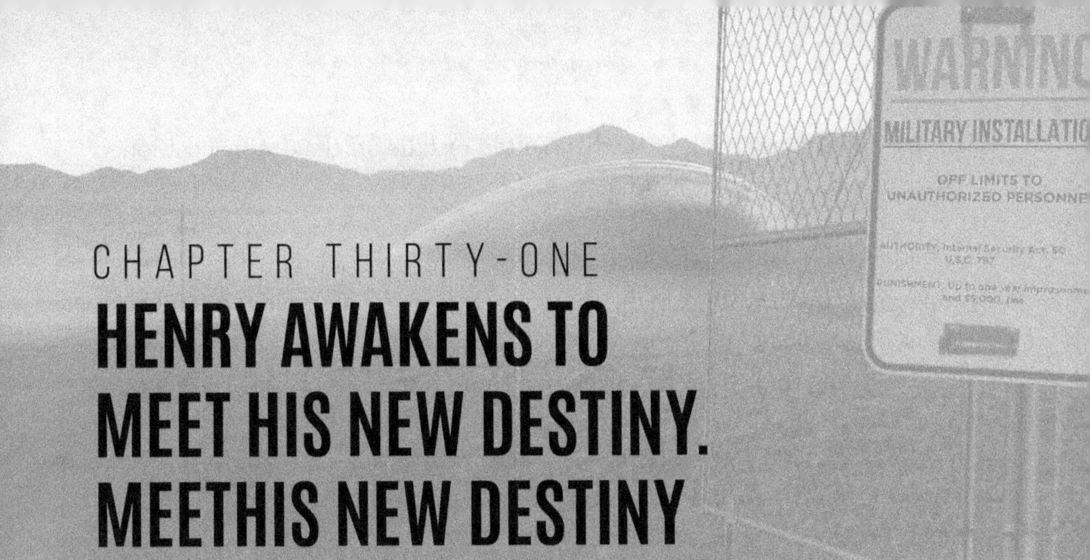

CHAPTER THIRTY-ONE
HENRY AWAKENS TO MEET HIS NEW DESTINY. MEETHIS NEW DESTINY

The atmosphere and all matters at the Henigson household are now quiet and serene. Jack and Mr. Xilx are in the library discussing how to approach Henry . They are very much aware of Henry's youth and immaturity of age, but they also recognize contrary qualities of maturity as well. Although Henry is young, he is wise and most mature for his age. His ability to reason and to be patient with the vicissitudes of life has encouraged their confidence in his capability to deal with the new, upcoming change in his life.

Mr. Xilx, being able to read Jack's mind, is keenly aware of his thoughts and his knowledge of Henry Wilson. Mr. Xilx's input on the task before them is concurrent with Jack Henigson's thoughts as well. There is no divergence. After all, they are into mind sharing, are they not? It is as though two heads are figuratively "speaking" with one mind! Their conversations are non-vocal. They communicate completely in silence, asking and answering mentally communicated questions only if they wish to do so. Otherwise, their communication is vocal.

They both simultaneously become aware of Henry's stirring in the other room. Although Henry is not fully awake, he becomes aware of the presence of the two beings near him. Jack and Mr. Xilx are in attendance in the case that Henry might be disoriented or falls off the deeply cushioned chair in which he took his nap.

Henry stretches and rubs both his eyes and gives a yawn. The yawn is a contagious disease of normality based on the power of suggestion and both Mr. Xilx and Jack Henigson caught it. They both find the need to yawn as well as giving the old limbs a stretch, although the latter is less a contagion.

Shortly thereafter, Henry reacquaints himself with his unfamiliar surroundings in a mild surprise. He gives Mr. Xilx a startled smile and a separate, but not startled, smile to Jack.

"Jack, how long was I sleeping?" he asked while still yawning and continuing to stretch his arms in the air like a television antenna array. He then blinked, looked at his companions and waited for an answer.

Mr. Xilx gave him his answer, "About an hour and a half!" He spoke in the lilting Cockneyed accent which expressed both cheer and applaud at the boy's awakening.

"One and a half hours!" Henry exclaimed in amazement. "I've got to be on my way! Fortunately, yours is about the last house on my paper route, but I am very late!"

Jack then joined in the conversation with, "Henry, I understand that you need to leave. We put you through your paces this afternoon, but it was necessary. I know that you can feel it or read it out of my mind. This is a new attribute for you, but one you always had and never knew about."

Henry responded, "Jack, I can read that you are worried about me. Please do not be concerned. Your thoughts and some of those belonging to Mr. Xilx have made themselves known to me. I understand completely."

Mr. Xilx answered, "That is very good, Henry. In time all that I told you will come true. All you must do is to be patient. This new-found ability of yours is only one of many to which you will eventually become accustomed. I can see in your mind that although you fully comprehend

Jack's thoughts as well as mine, that you are much less apprehensive than you were earlier. That is a good thing."

Henry acknowledged Mr. Xilx's words. "That is very true. It is an experience to which I am rapidly becoming accustomed. It is like a new sense. Instead of five senses I now have six!" Jack expressed delight, satisfaction, and surprise in this statement.

Henry and Mr. Xilx both laughed. Jack said, "It is good to see that you can laugh about all that you learned here. I also can read in your mind that your concern about Mr. Xilx has also waned quite a bit. That is all excellent."

Mr. Xilx added, "I too am happy about that. Henry, there are many different life forms in our universe. In time you will meet a few more. The best thing about this afternoon is that you, Henry, understand that there is a problem which we are destined to solve. We have gifts that not many people on Earth have. Additionally, as Jack said earlier, your Uncle Sam has called upon us to make the necessary corrections, whatever they may turn out to be."

Jack interjected, "I see that you comprehend this, and that you understand that we must meet again very soon. Use the intervening time to adjust to your "new" sense, as it were. Practice its use and learn what it may reveal to you about those around you and your environment."

Henry acknowledged Jack's grasp of the situation and he was thankful that Jack understood. Jack added, "Henry, be kind to those around you. Most of them are not like you or us. Do not be shocked or amazed that you are now able to read the thoughts of others, even though they do not possess the "gift". Be patient with them and try to understand them instead. Do not react to their unspoken thoughts because you will reveal yourself and shock them. If you do not do this you will lose your closest friends because they will fear and no longer trust you."

Jack continued as any serious teaching professor might, "Remember that only you possess the "gift" and no one else. That is to say this is usually the fact. You occasionally may come across others of our "kind", but they are very few and very far between. When you do, conversation is usually in silence.

You will know each other by one another's thoughts even without looking at each other face to face. The silent communication is a matter of security more than anything else. We are all "brothers and sisters" under the power of this gift. We never know who might seek to take advantage of us and our powers should it become known to the world outside our circle. It is our secret alone."

Henry took the ball and made a home run with his response, "I understand totally. I think we should meet again on the weekend, say Saturday morning in two days' time. What do you think? We could then be more at ease, and you can reveal the full nature of the problem in detail as well as our means of handling it."

Mr. Xilx was delighted and smiled his dog/cat-like smile, which made one think of the disappearing Cheshire cat in "Alice in Wonderland", but which was strangely pleasant, and said, "I think that is just perfect Henry. Please do not arrive before ten AM though. Jack and I both need our beauty rest, and who knows what evening chores we might be called upon to perform."

Henry acknowledged Mr. Xilx. He said his goodbye to Jack as well. Henry quickly bent over, grabbed and shouldered his newspaper bag as he headed for the door. Xilx and Henigson both waved him a goodbye and as the door shut behind Henry the two of them stood and looked at each other for a measurable moment in silence, conversing in the other's thoughts. They both sat down and began to plan.

Henry, on the other hand, was keenly aware of what had happened. It was a fact that he suddenly became aware of his powers and abilities. It was as if a curtain had been drawn on the next act of his life. His awareness hit him that quickly and without any warning. It was sudden, and Henry felt it was complete, although he was not sure of anything at this moment. He left the door open mentally that perhaps there might be more self-discoveries in his future. His newly found abilities were something he had suspected but did not really know until now. He contemplated his future and realized that his life had suddenly changed. He was not sure if it was for the better or for the worse. According to Mr. Xilx, it was for the better. Henry was not certain about such conclusions however but hoped that Xilx was right.

CHAPTER THIRTY-TWO

MARY DELEGATES BLACK LIGHTNING'S CARE

Mary continues her quest. She is very concerned that she still has not received follow-up telephone reports from HB, Seemore and Frank. Her early morning conversation with Larry Carl satisfied her qualms for only a few hours. The longer time passed, the more Mary became agitated. She finally decided. "I cannot just sit here and wait for their calls. I need to be proactive and take the situation in hand and find out what the delay is."

"Seemore was to give me a follow-up report as was Frank and HB" she thought out loud. "Where in the world are these people? Are they all right ? Have they been silenced by strange, unknown forces out there? What has happened to them?" Mary was becoming very concerned and worry showed on her face.

Mary paced up and down in her living room and finally said, speaking to herself as frustrated people sometimes do, "I need to get out of here. Perhaps I have a report at the office. In any case, that's where I'm going right now!"

Mary went to her car and sped off to her office. Mary thought, "These matters were not going as they should. There had to be a reason for the delay in her receiving these much needed follow up reports."

She called Wyatt and brought him up to date. She dialed Wyatt's cell phone. Wyatt answered after one ring. "Hello, this is Wyatt. How can I help you"

Mary responded, "Wyatt, I need to brief you on current events. Please meet me at the office as soon as possible. Some things are not going as I'd like to see them go."

Wyatt answered, "Certainly Mary. I already am at the office so just come up when you arrive. I'll be waiting."

Mary arrived at the DESE offices. She quickly parked her car and ran to the elevator that would take her to her floor. She had a special key that she used to trigger the elevator's rise to the unnamed and unlisted floor in the government building. The floor was omitted in the elevator panel and only those with special clearance knew that this special key would get them to the hidden floor.

Shortly thereafter, the speedy elevator rose to the floor level so fast that it almost left Mary plastered on its floor, but it did get her to her office quickly. The door smartly zipped open, and Wyatt was there to greet her.

Wyatt said, "Well Mary, what is the scoop? What is going on?"

Mary responded, "A lot is not going on. That is the problem. Have you received any calls or messages from Seemore, Frank or HB?"

Wyatt answered, "No, not one. Why? What is the problem, Mary? Please tell me what is happening!"

Despite the speed of her car, her ease of parking and the speedy elevator, Mary needed a few minutes to catch her breath and compose her emotional self.

"I have had initial reports from each of those agents, but there has been no additional information from any of them. As a result, I really have only half a report and some of those from their sub-agents and not our main contacts at all. It is as though they are incognito or disappeared off the face of the earth," Mary answered.

"Mary, did you try to make contact with them, or were you just waiting for them to call you?" said Wyatt.

Mary ignored the question but said, "They were to call me with an updated report, but I have yet to hear from any of them. I have partial reports involving strange happenings and reports of witchcraft that produced major climactic changes but there have been no reports thereafter. I am concerned for both the welfare of our agents and for our country." Mary added, in obvious concern.

"It seems to me that we should initiate contact and not just wait for them to call us. Especially if you are so greatly concerned about their well-being", proposed Wyatt.

Wyatt and Mary split the task of making calls to their agents, but neither made contact. Even the answering machines did not answer. Wyatt was starting to become as concerned as Mary regarding the mysterious lack of contact.

They tried to contact their agents the entire morning, but to no avail. Finally, they each looked at one another and both came to the same conclusion: they would need to once again visit their agents in person and learn firsthand what the problems were. What is the reason that they did not give timely secondary reports to tie up the loose ends of their assignments? It is a mystery which needs to be resolved, soon, if not immediately.

"Mary," Wyatt broke the silence which followed the lack of contact effort, "I think we should split up and get to our agents as soon as possible."

Mary answered, "Of course. You meet with the West Coast agents, Frank German and Seemore Manlein and I will meet with the East Coast agents, HB and Larry Carl."

They both readily agreed. There was urgency in their agreement.

Mary said to Wyatt, "We will need to take military aircraft to our destinations because we cannot wait for commercial and connecting flights. This is super important. I will make contact with the military air bases and arrange immediate flights. First, however, I will need to go home and pack suitably for perhaps a week's stay. You do the same. I will call you as soon as I have contacted the military transport planes. Let us say that we depart in about two hours from now, say two PM?"

Wyatt answered, "That sounds like just the right amount of time I'd need to pack and get to the airfield. It's a deal."

Each of them then left the DESE offices and went about their planned business. Mary went home and so did Wyatt.

As Mary approached her house, she noticed that Black Lightning was once again in the window waiting for her. She recalled her guilt in leaving the poor creature alone.

She went into her house and Black Lightning once again did the leg-rubbing thing. Mary knew what that meant. She went and filled the cat's dish with fresh wet cat food, which was called "Salmon Dinner" called and refilled the water dish as well. She just put the food down and the cat stopped rubbing her legs when the doorbell rang.

Mary went to the door and saw that it was Henry, the paperboy, who rang the bell. Henry said, "Hi. I'm here to collect for the week."

Mary was very happy to see Henry as also was Black Lightning who, surprisingly, left his dinner and came to greet Henry with a leg rubbing too. Mary was surprised at this because she thought that leg rubbing was a special thing Black Lightning had just for her. She was obviously mistaken. Somehow, Black Lightning already had a liking for Henry as well. Suddenly, Mary had a brilliant thought and she made Henry a proposition. "Henry, I am so happy to see you and so is Black Lightning. Would you do me a favor?"

Henry responded, "Of course. I would be very happy to do you a favor. What is it?"

"I must go away for at least a week. I hate leaving Black Lightning alone. Would it be all right for you to take care of him for me? You know, feed him and keep him company now and then. You could even take him to your house if you'd like. I just feel so guilty leaving him alone and without any companionship. I think he gets very lonely indeed."

Henry always liked Black Lightning. He readily accepted the request. Henry was very happy to do so. He did not have a pet at home. He bent down and petted the cat who responded with a loud purring and a raised tail. Apparently, it was a match.

Henry said, "I'd be very happy to help. I think Black Lightning likes me as I like him."

Mary showed Henry where the cat food was kept, and all the items needed to care for a cat. She told Henry that although she would not need the paper for at least the coming week, that Henry still should come by and care for Black Lightning anyway.

Henry said, "That's quite all right Ms. Kent. I am pleased finally to become more friendly with Black Lightning. Do not worry. I will take good care of him."

Mary showed Henry where the keys to her house were and then said, "Here is the pay for the week's paper and I am going to advance you some money to care for the cat. Right now, I've been packing to leave on urgent business. I hope you understand. I'll leave you here alone with Black Lightning so that you can become better acquainted. In the meantime, I will finish my packing and I'll be out of here in ten minutes. It is opportune that you stopped by, and I am very grateful for your help.

Henry said, "That is quite all right. The pleasure is all mine! I have been very curious about Black Lightning, and I am eager to know him better. So, you can see that I am very happy to be of service. I expect that I will enjoy Black Lightning's company as I hope he will enjoy mine!"

Mary was quite happy to hear these words from her prospective "cat sitter". She was only mildly apprehensive about leaving her long-time friend with a "stranger". Mary said, "Henry that makes me feel much better about leaving Black Lightning at home. I know now that he will not be alone and that he'll be with a good friend and a person who likes cats." With those words, Mary left for her bedroom and shortly finished her packing and said her goodbyes to Black Lightning and Henry and took her car to the military airfield.

Henry and Black Lightning were now together, alone in the house for the first time.

Henry said, "Well, Black Lightning, here we are, all alone. How are you, pussy cat? Are you all right? I need to leave to complete my paper route, but I'll be back, just like Schwarzenegger, in short order." Henry gave Black Lightning a petting stroke on the back to which the cat responded positively by arching his back and purring loudly. It was apparent that Henry had a friend in Black Lightning.

Henry also turned and left. Black Lightning did not like that and began meowing continually for several minutes. Black Lightning went back to the window in which Henry first saw him. He once again separated the curtains, saw Henry as he walked down the front path, and once again he waved. However, this time Henry had his back to the window and did not see the wave or the "look" of disappointment Black Lightning displayed. It is difficult for a cat to show disappointment, but this cat is as special as Henry and as a result, the emotional display of disappointment was noticed. Henry could not feel good about that. However, cats get over things like minor disappointments very quickly.

When Henry disappeared from view, the cat jumped down to the floor and began playing with his rubber band.

CHAPTER THIRTY-THREE
PLANNING

A man and a cat-dog are sitting at the dining room table, and they have their heads together, as close as a man and cat-dog might be able. They are deep in conversation, but almost inaudible. The other reads whatever words they fail to speak aloud as thoughts. Not a word is missed by either of them despite an occasional blank space in the conversation. That blank space exists only in the mind of an outside observer. Unless you are a mere mortal, with the usual earthly limitations, you would not have noted anything amiss. All appears as "normal" even though a human being and a cat-dog are sitting together. One might say that it is only a man and his favorite pet enjoying each other's company.

However, it is much more than that. They both concluded that Henry would need to be given all available information regarding our country's problems. Henry would need detailed facts to help solve the problems, as they now exist, and to protect himself from the possible wrath of the "enemy". It was a settled matter. Henry would mature even more at his next meeting of the secret trio at Jack Henigson's very quiet and peaceful house, the external appearance of which belied the truth of the happenings within. There could not be a place in which there was more turmoil encountered in the present and even greater turmoil will be encountered in the future.

Jack broke the silence, which meant that the telepathic section of their meeting was over, "We are to meet with Henry again on Saturday just another two days from now. I am not sure that I can wait that long. I am too much on edge."

Mr. Xilx chimed in, "I feel the same way. Do you think that Henry's abilities have developed to the point where he can read our feelings at a distance?"

Jack answered, "I cannot be certain. His abilities will grow at a rapid rate now that his discovery of the "gifts" has occurred. There is no telling how fast he will grow his talents."

Mr. Xilx answered, "I hope that he will develop them quickly. We cannot just wait around and do nothing while he grows enough to join our team."

"I know, I know." repeated Jack, yielding to impatient frustration under the continuing growing pressures they both felt was being placed upon them.

Mr. Xilx then said, "It is time to coordinate with headquarters as well. While you and I keep a low profile, there is still much going on, according to the information we have been getting from our boss. She is not getting her much needed reports from her agents on time. It has gotten to the point where she and her most trusted agents now need to go into the field themselves in order to practically "pull" those reports from her field people."

Jack replied, "This is true. Mary has been very unhappy that she has not had direct contact with her main agents as well as their original and follow-up reports. She is now asking us to help. That type of request from her is very rare. She must have her back against the wall to need to ask us to help her out."

Mr. Xilx replied, "That's for sure. I do not blame her for having unsettled feelings about the situation. She intends to get a detailed picture of the entire problem. She is a stickler for precision."

"That's true," answered Jack. "Henry has yet to know about Mary Kent, even though he sees her regularly."

Xilx answered, "Yes. Wait until he learns who Mary is and what she really does. It is fortunate that Mary does not have our gifts. If she did, she might not be able to hide her thoughts from the enemy and she might know our thoughts as well!"

Jack said, "I note that she has him watching her cat, Black Lightning. She has been taking care of Black Lightning ever since I gave him to her."

Mr. Xilx quickly replied, "I am glad that Black Lightning is with Mary. She has taken very good care of him. One would never know that Black Lightning is a staff member of my spaceship from the planet Ida."

Jack gave Mr. Xilx a quick look with a jerk, "That is true. I almost forgot about that. The more interesting thing is that Mary recently assigned Black Lightning to Henry's care! Wait until Henry finds out about Black Lightning's abilities! Henry thinks that Black Lightning is just another black cat. I would like to be a fly on the wall when Henry understands the otherworldly abilities Black Lightning possesses. It probably will come as a telepathic thought transference. Henry will be quite shocked!"

Mr. Xilx added, "You bet! Henry is in for two, not one, big shocks or at least surprises, is he not?"

"What do you mean?" Jack asked, puzzled.

"I mean not only does he need to learn about Black Lightning, but the really bigger surprise is when he learns that Mary Kent is the head of DESE and is a highly placed secret government agent. That is a double whammy! Isn't it?" Xilx answered.

"Here is this boy, who has innocently been delivering newspapers to this mature, classy businesswoman for several years now. There has been no suspicion as to what this demure customer does for a living. Wait until he learns that, between us and her, he is in the middle of what could be construed as a cloak and dagger spy ring!" Jack added.

"I think that he may not be able to survive the shock without ill-effects. Perhaps he should be forewarned after he is a little bit more deeply indoctrinated into our "club". Mr. Xilx replied, quite concerned about the effect all this information in such short time span could have on Henry.

Jack answered, "You are quite right. Now how do we do that?"

Mr. Xilx replied, "That is the sixty-four thousand dollar question, is it not? We do not need to reveal all the facts at once, do we?"

"No, we don't. That could be one way, but we need to get him working as soon as possible which means that he has to know all the facts just as quickly," said Jack.

"Of course, we could cheat and have Black Lightning produce some telepathic clues in Henry's mind," Xilx suggested.

"Perhaps. You forget that Henry is now developing the ability to read minds as well. He may be able to read what Black Lightning is thinking as well. When that happens, the whole matter will be in Henry's mind and he will know everything anyway!" Jack said.

"True," answered Xilx. "It will take a little more time for Henry to develop selective protection of those thoughts he would like to keep private. He has not learned to "cloak" thoughts he would not want to reveal to others yet. That takes a little more time to develop and will only occur after Henry has mastered his mind reading abilities."

Jack replied, "That is also true. It will keep him honest in the early stages and we will be able to know his thoughts in his pure initial development. He will not be able to hide from us, at least not in the beginning."

Mr. Xilx answered, "Yes, but now we need to accelerate his learning and development. I think the best way to introduce some of what he must know is by sending Black Lightning a thought transference message from the both of us so that he is aware of what we need to do and that we need to develop Henry's abilities and knowledge of our project as soon as possible."

"I agree," said Jack. "Let's do it now."

"O.K. Let's put our heads together and transmit our "M-mail," said Xilx.

Mr. Xilx and Jack then put their heads closer to each other, closed their eyes to help their concentration and started to emit their thought transference to Black Lightning. Henry will soon be getting the message, little bit by little bit, from Black Lightning, the innocuous black cat supposedly in need of Henry's babysitting help. That most certainly was an error. The staff member of an interplanetary spaceship most likely was very self-sufficient. His abilities were far more advanced than were Henry's. They should be because Black Lightning grew up with them and he had a lifetime to sharpen them. They were well honed and well-developed abilities that would take Henry as many years to equal in depth and quality. Nonetheless, the charade was necessary to conceal the reality that extra-terrestrials were here on earth. Was Henry in for the surprise of his life or not?

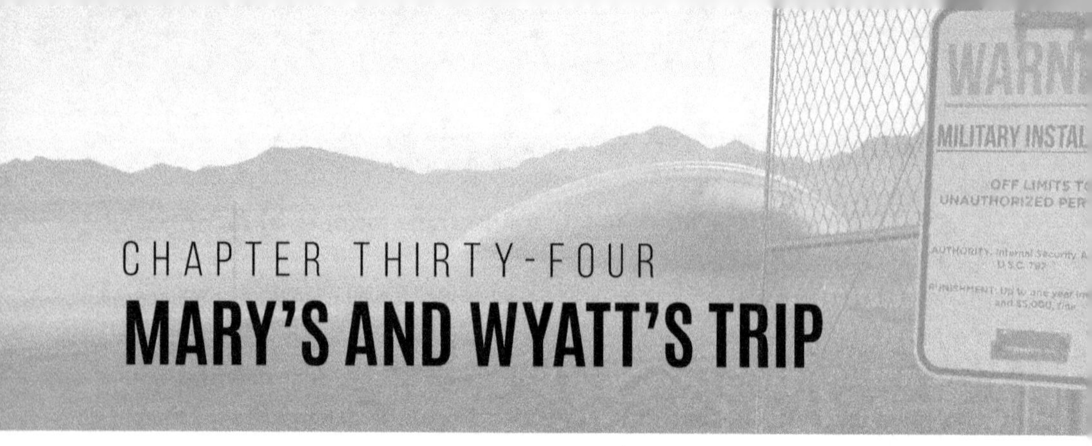

CHAPTER THIRTY-FOUR
MARY'S AND WYATT'S TRIP

Mary completed arrangements for a military flight to her field agents for herself and Wyatt. Wyatt was to land at the military base at the Los Alamitos Naval Air Station, just about in the middle of L.A..0 He would take a helicopter ride into the San Diego area and meet with Frank German.

Mary, on the other hand, had to fly up to Alaska to meet with Seemore and Hepseva, his wife. She did not really look forward to leaving her comfortable mid-Atlantic area for the cold of Alaska, but the lack of regular and follow-up reports made direct contact necessary. She had to know what was happening and why their reports were not forthcoming.

Mary was all packed up and on her way in short order. She told Black Lightning that she had to leave him alone again for probably another week. Apologetically she added, "Do not worry. I have hired a wonderful young man to keep you company and take good care of you. You have already met Henry and I think you will like each other."

Of course, Black Lightning already knew where Mary was going and why. After all, he reads minds! He even read thoughts that Mary did not ever vocalize. He read of her apprehension and lack of joy in having to go Fairbanks, Alaska in order to see to it that Seemore was doing his job. She was not even sure that Seemore was still there.

Mary was somewhat disappointed upon her arrival in Fairbanks. It was not what Mary thought it would be. There were almost no trees to speak of, although she thought they would have been there. She had envisioned Fairbanks as a land of verdant evergreens and thick woods. Several kinds of trees including nut bearing trees were able to grow here. There was an ample supply of berries, but the land tended to be sparse in areas and the growing season was short. Mary expected that the Manleins were probably all right in the region. Gnomes are naturalists. They are vegetarians, plant gatherers, and not meat-eating hunters. Mary remarked to herself that there had to be very little to gather here.

Mary shortly arrived at the Manlein's government residence. Her mind was open to any expectation. She knocked on the door and received no response. She knocked again and still there was no answer. She then tried the doorknob and it turned easily. The door was unlocked and she opened it without effort. That alarmed her. She first carefully looked inside and, seeing no one, she entered.

Mary received the surprise of her life. The place was vacant. Instead of finding the Manleins she found a large note taped to the wall opposite the front entrance which read:

"Mary, we have been so very much intrigued while reading the "Nome Nugget" that we simply had to go visit it. Nome, that is. Since we are "Gnomes", we want to see if we have any kinship up there. It is about 520 miles away. We will contact you upon our return and report.

Seemore"

Mary thought to herself aloud, "So the Manleins couldn't resist a visit to Nome, and all because of the minimal similarity between the words "Gnome" and "Nome"." Mary was amused on the one hand and gave a short laugh and smile. However, that smile was short lived. She had come more than three thousand miles on serious business and she was not really amused. This trip was not necessary. Her amusement changed to gross dissatisfaction and anger. She realized that when she enlisted the Manleins that this wanderlust was a probable risk, but she weighed that against the advantages Gnomes would have in their rapport with forest fauna. She still felt that this was an advantage.

Mary had no idea when the Manleins left, but she reasoned that it had to be shortly after her last conversation with Seemore and his current late reporting dateline. That would give them about a week long "vacation" from their duties.

Mary made herself comfortable because she was not only exhausted from her long flight, but the pressures she felt to uncover the reasons for strange national phenomena were great. She just had to have a release. She went to the cupboard, found some ordinary tea and brewed herself a cup. It was just what she needed.

Mary let out a sigh and sat herself down in a large, over-stuffed easy chair with an extendable ottoman, or footrest, attached to it and stretched out in cozy comfort. Mary thought "There is no one around. It is so quite." Mary slowly sipped her tea and shortly thereafter, dozed off.

Mary stirred and was surprised to see the sun in the East and not setting in the West, as she expected. "My clock is off", she thought. She then realized that the time change over the three and one half time zones had put her to sleep on Eastern time and she actually slept late into a sunny Western morning. It was the next day and not the day she arrived. That was gone. The benefit, however, was that Mary was refreshed and ready to do battle, as needed.

Her first step in battle was breakfast. Mary scoured the cupboards looking for something edible but found very little besides nuts. "Nuts!", Mary said with disgust. "Is that all the Manleins ate? How about something like Granola Bars or Cheerios! I guess that I either eat out at a restaurant or else I need to do some shopping for food. Thank God that the place is stocked with utensils and dishes at least!

Mary left Government House to go shopping in downtown Fairbanks. She found several places where she could food shop. There was the Farmer's Market on Farmer's Loop Road. She could possibly shop at the Great Alaskan Food Co. on Fox Avenue or the Riverview Quick Stop on Badger Loop Road, but their address of "North Pole" alienated her and she eliminated the "Quick Stop" from her itinerary. She instead substituted the Safeway Food & Drug - Bentley Mall, Bakery on College Road.

"That's where I'll go" she thought to herself. "It will be a place with people, warmth and cheery shopping. Perhaps I'll buy myself a souvenir like a cup or a hat or a sweatshirt."

Mary entered the Mall and made a very quick decision. She would find herself a restaurant in the mall and have a good, warm breakfast of bacon, eggs (over easy) and a small stack of pancakes which she did not need to cook. She would diet later at the Government House.

Mary was gone for several hours, both sightseeing and shopping. She had to buy herself a new pair of shoes. "That's a feminine rite, right?" she told herself. She rapidly agreed with herself and gave herself an introspective smug smile.

Mary was content for the moment. She was now well rested and well fed. She had shopped enough for the next two nights. She had no intention of staying longer. Mary entered the house and placed her shopping rewards on the kitchen table. She put away her cans, cereals and vegetables. She did not buy meats out of respect for the Gnome residents, but she did have meats in her canned goods.

Mary then sat down in the easy chair which had now become her favorite and took up the several newspapers she bought in town. She rapidly browsed through the "Fairbanks Daily News Miner", the "North Star Weekly" and the "Sun Star". She did not see much of interest to her. She put the papers down and made herself a pot of coffee. The aroma of the coffee percolating filled the room with its familiar smell and made the place feel less strange. Although it was not home, it was more comfortable, at least for the time being.

Mary checked for instruments that Wyatt had delivered to the Manleins. She found them and rapidly noted their data. There were changes in several of them. The solar jars had changed color and became heavier than they usually were. Mary checked everything else and then decided to relax instead.

Mary then once again took up her abode in the great easy chair with a second cup of coffee. Once again, she checked the newspapers but this time an article caught her eye. Mary did a double take. There was an article on a Fairbanks Witches' "Meetups". Apparently, there are witches here in Fairbanks. There was an article featuring people with the very strange names such as Glue Spirit, Moon Sapphire and Monrovian Wolf putting together a Fairbanks Witches Meetup. Mary was astounded. She thought aloud, "There are witches for real? Do they actually have group meetings? There are Shamans and Wicca all looking for a "Merry Meet"?

This means that the report from Larry Carl in West Palm Beach regarding a witches' gathering may not be off the wall at all." Mary read on at a feverish pace, rapidly turning pages excitedly to get to the continuing story. Although it was now either late morning or early afternoon, she was becoming restless. She went through the one article and sought out similar articles in each of the newspapers she bought. She did find them. They were there in the open for everyone to read; there was no attempt to hide them. A "Meetup" was arranged for just two days from now. The time and place was announced in the paper just as though it were a regular Rotary or Kiwanis Meeting announcement. "I will still be here", she thought to herself. "I will attend a meeting with them and learn more about this". Mary was becoming more than just restless, she was bordering on frantic and this was in middle of the day! "Wow!" she exclaimed.

Where was she to go with this? She was all alone and felt a great disadvantage at being without help. Mary put down the papers and threw herself back in a "favorite" easy chair engulfing herself in its soft folds. She loved the feeling of snug comfort and security it gave her, as false or as true as that might be.

"It is quite lonesome up here", she thought to herself, "but it's snug in this chair!" She sought retreat from the news as reported in the papers. She had a difficult time accepting what she read as a reality. Just as she became relaxed and settled, she heard a rustling at the doorway. Someone was turning the knob. Mary, being an Easterner, had already locked the door. If there were three or four locks on the door, she would have bolted all of them down tight.

Mary sat bolt upright in her easy chair, which was now not much of a refuge, and stared at the door for several, long measurable seconds. She ultimately summoned up the courage timidly to ask, "Who is there?" and "Can I help you?" Although she was timid, her voice was camouflaged to a feminine "booming", as only women can do.

The rustling stopped. The attempts at knob-turning stopped. There was silence. Only a soft wind was blowing outdoors which could occasionally be heard inside the building. Mary was now more alarmed than before. "What could total silence mean? Now even the wind outdoors was silent. The situation was becoming more and more ominous.

The silence was broken after a suspenseful several silent minutes with, "Hello in there! Who is in the house?" the outside voice sounded quite harmless and mild. It then added, "Who is in MY house. Please answer."

Mary was now much relieved. The Manleins had returned from their journey to Nome. Mary quickly rose from her chair and went to the door, peeped out to make certain the voices were as she thought they would be. (Easterners are very careful people, especially city or near-the-city dwellers.)

"It is the Manleins!" she thought excitedly to herself. "Thank God they are here. I would have hated to spend another lonely night here." Mary went to the door and unlocked it. When the Manleins saw her, they were overjoyed. There were smiles, hugs and kisses all around.

The Manleins were carrying small satchels with them that they carefully placed on the kitchen table. There were four in all. Seemore said, "Mary, I'm sorry that I left you that note, but the lines of communication were down. We had a storm just before we left, and it affected the phone and cable lines in the entire town. We were out for several days. I thought that you would have known all about it back in the "States". There was no other way to contact you and we felt useless here. That is why we felt it was an opportune moment for us to make a visit. This is a place where the name has intrigued us both for some time. So we went!"

Mary was so happy to see them that she forgot her earlier fit of anger. She said, "I was a little disappointed when I arrived, but I am so relieved that you are all right and still here. We need you now more than ever."

Seemore responded, "Of course we are still here. Mary, strange things have been happening. The Northern Lights are sometimes in the Southern sky. The temperature occasionally has become almost Florida-like, but only for a very short and unexplainable moment. The instruments sometimes appear to go haywire. I cannot be certain that they are working properly.

My good friend, Peganni, has told me that sometimes the Northern Lights have started in the Northern sky and then suddenly switched themselves over to the South. It has never done this in all written history. There is something unexplainable going on here."

Mary was giving Seemore her full attention, but her curiosity got the better of her, "Peganni?" she asked quite inquisitively. "Who is Peganni?"

Seemore answered, "Peganni is my very good friend. Sometimes Peganni gives us a lift so that we can go to places that mere mortals cannot, and more importantly, the public does not get to see us. When we travel with Peganni, we travel so fast and in such a magical fashion that we become invisible to man. Peganni also scouts for us and brings us back news of local happenings and where the largest haul of berries or nuts might be."

Mary was even more intrigued and did not know whether to believe Seemore or not, but she was most curious and could not help herself from saying, "Peganni surely sounds like a very interesting person. What is he, a magician or what?"

Seemore answered, "He is neither a "magician" or a "what", exclaimed Seemore, apparently offended in his friend's behalf and getting a redder flush in his already red face. He is simply Peganni! He is a magical being, made from the will of the Almighty. He is all spiritual and animal at the same time. He is only good. Evil has no affect on him but the reverse is true. He affects evil with good. What is good by definition is never able to be evil. Peganni is all good. Mary", said Seemore in serious earnest, "You need to understand that!"

Seemore emphasized this last part with a pounding of his fist on the table and looked Mary squarely and unflinchingly in both of her eyes and less than a foot away from her face. Mary got the point.

Mary said, "I would like, most emphatically, to meet this Mr. Peganni. He seems to be a being like no other. I most certainly would like to meet him."

When Mary said that, Seemore jumped to his feet so quickly that a frightened Mary did an equally backward jump away from Seemore. He jumped so close to her that they almost collided. Mary said, "I'm sorry Seemore! Did I say something wrong? What did I do? Why did you jump that way? You frightened me. Is everything all right?"

Seemore looked down, sheepishly, and replied, "No Mary, you did nothing wrong. I just so happens that Peganni flew us back from Nome! He is outside right now and waiting for us! Would you like to meet him?"

Mary was quite astounded. I would definitely love to meet this Mr. Peganni!"

They all rose to meet and say hello to Peganni. Hepseva, Seemore and Mary each put a warm jacket over their shoulders and went to the door, behind which a patient Peganni stood quietly.

When the door opened, Mary almost fell over in extreme shock. Mary expected another Gnome or a human being on the other side of that door. The creature before her was neither human nor a Gnome. Her imagination would have a difficult time even placing this creature in any of her wildest dreams. Since she joined DESE she had a multitude of wild dreams. She guessed that wild and disturbing dreams was part of the job. In fact she could not believe that she was seeing what she saw. She thought that she had to be hallucinating and actually did fall over, but Seemore quickly grabbed hold of her and prevented her fall.

Mary looked up into the eyes of the most beautiful and magnificent and beautiful creature she ever saw. Before her stood a winged horse, a Pegasus! However, there was much more. This horse had a single spiraled horn in the middle of its forehead, resembling the horn of a Narwhal. It was also a magical Unicorn! Beyond that she still had to say that there was even more to Mr. Peganni. Mr. Peganni actually sent forth light. He glowed like both the setting and rising sun at the same moment. He was a brilliant, unblemished white and looked like a creature from Heaven itself. The light just radiated in all directions from his body, in shimmering colors of pink and yellow and orange, but mostly a shining white. His wings were large and magnificent, even folded up. They were immaculately white. Not a feather was out of place. Each feather was long and emitted white light from underneath surrounded by a faint orange-pinkish glow.

Mary now completely understood what Seemore was talking about and why he was both protective of Peganni and offended at the naiveté of her crude references to their friend. Mary said, "Mr. Peganni, I am very happy to meet you. The Manleins need told me so much about you." Mary did not know what to say. She never heard of anyone talking to a horse, except for Mr. Ed that is. Mary did not know what to expect, but very shortly, her questions regarding the unknown were answered.

Mr. Peganni shuffled his hooves and moved his head back and forth, side to side. He looked directly at Mary. The combination creature of Pegasus and Unicorn embellished Mary's surprise when he began to speak. His eyebrows developed an almost human seriousness. He looked earnestly at Mary and said, "Mary, the Manleins need told me all about you as well, but I had the advantage of knowing in advance that you are a human being. You did not have that advantage. I know that you must be very surprised at my existence."

Peganni continued, "Humans have only thought of our species as mythology, but here I am. I am quite real as you can see. This is as it should be. My secret has to be kept a secret. My actual existence has to remain a legend and that legend has to live on for all human generations to come. If too many humans know of my reality they will fight over me and my brethren. This cannot be. There is no power in me but I do have powers."

"Humans cannot own me or others like me. I am a free, but supernatural, being with my own thoughts and goals. My goal is goodness and truth. The powers I do have emanate from the need to develop that goodness and truth in all the peoples of the earth, now and for the life of the earth itself. That is your goal as well, Mary, is it not? We are on the same side and that is why the Manleins were given permission to introduce you to me. I am at your service, Mary, only to do good in this world. That is my mission. That is your mission as well. We have the same goals." Peganni bowed with grand flourish.

She had the extremely rare opportunity to meet this extraordinary and very special individual. They were "mythical" which implies "not real" and "fairytale". He is instead a very real creature but like no other. I have heard of Unicorn and Pegasus, but I have never seen one and I most certainly have never met one much less a combination of both!" They really were not supposed to exist. Human beings are not even supposed to be cognizant of such entities as a reality. They are written and read about in mythology books that humans relate to as fantasy.

That is all that Mary had done in her lifetime: read about such mythical beings. Seeing one is a very special rarity and a privilege. Meeting one had to be impossible. Yet Peganni's parents were creatures which she could only read about. The dividend this time was that Peganni was more than just simply one of those magical creatures. This creature is a blend of two mythical and magical creatures. Mary answered, "I most certainly find it an honor to be so blessed as to be your friend", Mary humbly replied to Peganni."

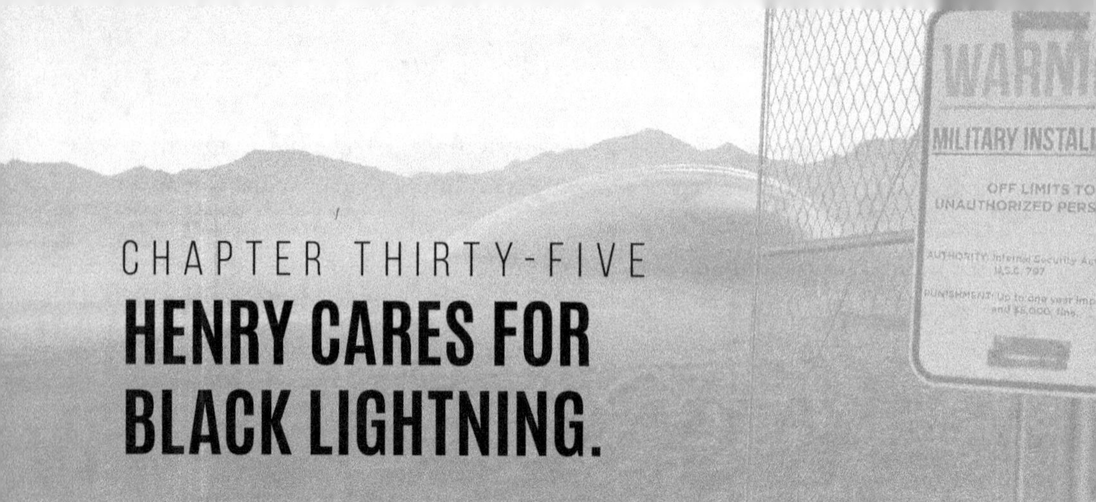

CHAPTER THIRTY-FIVE
HENRY CARES FOR BLACK LIGHTNING.

Mary was only gone for several days. Henry was at Mary's house on day three of her absence. Black Lightning was just as nice and as cute as ever. Henry would still swear that the cat could not only wave at him, but also smile. That "smile" was hard for Henry to accept, but part of him agreed with the concept. Henry really liked BL and it was apparent that the reverse was equally true.

When Henry came into the house to service BL, the cat would always jump up and down, purr and rub against Henry's legs. Henry would bend over and pet the cat, as humans do, and the cat would respond positively, showing its pleasure.

None-the-less, Henry acknowledged that the cat's real motive was not to show affection or to be friendly, but just to beg Henry for its next meal. Henry dutifully went to the cupboard and took another can of Gilmore Gump's Tuna and Shrimp Mix from the cabinet. That excited BL even more. The cat almost went in to a whirling dervish pin wheeling, almost without stopping until the food dish was placed before him. Then he quickly attacked it. The served meat was gone in short order.

Henry noted that several other cans had been opened, although he did not remember opening them himself. He assumed that Mary had opened them and left them in the refrigerator. That is where the remaining portions of the canned meats were placed. The lids were not perfectly in place over the opened remains of each can, but they were covered adequately enough for storage of the meat without excessive drying out or oxidation.

After Henry placed the dish before BL, he sat up in a chair and watched BL make short work of the food. Henry felt that he had to serve BL water as well and he took one more of BL's dishes and filled it with fresh water and also put that before BL.

Strangely, something prompted Henry to say "You are welcome" to BL. BL just quickly shifted from meats to water without missing a beat or even acknowledging Henry's service at all.

Henry thought out loud, "This cat certainly has the world by its ears. Service and all: food, water, shelter. A nice place to live in and people all around him to take care of his needs!"

At the very moment Henry had completed that thought, BL quickly jerked his head around and looked Henry directly in the face. Henry felt that it was as though the cat understood what he had just said and either took offense or was going to respond or both!

Henry did not have long to wait to have that answered. BL was staring directly into Henry's eyes for almost a full thirty seconds, a moment commonly called a "pregnant" pause. Then Henry thought he heard a voice, although there was no sound coming from anywhere in the room! The voice was a pleasant, lady-like voice, like an announcer on the radio, but there was no radio!

The "announcer" said, "Mr. , I want you to know that I DO appreciate all that you do for me. It is not that I am helpless. You would be surprised at what I am capable of doing."

Henry looked around the room. "***MR***. indeed? Who in the world would ever call me "***MR***"?" Henry asked a rhetorical question of no one because no one was there. Except the cat, that is. Henry looked down upon the friendly Black Lightning and asked quietly and without any alarm, "Is that you I hear in my head? Are you the cute, fast moving Black Lightning I have come to know and …… ?" Henry stopped from saying "love", but he thought it just the same.

Black Lightning responded, "Yes indeed. It is I, the one you know <u>and</u> <u>LOVE</u>. Even though you did not say it, I know your thoughts. Henry, I can read your mind, and if you cannot yet do it, you can read mine as well. Actually, that is how you can hear me, although I can also speak vocally, that is. I actually can speak several languages as a matter of fact, including some which do not come from this world!"

Henry received another shock. Not only did he recently meet Mr. Xilx, but he now meets BL, who can also claim existence as an intelligent being. "What is going on here?" he thought to himself. "Where did these cats come from? Why is it happening anyway?"

BL intervened telepathically into Henry's thoughts, "It is happening now because the time is right and the need is urgent. We do not have time to play games. Henry, I am part of Mr. Xilx's extra-terrestrial, space ship staff. Mr. Xilx has communicated with me just as you and I are doing right now."

Henry sat back in his chair and looked at BL. BL was not speaking aloud. This little cute cat was not at all what he seemed. As the thoughts came into Henry's head, all the evidence Henry could ascertain was that the cat was actually originating this telepathy was that the bright yellow eyes seemed to develop a momentarily more intense yellow which added to a spiked brightness as each thought or point was made. Then that bright intensity would fade for a second until the next point was raised and made. It almost seemed like a visual Morse Code!

That this cat was actually speaking with Henry was unquestionable. Henry was once more at a loss for words. It had only been several days that Mary had left here and only a day or two more that Henry had his most revealing meeting with Mr. Xilx and Jack Henigson. The realization came to Henry that there was something very big happening about which Henry had to know more. He realized that these events could not just have happened to him for no reason. He now knew that he had been gifted and, as a result, he apparently had an obligation to use that gift in the best ways possible.

"Know more?", BL once again interjected into Henry's thoughts, "Indeed you need to know more!" BL's telepathic words were emphatic. "You need to know much, much more. This is just the beginning."

Henry asked, this time telepathically, "What exactly do you mean? Who are you anyway? What is your real name and how did you say you know Mr. Xilx?"

"My real name is Agent Eight Five Seven Five. I arrived here a while ago on a space ship with Mr. Xilx who is the master of our ship. We came from several light years away from Earth. Our home planet is the planet Ida. We are known as Idaians." BL explained.

"Yes, go on." Henry said as BL paused.

"We ran into a proton created magnetic-electrical storm near your planet and lost power. We crash landed near the place you call Roswell, New Mexico. Our spaceship uses both inter-planetary polar magnetism and interplanetary force and varying forms of electricity to both navigate and power our ship. Your most recently revealed friend, Jack Henigson, rescued both me and Mr. Xilx. He first discovered Mr. Xilx. It was a bit later when Mr. Xilx was able to tell Jack that I was also aboard the vessel."

"Very interesting indeed. Tell me more!", the incredulous Henry begged.

"Very simply, Jack went back to the crash site and looked for and found me. He also rescued me. I joined Mr. Xilx at Jack's house and there I recovered." BL said, thus ending his explanation.

However, Henry still needed to know more. Somehow, the connections did not seem complete. There were still unanswered questions and Henry asked BL to explain those connections and answer the questions. All this was going on telepathically. There was no sound to be heard.

"Well, Agent Eight Five Seven Five, I still intend to call you BL. Your name is too cumbersome." Henry stated. "How and why did Jack keep the two of you and why did he not turn you over to the government?" Henry went on, "How and why are you here in Mary Kent's house? Does Mary have any idea of who you are? Does she even have the slightest hint?" Henry asked in near despair. "Poor Mary. When she finds out, she will be shocked beyond all belief!"

BL was not surprised by these questions. He would have been disappointed if Henry did not ask them. There was so much that Henry needed to know, and these questions made explanations much easier for BL to follow up.

"Good questions!" BL exclaimed. "Jack took both me and Mr. Xilx to his house because he did not want the government to dissect us and our mentality. First Jack thought Mr. Xilx was just a metamorphosed mutant cat. He became aware of Mr. Xilx's real being as he was driving him towards the military laboratory. He did not trust that the government would not destroy our bodies and our minds in their investigations. After all, we looked only like earth animals to them. That is why he took us to his home where we could recover."

"There has to be more." Henry continued, "How did you get to Mary's house as Mary's pet?"

"There is more. Brace yourself, Henry, for an even greater surprise. Mary Kent is not who you think she is. Mary is a special United States government agent who heads up a very secret and very confidential government agency. It is entitled "The Department of Extraordinary Situations and Events" said BL. It is quite secret. Only the President of the United States knows about its existence and knowledge of that existence is passed on only from president to president. It is more clandestine than the Department of Homeland Security and deals with threats to our nation that are not as apparent or as obvious as those the DHS will deal with.

"What!" Henry exclaimed. "Is there no one in my life that does not know of these events? Are all these people "agents" and connected with out-of-this-world extra-terrestrial life? Is there any part of my world that still only belongs to ordinary human beings?" A dismayed Henry asked plaintively while in a continued shock phase.

BL responded, "I do understand how you must feel. You have had a lot of information just simply thrown at you. Most of which has to be very astounding especially since you learned of all of it in a very short time." He continued, "Do not be concerned." BL said, assuring Henry. "It will all work out and you will ultimately have a greater understanding of the entire matter. Your life will never be the same again."

Henry replied, "Sure, it's easy for you to say but how about me? Do I still have a home, a mother, a father, friends, and buddies? What about school? What about college? Do I still have whatever is left of my "childhood"? Where do I go from here? What's to become of me? Where do I go from here?"

Henry was in plaintive, complaining and in agonizing despair. He did not enjoy all the new and strange situations that surrounded him. He looked at BL for answers. He hoped that some were coming to provide him with at least a little relief. BL just sat and stirred a bit and played with his "rubber band" in the manner cats play with little things.

However, this "little thing" was different. Henry was amused. The supposed "cat" was playing just like any cat would with a favorite plaything. He tossed the rubber band around and into the air. He then scooted in true "black lightning" form from corner to the middle of the room and back again. Henry thought, "Was I imagining that this cat was really "talking" to me or is this just another cat? This is ridiculous! Of course, he is just a cat!"

Just as this thought was complete there was a bright flash of light and a loud beeping sound which increased in crescendo! Suddenly the rubber band emitted a super heterodyne sound, screaming and squealing as a radio type frequency apparently "tuned" itself in. Then the room filled with light and full-sized three-dimensional images began to form a circle of four to five feet diameter and apparently projected several feet in front of the rubber band. Henry was both amazed and awed at the suddenness of the sight before him.

There was Mr. Xilx, along with Jack Henigson clearly visible but in an ethereal fog. They were talking among themselves, but they both stopped and looked directly at BL and Henry. Henry could see that they were still in their living room and the large, comfortable chair in which he had fallen asleep was clearly visible.

BL now spoke out loud and faced the images as though they were real persons and said in a conversational vocal tone, "Mr. Xilx and Jack; I need told Henry here, some of the facts of his surroundings. He is now aware of Mary's role in DESE. He managed to survive the shock, which is commendable because he also had to live with the realization that this "cute" cat is an extra-terrestrial being with incredible abilities.

These two revelations were loaded upon him almost simultaneously. He was unhappily shocked, but he did manage to absorb the reality of the situation, I am quite pleased to report", BL said proudly while strutting with his tail up straight, marching back and forth before the holographic images and displaying as much of a puffed out "chest" as a cat could ever show. It was obvious that BL was not shy about "bragging" at all.

The images responded in kind. Jack spoke first, "Henry, I hope that you are now aware of the seriousness of the world about you. We have a mission to secure our country and keep our people safe. There are extraordinary events happening all around us. I would not think that any of them have happened where you are. That is, none have happened up to now. Our country is really only feeling a "nuisance" type of assault. It is almost subliminal, but it is real and it can become devastating if those of us who have gifted abilities towards the extraordinary do not intervene and stop wherever it is coming from. We must destroy the causes at their base. We must stop its spread and keep our country and our people safe!"

Although Jack was a three-dimensional holographic image standing in front of Henry, the earnestness and seriousness of his demeanor came through very well. Henry most certainly sat up and took notice. The "rubber band", with which BL was playing, was on the floor, but steadily flashing different and very bright colors, similar to a movie projector all the while Jack was speaking. It became obvious to Henry that this was much more than just a rubber band!

"Jack is quite right, Henry," Mr. Xilx said. "We all have a job to do, and as sure as Fish and Chips, as well as Bangers and Mash, we'll get it done. We will not only do our job, but we will do it very well. You'll see, Henry!" The Cockney accent was as bright as ever and came through the holographic transmission very clearly. Henry most certainly knew that the voice was authentically that of Mr. Xilx.

"Well," Henry started, "I keep hearing all about the so called "attack" on our country and the "seriousness" of certain "happenings" and the need to "protect" our country, but so far no one has given me any information on what the problem really is or why it is or where these "happenings" have occurred." Henry said in an exasperated and challenging tone. He continued, "I am totally in the dark, so would one of you three "geniuses" come forth with all the information you have so that I can intelligently join your group. In short, would even just one of you give me all the available data so that I can be of some real help as well."

Henry went on, now becoming a bit perturbed over the intrusion into his formerly tranquil life and over what seemed like an extreme lack of organization and almost no pro-active investigation into the "whatever" program. "Where is the danger? What is the danger? Where is the danger coming from? The biggest question of them all is where and why does it exist?

Mr. Xilx responded, "Henry you are asking very good questions and we all wish we had the answer. Mary is currently on an investigational trip along with her aide, Wyatt. When they return, we should have the answers to at least some of our questions."

Jack once again walked towards the front perimeter of the holographic projection and said, "Henry, we all need a meeting after Mary's return to discuss the findings both she and Wyatt will share with us. Mary does not know that BL or Mr. Xilx has these gifts or attributes. We would like to keep it that way, at least for the time being. Mary does not even know about you, Henry, although she knows a lot. I think that we probably must let her know that you are "gifted", as it were. That way we will be able to have you be of great help for "our side".

"Henry, DESE has agents in different areas of the country. DESE is a national supernatural defense agency. Its very nature prevents it from being in the forefront of the public realm. I mean, who in the world in our country, that is to say, would ever believe in the supernatural. We, who are part of DESE, sometimes have a hard time believing what we see, hear, and learn. It all becomes easier to understand when we can place events and people in a factual setting that is more in line with rational, scientific thought. In short, we do not discount the "supernatural" one hundred percent, but we do try to bring such "happenings" into our current world of conventional "reality". Most of what happens has a natural and not a supernatural cause or causes. It is our job to sort out the reasons for either event. Whether or not such an event may be caused in nature or not. If not then we must deem it supernatural or "extra-natural" said Mr. Xilx.

Jack now interjected, "Henry, I do not want you to think that there are no supernatural events. It is really unbelievable that about ten to twenty percent of our investigations are from and by causes outside of nature, and as you can see by the presence of Mr. Xilx and Black Lightning, that some of our findings are in reality and "out of this world" so they are more than just supernatural. They are sometimes "extra-terrestrial" as well."

Henry took all this in stride. Fortunately, he was mature minded for his age and was able to comprehend all that came his way with ease. He realized that it was true and that his life would henceforth be permanently changed. He wondered how these changes would affect his relationships, not only with his parents, but also with his closest friends. He realized that simple ball playing was really child's play and for those with fewer cares and responsibilities to his fellow man and country.

Henry now spoke. He said, "You really mean that ten to twenty percent of your investigations are well founded in the quasi-fantasy world of the supernatural, magic and the extra-terrestrial. How very strange indeed. I do not find it funny, but I do find that number amazing."

Jack answered, "Do not misunderstand. The percentage we quote is only a miniscule number with regard to the amount of cases our government actually investigates. We do not get them all. We only get the ones that our more public government agencies find either hard or impossible for them to solve. Out of about one thousand cases a year, we may get one to two hundred of those cases for ourselves. We solve just about all of them, but not all. Our rate of problem resolution is about ninety-eight to ninety-nine percent. Of those about eighty-five percent or so are solved by scientific or natural fact and are not extraordinary at all. The other fifteen percent are either supernatural or out of our world occurrences."

"Wow", exclaimed Henry. "That is amazing." Henry went on, "What is it that I can help all you extraordinary people with? Wait a minute. I did not mean "people" because Mr. Xilx and Black Lightning are not people. I do not know what they are. They are neither dogs nor cats. What are you guys anyway?" Henry asked plaintively and hoping for a reasonable answer.

Black Lightning responded almost indignantly, "We ARE people. We are the representative people of the planet Ida, a very lovely place, a lot like earth. We are Idaians and you should respect us as such. Of course, if you do not think of us a people because of our form, perhaps a change is in order!"

Black Lightning was bordering on being angry, but did not really get there. He continued, "If you need a change, Henry, watch this!"

Suddenly there was a poof of smoke right where Black Lightning was standing and he disappeared, just as in a David Copperfield trick. He was nowhere to be found. The image-projecting rubber band still played its light show of Mr. Xilx and Jack. It began to quiver and shake and rotate, still making its projection of Jack and Mr. Xilx visible and steady, despite its movements. Suddenly Henry saw a form emerge from the center of the rubber band, but outside the circle of the Xilx and Henigson projection. The form began small and grew larger and larger by the second. When it stopped forming itself, Henry saw before him the most beautiful girl he ever laid eyes on. Henry was immediately in love!

Her long hair draped over her shoulders and was a brown-red streaked golden blonde with incredibly shiny highlights. She was about Henry's age and height. She was modestly clothed, but not so much that Henry could not see her most ideal, hour-glass form. Henry was left with his eyes wider opened than just wide open. His mouth followed suite, and he stood there, dumbfounded and gaping at this new figure standing before him.

Henry stammered, "Who are you? Where did you come from? Where is Black Lightning? What did you do with him?" Henry backed away from the figure before him. He did not know what to make of this person.

The figure answered in the most dulcet tones which just melted one's heart away, "Henry, who do I remind you of? Do I look like a relative of yours? Do I look like any of your friends? Who, Henry, do I remind you of? Tell me Henry. Please tell me!" the figure asked plaintively.

Henry did not know what to say. His answers did not come quickly. Instead of looking at the girl, he looked towards the holographic projection of Mr. Xilx and Jack. Henry asked the projected images, "Jack, Mr. Xilx, what is going on? Where is Black Lightning anyway? Where did he disappear to? I liked Black Lightning. What did she do to him?"

Henry was quite upset. After all he was to take care of Black Lightning in Mary's absence. How in the world would he ever explain his disappearance? Black Lightning was his "buddy", even if he were from "out of this world". To Henry, he was still just a cat.

The girlish figure before him advanced and Henry retreated. The girl came one step forward and Henry responded in near fright with one step backward. Then the girl spoke again. "Henry, don't you like my blonde hair? Don't you like me......?"

The pause that followed was so silent that one could hear a fly scratching on the wall, that is, if flies do scratch!

The girl continued with ".....any more?"

Henry was shocked. It is a good thing he is young and that his heart is strong. All the events of recent times would put almost anyone into the hospital. Henry asked in fear of the girl's response, "what do you mean by "any more" anyway? What do you mean by that?"

The girl said, "You used to like me very much, Henry."

Henry was puzzled. He asked, once again, both timidly and fearfully, "I do not think that I even know you. We have never met before. What in the world are you talking about? Are you mad? What is your name anyway? Where did I ever meet you? I would not have forgotten."

The girl answered, "Henry, it is me, Black Lightning. You thought that a change might be in order, and I ordered and created the change!" The girl did a smart and quick pirouette followed by both a bow and curtsey. "You like?" she asked.

"Black Lightning!" Henry yelled out. "I must be dreaming! How could you be Black Lightning? What did you do to that cat? What will I tell Mary when she returns? I am going to be in big trouble!" Then Henry asked the holographic figures, "Is this true? Is this really Black Lightning? Is Black Lightning a girl?"

Mr. Xilx answered, "Now, now Henry. It is not so bad, is it? No one ever told you that Black Lightning was either male or female. You just assumed and your assumption was wrong."

Henry replied, "This is just too much. I cannot handle any more. I need a rest!"

Jack now entered the discussion. He said, "Henry, it is not so bad. The three of us, Mr. Xilx, Black Lightning, and myself, have decided that the time has come to disclose the existence of our abilities and who Mr. Xilx and Black Lightning are to Mary when she returns. We feel that it is necessary for us to coordinate what we know and who "we" are with what

Mary knows. The "we" will also need to include you, Henry. She has to know that there is an arsenal at her command that will help her. She must know that people exist with extraordinary powers, such as you and me. It will all need to wait until Mary and Wyatt return."

Henry said, "I guess that is the way it has to be. Since we do not know all the problems and their meanings or origin, coordination with Mary and her work has to be a first step for all of us. In the meantime, I am going home and get some rest. I need to collect my thoughts and refresh my mind with a good night's sleep."

Jack and Mr. Xilx agreed and said good night to Henry. The projection blinked several times and then disappeared. Black Lightning was still in her girlish form and said "Good night, Henry. Have pleasant dreams!" Then she blew him a kiss! As she said those words, she changed back into the familiar cat that Henry liked. He liked the girl too, though. He found it hard to let the girl disappear without knowing more about her, and that bothered him at least a little bit. Knowing more about her would require another day and another time. Right now, Henry had to get out of there, and go to familiar surroundings and the security of his own house, his own family and his own bed.

Henry smiled as he snuggled under his covers in a near fetal position. He felt secure from the real and supernatural world to which he was just exposed. He snuggled into the folds of his blanket as he pulled them securely about his neck and shoulders. He felt warm and fuzzy. He was now contented. e was going to have pleasant dreams.

He thought of Black Lightning as the girl and not the cat. The thought put a smile on his face which slowly faded into a calmness as Henry fell off to a peaceful slumber.

CHAPTER THIRTY-SIX
MARY'S TRIP CONTINUES

Mary was having a ball, becoming reacquainted with the Manleins.

Peganni was an incredible dividend! It was because of such mythological creatures such as Peganni that Mary entered a government service with the incredible name of "Department of Extraordinary Situations and Events". She never really believed that such beings existed, but always hoped, in her heart of hearts, that they did. Now she knew they did exist. That made her day. She wondered how many other such creatures she might ultimately meet in her career at DESE. She felt that if one existed, then the chances had to be very good that there were more. It would be only a matter of time, she thought to herself. She thought "I may not get to meet them all, but I'm certain that I will get to meet quite a few of them." Mary was very eager to meet more such creatures.

She realized that the job she had as the head of DESE simply had to lead her into more and more extraordinary adventures of the same sort as meeting a mythological creature which had not even been introduced to the world. Imagine, both a winged Pegasus and a Unicorn in combination! The production of such a marvelous creature had to be as the result of an extraordinary love between two marvelous creatures of mythology. Peganni's very presence proves that the Pegasus and the Unicorn were not mythological fancies but real living creatures. They were not only living but possessed unbelievably extraordinary powers both supernormal and supernatural. Perhaps they lived in a parallel dimension with the human world, entering and leaving it at their pleasure.

"Seemore", Mary exclaimed, "How long have you and Mr. Peganni known each other?" Mary was very curious about this. The answer she received was one she did not expect and never would have imagined.

Seemore replied, "Oh, Hepseva and I have been very good friends with Peganni for about nine hundred years now. We met him after our move to Sweden had passed three hundred years or thereabouts."

Seemore said this in a matter-of-fact manner. It was as though there was no great deal in being more than fifteen hundred years old! Mary was amazed and surprised. She had no idea that Gnomes had such long lives. In any case, it was now known to Mary that in the least, these Gnomes lived that long and perhaps even much longer because they moved to Sweden from someplace else. Mary was afraid to ask where they came from and how old they actually were. The information they just revealed now was enough for one day, she thought.

Seemore went on, "Peganni is only one of the many unusual beings we have known. Of course we know several Centaurs, Faeries as well as several Leprechauns that we met when we were in Ireland, the Emerald Isle. We also have several Wispy Whisperers as our friends as well. They are all over, but very shy and secretive."

Mary could not contain herself. She was amazed at what Seemore was revealing to her. Every word he uttered had her full attention and was a jewel in her glossary of knowledge. Mary asked with only slight trepidation, "What are Wispy Whisperers? Where do they live? Who are they?"

Seemore responded, "Wispy Whisperers are almost spirit like. They have an almost gossamer-like body which means that you can almost see through them, but not quite. They are thin, wispy, and not very big, but only about two feet or so tall. Some are taller and some are shorter. They can fly like faeries, but they do not have wings. They hide in high winds as they can be blown away because they are feather light. They are benevolent and kind creatures and influence humanity for the better. Their goal is as is Peganni's and ours: to improve the goodness in the world and to better the lives of man as well as all of earth's creatures. They are placed here by the highest power in the universe for that purpose. They "whisper" thoughts, not words, to influence the mind of man to achieve the highest goals. They are something like muses in that way, but they are much more powerful."

Nymphs go along with the Wispy Whisperers and help them along their way. The nymphs are stronger and more worldly wise than are the more innocent and naïve Whisperers. They are protectors of the Whisperers and escort them to places of greatest need. They go to where malevolent thoughts or evil actions are being forced upon innocent humans."

Seemore paused. He had been speaking for longer than expected. He thought that perhaps all this history would bore Mary, so he looked at her quizzically for her reaction. He was quite wrong. Mary was very interested.

Mary asked almost urgently, "Is there more Seemore? Is there more? I find this very fascinating. I want to know all there is to know." Mary was very interested. This kind of information is her department's concern. Everything that Seemore was telling her was almost certain to be used some day for sure.

Seemore continued, "Well, Mary, there is more, but it sometimes borders on the dark side of the universe. I may have left out some of my friends, but there are really so many. The existence of witches is something better known to humankind. You, and human society, have known of them for some time now. What you may not really know is that there really are two kinds of witches, good and bad. I have known both kinds. Unfortunately when I meet the evil type no good comes of it. Sometimes I can get one of my nymph friends to bring one of the Wispy Whisperers and influence them to the good, but that is not always expedient.

However, Mary now that I have use of the Cogito-Lector device I have from DESE it is not always necessary for me to call the Nymphs to help me get a Wispy Whisperer to induce beneficent thoughts into the mind of a potentially evil witch. The Wispy Whisperers are neither happy nor unhappy about this decrease in their employment, which is really a minor factor for them because they are in such high demand around the world.

DESE does not have that many agents and the few that we are does not impinge greatly on Wispy Whisperer employment."

Mary did appreciate this more than expected explanation from Seemore, although she was quite surprised by its extensive detail and new, never before known, information, especially about the creatures called "Wispy Whisperers". These were a completely new entity in her lexicon of mysterious and quasi-supernatural creatures.

Mary replied, "Witches! Witches indeed! I must know more about them, Seemore. I have had reports of goings on regarding them from other parts of our country. Whatever you can tell me about them and your relationship with them could be of great value in solving the current events before they can become critical." Mary paused and continued, "So please go on Seemore and tell me all that you can."

Seemore turned his ruddy, bearded face towards Mary and said, "Mary, I am not sure that you want to know all that I can reveal. Some of it may not be very nice and some of it can fully change your mind regarding the stereotypical notion of witches." Seemore paused. "Are you sure that you want to know all that I can tell you?"

It was Mary's turn to answer, and although she was cautious about Seemore's warnings she timidly answered, "Yes Seemore, it is my job to know all, and I mean everything, there is to know. Please leave nothing out."

Hepseva almost turned white. The color left her reddish complexion and she let out a near fearful "Ohhh!" and said, "Please don't mind me. I have heard it all before and I find it somewhat unpalatable, so I am going to leave the room while Seemore tells you "all". Good luck Mary."

With that, Hepseva left the room and stepped into the safety of the peaceful, tranquil outdoors.

Mary looked towards Seemore. Curious inquiry showed in her face with her brow furrowed and her eyes almost "squinty". She waited, with an anxious uneasiness for Seemore to reveal his "secrets". Mary wondered why Hepseva felt that she had to leave the room and why she wished her "good luck".

Mary waited and Seemore turned towards Mary and with a very serious and solemn look, he at last started to speak. The happy eyes, which usually had a twinkle, became very somber as he began. The twinkle was gone.

CHAPTER THIRTY-SEVEN

WYATT'S TRIP GOES ON

Wyatt was all packed and on his way to San Diego to interview Frank and to determine the facts behind Frank's report. San Diego: the most perfect climate in the United States. That's its reputation. When Frank told Mary of the snow and the risk to San Diego's crops and reputation for fine weather, Wyatt could not believe it. It was one of those things a person had to check out for himself.

Wyatt took a limo out to JFK airport. He did not care for military transportation. He was dropped off at terminal six, the Jet Blue terminal, went through security and boarded the airplane when the flight was called. Wyatt liked Jet Blue so much that he decided to take it to Long Beach Airport followed by a leisurely, scenic drive to San Diego. Jet Blue flight 209 left JFK right on time at twelve noon, or so they reported, but it really was twelve twenty-four instead. Wyatt enjoyed the time aboard without stress. Peanuts, sodas and a small color television set in the seat back front of him was all he wanted. He just wanted to rest his mind on senseless things. He would have enough to cope with when he had his meeting with Frank. He wanted to rest if he could. Flight 209 did manage to arrive early at Long Beach Airport despite its tardy departure from New York. It was to arrive at two forty-five PM but arrived instead at two thirty. Wyatt appreciated the extra few minutes for himself before meeting Frank again.

He had already arranged for a car rental at Hertz, an interesting small, blue PT Cruiser convertible that had just enough room for him to carry his luggage. Although he liked Jet Blue, he already arranged that his return flight would be from SAN to JFK. Unfortunately, Jet Blue did not leave from SAN, so he already arranged for an American Airlines flight back home.

He stopped off to see his buddy, Matt Ovlas, his surfer dude friend who moved to California shortly after graduation from the University of Connecticut and now is living in Huntington Beach. He missed Matt, and the visit would be a welcome change of pace from the chores of service in DESE. The other-worldly adventures and reports he had already experienced and had knowledge of at DESE would make the most courageous and battle-hardened service men cringe at what DESE came across.

Matt was very happy to see Wyatt one more time. He greeted Wyatt at the entrance to his apartment complex with a big, very cheery smile and a can of cold Coors Lite in his hand. He raised his right hand in a high five and followed that up with the "secret" handshake they shared which was somewhat complicated with closed fist upon closed fist followed by open palm passing each other's hand in a brushing "flyby" motion. Matt passed the Coors Lite to Wyatt who took it gratefully. He was slightly tired from the long six-hour flight and was thirsty and famished as well.

Matt said, "Wyatt, I am so very happy to see you! To what do I owe this pleasure?"

Wyatt answered, "Just mixing some business with pleasure. Visiting you is the pleasure."

Matt asked, "Really? What kind of business may I ask? Jobs around here are a bit hard to land, especially if you have something specific or a specialty needing experience and ability to cope with the competition for that job."

Wyatt replied, "I already have the job. I need to interview one of our reps in San Diego the day after tomorrow. Nothing very significant."

Wyatt knew that was not true. He just did not want to pursue the matter with a friend. Matt had no idea what kind of work he did and that is the way Wyatt wanted to keep it. After all, this was not just "business" but very serious "business" indeed. Matt did not need to be concerned about the threats to his well-being as they may not really exist at all. Wyatt could not really assess the situation until after his interview with Frank. He wanted to set his mind in neutral and cleanse it of the knowledge he held, and which kept popping into his consciousness. He wanted to be a "clear" person when he dealt with Frank. He did not want to be viewing Frank's facts with what he already knew.

He continued, "Well, what do you Californians do here anyway besides sitting in the sun all day and drinking beer?"

Matt replied, "Wyatt, this is Surf City USA! What do you think we do? We really do work." Then he quickly added with a smirky smile, "Then we do surf, but only when the waves are up!

"Matt, that all sounds great. Right now, it's a little after four PM. I am hungry. Where can we go that is pleasant and we can get a bite to eat? I am starved", said Wyatt.

"What do you say to a short tour of my California Street area, and we can wind up down at the Huntington Beach Pier Restaurant for a little something to remove your hunger pains! We can park your blue chariot on Main Street and walk the short distance to the restaurant at the end of the Pier. It'll be a pleasant, leisurely outing. You'll enjoy it." Matt offered.

They both finished their beers and put the cans in the recycle, piled into Wyatt's car, and headed to the downtown area that was only several blocks away. They managed to park diagonally on the main drag, fed the meter and walked about.

There were the usual touristy attractions. The novelty stores sold Huntington Beach memorabilia and novelty gifts. The surf shops are very well inventoried. You could get just about anything you'd want in surfing. They had it all. The main street was only two lanes wide, with only one lane in each direction, thus giving the area a small-town feeling. The diagonal parking was also unique and made the driving lanes a little narrower. The restaurants catered to "on the sidewalk" tables, set in a "private" area, sometimes roped off or fenced in and closer to the street. Pedestrians would need to walk between these areas and the front of the restaurants. It gave the place a more friendly feel.

The main drag was perpendicular to the beach and the major north-south street which passed between the main part of town and the beach. That macadam highway was four lanes wide with parallel parking and an esplanade between the north and south lanes. Matt and Wyatt took themselves across the Pacific Coast Highway to the Pier, the entrance of which lies directly across the PCH and is a continuation of Main Street.

The pier is nearly fifty feet above sea level and about three hundred feet long. It is constructed of heavy planked wood, grey in color having been aged and weathered by the elements. It is wide enough to handle two- and one-half car lanes. and the public is protected from falling into the ocean by chest high three-inch diameter pipe fences. There were people doing all sorts of things from fishing, just strolling and shopping in the few shops it carried on its back.

The Pier restaurant was at the end, painted in a deep maroon-red color, and constructed in a more modern circular shape. Wyatt and Matt took their time in getting to restaurant, meandering their way walking from one side of the pier walkway to the other, checking out the fishermen's pails out of curiosity to see what they caught. Only a few fishermen hooked anything this day and there was nothing notable in their pails.

Matt and Wyatt finally made it into the restaurant, Ruby's Diner. The motif was that of a nineteen-forties NASCAR, racing diner. There were checkered flags around along with race cars and driver's pictures. Its décor is to recapture the "good old days".

They were ushered to a seat by a waitress clad in a forties type uniform with a trim white blouse and wide red and white vertically "candy striped" short skirt which was held up with red and white suspender-like straps crossed over each other in the back but perpendicular in the front.

She was a pert red head coiffed in a short-hair style which added to the pert look. She asked in a snappy, "Can I get you something to drink?" She passed out menus to each of them.

Wyatt responded, "I see that you have fish and chips. That is what I'll have along with a Cola."

Matt chimed in, "I'll also have a Cola, but a cheeseburger, instead of fish and chips, but with Cole slaw instead of fries."

The waitress did an almost military about face and went forth to fill the order.

Matt then turned his attention towards Wyatt and continued their conversation. Wyatt started by asking, "Matt, how are things around here? Is everything all right and the same as usual every day?"

Matt looked at Wyatt as though he had a screw loose. Matt answered, "Wyatt are you o.k.? Everything around here is boringly the same every day. The "same as usual" is an understatement. It's so usual that it's monotonous. We have sun almost always. A cloudy day now and then, especially in the winter, does happen, but it's never that tough to get through."

Wyatt said, "I did not mean to upset you. In your case, "usual" is the way things should be. Nice and safe, even if it is monotonous. There have been reports of strange weather events in different parts of the country. I just wondered if you have noticed any strange weather around here, that's all."

"No, Wyatt, as I said each day seems to be the same as the next. It's interesting when you first move here, but after a while, it gets to you. I like it though."

The red and white trimmed uniformed waitress returned with their order and the two of them immediately dug in and grabbed their meal with voracious delight.

When they had completed their meal, Wyatt exclaimed, "You know, I'd like some dessert as well to finish this meal." Wyatt then motioned to the waitress to return, which she did quickly.

The pert young thing asked, "What can I do for you?"

Wyatt smiled and said, "I'd like to order desert. May I have a Vanilla, Chocolate and Strawberry ice cream dish?" He then looked across at Matt and saw that he most likely was interested in just about the same thing.

Wyatt asked, "How about you Matt?"

Matt replied, "You bet. I'd like a banana split!" Then he smiled a happy, satisfied smile at the waitress, who smiled right back.

The waitress said, "Very good. I'll be right back."

While Matt and Wyatt sat waiting for dessert, they both stared at the Pacific Ocean scene outside. It was so peaceful and serene. Surfer dudes were happily floating over the waves, which were supplying an eclectic number of waves of varying heights. These dudes were surfing in extraordinary delight. Matt had a greater appreciation of the scene than did Wyatt, him not being a surfer dude.

The tricolor ice cream and banana split arrived at their round, brilliant, white Formica table and the waitress gave each of them an appreciative smile. The two dived into their desert and made short work of it. They then rose, left a tip and Wyatt paid the bill.

They stepped outside, into the warm sunshine, and under the blue sky. There was not a cloud in the sky as far as they could see. Wyatt noted the oil wells set out into the ocean, short of Catalina Island, and thought at first that they were sailboats. The fact that they never moved whetted his curiosity.

"Matt, why are those sailboats not moving? I've been watching them ever since we arrived here. They have never moved all that time! Are they anchored out there, far out in the ocean?", asked Wyatt.

Matt did not reply immediately, but just laughed. "No, Wyatt, they are not fishing boats at all. They're oil wells, pumping out oil for our cars and industry!" He then added, "It's true. You can easily mistake them for sailboats at this distance."

"It is a gorgeous day here. It makes a Northeasterner want to leave the gray and dingy area back home for the sun and sea out here! Look at that beautiful blue sky!", said Wyatt.

Just as Wyatt uttered his last words, he felt a cold spot on his nose which he quickly brushed away with his hands. Wyatt thought nothing of it until a second cold spot followed the first, and then another and another. Wyatt was shocked.

He shouted out, "Matt, it's snowing! It's snowing!"

Matt answered, "No, it can't be. This is Southern California. It does not snow here except up in the mountains, far inland."

Matt extended his hands out, palm upward. His hands were rapidly becoming covered in snow. The Pier was being covered in snow. Matt was amazed. It occurred to both of them that they were cold as well.

Matt said, "I'm freezing. Let's get out of this!"

Wyatt chimed, "You bet."

They made a beeline for their car parked on the other side of the Pacific Coast Highway and climbed in and quickly slammed the car doors shut.

They both exclaimed at the very same moment, "Wow!", and then stared at each other in surprise, but shock is probably a more appropriate description indeed.

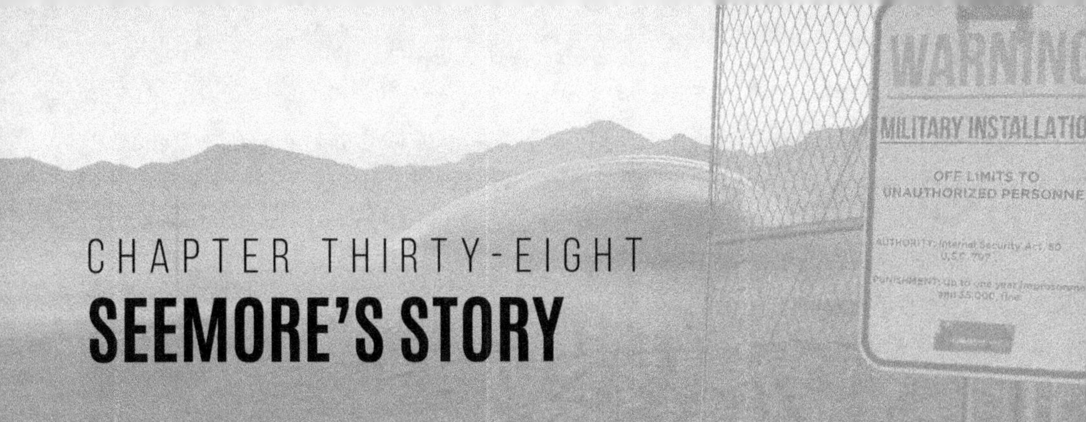

CHAPTER THIRTY-EIGHT
SEEMORE'S STORY

Mary sat like a bump on a log. She waited with the proverbial bated breath for any sound out of Seemore's mouth. Seemore was not easily forthcoming with his story. It was obviously difficult for him to communicate with Mary, either because of the complexity of what he had to say or because he was emotionally conflicted and the information he had to relate to Mary was painful for him to reveal.

Finally, after a long and perspiratory pause, he said, "Mary, the most important matter which bears on the current state of events and your office, is that which is the Veneficum and their misguided goals and causations have revealed to the world."

He paused a second, but just long enough for Mary to ask, "Venificum? What are the Venificum? I have never heard of that word before."

"I'm so glad you never heard of them before, because no good could ever come of that knowledge. Nevertheless, the time has come when you need to know about them. I first met them almost one hundred fifty years ago when I was a much younger lad and not approaching my prime as I am just beginning to do now." Seemore paused.

Mary prompted, "Go on. Go on Seemore. Please tell me more, please. I need to know all that you can tell me."

Seemore hesitated once again, but he continued nevertheless, "In 1917, October 13th, the Miracle at Fatima occurred. The Venificum were there. They did not believe what they saw. The good guardians of the earth and its heavenly creatures, the angels of heaven, as well as the good witches of the earth, were also there. The good witches did believe and they saw the angels flying about Mary, although none of the other human spectators did. The Venificum sought, through witchcraft and the summoning of even more evil spirits than themselves, to prevent the event from even beginning. They would destroy, maim and murder anyone who stood in their way. The good witches, being on the side of goodness and virtue in this world fought not only the evil witches' efforts but also those of the evil spirits summoned by dark incantations and chants. The good witches, and I (Seemore added proudly), succeeded in repressing the efforts of the Veneficum to both suppress the event and deny that it ever happened as well as attempt to refute its reporting in history. I was there and I was on the side of the good witches. The powers of Heaven were enough, by themselves, to defeat the evil. We, the good witches and I, Seemore added unabashedly, did our very small part to create the victory. I did not need to have any events shown to me beyond what I saw to prove that it was a real miracle.

The Heavenly powers revealed that day far surpassed those of evil, and so it will always be."

Mary was completely intrigued. Seemore had her full, almost mesmerized, attention. She interjected, as Seemore paused to both gather his thought and take a breath, "Interesting. Please tell me more." It was as though Seemore was telling Mary a bedtime story as to a child. Mary was wide awake, however and impatient for more.

Seemore went on. "The whole world reported the event. A quote from Dr. Joseph Garrett, a Professor of Natural Sciences at Coimbra University stated, *"The sun's disc did not remain stationary. This was not the sparkling of a heavenly body, for it spun round on itself in a mad whirl, when suddenly a clamor was heard from all the people. The sun, whirling around seemed to loosen itself from the sky and advance threateningly upon the earth as if to crush the people with its huge fiery weight. The sensation during those moments was terrible."*

Dr. Formagio from the seminary at Santarem was also quoted. *"It was like a bolt from the blue, the clouds were ripped apart, The sun at its zenith appeared in all its glory. It began to rotate creating a dizzying sensation upon its axis as a most magnificent fire wheel ever imagined. It revealed all the colors of the rainbow and emitted bright flashes of spectrum colored light, creating a fantastic effect. This spectacle was repeated three distinct times. Each lasted long enough to impress all the crowds and endured for about ten minutes each time. The multitude were overcome by evidence of such a phenomenon and fell on their knees before the power of heaven."*

Mary was eager to hear all that Seemore could relate to her. She certainly heard of Fatima, but who could ever imagine that she would ever speak with an actual eyewitness and a participant behind the scenes!

Large numbers of people made additional statements. Some were from a crowd at the Cova da Iria and even more from areas very much further away. Witnesses over such a large area mean that this phenomenon is not explainable as crowd hysteria or hypnosis. The absences of reports from a wider area and from distant scientific observatories reveal that the phenomenon was local to Fatima."

Seemore continued, "There are two possibilities. Either remarkable atmospheric phenomena was arranged by an intelligent agency at a time announced specifically in advance or coordinated hallucinations in thousands of people were similarly arranged at this time. By either interpretation, it is hard to fit these phenomena into the framework of modern science.

In 1960 the Rev. Joaquim Lourenco, a canon lawyer of the diocese of Leira, described what he saw as a boy in the town of Alburitel, some nine miles from Fatima and was in agreement with those immediately on the scene.

Seemore answered, "Mary, the Venificum are a loose, but still vaguely organized, group of witches that have only hatred, vengeance and evil in their hearts. That is, if they have hearts. They are cold and unfeeling. Whenever they are about, you will notice that the weather changes, and never for the more pleasant. It may be a warm sunny July day, as happened recently in the Florida incident you reported to me. Then suddenly, the weather would change, the skies would darken and cold or snow could descend upon a land which almost never saw it before."

Seemore went on," Mary, I believe, and our instruments show, that it is most likely the efforts of the Veneficum, and their associates, which have created the climatic and celestial changes we have recently witnessed. While it is not the only explanation, it is the one that makes the most sense. I think that further investigation is needed. The changes in the Northern Lights position and snow in Southern Florida is right up their alley. It is the kind of thing they would do, but I think that they are just beginning. I think that they want to create serious and massive havoc and destruction.

This story had Mary actually sitting on the edge of her chair. Seemore's relating the Venificum to the Florida incident was exactly the kind of explanation that Mary was seeking. Perhaps she was getting her answers, at least in part.

Seemore continued, "I took several photographs of the Northern Lights Phenomenon. The camera I used is the special one your department issued to me. It is the one which permits continuing intrusive investigation even after the picture is developed and viewed. Your department calls it the "Time Store Photographic Capsule" camera or "TCC". I have enlarged one of these pictures to twenty by thirty feet. We can see it here."

Mary said, "Of course. That is a very recent development produced by the nuclear scientists and physicists. They developed it for space probing and exploration. We saw the covert applications it might afford in our department and as a result, we are using quite a few of them. They are fascinating but they can be dangerous as well."

With that statement, Seemore opened a large, combination locked drawer. He concentrated seriously as he turned the dials left and right, muttering the numbers under his breath and adding an occasional expletive when he dialed an error, and took out a large, almost museum sized photograph. Mary was quite amazed because the drawer he opened was only two feet wide and definitely not more than two and one-half feet deep. Still, as he extracted the photograph from its home, it rapidly expanded to life size and achieved its twenty by thirty foot dimension. It virtually filled the room with its mass. Mary could see the Northern Lights as they were when the photograph was recorded. She was surprised to see that they still were moving and flashing in the photograph, like a moving picture.

Seemore invited Mary towards him and the photograph. Mary moved forward and he held her gently by the hand. The even greater surprise came when Seemore suddenly pulled Mary's hand and they both jumped into the photograph! They were in and actually a part of the living photograph!

"Seemore", Mary shouted. "I'm sorry but I feel a little woozy. I need to pause a moment and sit down and rest a little while."

Seemore replied, "I most certainly understand. Apparently, you have never been inside one of these "living" photographs. I am not surprised because most people never know how to use their own equipment and all its nuances. Mary, this is one of the pieces of equipment you have given me. You really never knew how it worked, did you?"

Seemore laughed and Mary blushed. Mary had to admit to herself that he was quite right.

Mary gathered her senses and looked around to determine where she was. She knew that she had to leave the picture and the spot she was in was the exit area. Mary was not happy that it was not labeled "Exit".Although she was certain that Seemore knew the way out as well, she did not want to trust herself to chance in any way.

Seemore reached down and took her hand. Since Seemore was not very tall he hardly had to bend over to reach the hand of a seated Mary. Mary took his hand and rose off her seated position and they both looked about and marveled at the shimmering lights.

Seemore spoke, "Mary this is what the Northern Lights look like. This is north and that is south." Seemore pointed southerly towards the moving light show. There was nothing but darkness in the northern direction. "That is not the way it is supposed to be. The opposite is what should be and not this." Seemore shrugged his shoulders and held his palms outward towards Mary in despair.

"Mary that is not all there is. If we walk further into that small bramble of bushes behind you and to your left, you can see what really is bothersome to me and why I took this picture." Seemore turned very serious and urged Mary to follow him towards that thicket. Mary did so.

The approached the thicket and stopped just a few feet short of it. Seemore cautioned Mary to be quite and to move slowly and silently.

Mary followed Seemore and they both peered cautiously over the bushes. They saw a small bonfire about five hundred feet away from their position. There were strangely hooded and gowned figures prancing and dancing about the fire. They were chanting, sometimes softly and sometime loudly. Mary could barely make out their words, but she thought she heard, "Curses to the Bedraglers in Boston, to the Deneyers in Washington, to the Sousicos in San Diego. Activate the San Andreas fault! Light up the sky to the south to show us our powers will work. Move the hurricanes into New Orleans! Flood Pittsburgh! Shake the sky! Let there be meteors pummeling the earth in the dishonorable areas." They shouted and screamed in unison while waving short sticks up toward the skies and down towards the earth.

They chanted and chanted. Mary and Seemore stayed there for a good fifteen to twenty minutes and still the figures continued their cursing. They were joined by smaller and larger than normal individuals who seemed to emerge from the center of the circle. Some were twice as tall as the average man. Some had arrow-pointed tails and Mary thought that she even saw pointed bulges over their foreheads and under their hoods. "Were those horns?" Mary wondered. She thought they were red men, Indians perhaps, or people who had been out in the sun too long because they looked like they had a severe reddened skin and sunburn. Mary did not take too long to realize that what she was looking at were not even men. The bulges under their hoods and the pointed tails and reddened skin proved to her that they were demons from beneath the earth!

Mary shrunk down kneeling behind the bushes. She was shaking after realizing what she saw. It was more than simply supernatural. It was super spiritual in an evil way. Seemore knew what Mary saw. He had seen it before when he took the original photos and entered them a while back. Mary was deeply troubled. This was much more than she had bargained for. Of course, she never bargained with anyone. It was just that she never realized that her job would involve such creatures, both good and bad.

CHAPTER THIRTY-NINE
SECRET MEETING

Mary really did not know how the "living picture" camera device worked. Here she was, inside a photograph that was kept in a small drawer, then which grew to great size upon removal and was a picture into which she entered. That she entered it with a Gnome was not remarkable considering where she now was. What was remarkable was that she was actually seeing an event in the past, recorded on a "living photograph" that was one in which she could interact on a real time basis!

Mary slowly recomposed herself and looked up at Seemore. He had been keeping a watchful eye on her as she shuddered in her crouched position. She had somewhat recovered from her shock and was ready to address the situation.

Mary whispered to Seemore, "Is what I am seeing real? Is this really happening or did it happen some time ago? Am I able to interact with these people or whatever creatures are there?"

Seemore replied, "Hold on, Mary. One question at a time and one answer for each in its own time." Seemore said as he raised his hands in a "stop" signal. "What you see is very real. It did happen weeks ago when the last shifting of the Northern Lights occurred. The third part of your question is the most interesting. You can actually interact with these creatures on a "real time" basis just as though you were back in time and present when it actually happened. Conversely, they can interact with you as well. That is where danger lies. You need to understand that while we are in the photograph, they can hurt us badly. They can even kill us. In that case we will not return."

"These are not nice beings. You can see that some are from the deep underworld and are demons. They are the most evil of all, excluding their master of course, the head of all demons. All these beings have magical powers. That means, in short, that they can cause us harm. We must be very careful not to be discovered here because this is a secret gathering to which only the evil can attend. It is like positive and negative electricity. They are negative and we are positive. Should we meet, there will be a great figurative "explosion" as it were , and one we do not wish to precipitate because we would lose and they would win. Therefore, be very careful."

Mary considered Seemore's words. She decided to err on the side of caution. "Seemore, could we come back to this picture at any time? Is this a one time and "now" only occurrence?"

Seemore answered, "Mary, it is just a picture, quite extraordinary, but still just a picture. We can put it away and come back to it at any time we wish!"

Mary was relieved. She then said urgently, "Seemore, then let's get out of here right away and out of this picture to where we are safe. We can talk about this then." She then turned around and started to walk back, not even waiting to see if Seemore followed. She was in that much in a hurry to get away from there.

Fortunately, Seemore agreed. He quickly took Mary's hand and led her out the way they came. Once again, after they stepped out of the picture, Mary had to sit down to gather her thoughts and compose herself. She would address what Seemore just revealed to her after a rest. She had to rest. Although there was minimal physical exertion, the mental and emotional response had shaken her so severely that she needed a rest and also a nap to recover from it all. Perhaps that was a protective form of escape for her, but she had to do it. They went into the other part of the room where there was a second cot. Mary laid down and almost immediately fell fast asleep just as though she were drugged. She was not, of course, but just emotionally and physically drained.

Seemore watched helplessly as the exhausted Mary fell into her slumber. He understood the stress she had to be under also considering her traveling to a distant location, running the DESE organization and doing the research and coordination of results needed to come up with an answer to the strange happenings around the USA. He thought that it was a good thing that she was healthy, vigorous and energetic to boot. She would need all those qualities to get through whatever lies ahead.

Mary slept deeply and motionless for the first two hours and then she started to stir and mumble. Seemore was nearby, examining results from the exotic equipment DESE had sent to him. He heard Mary stirring and he expected that she would be awake soon. He tried to anticipate what her thoughts would be, especially with regard to what she saw in the expanded photograph.

Mary sat up but not leaving the cot on which she had napped. She saw Seemore on the other side of the room and said, "Seemore, I want to thank you for all the adventures I have had since I have come to visit you. I could never have imagined what I have seen since I have been here. But nevertheless, what does it all mean? What you showed me was really an interactive recording created in the past, but still with powers to affect the present. That seems absolutely incredible."

Seemore replied, "Certainly does. I remind you Mary, it's your equipment!"

Mary continued, "Seemore, did you use the Cogito-Lector to learn anything at that demonic gathering?"

Seemore answered, "Mary, I most certainly did, and I can go back again and again to set in good thoughts and read if there have been any changes since then. I have also used the Cor-Cordis to get an assay on their emotions, especially all their feelings and thoughts."

Mary showed a pleasant surprise. "Well Seemore, I am happy to see that you have taken to the DESE diagnostics supplies. What did you learn?"

Seemore beamed a broad, bright toothy smile, except for the three yellow gold ones right in front, the rest were a kaleidoscope of colors. He gave into those, because, as you recall, Gnomes love jewelry. He thought of it as "body art". He was ahead of his time.

Seemore answered, "I learned a lot. I learned that these creatures, especially the witches, want to destroy the United States. They are resentful that the USA has not recognized their care of the environment and their use of magic to help the various natural disasters and afflictions upon the earth, both in the present and the future as they see it. They are very angry over the persecution of witches, both good and bad. One of the things they plan to do is to make the "Freedom" statue atop the congressional building to come to life and to fly away."

Seemore continued excitedly, "They are vengeful and vindictive. They are simply using their efforts here in the USA as a testing ground for their powers and to check on the effects they have and the results they can produce. They are angry that what they see as their domain, their stewardship of the earth's natural environmental resources, as being destroyed for all time. They are unhappy about acid rain, water pollution, perforation of the ozone layer in space, buildup of "greenhouse" gases, the manufacturing that creates water and air pollution, the ignoring of "global warming", the lack of recognition of their kind as well as persecution because of their beliefs, et cetera. The demons are there to goad them in their destructive and malicious goals in their progression towards collect the spirits of the evil witches to their nether world. I could go on and on. In short, the demons are there only to gain the spirits of the evil witches for their own demonic glory!"

Seemore had to pause to catch his breath. Seemore did go on, "Mary this is only a test site. Their plans are to revert the advances of society to one of dependence on nature and not on man's mechanical, chemical and other physical contrivances. Mary, they'd be happy to see us live almost back in the dark ages! They most certainly would like us to return to the mid eighteen fifties."

Mary interjected, "Are you serious, Seemore? You cannot believe that, or do you?"

"Mary, if this "test site" action works for them, they will then go after the other parts of the world and create havoc. Right now, they want us to go back in time and into the dark ages when the toilets were outhouses and you got your water from a well, you farmed your own food, grew, and butchered your own animals for meat. Heat was provided by chopping your own wood and light at night was provided by candles. That is if you made your own candles."

Seemore paused and reflected, "You know Mary, I recall it as something of how we lived in Sweden before coming over to the USA. It was a very natural way of life!"

Mary answered, "I know, but I think you have modernized yourself by now. I hope that I did not spoil you too much. You now live in a "modern" house with modern equipment. Something tells me that although you like the "natural" ways, that you will never go back to that way of life one hundred percent."

Seemore continued his reflection, "I think you are right, Mary. I do not think I'll miss it a lot, but you are right. I will engage in some of the old ways, but not one hundred percent."

Hepseva, who was in the kitchen section of the building, silently dealing with cleaning and cooking the evening meal finally cranked up, "You're very right. There is no way I'm going back to the outhouse and have no dishwasher or vacuum cleaner! Mary, if you think that Seemore is modernized you do not know me! I'm more "modern" than him!"

Mary could not stop herself from laughing. She told Hepseva, "Us modern women need to stick together, don't we?"

Hepseva humorously said, "You're darn right Mary. You're darn right." She then joined in with Mary's laughter. Seemore just stared at the two in dismay and dared to say nothing!

Mary now turned serious. Seemore, have you taken any more pictures with the DESE "camera"?

Seemore popped up. If he had dog ears you would say that they "perked up". However, Seemore did not have dog ears, but he "perked up" anyway and said, "You bet, Mary. I most certainly did. I have a few more real doozies. Your realize, Mary, that all of these can have varying degrees of danger in them because they are interactive, but we have the upper hand with the DESE equipment. Now that you're somewhat more familiar about how the these "pictures" work and have gotten over what had to be a shock to you it will be different for you. The next time we venture into one it will be easier for you to deal with, since you're now "experienced"".

Mary answered, "You bet. Let it wait until tomorrow though. I think I can only take this adventure just one at a time.

CHAPTER FORTY

HUNTINGTON BEACH SURPRISE, EXPERIENCE AND MOTIVATION

Matt and Wyatt just sat in their car for several long minutes, just staring at the incredible snowfall. They were shocked into speechlessness. However, they eventually gathered their senses and recovered from the shock of the unbelievable weather change.

Matt spoke first, "I have changed my mind. Some days are not the same as other days. This is certainly not an ordinary Southern California day! The daily drudge and the constantly monotonous weather does not exist today!

Wyatt responded, "This definitely is not what I ever expected to see in Southern California at all, ever!"

The interior of the car gave them shelter and a means of escape from the inhospitable elements. They cut short their excursion to downtown Huntington Beach. The Pier was now empty of all its sightseers and travelers. The snow on it approached six inches, which is a decent amount of snow even in the Northeastern USA. Californians who were still traversing the sidewalks were slipping and sliding all over the place. They rarely experienced such weather and other people, that were more experienced and that had escaped from colder, snowy climates, were maneuvering themselves almost expertly on the sidewalks.

The Main Street was now almost emptied of cars and patrons were deserting the outdoor eateries and sundry shops lining the street. Wyatt decided that leaving the business area was a good idea before he experienced an automobile accident he did not need. He managed to operate his car very well compared to the Southwesterners, many of them skidding here and there. He did, after all, come from the snowy Northeast and had no problem getting back to Matt's apartment.

When they arrived, there was most definitely a good six inches of snow on the ground before them. They were still dressed in Polo shirts and shorts. They were very cold indeed.

Matt and Wyatt ran from their parked car into Matt's California Street apartment at great speed. The cold had not penetrated the building yet. Nevertheless, Matt turned the gas heater in the hallway on to seventy-two degrees. It was now six o'clock in the PM and night would be falling. The snow would probably not melt overnight, even if the cold air let up. Matt said, "It has to be a good twenty-five to thirty degrees outside. I never imagined that this could happen here."

Wyatt turned on the TV to check the news and weather. Several of the stations had lost power. They did find a station broadcasting news and they learned of the extent of the destruction such a snowfall caused in defenseless coastal California.

Ironically, San Diego and Los Angeles Counties were the only victims of the surprising snowfall. The entire Los Angeles and San Diego Counties had been covered, strangely to the limits of their political boundary lines and not beyond. It was as though someone had cut a "pattern" in the shape of each county and designed a "snowfall" to fit it exactly.

There were accidents all over the place. Some buildings had roofs, which were never made to resist the weight of any heavy snow, collapsed and injured people who were unfortunate enough to have sought shelter under them.

All roads, except major highways, were closed and because it is Sunny Southern California, there were virtually no snowplows or snow removal equipment to be had. Californians had to stay where they were and made the best of it. No one knew what was going to happen tomorrow or even if the snow would melt.

The weathermen apologized to the citizenry for not having foreseen this snowfall. They said that there was no warning whatsoever. The Doppler radar screens were blank. They admitted that they were puzzled.

Wyatt thought on this a bit. He remembered that when he left the restaurant the sky was a crystal clear blue and without even one cloud in the sky. He was troubled. He further remembered that the snow fell on his nose and that when he looked up, there was still not even one cloud in the sky!

Wyatt thought, "This is impossible. There cannot be snow or rain without clouds, or could there? He had to make contact with Mary and let her know of this happening right away and have the benefit of DESE counsel as well as her research and her opinion.

Matt said, "Well, welcome to Southern Cal! I have never heard of such a happening!" Matt was visibly disappointed. After all, he came in February to escape the Southwestern Connecticut winter. This snowfall rivaled many of the snowfall experiences of his Northeastern life! It was no escape at all!

Wyatt read his disillusionment. His face could have had a poster over it exhibiting his disappointment. Wyatt offered, "Matt don't be too upset. Something like this occurs very rarely if ever. It must be due to some freak of nature or even something "strange", certainly an unnatural occurrence of some sort. Eventually such occurrences will be scientifically explainable. If the snow lasts beyond tomorrow there will probably be a big problem."

Matt appreciated his friend's attempt to cheer him up. Nevertheless Matt already realized that Wyatt's statements were quite realistic. He hoped beyond hope that the snow would be fully gone by morning, although the existence of snow on his window ledges made him wonder at the reality of his wish for a return to the daily monotony of seventy plus degrees, sunshine and blue skies as soon as possible. Matt was more than just concerned. He was scared.

"Wyatt", Matt began, "I need to admit that I am very bothered by this snow. Wyatt, when we left the restaurant, the sky was cloudless. Where did the snow come from? It came down so fast and thick that you could not see the sky. Wyatt, did you notice any clouds? Where did they come from? You heard the weathermen report that they saw nothing on the Doppler radar screen. Wyatt, what is it all about anyway? What happened?"

Wyatt shrugged his shoulders. "Matt, I have no idea, but I'm sure that it's explainable somehow and we'll probably get the news tomorrow or the next day. Things like this just do not happen without reason, you know. There is an explanation that will put your mind at rest. All of us will just need to wait for the authorities to investigate and come up with the answer. Please be patient. I'm sure that we'll get the news by tomorrow morning."

Wyatt spoke with an almost authoritative certainty that made Matt immediately feel better about the storm.

Wyatt was not sure if he should reveal to Matt exactly what his mission was. He struggled with the thought and decided that he did not need to make that decision right away and that he would continue to consider it as an option.

"Hey Matt!" Wyatt exclaimed loudly with an explosive start to get the thought of revealing himself to Matt out of his mind.

Matt jumped at the sudden loudness of Wyatt's voice. "What? What happened? Did something happen that I did not notice? What's wrong?" Matt was very surprised at what seemed to be an alarm from Wyatt. True, it was an alarm, but not for any reason except that Wyatt had to stop himself from revealing his truth to Matt.

Wyatt answered, "Nothing, Matt, nothing really." He added, trying to lessen the shock of his explosive outburst and added "What are we going to do tomorrow? Want to go skiing? Look at it out there. It's a winter wonderland. It's pretty. Unfortunately, it's not winter and it's Southern California and it should not be at all!"

Matt looked out and it was true. Matt said, "It is truly very pretty. It is also very bad. The agricultural and tourist industry will hurt because of this. I hope it doesn't last long at all. It has to be a freak of nature or something. It can't last at all!" He raised his hands in a flair of despair and looked at Wyatt for support.

Wyatt's thoughts were returning to his business. He had to get in contact with Mary right away. She had to know about this right away. He was sure that this had to make the papers all around the world and that she would most likely know of the event any way, but he knew that he needed to confer with her in any case, and very soon. Unfortunately, Wyatt had a dilemma in how he would work out making a private call to Mary in Matt's presence. Matt would get a very good idea what Wyatt's business is. Perhaps it would not make much difference if Matt did actually get to know what Wyatt's job really is. Wyatt thought to himself, "I've known Matt for a number of years now and there is not any reason to worry about security wise regarding Matt." He reasoned that "Matt might be useful in Huntington Beach and assist in my work for some compensation from DESE." Wyatt decided that he would enlist Matt Ovlas in his service after all.

"Matt, I need to make an emergency phone call after which we need to have a very serious, private and secure discussion" Said Wyatt.

Matt was puzzled, looked at Wyatt and nonchalantly said, "OK".

Wyatt went to his suitcase and took out his telephone, a satellite telephone, and dialed up Mary in Fairbanks. Mary answered after about a dozen or more rings.

"Hello", Mary hesitantly spoke into her telephone. She was worried that when her satellite phone rings when she is away from her office, there is almost never good news that comes her way via that telephone. "Who is this?"

Wyatt answered, "Mary this is Wyatt. I am in Huntington Beach, California visiting my good friend, Matt Ovlas."

Mary said, "Oh yes. How are things going?"

Wyatt responded, "Almost too well Mary. You know that I am on my way to get a report from Frank in San Diego. I stopped here because I needed a break. Now I think I need another break!"

Mary laughed and said, "Another break from a current break? Why? What happened that you need a break from having a break? Are you all right?" Mary was now concerned.

"Mary, you know that Huntington Beach is South of LA?" Wyatt asked rhetorically.

"Yes, Mary said, "Go on."

"Well, it is usually warm here with palm trees, blue skies and warm sunshine." Wyatt went on.

Mary said, "Yes, Yes, Go on."

"Mary it is not like that here now!" Wyatt exclaimed.

"What do you mean?" Mary was eager to get to the bottom line of this conversation. Wyatt was not making it easy.

"Mary, since I really don't know how to say this any other way so I'm going to say it right out. Mary, there are six inches of snow on the ground out here! What is happening? Do you have any reports from the head office about this?"

Mary shared Wyatt's shock. She had been in LA many times. She knew that snow was not part of its makeup.

"I guess I do not need to ask if you are sure. Six inches of snow is six inches of snow. You cannot be certain that what you are seeing is not an illusion. Is it?" Mary asked, hoping that it was not real.

Wyatt answered, "Mary, it's cold, wet and people all over the place were slipping and sliding along. It's real all right. It's real."

Mary responded with a simple, "O.K."

Wyatt went on. "Mary there's more. There were no clouds, Mary. The weathermen saw no Doppler effect on weather radar. The snow has no basis for its existence, especially here in Southern California!"

"No clouds?" Mary asked incredulously. "No clouds?"

"No clouds", Wyatt resonated. "No clouds."

"Wow." Mary said. "I'm going to check with DESE and see what they have. In the meantime you need to get Frank's reports in San Diego."

"I know, Mary. I know that I need to do this right away." Said Wyatt and added, "There's more. I want to engage Matt here to help. This snow shows the need for an added assistant here. Matt is quite trustworthy and I hope you approve should I enlist his services."

Mary answered, "Wyatt, if you think that you need additional help in Huntington Beach and you choose Matt, then it's all right with me." Then after a short pause Mary asked, "Is he reliable and trustworthy?"

"Of course! I would not have recommended him if he were not, would I?" Wyatt answered almost indignantly.

Mary responded, almost apologetically, "Sorry Wyatt. I know that your choice has to be impeccably accurate."

Wyatt returned with, "Then I am going to brief Matt on the current "happenings" providing he agrees to help us. Will that be all right?"

"I would expect that you would need to, considering that you are going to enlist him as one of our California agents." Mary went on, "Wyatt, I have had some communication with HB in West Palm Beach and as you know, I am currently up here in Alaska with Seemore. Here we both have seen witches, and the like, who may be creating spells that are producing severe weather changes in different parts of the country and none of them good. I suggest that you do some investigating there in Huntington Beach before going to Frank's interview. The cloudless snowfall you reported seems to be right up the witches' alley. I would not be surprised if you learn that you might locate a coven there which may have had some connection to it and even may have caused it."

Wyatt took Mary's words to heart. He had at least another day here in Huntington Beach and he would use his remaining time to conduct such investigation.

Wyatt and Mary said their goodbyes and hung up the telephone. Wyatt knew what he had to do. Fi rst he had to bring Matt into the picture and after he gained Matt's cooperation, he would need to start his investigation. He expected that Matt would be eager to help.

Wyatt turned to Matt and said, "Matt, it is now time for that serious conversation I told you about before the phone call."

Matt said expectantly, "Yes? Go on."

"Matt, do you have any idea of how I earn my living?" Wyatt asked.

"Not the foggiest." Matt answered.

"Matt, you had better sit down. As a matter of fact, we both had better sit down. I want you to gain a full understanding of what I need to tell you." Said Wyatt.

"I'm sitting." Said Matt.

"Good." Said Wyatt. "Matt, you are aware that I do a lot of traveling."

"Yes, yes." Said Matt impatiently.

Wyatt continued. "You need to promise me first that you will not reveal to anyone the information I am now going to impart to you. It is highly secret and sensitive information and I need your word and promise of maintaining that secrecy."

"Of, course Wyatt. If you ask me to do so, I most certainly will comply!" answered Matt now becoming very curious as to what Wyatt had to tell him.

"Matt, I work for our government." Said Wyatt.

"What? You don't work for the Internal Revenue Service, do you?" Matt answered quite concerned and alarmed.

"No, Matt. Nothing like that at all." Wyatt went on. "I work for a secret organization within our government. It is so secret that Congress is not even aware that it exists."

"Oh, really?" Matt answered in a challenging tone. He thought that Wyatt was pulling his leg.

"Really.", said Wyatt matter-of-factly. "The name of the organization is the Department of Extraordinary and Situations and Events, commonly known as "DESE" for short. That's what we do. We investigate and determine the cause of such "extraordinary situation and events.""

"Really." Said Matt, still not certain if Wyatt was kidding with him.

"Really." Answered Wyatt. "Wouldn't you say that today's snowfall would fall into the category of an "extraordinary event"?

Matt did not need to think twice about it. He exploded with a "Yes! Are you kidding? It was super-extraordinary!"

Wyatt continued. "Matt that is the kind of thing that we constantly, but unfortunately, investigate. We investigate the "why" of such events as well as the "how". Could I count on your helping with investigating why today's snowfall occurred?"

Matt became a little wary and asked, "What do you mean? How does one do "investigation" in your field anyway? What exactly is involved?"

"Fair question", Wyatt responded. "We have special equipment and techniques to conduct research into such events. Some techniques are involved and some are simple. The same is true of the equipment. Most are easy to use once you know how to use them."

"For instance?" Matt questioned.

"Unbelievably, we have equipment that can read thoughts and change minds. We have equipment that can relocate a person to distant places in the snap of two fingers. We have survey equipment to detect changes in the atmosphere and also the moods of people in a certain area. I could go on and on. I think that it would be best if you get slowly introduced to each piece of equipment as the need to use it arises. That would be the easiest way to learn." Wyatt concluded.

"All right. I'll give it a go. Now what do you have in mind, Wyatt?" said Matt eagerly.

"Matt don't get too shaken up. Mary Kent, my supervisor, said that she had received reports from different parts of the country which have had similarly strange and contrary environmental events occur. The part of it which may shake you up a bit is that there is some evidence that witches and witchcraft are involved."

Matt jumped up at this revelation. "What? What did you say? Witches? Witches indeed. Now I know that you are pulling my leg. Witches only exist in fairy tales and the "Wizard of Oz"! What you are saying has to be pure nonsense." Matt started to laugh an extended and hearty laugh. "Wyatt, you are a jokester of the worst kind. You really had me believing that this "DESE" and the government job was real! Wyatt you are a card!" Matt could not stop laughing.

Wyatt was not laughing. He did not find anything funny about what he was saying. He was very, very serious. Matt kept on laughing a gut-breaking laugh, pointing his finger at Wyatt, his face reddened. After a while, Matt noticed that Wyatt's disposition and facial expression was very serious. His laughter started to fade. Eventually, he stopped and stared at Wyatt.

"Wyatt, you are serious, aren't you?" Matt asked, slowly getting his face and disposition back to normal.

"You had better believe that I am serious. DESE does exist and I am a government agent. See!" Wyatt took out his badge contained in a black leather folding wallet made just for holding badges as he said that and showed Matt the badge along with his government ID. "Now what do you say, Matt?" asked Wyatt.

Matt sat quietly, obviously impressed. Finally the reality of everything Wyatt told him sank in. Matt thought, "Wyatt is for real. He is not just fooling around. Everything he told me is true!" Matt was shocked as well. The realization of the reality of this truth sobered him up instantly. He knew that he would need to get involved in a big way to help Wyatt.

"All right, Wyatt, you have convinced me. What do we need to do?" said Matt.

Wyatt answered, "Matt, the first thing we should do is to go to the library and look up old newspapers in the events sections. Sometimes you might find an announcement tell the public where and when meetings take place."

"What kind of meetings? What kind of announcement?" Matt asked.

"I don't really know. They call them "Meetups" and they happen all around the country." Said Wyatt.

"Meetups?" said Matt.

"Yes, meetups", responded Wyatt. "Have you ever heard of places where strange meetings are held? Have you knowledge of strange organizations espousing pagan/witch events happenings and meetings? Possibly some meetups are just organizations in which people simply have a common interest. There may be nothing pagan or witch-like about a particular "meetup". However there are "meetups" where witches do meet and some of them might be responsible for the spell which caused our cloudless snow storm."

"Are you serious, Wyatt?" interjected Matt.

Wyatt continued, ignoring Matt's question, "Usually, from Mary Kent's reports, the witches need the power of a group of witches to affect the environment with simultaneously chanted or spoken spells. It seems that the spell has its power multiplied by many witches chanting the spell at the same time. It's like an amplification device and apparently it works. The point is where does it go from here? What will their next target be? Our government is concerned and public safety is involved as well as national security. We need be on top of this and any developments which come from them."

Matt was silent for a short while. Matt then raised his right hand with his index finger extended and shaking it towards Wyatt, he said, "You know, come to think of it, there is this place here in Huntington Beach called Fitzhews Sports Bar near Fountain Valley. I think that we might get some information there. I have heard that sometimes very strange people meet there occasionally."

"What do you mean by "strange", Matt?" asked Wyatt.

"Matt answered, "I know that the people who meet there like to read palms, tarot cards and those stones which are used to tell the future. They call them "Runes". They mostly go by strange and unusual names like Sky Dancer, Newts Blood, Mealyworm, Wicca Dragon and such."

Wyatt did a double take on the "Wicca Dragon" name. He quickly rose to his feet and exclaimed, "Wicca Dragon?"

Matt responded with excitement and mimicked Wyatt's response, "Wicca Dragon. What's so exciting about that? Yes, Wyatt, I know that is the name of one of them because I have met her on one of my very few "fun" nights out on the town!"

Wyatt explained, "Matt, the name "Wicca" is not just another word. It refers to the persons who create witchcraft. The word "Dragon" is obviously a reference to Dragons. Some of the Wicca may be good people and as "naturalists", and I use that word cautiously, they look after the environment. They do it through creative magic, spells and objects they use as instruments which are to help them to achieve their goal.

It has come to my attention, and the attention of DESE, that not all their goals are meant to benefit the environment or mankind. Instead, there is destruction of the environment and destruction of the interests, security and financial welfare of certain parts of our society. I am guessing that the malevolent witches are still in the "experimental" stage because all we have seen so far across the USA are nuisance environmental problems that have caused only minor destruction. The problem is that no one has any idea of what they really are planning, if indeed they are planning anything at all, that is."

Matt expressed concern. "Wyatt, you cannot be serious. These are just people, like you and I. They cannot be doing much in the way of damage to environment and people. I don't believe you. I had a very nice time with this "Wicca Dragon" woman. She was very kind and very likeable, and I did, I mean I do like her. We got along perfectly."

Wyatt answered, "I understand where you are coming from. I know that it is hard to believe, but you need to believe it. Where do you think that snow came from? There were no clouds. It did not come from heaven. Once again, Matt, where do you think it came from? I'd like to have your answer."

Matt remained silent. He could say nothing. He had no answers. He simply put out his arms to the side, palms outward and upward and shrugged his shoulders.

Wyatt went on, "It materialized out of nothing. No, that's not true. It materialized out of something and it had to materialize out of magic and not White Magic."

Matt said, "White Magic? What is that?"

Wyatt turned towards Matt and further explained, almost pleadingly, "Matt "White Magic" is the kind of magic that might do good and not bad, to either people, animals, the environment or things. It is the magic of the "Good Witches".

Wyatt paused and looked at Matt for a reaction. None was coming and that is the way it stayed. Matt's face displayed a blank and dismayed expression

The opposite kind of magic is evil and does nothing good for anybody." Wyatt continued, "It produces whatever the evil-doer wants to have happen. You have heard of this magic. The whole world had. It is appropriately called "Black Magic". It is the kind of thing the witches in "Snow White", the "Chronicles of Narnia: The Loin, the Witch and the Wardrobe" and "The Wizard of Oz" do. It hurts innocent people for some malicious goal the witch wants to have happen. Such witches are evil and have no goodness in their soul at all. It would take a miracle to have them change their goal orientation. Their mind set has to change."

Matt asked, "What do you mean?"

"Usually such deeds happen because these people hate, are angry, disappointed and unhappy personalities." Said Wyatt. "They want to hurt and maim physically, emotionally and financially. They really do not care who or what they destroy. They want their revenge and to attack their "enemies", real or imagined, with their "Black Magic". I can only ask you to keep an open mind and keep your eyes open."

Matt did not exactly recall where Fitzhew's Bar was located. They had to ride around downtown Huntington Beach for a while but they found that it really was on the outskirts of Huntington Beach near Fountain Valley. This was after almost twenty-five minutes of touring streets that Matt visited infrequently.

Wyatt and Matt left for "Fitzhew's Bar" driving South on Adams after making a right turn off of Beach Boulevard to learn whatever the evening would reveal to them.

The bar was in the middle of a strip mall and its entrance was very interesting with small windows to improve privacy within.

The entrance to the bar was unremarkable. There was nothing special about it except that it was very ordinary. They entered the bar through a single door, which opened to the left. They both stepped inside. The bar was to the left and pool tables were to the right. A large projected television screen was in the rear and behind the bar over a polished wood dance floor. Behind the bar and to the left was a beaded curtain doorway behind which was an additional dark cloth curtain. They found themselves in front of the bar proper.

A female voice spoke in a husky, almost come-hither, tone. "Welcome, gentlemen, I am so very happy to welcome you."

Matt and Wyatt were both startled because they did not remember seeing anyone in the bar at all. It was a shocking moment when they turned towards the source of the voice. There was no one to be seen. The only living thing they saw was an uncaged parakeet. Wyatt and Matt both thought an uncaged parakeet could possibly be a sanitary problem. They also wondered what could possibly keep the parakeet from leaving and escaping the confines of the bar.

The parakeet fluttered towards the curtained doorway. The parakeet flew to the floor and strutted behind the curtain. The voice now was apparently coming from behind that curtain. Although Wyatt and Matt could not see through the curtain, it was obvious that the person behind it could see them quite clearly.

The voice went on, "Please make yourselves at home and someone will be in to take your order shortly. Please take one of the tables just behind you."

"Just behind us?" Wyatt responded. "How do you know where we are and where are you?"

The voice said, "I am right here, just behind the curtain."

"Just behind the curtain?" Wyatt retorted.

"Yes", the voice said. "I see you quite well and I will be out shortly."

A few moments passed and the curtain started to open. It was behind the thick beaded curtain made of multi-colored thick and thin crystal-like beads.

A beautiful young long-haired blonde woman wearing hip hugger dungarees, with a butterfly tattoo near the end of her visible spine, made her entrance to the bar proper.

"Hello, gentlemen." She said in that same husky voice that welcomed them to the bar. "My name is Juday. What can I get for you?"

Wyatt and Matt did not really know what to say. They were on an investigatory mission and not one where they wished service. What they really wanted was information. They hemmed and hawed a bit and virtually stuttered a response. They felt if they did not order anything that future visits would be viewed with suspicion.

"Well, uh", Matt started, "Could you give us a second or two so that we can look at what you need to offer? We'd like to talk between ourselves, and do you have a menu?"

Juday answered, "But of course. Take your time. There are menus to the end of your table. I will be back in a minute or two. No hurry."

With that, Juday disappeared again behind the beaded curtain and its darker, less remarkable hinter companion curtain. Both the young men were surprised when shortly thereafter the parakeet strutted out again and sat on the beer pull faucets on the bar. It looked like it had a preference for the Heineken handle with its fancy colors and all. The silly bird looked as if it were in attendance for something or other and moved between the Heineken handle and the Guiness and Lowenbrau handles. Apparently, the bird had a liking for beer!

Matt spoke first. He put his hand up to his mouth and whispered into Wyatt's ear. "Wyatt, there is something strange here. Let's just order a snack and a beer and come back later. We need to discuss what is going on here."

Wyatt looked at Matt with no surprise at all. Wyatt answered also in the same secretive mode but in a very soft whispered voice, "Matt, I fully agree with that! This place almost gives me the creeps!"

Matt said, "Hello, Juday! We're ready to order."

Matt and Wyatt just sat there for a second and stared at each other. They were silent.

They were very surprised when Juday responded to them from the far end of the bar near where they last saw the parakeet. They were both quite certain that Juday was behind the curtain, which separated the bar from the back room. Nevertheless, they ordered. Juday once again came out from behind the curtains and went to their table.

Matt ordered first. "I'd like to have a Budweiser and a B.L.T., and no fries, please."

Wyatt ordered, "That sounds like the ticket. I'll have the same."

Juday said, "Thank you. It will be just a minute." With that, she again , disappeared behind the curtain.

The boys noted that the parakeet was nowhere in sight. "Where did the parakeet go?" they both asked the very same question of each other at the same time and in unison. They both shrugged their shoulders also at the same time and made the expression which said "Who knows! I don't know anything!" They then both laughed an exasperated, uneasy and fearful laugh.

Shortly, Juday returned with their order. It only took about twenty minutes or so for her to complete it. She presented herself at the table with the orders and a big smile.

"Here's your order, gentlemen. Enjoy!" she said in an apparently good mood.

The two minimized their conversation and actually did enjoy their beer and sandwiches, which they devoured with gusto. When they were fully satisfied, they rose, paid their bill and left a generous tip. Then they exited the bar in a good mood themselves, smiling and joking between themselves. They took care not to let on that they felt the bar was strange or suspicious or anything of the sort.

CHAPTER FORTY-ONE
MARY ENTERS A NEW PICTURE

Seemore woke up early the next morning. The sun was just barely cracking the sky open. There was only a slit of light at the horizon, but the clouds surrounding it were brilliant with red, orange and pink colors.

It was going to be a good day, despite the sailor's "Red Sky in Morning" warning, and Seemore was quite eager to get started on the day's adventures. He was very anxious to show his pictures to Mary. However, he knew that awakening her at this ungodly early hour would not make her happy. Furthermore, if he woke her at this hour, it would be he who would be even more unhappy than her. He decided to wait to a more reasonable hour instead.

Seemore rose and went to the picture drawer. The drawers defied the actual dimensions of the pictures they contained. He searched through the labeled tabs at the end of each of the photographs for several minutes. He eventually found one that satisfied his interests and one that should keep Mary in impressive memory long after she left Fairbanks.

A broad smile spread across his face as if he were greeting a long-lost friend, although the photograph was no more than four weeks old.

"Ah ha!" Seemore exclaimed, being quick to stifle his exuberance, not wanting to awaken either Hepseva or Mary before they were ready for arousal by themselves. The previous day was stressful enough for Mary. Seemore already knew what the pictures contained and their significance. After all, he was the one who took them!

The picture he withdrew from the drawer was labeled "Action in Miniature" and dated only four weeks previous. He could barely wait for Mary to wake up. He was like an excited little boy at Christmas time. The temptation to awaken her was great, but fortunately for him, he was able to resist it. He put the picture down and attempted to join them in sleep and doze off a bit as well.

It was almost mid-morning when Seemore finally re-awakened. He really dozed off and slept much longer than he wanted to, much to his shock and amazement! He guessed that the anticipation of having Mary with him and exhibition of the photograph was too much for him and the prospect exhausted him.

Seemore was even more surprised that the women were already awake and did a turn about by letting Seemore sleep as long as he felt the need. That was what Seemore was doing in regard to the women! He was going to let them sleep to their fill. However, the women turned the tables on him and reversed the well-intentioned deed.

Seemore stirred and the women uttered a joint cheer: "Well, hooray and huzzah, Seemore the Great is with us hoorah!" They then followed that up with "Well, hooray and huzzah, Seemore the Great is with us hoorah!" They repeated the chant several more times. Seemore got the hint and gave a loud, cheerful laugh! "All right you two. That will be enough. I appreciate your letting me sleep longer, but the day is fully awakened as are we all."

Then in a change of mood, Seemore cheerfully asked, "What's for breakfast?"

The women were also apparently well rested and cheerfully responded, "Don't you worry about it! You will be served shortly. We have been busy getting your highness's breakfast, and ours, ready while you slept. Just rise, rub your eyes and get to the table and behave." Hepseva scolded Seemore with a smile and kiss on his forehead. Seemore silently complied, happily returning the smile.

Their breakfast was one of granola and different wild berries in goats' milk. Although it was a cold cereal, they ate hearty, followed by muskmelon slices from one that Mary had brought with her.

Seemore had a gleam in his eye. He looked at Mary and said, "Well, well Mary, it is time for us to take up where we left off yesterday. I have selected a picture for you in which I know you will have a very great interest."

"Really", said Mary. She was interested, but not excited about it at all. As a matter of fact, she showed a little apprehension regarding interactive photographs from the past which could affect her and the future. Essentially, these scientifically magical photographs could rewrite history! This was something that Mary felt was up to supreme powers and beyond the realm of humanity. "What is it about?", she asked curiously.

"Oh, you need to be in it to believe it!" teased Seemore.

"All right, Seemore, let me see what mystery you have that intrigues you so much." Mary quickly added, "This is the last one I'll be able to see."

Seemore agreed. "These photographs can be very taxing, and they are also very dangerous, both emotionally and physically. We always need to be very careful not to change history and for our own safety. The people we will be seeing are not angelic and beneficent beings. Unfortunately, they are quite the opposite and if we are discovered, we will be in danger. One thing we do not want to do is to meet them. We are to avoid them completely. There is danger. We may never leave the picture. Once again it is very serious and very dangerous."

With that, Seemore led Mary to the far end of the room where the chest of drawers was. He reached out and seized the photograph he had discovered earlier that morning. "Action in Miniature". He grabbed the rolled up photo and withdrew it from its container. Once again, as he did so, the photograph snapped up in a flash of light, unrolled itself, lengthened and increased in height. These photographs were in color and a virtual reality. It was sometimes questionable whether it was not real. The situation boggled the mind.

Once again, Seemore gently took Mary by the hand, and they gingerly and carefully stepped over the picture's white border and into the frame.

Immediately, everything in the picture came to life. The sound of crickets and moisture on the leaves and grass touched Mary. This picture was now living. Once again, they were behind a bunch of bushes. Entering a photo and being protected behind bushes or other barriers was apparently the experienced Seemore's vantaged view. Mary was grateful for hidden safety. It was a place where they would have some protection from the powers of those they were spying on. Mary was grateful for that. She was happy to be concealed somewhat, rather than being out in the open to be easily spotted.

This photograph was taken at a different location than the first as the scenery was radically different. It was high up on a steep hill overlooking Catalina Island in the Palos Verdes Estates area. The pleasant smell of wild fennel and eucalyptus wafted through the air. Looking down from the highest part of a hill they saw that there was a fire in the center of a group of people who were somewhat more relaxed than at the first photograph viewing. Some were sitting and some were standing. They were discussing a happening. Mary had no idea what they were talking about.

The one who was standing before a seated figure was gesturing and waving his arms as though he were describing something. The seated figure was on an opulently draped gold and jewel encrusted throne. The easily read name "Leroi Barrbberi" was carved upon it in gold filled letters and in angular German script the words "Master of Evil, Deception, Dishonesty, Deceit and Betrayal" were inscribed below the name. On the inferior edges of each gold letter one could see oozed stagnated liquid in coagulated red droplets. Mary struggled, along with Seemore, to hear his words.

Seemore surprised his companion when he took the Cogito-Lector out of his bag. That made it quite easy to understand what was going on.

"Master", the standing figure addressed the seated figure, "Our coven has come up with a strategy to deal with our oppressors. We have been in communication with our comrades in the various parts of the United

States and Canada. We agree and want to join all our powers to settle the score as we have been eager to do over these many centuries."

The seated figure turned, stood up and raised his reddened face to the other while at the same time raising both his hands to shoulder height and towards the figure standing before him. He was almost touching him. Suddenly there was a flash of light between them and the sound of thunder, although there were no clouds anywhere in the sky. What appeared to be a broad, feathery-like spark flew from the Seated One to the other. The light from the spark illuminated the entire gathering.

It was as though some magical medium transferred from the seated one to the other. The former Seated One spoke.

"My child", the Seated One said in a benevolent and caring tone, "It is good to hear you speak of vengeance. It is music to my aged ears. However, you must be sure that whatever is to be done is done without connection to you or to the coven. Should it ever be known that your actions are a result of our creation, the consequences set upon our coven will be most undesirable. We have suffered through the ages because of our caring for the environment and nature. We have caused man to be responsible for his damage to the environment and many do not like that nor accept it. Thus, they attack us. Vengeance and retribution are long overdue. We are happy that some of us seek it."

The Seated One slowly returned his extended arms to his side and reseated himself, still looking at the Younger Standing One. He asked of the Younger One, "What are you planning? What exactly are your goals and how do you plan to achieve them?"

The Younger One replied, "That is the delightfully easy part. We have been guardians of nature and the environment throughout all our history. We plan to use what we have learned of the environment, over our many generations, to turn the environment against those who offended, insulted, and persecuted us. It is time that humankind be aware of what our protection and care of the environment has saved them and how much they have benefited from our caring."

"You are quite right." The Seated One responded affirmatively.

"We will radically change what they expect from the seasons, from the sun, from the sea and from the forests so that they are aware of the unnaturalness of the events we will cause." The Younger One spoke in a firm voice, obviously firmly dedicated to his cause.

"But how can a small coven significantly affect the environment to an extent that it will be noticed, not as a serious event, but one that is notably abnormal and serious?" The Seated One asked.

"Master", the Younger One explained, "We will not be alone." Then he gave a squinty-eyed smile which reeked of evil and menace while rubbing his hands together in delight. "We have organized!"

"You have organized?" the Seated One inquired.

"We have organized." The Younger one replied. "We have organized very, very effectively indeed."

"What do you mean by "effectively"? What exactly does that mean anyway?" the Seated One asked incredulously.

"Master", the Younger One replied, "we can change a climate at will. We can make it rain without clouds. We can move the Aurora Borealis at will. We can make rivers flow backwards. We can create tornadoes and hurricanes where they never have been before."

"Are you serious?" The Seated One was incredulous and although it might have sounded like he was indignant. What he really revealed was his amazement at what he was hearing. He simply could not believe it.

"I am quite serious. We have recently caused a tornado to occur in a very unusual place. One where one almost has never happened!" the Younger One said with proud satisfaction radiating creating a luminous glow from his face.

"Really?" the Seated One asked.

"Really." The Younger One firmly retorted.

"Explain." The Seated One virtually demanded.

"We have caused a coven-created tornado to move from the hills in Ringwood, New Jersey to travel across Nyack and Tarrytown in New York through northern parts of Westchester County and White Plains, New York as well as across Northern Greenwich, Connecticut. It was a delightful display of our powers. Regretfully, it did not cause as much damage as we wished, but it is only a test of our, not yet fully developed, abilities. We are working on it though!" The Younger One said both proudly and apologetically at the same time.

"That is very impressive." The Seated One said in appreciation.

"That is not all, Master." The Younger One continued. "We have created a very significant snowstorm in Huntington Beach as well as San Diego, California."

"How did you do that?" the Seated one timidly asked.

"That is not important. What is most significant about that event is that we did it without any clouds in the sky! Now that is an event which has should be recognized by everyone as being fully unnatural and noteworthy." said the Younger One exhibiting even greater pride, which almost bordered on conceit, although his attitude was deservedly the result of accomplishment.

The Younger One continued. "It is the combined power of all the covens throughout the USA and Canada and the simultaneous creation and calling up of our spells in that one moment that has given us the power to produce such significant events. It is an amplification methodology we have recently found to be very effective. We can use such power virtually to control every nuance of nature in just about every way and in every sphere. We are working on improving it and extending it to human events as well!"

Mary gave out a low and muffled "My goodness". She heard more than she needed to hear. It was more than enough. She tugged at Seemore's sleeve . "Let's get out of here quickly, Seemore. I do not wish to be here any longer." She turned without waiting for Seemore and even started to leave the picture alone. Seemore saw that she wanted urgently to leave and thus he immediately turned to follow her out and help her. The last thing they needed was to be discovered. Her unguided steps were risky. Seemore was very concerned about being discovered. It was a danger that he wished never to test.

CHAPTER FORTY-TWO
WICCA DRAGON

Matt and Wyatt were soon out of sight of Fitzhew's Sports bar. That is when they let each other know what their feelings were.

Uncharacteristically, Wyatt spoke first. "Matt, did you see what I saw? Are you thinking what I am thinking? I don't believe it. I could not believe my eyes. That was a creepy place!"

Matt answered, "You bet I saw what you saw. You are right. It still is hard for me to believe or even understand what it was that I saw."

"You saw the parakeet?" Wyatt asked.

"I saw the parakeet. Do you think that I am blind, or what?" Matt answered indignantly.

"No. I do not think that you are blind at all. It is just so incredulous! I mean first we go into a deserted bar and there is no one in there but a loose parakeet. Then we hear a voice but see no one." Wyatt paused for a pensive moment. "Then the voice tells us where we are and where we are to sit, just as though the person was seeing us all the time!"

"True." Said Matt. "It was really as though eyes were upon us every moment upon our entry into that tavern."

"Not only that, but the parakeet flew down from the beer handles and actually strutted behind the two curtains", Wyatt continued.

Matt shook his head in agreement. "It was then that the voice really seemed to come from behind the curtains instead of just from somewhere in the room and we did not see the parakeet again! Did you notice that?"

"I did. Are you thinking what I am thinking or are we going insane? Perhaps it was just a trick of some kind", Wyatt said hopefully.

"No, no, no," scolded Matt. "There was no trick. It was exactly as we thought. That parakeet and the woman were one and the same!"

Silence fell over both. They realized the same thing, but it took Matt to say it. Wyatt, although he said nothing, was in full agreement. There could be no doubt whatsoever. It was a little more than one minute before either one of them could speak. The mutual realization of the same fact put both in awe and fear of the unknown entered into each of them.

Wyatt spoke first. "Matt, I must report this to my boss. This is serious business. This woman has the power of transmutation. That is very powerful magic. If she can do that, she probably could do a lot more. Some of what she could possibly do might be dangerous."

Matt agreed. "Not only that Wyatt, but she is also most likely not alone. We may have hit upon a mother lode of the source of our snowstorm and who knows what else! Wyatt, you need to remember that this was the place where I first met Wicca Dragon."

Wyatt and Matt were of one mind. Their course was set before them by the circumstances presented.

Matt continued, "I agree. There is more Wyatt."

"What more could there be?" Wyatt responded.

"Wyatt, think. We have not really completed our investigation of Fitzhew's bar. We need to go back, but I think that we first need to get in touch with the powers that be at DESE and give them an initial report."

Wyatt answered, "Of course. I agree. You are developing your mettle, Matt. I am a pro, but your advice is well taken. We should do that simply to protect ourselves. Who knows what is going to happen."

Matt said, "Right. DESE should be aware of what we have discovered. We need to make a report right away. We have no way of protecting ourselves, except for our wits, and that may be limited!"

They both broke out into laughter at that comment. They needed a break from the tension of the day. That was the stress breaker. They were both grateful for the few moments of relief it allowed them.

Matt and Wyatt returned to Matt's apartment on California Street. They parked Wyatt's car in front, facing west and on the right-hand side, walked up the eight foot wide walkway which was fenced in on the easterly side and passed a small court yard and building, which almost encroached on the walkway, on its westerly side. They reached Matt's unit and swung open a planked gate which was part of a ten foot, painted grey, shoulder high fence that enclosed an additional small private courtyard as part of Matt's living quarters. Matt unlocked the entrance door to his apartment on the right side of the courtyard. They entered. They both exhaled a sigh of relief and Wyatt spoke first.

"Matt, I need a moment or two to gather my senses and my thoughts before I can call the head of my department, Mary Kent. I need to call on the scrambled satellite telephone connection. This is highly classified, sensitive, and very secret information I need to give her."

Matt acknowledged Wyatt's statement with a nod. He was also emotionally exhausted and needed a few moments of his own to recuperate from the shock of their unexpected adventure. Matt went into his room and laid himself on his bed to gain some rest and hopefully peace of mind as well. He left Wyatt with "I'm going to leave you alone for a few minutes. I'm going to try for a short nap or something. I need to rest for a second or two. You should do the same. Don't call Mary yet. I want to be around when you call. Since you now have me on the DESE payroll, I want to know all that there is to know about my job and what concerns it."

Wyatt replied, "Definitely. I also need a rest and I will take your advice. A nap and a fresh perspective on recent events will probably come with a few moments of rest as well. Will do, Matt, will do. I also am going to take a short nap and I'll wake you when I make the call to Mary."

Wyatt then turned and went to lie down as well. Both were asleep in minutes. Their stressful emotional experience took its toll on the two of them and sleep is a welcome solace.

They both awakened about one hour later. Neither one of them had a fully undisturbed sleep. They stirred, tossed, and turned throughout the hour, but still managed to refresh themselves somewhat despite their mutual anxiety.

Wyatt woke and addressed the dreary eyed Matt, "Matt, I am ready to make that call to Mary. How are you feeling now?" Wyatt was solicitous of Matt's mental and physical condition. He wanted Matt to be fully awake and aware when he spoke with Mary. First, he did not want to need to repeat anything and secondly, he wanted to share the call with Matt so that Matt could be fully informed on all matters.

Matt responded, "Quite all right, Wyatt. Make your call. I am eager to know what Mary's response will be, most likely as much as you!"

"Right-on." answered Wyatt. Wyatt then dialed Mary and entered the necessary codes to access the private satellite communication system. Mary answered after four rings.

"Hello" Mary answered. "May I help you?"

"Mary, this is Wyatt calling. I have some information which will be of great interest to you."

Mary responded, "Excellent. I also have information which will be of great interest to you as well. You go first."

Wyatt started, "Mary, I have not yet been able to visit Frank in San Diego. My short visit here with Matt in Huntington Beach has provided us with some very interesting and most likely very important, leads and information."

"Really?" Mary answered in surprise. "What do you mean? Please explain."

Wyatt went on. "Mary, you do recall that I earlier reported snow from a cloudless sky here in Huntington Beach?"

Mary responded, "Yes, I most certainly do. That would be hard to forget."

Wyatt continued, "This is a follow-up on that report. I have been in conversation with Matt and he told me that he had met a person who call herself "Wicca Dragon"."

Mary quickly interjected, "Wicca Dragon?" Mary's interest had peaked. She knew that "Wicca" in some way, or another, referred to or meant witchcraft and associated events and persons. She also related the "Wicca" term to the events Seemore was revealing to her in the living photographs. Mary was all ears and very anxious to learn more.

"Tell me more Wyatt. What about this "Wicca Dragon" person?"

"I really do not know who this person is. It is a person that Matt met at a "social" event at a bar here in town." Wyatt answered.

"Well, then, what is her significance anyway?" questioned Mary.

"I really have never met Wicca Dragon. Matt has though. Mary, we decided to visit the place where Matt met her. It is supposedly a location where "Wicca" meet. What is of interest is what happened when we went there to investigate further," Wyatt responded.

"Really?" Mary asked. "What happened there to pique your interest and why are you so concerned?"

"Well, there was nothing there that was harmful to us or anything like that. What happened there was not "normal" or even an ordinary human event. Mary, what happened was quite extraordinary!" Wyatt responded, now flustered, because it was difficult for him to come up with an explanation that made sense to himself, much less to Mary.

Wyatt paused.

"Go on, Wyatt, what exactly do you mean?" Mary was becoming a bit impatient with Wyatt's lack of adequate relation of the event.

"Mary, we went into this Fitzhew's bar in Fountain Valley which is where these "Wicca" are supposed to meet. There was no one in the bar when we entered but a loose parakeet, sitting on beer handles behind the bar. Then this voice came out of nowhere to greet us and told us where to sit. When we inquired as to who was speaking to us, because there was no person to be seen, the parakeet flew down and walked behind a curtain. All the while, the voice claimed that it could see us plainly. Shortly after the parakeet disappeared, a very beautiful woman came out from behind the curtain and took our order. We never saw the parakeet again." Wyatt answered.

"Perhaps the lady put the parakeet in a cage out of your sight. Perhaps it was nothing extraordinary." Mary offered in explanation.

"No, Mary. Matt and I are convinced that the lady and the parakeet were one and the same! Matt and I were there and we both came to the same conclusion." Wyatt protested.

"Well, it could be an illusion. One never knows. What do you plan to do next?" Mary answered.

"Next?" Wyatt asked. "Next?" he reiterated. "Easy. Next we will go back and continue our investigation. We wanted you to be aware of our activity." Wyatt paused and then went on, "Just in case something happens to us and we call for help."

"Really!" Mary asked. "Do you think that what you are doing can put you in danger?"

"I don't know", Wyatt answered. "I have never witnessed anything like what I witnessed today. I guess that anything can happen!"

Mary then said, "Wyatt, my experiences up here with Seemore are quite amazing to me as well. Perhaps we need to expect witnessing amazing things when we deal with the people we are investigating."

Wyatt now had his turn to inquire of Mary the facts in reality. "Mary, amazing is the word all right. That's a good description of Matt and my experience: amazing."

Mary continued with no pause. "Seemore has this DESE camera that can take pictures."

Wyatt laughed. "Mary that is what they are supposed to do!"

"You don't understand. This DESE camera takes compressed photo-event recordings that are interactive somewhat like a Sun Microsystems' Java Script program. The viewer can become very involved with these highly specialized photographs. However, any interactions can affect the present and the future as well."

"What do you mean by that?" Wyatt asked, becoming concerned for Mary's mental and emotional welfare.

"What I mean is that we can enter an uncompressed photo and witness the events taking place. Wyatt, we can be a part of the event if we choose to be. We can hear what people are saying. We can even use the Cogito-Lector and read their thoughts as well. It is as though what was recorded in the past is happening in real time, that is, right now! It could have been recorded years ago, but we can enter the "picture" and even change events. They can be changed then in the past and result in a change in the present time as well." Mary continued, becoming more excited with each word.

"You need to be kidding!" Wyatt responded.

"No, I am very serious. The drawback is that the interaction goes both ways. They can harm us in the present even though the action and photo recorded could have been from years ago." Mary said. "They can only affect us while we are in the picture with them. Once we step out of the picture, they cannot influence us in any way, and they cannot exit the photograph. In a sense, they are captured in the moments of the picture itself and within the limits, both geographically and chronologically as well.

"That sounds extremely dangerous Mary," Remarked Wyatt. "Are you safe? I mean how do you protect yourself from danger?"

"Seemore is quite protective, and he has had experience with these photographs. After all, he is the one who took them. He has witnessed the goings on at the time the photos were taken." Mary said.

Wyatt went on, "So you entered these DESE photographs. What is their significance anyway?" Wyatt asked curiously.

"Well, there would be almost no significance if they were photos of people going on a picnic or fishing or something like that." Mary answered.

"So, what do they signify? Why did Seemore take those pictures anyway? He must have had a reason. At least that would be my guess." Wyatt said.

"Oh, there most certainly was a reason. I only saw two of them and they were more than enough for me to deal with. They will need to be sent back to DESE headquarters right away and we all want to meet there and discuss what is threatening to be a major environmental and societal threat." Mary said.

"What do you mean, Mary?" asked Wyatt.

"Wyatt, the pictures were of witches and covens having secret meetings. Their meetings were about planning injury and mayhem on our society and various interests, both environmentally as financially. They want to affect our environment in such a way as to upset business, agriculture and the very integrity of our society. They do not care who they hurt."

It was now Wyatt's turn to say, "Really?"

"Really", Mary responded. "They even spoke of their creating the snow storm you experienced at Huntington Beach! They also bragged about the cold snap in southern Florida as well."

"We just now have a line on a group of witches here in Huntington Beach! How could witches in Alaska affect the climate here in California, much less Florida?" Wyatt protested. I also still need to visit Frank in San Diego as well. I still need his report. You know we cannot need too much in the way of intelligence, Mary" continued Wyatt. "We need all we can get."

"You are right, Wyatt. I want you to continue your investigation at Huntington Beach to your satisfaction. Then, when you feel that you have completed all that you need to in the way of investigating, especially the "Wicca Dragon" person and the barmaid, that you make your visit to Frank in San Diego." Mary offered.

"All right! Mary, it will be done just as you say. That is exactly as I wished to proceed as well." Wyatt concurred.

"We will meet at headquarters after all investigations are complete. You are to keep in contact so that I will know when to schedule our meeting." Mary said.

"I will check in with you after I have met with Frank. I will report on what I learn from Frank at that time unless it's an emergency." Wyatt continued.

"Agreed." Mary said. "Stay well and watch out for the unexpected. That seems to be the watchword. Please be very careful. That goes for the two of you."

"Will do", Wyatt said.

They then said their goodbyes and the telephone conversation ended.

Wyatt turned towards Matt and said, "Matt, we have our marching orders! Let's talk."

CHAPTER FORTY-THREE
MARY RETURNS

Mary had more than enough information and experiences at Seemore's place to suit her for a lifetime. Between the mythological creatures and the witches' goals in the "living" photographs, Mary knew that she had an emergency situation which needed tending right away. However, she had to await Wyatt's return and Frank's report. Then there was also HB Gaunt in Palm Beach along with Larry Carl. The problem at hand could not be properly dealt with if all available reports were not made, understood, and analyzed. She knew that she needed those reports to reach any conclusions and to make any plans whatsoever. She would wait.

She would use the time before Wyatt's return to collate and finalize the reports between them. Eventually the meeting at DESE headquarters would involve all parties and all investigators. All parties would need to meet with all their reports, all their data and in Seemore's case, living photographs. Once these were known, a plan of action to deal with the threat could be reached. Right now, Mary had no idea whatsoever as to what plans to combat the threat, as she already knew it, could be developed. She knew that action was necessary with the few facts of which she was already aware.

Mary estimated that at the most she would allow would be another two weeks or so, depending on need, for Wyatt to complete his investigation at the Tavern, the Wicca involvement, and the report from Frank German. She decided to slate a meeting at DESE headquarters in three weeks. In the meanwhile, she planned to contact the Floridian group of agents, Jack Henigson, his group of agents and of course Seemore and Hepseva. She would tell Wyatt to inform Frank German and Matt Ovlas about the need to meet as a coherent unit at DESE to coordinate all the various data collected by meeting time. She knew that she could count on all her agents to attend. They had to. DESE would arrange all transportation and accommodation needed to comfortably house and take care of all agents' needs.

In the meanwhile, she would call on HB and Larry Carl in the Palm Beach area and reconnect for an update.

Once again, her prelude to making her call to Florida was to take a nap in advance of her travail. The calls to HB were not always easy. HB had a slightly caustic attitude, somewhat like Dr. House on the TV Medical Drama Series. Like Dr. House he also had the ability to question and amuse himself with both his own answered foibles as well as those of the people around him as well as any new acquaintances.

Black Lightning was there to console her. Mary was grateful for Henry's attendance in the care of Black Lightning. Black Lightning meowed and walked back and forth, as he rubbed against Mary's legs to show pleasure at Mary's return. She had missed Mary very much.

There was not much that Black Lightning missed. Black Lightning knew every thought Mary had and everything on her mind as well as her goals and apprehensions. Mary was quite on her guard whenever she would call HB because sometimes, he could be quite gruff, although he never showed her the full extent of his available coarseness. Mary was not aware that HB could be "gruff" at all, because she had never seen it. However, there was some subliminal information and she sensed that such could be the case. She just wanted to be well rested before she had to deal with HB. Larry Carl would be no problem whatsoever. Larry was always the mellow, happy-go-lucky sort with bright blue eyes and an effervescent smile. He gave everyone the idea that his life was one without a care in the world. That is until Mary showed up on his doorstep with her job offer.

She plopped down on her pillow-top bed, which is covered with a light pink, very thick, hypo-allergenic filled comforter. She was comforted indeed. She was so comforted that she almost immediately fell asleep. It was a sleep that was much needed. Her mind was all a-jumble with all the events, happenings, and adventures she recently had. Thinking of how to deal with each one simply proved too exhausting. She thought just prior to laying down ,"Oh Morpheus, thank you for the relief of this stress and please make my mind a blank page, at least for a few hours!"

Morpheus came into her life almost immediately. She simply closed her eyes at the end of that thought and was in the deep sleep that the exhausted cherish.

Her sleep was so good that it was almost midnight when she awoke. She thought to herself, "Doggone. It's too late to call anyone now. It will need to wait until the afternoon." Her thoughts went on, "Perhaps I can go over my information and plan my conversation with HB before I even make a call to him. That's a very good idea. I will try to foresee any objections or criticisms before I even call him, but it will need to wait until morning because HB is probably cranky in the morning. It's bad enough to try to communicate with him in the afternoon, but that's a much wiser time to speak with him."

There was no one in the apartment with her except for Black Lightning. Her thoughts went on "I guess I took a nap before I went to bed for the night!" She laughed to herself at the idea. It was a strange set of events, but one she had experienced before. Her work and her travels were almost always quite exhausting. Being so tired at the end of one of them was something she was becoming accustomed to but not welcomed.

"Well, what do you think of that?" she rhetorically asked Black Lightning. She did not expect an answer because Black Lightning was just a cat, and a homeless one at that.

Nevertheless, Black Lightning gave her a look as though he understood what she was saying and what she was feeling. She did not suspect that Black Lightning was anything more than just a cat. Her thoughts on Black Lightning were being reconsidered in her mind. After all, she did meet a flying Peganni at Seemore's. Now she thought that Black Lightning was communicating with her as well.

Black Lightning knew that the time was coming when her domain at Mary Kent's house would be more than just that of a house cat. She knew, from reading Mary's mind, that a meeting of all agents would be arranged soon. Black Lightning knew that then she would need to reveal herself as who she really was. The time would shortly present itself when Mary would need to become aware of all the "Sub-agents" in DESE's service under her "Known" agents' list. The Sub-agents had to be eventually revealed. It was Mary's time for still another surprise.

It was with this thought in Black Lightning's mind that she interjected into Mary's mind the thoughts that he felt. She wanted to lessen the shock Mary would have when she eventually learned that the starship cat, Guiness, was a Starship agent from outer space and not just a cat. Black Lightning wanted to bring Mary's mind into the true realm of her surroundings, but slowly. Slowly, gently, and carefully she intended to "nurse" Mary into her Black Lightning reality.

In the here and now she let Mary know that everything would be all right eventually. Black Lightning subliminally assured Mary that she would be very capable in her communications with HB and Larry Carl. She encouraged Mary not to question her ability to deal with the problems before her and to have a peaceful night's sleep in continuance of her earlier "nap". She would not yet engage Mary in a conversation, neither a mental nor a vocal one. She just wanted to plant the seed in Mary's mind that her cat was her friend and an understanding, caring, and loving one at that. Mary never questioned that her mind's thoughts were not hers. She guessed that it was her own spirit reassuring her that comfort, security and the warm, cozy feeling she had just before dozing off was of her personal mental ownership. She never guessed that Black Lightning, of all creatures, had planted those nice thoughts into her mind. Mary did not have the slightest clue whatsoever.

CHAPTER FORTY-FOUR
FLORIDIAN DIALOGUE

Mary awoke hale and hearty the next morning. She had not drawn the blinds in her bedroom and the sun came beaming through her windows in glorious rays of light. There were no clouds in the sky which simply glowed a deep azure blue. She stepped out onto her balcony and deeply inhaled the cool, crisp, fresh morning air. She sipped her Fresh Market freshly brewed Amaretto flavored coffee which she bought while on a trip to Asheville in western North Carolina and seated herself on one of the very inviting, welcoming, comfortable patio chairs that were waiting for her and contemplated the last evening's events. She did not resist the invitation.

Her mind was clear. Morpheus did his job. She was fully refreshed for a change and felt like a new woman. She was eager to meet the day. She thought, "Watch out, HB, here I come!" However, it was the opposite of last night's timing. It was now too early to call HB. He was always best called in the early afternoon. That would be when he was fully awake and aware of what was going on around him and when he would be less likely to develop any contesting of what Mary would need to tell him or ask him. She needed his final report and his presence at the DESE headquarters upcoming meeting.

In the meanwhile, she set herself up with a good breakfast of bacon and eggs along with two pancakes and another cup of coffee. She thought, "I'll call Larry Carl up first. He is up early in the morning, but I'll give him another hour before I call just to be certain that he has had his breakfast too. I want him to be fully charged and in command of his faculties before I ask him for a report as well."

Mary finished her breakfast, took a leisurely shower, dressed, and made herself comfortable. Then, when she had met all her needs, she sat at her desk and dialed Larry.

"Hello, Larry?" said Mary when the call was answered.

"Hello. Who is calling?" asked Larry.

"Guess who!" said Mary playfully.

"Mary! It is you. How are you and what is happening? Are you all right? I heard that you were traveling a bit on "business". Is everything OK?" asked Larry.

"Yes, Larry, everything is quite all right." Mary went on. "I have had a most interesting visit to Alaska"

Larry responded, "Pray tell."

"Well, I will tell you, but not now," Mary continued, "It seems that there are events which need deep explanation and discussion. Each event must be gone over between each of us with complete and detailed clarification and in person."

Larry was now intrigued. "Why? What do you mean?"

"I simply mean that we all need to have a joint discussion and a joint revelation of what each of us has experienced. We need to make plans as to how we are to deal with likely pending disasters." Mary quickly answered. "The discussion material will require a full evaluation of everything each one of us has experienced." Mary went on.

"What happened, Mary?" asked Larry, now a bit concerned.

"Many things materialized, Larry. Things that no one could ever believe unless it happened to them. That is one of the reasons we all must get together. Each one of us has to fully reveal to our group exactly what happened to them. We cannot hold back anything, however ridiculous or minor, because we may fear ridicule. There is nothing funny about what is going on. There is nothing to laugh about. Each one of us must come completely clean and honest and fully reveal our experiences without any reservations." Mary went on emphatically.

"Well, Mary, you know about the witches meeting in the swamp, do you not? Larry asked.

"Yes. You already told me all about it. I have yet to speak with HB and get his report on the matter, but that is what I will be doing shortly. Right now, I want you and HB to come up to headquarters along with all the other agents across the country. We urgently need to get together. What do you say?" Mary asked in a very authoritative voice.

"Of course, Mary. I consider it my national duty to help deal with the problem. I can most certainly understand the seriousness of the situation, especially after the witches' meeting." Larry said without hesitation.

Mary responded, "Great. I will set the date in about one to two weeks from now. The government will take care of all transportation and housing. You have nothing to worry about except to be ready when the call comes. I will try to give at least a few days' notice before the shoe drops!"

"All right Mary. Let me get onto producing a written preliminary report for you and the meeting. I'm sure that I will find it very, very interesting," said Larry.

Mary answered, "Larry, you have no idea! Even with what you do know, there is still much more for you to learn. We will have some surprises for each of you."

"Looking forward to it Mary." Larry said.

"All right Larry. I'm off to call HB right now and I'll be in touch with you in short order. 'Bye." Mary signed off.

"'Bye, Mary. I can't wait." Larry signed off.

Mary took a few minutes to relax and gather her mind before making her call to HB. Mary grabbed another cup of her favorite coffee and again sat herself at her desk and began to dial HB's telephone number.

Her fingers did the walking. First "561" then "555-5555". Her telephone hummed a buzz, buzz, buzz. HB answered after the fourth buzz.

"Hello. What do you want?" HB answered in his usually gruff tone, intended to intimidate any solicitor, make that poor solicitor turn around and head for the hills with the caller saying a rapid and apologetic "I'm sorry" followed by a very quick hang up at the other end. However, Mary was not intimidated this time. She remembered her first telephone call to HB and understood it to be all a ruse. It was a false front. HB was really a teddy bear and a soft one at that!

"Hello, HB. How are you?" Mary asked with neither fear nor hesitation this time. HB was not going to get the better of her any longer.

"Who is this?" HB demanded.

"HB, I am very surprised and offended." Mary faked her dismay. "Don't you remember our trip to the Breakers?"

"Mary! Mary Kent!" HB exclaimed in virtual joy which was not faked at all. He was indeed very happy to hear from Mary. He had a lot to tell her and had wanted to call her but did not because he did not want to disturb her. In any case, he did not know where she was anyway. Now she finally made contact with him and he was overjoyed.

"I remember our trip to the Breakers. How could I forget?" he asked rhetorically. "Mary, I have been waiting for your call for some time now. I understand that you spoke with Larry, and he told you some of what we have been experiencing.'

"Yes, he has" Mary said.

"Well, what he told you was only a small part of the story. Did he tell you about the witches near the Burt Reynold's Ranch? Did he tell you about the pelicans and seagulls that were dropping clams and other shellfish on unsuspecting cars and people on Interstate 95 and at the City Center? Did he tell you about the birds which came to the witches' celebration and then transformed themselves into witch attendees?" HB was now very excited. He could barely stop talking. Mary couldn't get a word in edgewise, even if she used a hammer! HB now paused just to catch his breath. That let Mary speak.

"Yes and no. He told me about the witches' meet but nothing about pelicans and corporeal transformation. He certainly did not say anything about pelicans bombing people and cars either." Mary interjected.

HB went on, "Did you hear about their intent to influence people's minds and have them act as their agents of destruction as well? They will affect our own citizens to act against our society. These people are very, very scary and dangerous. Imagine: turning our own citizens, our sons, and daughters, against us all!"

"No." Mary answered, now in awe of what might come next.

"Mary, they want to affect the phenomena called "global warming" by dealing with their connection to the environment. They want to influence foreign entities to attack our nation in exceptionally extreme violence. They are opposed to our society and all its forms and attributes. They want us all to live in tents and back to using outhouses or worse! They are vehemently vicious to the point of being rabid. Our country and all our people are in tremendous danger, and nobody is aware of any of it!" HB was almost out of breath. He was obviously emotionally involved at this point. He even paused for Mary's reaction to all he had said.

Mary did react indeed.

"HB", she started, I need you to get all the readings you have and put everything together. It has become almost an emergency, especially after I hear what you just told me. I am waiting to hear from Wyatt who is out in California meeting with Frank German. We need to meet up here as soon as it can be arranged. We must deal with this threat now and not later. Will you please come up? Our Uncle will pay all expenses and make all arrangements for transportation, lodging and board." Mary paused. She did not expect HB to give her any grief at all.

"I will. I have never hesitated when my Uncle calls me, have I?" HB answered.

"I guess you haven't. This is another call. It is one quite different from your earlier service to our country, but it is one that is very urgent. It is also possibly more threatening than anything we have seen before. In any case, it is definitely quite different," said Mary.

"Wilco!" answered HB. That's old air force lingo for "will comply", just in case you didn't know Mary!"

Mary went on. "I know. I do not live in a vacuum you know, and I am around government pilots and agents all the time. If that was not enough, I also have seen my share of war movies too!" shouldMary was only playing with HB and he knew it. They both had a short laugh and Mary continued. "You need to know that what you need told me, although quite remarkable, is just the tip of the proverbial iceberg. You will learn many additional surprises when you show up at our meeting. By the way, please know that this meeting will be quite secret. Security will be at a very high level. Please keep it that way."

"Certainly, Mary. I have been there before. The saying is "been there, done that" HB answered.

"I expect that Wyatt will be back in less than two weeks. We will hold our meeting at that time at DESE headquarters," said Mary. "Security will be heavy. I will inform the President right away. He needs to know all of the details."

"George is an old fly boy along with me. You have it right. He must know right away. No one knows when these people will strike and we must be ready," answered HB.

"Great. We are both on the same page. I will be in touch with you within the next week with all the arrangements and instructions. Can't wait!" said Mary.

"Neither can I!" responded HB.

Once again, each said their goodbyes and phones were hung up at both ends.

CHAPTER FORTY-FIVE
WYATT REPORTS

Mary spent her time while waiting for Wyatt's report working at developing a format for the coming meeting at DESE. She wanted it all to go well and with no hang-ups. She most earnestly wanted to have each reporter fully disclose their experiences including those they might feel embarrassed to disclose. She already probably had the most unbelievable experience of any of her agents. After all, who could believe in a flying combination Unicorn and Pegasus? She thought that if she could tell that story, then the remaining agents should have no fear in completely revealing their most incredible experiences. However, she could not be one hundred percent certain that the other agents did not have just as extraordinary experiences as well.

It was agonizing just to wait for Wyatt's final report. The days just dragged on and on. Mary was at her wit's end. She was hoping for something, anything to break the monotony of one day passing into the other.

Her conversation with HB was enlightening, but she knew that he left out much more than he revealed. HB did not tell her everything he knew. She was certain of that. She could barely contain herself to meeting time. She saw it as a time of excitement, obtaining new knowledge and creation of a plan that would make long-term sense in controlling these otherworldly creatures and people who were angry at our world to the point of enlisting the aid of the real underworld. It would be. At the very same time, it will be an adventure into the unknown.

It would be a venture into new fears and each one of the agents would approach any new idea with much trepidation. After all, not all the opposition was from our world. It was most certainly not the world each of us knows daily.

While all these thoughts were running about in her head, Black Lightning came into the room. Black Lightning was fully aware of all the thoughts Mary was having. He thought, "Would it not be something if Mary really knew who I am? Perhaps I should tell her. She would need to know eventually, and that eventuality would be real soon. All would need to be revealed at the DESE meeting."

Black Lightning just stared at Mary and sat on his haunches in the fashion cats sit when they are thinking deep thoughts in silence. In Black Lightning's world, his thoughts are not always his alone. This time his thoughts were in advertently transmitted to Mr. Xilx back at Jack Henigson's house and a conversation of sorts ensued.

"Agent 8575", Mr. Xilx thought transferred to Black Lightning. It was a very stern and strong thought transference Mr. Xilx scolded, "what in the world are you thinking?"

Black Lightning snapped to, just as if he was in the army. He snapped to attention! Since he was cat-like, he suddenly stood stiffly and smartly on all fours.

"Pardon Sir. I did not mean to transfer that thought to anyone. I was just sort of day-dreaming. The thought just kind of escaped!" Said Black Lightning apologetically. He was obviously shocked that anyone "overheard" his thoughts!

"No, don't apologize. Your thoughts bring up a very valid point. If Mary learns who you really are, she may not be able to sleep at her house at all with you around. She would have no problems with you as a dumb animal. She may even want you out of her house, period! Then where will you go?" continued Mr. Xilx.

"Jack's house?" asked Agent 8575. "Would that be possible?

"I guess that if it came down to that, we would need to accommodate you," said Mr. Xilx.

"It would be quite all right" Jack Henigson chimed in.

Black Lightning did a double take. "Hello there, Jack Henigson! How are you? I did not know that this was a party line!

"Sorry", Jack said. "I did not mean to intrude. I could not help "over-receiving" your thoughts. Please forgive me!"

"No problem. You are welcome. I need all the help I can get on this," said Black Lightning.

Jack responded, "You most certainly do. If you let her know who you are outright, she could die of shock. You cannot do that, can you? We need to keep her alive."

"Right" said both Black Lightning and Mr. Xilx in the same moment. "We need her very much."

"What do you say that we try to get her weaned onto who we are very slowly? You know. Feed her a thought now and then until she starts to suspect our intelligence," said Mr. Xilx.

"Good thought", responded Jack. "Let her slowly suspect that you are much more than just a cat. You can do most of that via cognition induction. You do not even need the "cogito-lector" to do it because of your natural talents.

"Right", said Agent 8575. "Right" he repeated. "We do have that talent, don't you know?"

"Black Lightning!" Jack called out.

"Yes", answered BL.

"Please get it done before we all meet at DESE. That way Mary will have one more revelation under her belt and not wait for the meeting to have her shocked even more!" said Mr. Xilx.

"I know that she already suspects me to be an extraordinary "cat". If she only knew!" thought BL reflectively. He followed up that random thought with "and she will know eventually. That eventuality will be very soon, will it not?"

Jack and Mr. Xilx answered in a united and resounding thought, "Yes!"

Mr. Xilx followed that up with "Definitely. You havshould to start right now. Begin this minute. We have only a short time to introduce her to our world. She already has been through a lot in her adventures into the world of the strange and supernatural. Her experiences will have been stressful enough. She has even more experiences to witness when we all get together."

Mr. Xilx and Jack signed off thinking "goodbye" to BL. BL returned the thought and communication ceased.

BL thought transferred to Mary, "Mary, don't be so stressed. You have friends that will stick by you through thick and thin. You will eventually get through this, and everything will be all right. Just relax and take everything in stride." Then he tried a subliminal thought "be good to your cat. He is your best friend."

Suddenly a strange feeling came over Mary, she felt a calming force over her entire body, and she started to relax. "Wow!" she exclaimed. "What is happening to me? I suddenly am at peace. I have no doubt about the DESE meeting. Everything will be OK. The meeting will go well. No worries."

BL took pride in his influence over Mary's thoughts. In a show of "strength" he rubbed against Mary's legs, the way cats do, and purred loudly. Mary bent over and picked him up. "And how is my best friend?" Mary asked in a new appreciation of her usually abandoned cat. "How has Henry been treating you? Has he been taking good care of you? I have not seen him for a while now, but I suppose I will be seeing him soon now. He does not know that I have returned. I expect that he will be coming over to check on you any time now."

BL, the cat, just simply enjoyed the attention and continued purring even louder. He thought, "Mary, this is a very special cat. This cat is intelligent and very protective of you. This cat may even be an agent from outer space. He is that special indeed!" He fed that thought to Mary.

Mary was startled. She said gleefully "BL, you are most certainly a very special cat. You are smart and you look after me. It is as if you were almost human! However, you are not, are you? You are just a cat, aren't you?" She then put BL down on the sofa and looked directly into his eyes. She was considering the thought that BL was an agent from outer space. "No", she said to herself. "It cannot be. You cannot be an agent from outer space, can you? After all, you have been here about a year now."

BL did not transmit any thoughts. He decided to let Mary's statement stand without challenge. He felt that just planting the seed in Mary's mind as to the possibility that he could be from outer space was enough for one day. Tomorrow is another day. He would let Mary sleep on the idea tonight and possibly insert another thought tonight while she slept. He would eventually feed her dreams with graphics as to where he came from. The planet Ida would be introduced to her, as well as who he is. Mary would awaken refreshed and further enlightened. She would think that the dream was her own fantasy. That would make the shock that she was living with an intelligent extraterrestrial a little easier to accept. That was the way BL wanted to go: slow and easy. Tomorrow was another day.

Mary took a hot bubble bath to help her relax before going to bed. She dried herself with her heavy napped thirsty Turkish towel, got into her comfortable silk nightgown, and placed herself into the cleft between her blankets and her sheets. Placed her head on her soft down pillow and soon was visiting lullaby land.

It did not take long for BL to go to work. He would enter the sleeping Mary's dream and embellish what she experienced with facts from his life.

CHAPTER FORTY-SIX
WYATT'S REPORT

Mary awoke the next morning bright and early as she usually did. Once again, although she was quite rested, she did still feel the burden of her duties weighing heavily upon her. They were stressful enough to make her want to go back to bed. However, she knew that if she did so she would not sleep. Her mind was running at the speed of light and that light would keep her awake. Her thoughts were centered at the threat to her country and the upcoming DESE meeting.

This morning was somewhat different. She felt that she learned something new. She could not place her mind on exactly what it was, but she felt that it was important.

"Oh well, just another thing to keep me awake and alert! Another day and another dollar spent! Let me just save our country from calamity!" Mary said aloud and to herself.

BL was nearby and knew her thoughts and her feelings. She could hide nothing from him. Her mind was not only an open book to him, but a very well illuminated one as well.

Mary turned and placed her feet on the floor and into her fuzzy slippers. She then grabbed her fuzzy collared night robe from the chair next to her bed and stood up. It was then that she saw BL. BL looked right back at her. He did not behave like a cat this time. Mary was not certain what that look he gave her was all about. It was as though she was looking into the eyes of a very intelligent being and not an animal. The thought surprised her, and she once again shrugged off the strangeness of this cat's character.

"No way" she said out loud and to herself. "There is no way that you, BL, are anything more than just a cat. No way, no how!"

She was surprised and stopped in her tracks when she heard the response, "That is what you think!" coming from BL.

It was not vocal. There was no sound, but Mary was certain that it was BL who planted that thought in her mind. Once more, she shrugged it off as being her own mind playing tricks on her and just her imagination. It was not real. "My goodness! she exclaimed. "I need my cup of coffee badly!"

She then went off to her kitchen, approached her pre-timed coffee maker and poured herself a cup of the Asheville Fresh Foods' Amaretto flavored coffee. It was her favorite. Then she went back out to her patio, resumed her seating on her comfortable chair, and slowly sipped her coffee while contemplating her day's plans. The thought of BL was no longer on her mind.

It was now almost nine o'clock in the morning and she had not accomplished anything so far. That bothered her. She decided to have a light breakfast this morning. She felt that a heavy, full breakfast would slow her down and she wanted to perform at high speed this morning. Her thoughts went to Wyatt and his lack of any report or any call. That thought only lasted a moment or two because the telephone rang. It was almost on cue. Wyatt was on the telephone much to her surprise!

"Wyatt! How nice of you to call" she said. "I have been very concerned about you. What in the world is happening out there? I have been on edge just waiting for your report. Has something happened out there? It must be a little after six in the morning out there. What is going on? Is there a problem?"

"Mary," started Wyatt, "there are several things of significance that I do need to report. The rest can wait until I return."

"Shoot" said Mary. "What is the news?"

"You do remember the snow at Huntington Beach, correct?" quizzed Wyatt.

"Of course I do." said Mary. "How could I forget?"

Wyatt went on, "Well we had some of that here in San Diego but it went even further. Mary, we even have ice storms here. We have clouds in the sky when there are usually either very few or none at all. Tropical vegetation is freezing and yet the sun is warm. It is a contradiction!

The farmers are in big trouble. They are looking to the immigrant workers only to help clean up the frozen debris. They have lost almost their entire crop of berries and fruits to say nothing of their vegetables."

"That is one thing. Then there is another. Overnight all the traffic lights have turned upside down. The green light is on top, and the red light is on the bottom of every traffic signal. The only thing that is the same is the yellow light in the middle! If that is not enough for you there is more. The one-way street signs are all reversed. The old one-way is now the other way! Mary, it is a real mess here. The police have no clue as to what happened. We are all willing to leave for a hopefully saner location, like DESE headquarters. Frank, who has spent most of his adult life here, is also ready to leave in a hurry." Wyatt continued his impromptu report.

"Wyatt, come back as soon as you can. We need to get all of this together so that we can deal with the problem." Mary virtually ordered.

"Mary, the witches here are advertising in the papers as well. Frank and I witnessed a witches' meetup here in the outskirts of San Diego. It was advertised as "Greet your local coven of witches, wiccans, pagans, and other practitioners of The Craft. Meet those of the Old Ways and who follow the path of the Ancients." There is no attempt to keep these meetings a secret," continued Wyatt.

Mary answered, "I have heard all this before. It is not new. Did you hear anything in particular?"

"Yes, Mary we most certainly did. Mary they are angry at the hundreds of years that the non-Wicca public have been persecuting them. They have increased their membership numbers based on their supposed environmental concerns. They have developed the ability to magnify their spell powers by unifying their chanting and spell making at the very same moment in time across the country! They have discovered this as an amplification technique and verified the results via the internet. The technique was stumbled upon quite accidentally and the internet allowed them instant communication everywhere a coven exists!" Wyatt continued.

"I have been made aware of their anger from other reports. I know all about their attitude. I am very much concerned, however, at their retaliation on a helpless and unknowing public. Do you have more?" asked Mary.

"Yes", said Wyatt. I knew that my time in San Diego is limited so Frank took the "TCC" recording camera with us to peruse the event later. We will bring it with us to the DESE meeting so that we all can inspect it for additional clues to their plans and intentions. Frank and I just wanted to get out of there before we were discovered. We did take a long period of photos in any case. I know that it will be more than enough to satisfy our DESE colleagues."

Wyatt made that last statement with satisfaction and a bit of pomp as well. He was obviously tired from all his West Coast adventures and who could blame him?

Mary then said, "Wyatt, I expect that you will be back within the next several days. I will arrange the meeting for about five days from now. That should give everyone time to complete their duties, both personal and government, and get to Washington for our meeting. I will arrange everything for them all. Does that seem all right to you?"

"That time seems workable. As a matter of fact, I am just about ready to return right now. Frank, however, is a different story." Wyatt said.

"How so?" asked Mary.

Wyatt responded, "Well, he wants to make Leslie aware of what is happening. They need to get packed and all, you know! Nevertheless, I think that time will work just fine."

Frank nodded his head in agreement. He heard both sides of the conversation since Wyatt used an amplification telephone.

"Very good", answered Mary. I will make arrangements for the rest our team to get here and to develop our plans to deal with this threat.

"Great", responded Wyatt. "I'll be seeing you very soon. I will accompany Frank and Leslie to the meeting to make sure they don't lose their way!"

"Right", said Mary. They then both said goodbye to each other and hung up.

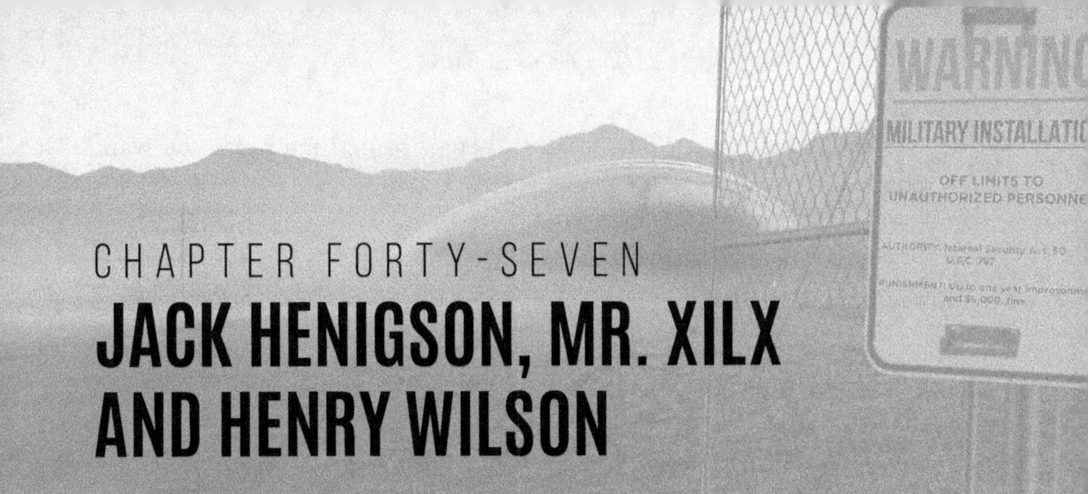

CHAPTER FORTY-SEVEN

JACK HENIGSON, MR. XILX AND HENRY WILSON

Henry approached the Henigson house one more time walking up Rockridge Road instead of cutting through the back yard of houses this time. "Today was special," he thought. Today was collection Thursday. He would get a good tip from Jack, especially since their relationship had changed to a higher level. Henry was no longer the young boy he was several weeks ago. He knew it, Jack knew it and Mr. Xilx knew it.

The house seemed different this time. The curtains were opened and Jack was sitting on the porch. Mr. Xilx was lying on the porch next to him. They already knew that Henry was on his way because of their powers of mental communication. They already knew that Henry hoped for a good tip as well. They both found that amusing.

"Hi, there, Henry!" Jack greeted the unsuspecting Henry. It did not take Henry long to know what was going on because Henry had also developed mental communication abilities as well. His was not as fully developed as his companions were yet, but he was constantly improving. He had not yet develop that ability to communicate a great distances yet so he was not aware that Mr. Xilx and Jack were waiting for him at all.

"Hi", responded Henry. "I'll take the payment for the week's papers first, if you don't mind."

"I do not mind at all, Henry. What is more, I also have a "good tip" for you as well." Said Jack pleasantly.

"Great", Henry went on, "I think there is something more you want to tell me."

"You bet there is, Henry. It is time to go to work," answered Jack. Mr., Xilx remained silent.

"All right, let me have it in words, please" responded Henry.

"Henry, please take a seat," said Jack. "Henry the word is that we are to meet in Washington early next week. All agents across the USA are to attend to deal with the threat to our country. We will develop a plan to cope with that threat at that meeting. You, however, have several chores to finish before that time."

"Such as what?' quizzed Henry.

"Such as Mary Kent and BL and you. Mary has no knowledge of our extraordinary functions or our extraordinary existence and abilities. We need to introduce her to the full truth concerning the little world about her and more importantly, about all of us," answered Jack. "I am afraid that it will be a bit of a shock."

"Do you mean to tell me that she does not have a clue as to what we can do?" said Henry, now anxious about the matter.

"Correct, Henry. She has no clue. Right now, we are working on having BL reveal himself to her, but she is doing that very slowly. Apparently even that must be sped up since the DESE meeting is coming up in the next few days," answered Jack.

"How do you suggest I do that?" quizzed Henry.

"You will do it slowly. We will ask BL to introduce the thought to her as well. She will introduce you to Mary via thought induction as one of us. Mary will understand because she already knows about me. It is just my extrasensory abilities of which she is not fully aware," answered Jack.

"I need to go to her house and make my collections there as well," remarked Henry. "Will BL give her a clue today, before I get there?"

"BL is giving her clues and feeding her thought processes regularly. I expect that the "cat" will be out of the bag within the next forty-eight hours. We need to have Mary fully informed about the "agents" unknown to her and their real nature. That includes Mr. Xilx, BL and even you, Henry. She does not know about you at all. She does not know your real potential and the full extent of your "gifts" either. As a matter of fact, Henry, even you have not yet realized the completeness of your abilities and powers. You are still growing into them, Henry. Your shoes are not yet fully filled, but they will be and in a very short time!" said Jack.

"Do you mean that Mary does not even know about BL? What is the hurry to get her informed anyway? Why don't you just take it easy on her?" Henry asked.

"We want to have her fully aware of all her assets before the DESE meeting. She needs a full armamentarium to deal with the problems we currently have." Jack answered.

"What is DESE?" asked Henry.

"What is DESE? What is DESE? What is DESE? You are asking me what DESE is?" asked Jack somewhat flustered. "Do you mean to tell me that no one has ever told you about DESE? DESE and Mary, go together. Mary is the head of DESE, Henry. DESE stands for the "Department of Extraordinary Situations and Events".

"No one ever told me." Henry answered sheepishly. He guessed that he should have known, but it could not be his fault at all. After all, he was just introduced to this weird fraternity only a short time ago.

"Henry, it is not your fault. It is ours. We assumed that you were fully aware of Mary's heading up DESE. That was our error and not yours. We apologize. Now, since you know about DESE you also must know that we have a problem which affects us all. Has anything strange ever happened to you? Anything weird or unexpectedly abnormal ever happen to you at all? In short, has anything happened, that you have witnessed which was out of the ordinary?

"No", Henry answered quickly, only to follow it up just as rapidly with a "Yes, maybe."

"Yes, maybe what? What are you thinking of Henry?" queried Jack.

"There was this one time, when I was handling my pigeons a long time ago that one looked me in the eye and his eyes flashed bright red. I thought that his eye actually radiated a red light beam right at me. It lasted only a short second and I put it off as reflection from the sun beaming down into the pigeon coop," explained Henry. "My friend, Joe King and I both witnessed it. It was strange but the lit-up eyes fully illuminated the pigeon coop."

"How did you feel after that? Did you notice anything different about yourself?" asked Jack.

"Not really, but I felt good about everything anyway. Anyway, everything I did went very well for me after that time. Maybe I did not really acknowledge an influence at that time. Looking back, I may need to really rethink it all", responded Henry pensively.

"Henry, you were zapped. Your pigeon was not a pigeon at all, but a transformed Wicca who saw your potential. You are not an ordinary boy, Henry. You have gifts very few people have. They are "gifts" only if you use them in the interest of mankind and our world. If you use those "gifts" only for your own selfish interests, then the gifts will be a curse, not only on mankind but also on you. Good can only come from good, Henry. It is very hard to have good come from bad. I know from what I have seen of you in the past and learned from scanning your mind that you are the "good" sort and as a result, you are invited into our midst. We welcome you, Henry." Jack continued.

"Aye", said the quiet Mr. Xilx, in his Cockney brogue. You are very welcome indeed. We need your help and perhaps even the help of some of your friends as well!"

This surprised both Henry and Jack.

"Some of my friends? What do you mean by that?" asked Henry.

"Some of your friends can be of some help to us in dealing with the problem facing our nation. Some, though either not gifted or even slightly gifted, have potential. None, however, have your abilities," stated Mr. Xilx with authority.

"Really?" puzzled Henry. "Who for instance?"

"Your pigeon buddy, Joe King. Your good friend, Mickey Tedesco. That's just for starters. There are not many more though" Mr. Xilx snapped.

"Really?" repeated Henry.

"Really" repeated Mr. Xilx.

Henry asked, "How can my friends help anyway? They only play baseball in the street with me and sometimes we go fishing. Besides, they are not that smart and certainly not that "streetwise". The quasi-supernatural and extraordinary situations we are becoming aware of are just about bearable for me. I'm not sure that they would or could understand what may confront us. I think that they will just "fold" away. That would not be a good thing, would it? I cannot see why you think that they might be of any help at all. That is a respectful opinion Mr. Xilx."

"Probably not a good thing if they just "fold" away as you say", answered Mr. Xilx. "It would be good to have the vitality and the power of youth with us. Youth power is a great amulet which will work well under the circumstances."

"Really?" remarked Henry.

"Really" said Mr. Xilx. "You see, we will be dealing with spells and non-benevolent witchcraft. Youth power is what that creature within that pigeon of so many years ago saw in you." Mr. Xilx continued, "And that is what we, Jack, BL and I see in Mickey Tedesco and Joe King. We see the same thing. We also see it in those friends we have just named."

"Are you serious? How did you know their names anyway? "You have never even met them," said the shocked Henry.

"We have met them through you via your mind Henry. We know them better than even you do! "We are both very, very serious", answered Jack Henigson, interjecting himself into a momentary lull in the conversation, wedging his words between those of Mr. Xilx and Henry.

"Right now, that involvement of your young friends should wait until we have our DESE meeting. The first matter at hand is getting Mary Kent online with the real nature of the people around her. We need to have everything online. You know, dot the "I's" and cross the "T's" sort of thing" continued Mr. Xilx, carrying on where Jack left off.

CHAPTER FORTY-EIGHT
MARY'S REAL WORLD

Mary had changed from hanging around just waiting for Wyatt's call. She was now a very busy beaver. She was busy arranging travel for her agents by contacting military transports around the country with the help of the former Cos Cob accountant, Jim Barrett, the man from the Government Accounting Office who arranged payment for all expenses in DESE.

Mary would now need to contact each of her agents only after Jim Barrett managed to arrange air transport and then let her agents know when and where they were to meet their transportation. She would then need to arrange accommodations around the Washington, DC area for her agents to stay while they attended the DESE meeting.

Mary wanted her agents in the same hotel. That was to be designed to allow traveling to the DESE headquarters to be a bit less traumatic and easier for everyone.

She contacted Seemore and Hepseva in Alaska, Frank German and Matt Ovlas in California, Larry Carl, and HB in Florida. She also wanted to have Sam and Liz Ham from the Chicago area as well as Val and Samantha Ovlas from the New Canaan region also attend.

All the while she is making those preparations, BL is busy rubbing her legs and demanding attention, both purring and meowing loudly.

"Guiness", said Mary, "what in the world do you want anyway? Can you not see that I am very busy? Oh, Guiness, I am sorry. I did not mean to scold you. What can a dumb animal know anyway? It is not your fault that you want attention. It is mine. I am sorry Guiness."

Suddenly Mary was once again surprised. She would have sworn that she heard a mental voice saying, "Mary, oh Mary. If you only knew that this "dumb animal" is not so dumb at all. Would you like a demonstration, Mary?" the voice asked.

Mary was dumbstruck. She said to herself, "I must be under too much pressure. I think I need a nice, long, peaceful vacation."

The voice persisted, "Yes, Mary, we all do. Why don't you check out that travel magazine on the table next to the sofa?"

Mary responded to herself aloud, "That's a good idea I have. I will relax a bit right now and take a short break from all this arranging and planning. Let me look at that book!"

As Mary said those words, the travel magazine left the table and floated to her while she still remained seated at the desk where she was making travel arrangements for DESE agents.

"What?" she both questioned and exclaimed. "What is this? What is happening?" Then she looked around the room and there was no one there but Guiness, the black cat.

Guiness just sat on his haunches and looked her directly in the eyes.

"This dumb cat just did that Mary. This dumb cat is not a dumb cat at all." BL mind transferred the thought. "This dumb cat is your friend, though. Mary please do not be alarmed."

"Really!", said Mary aloud.

"Really", thought transferred BL.

"I am happy that I am still sitting down, but I need to lie down instead. I think that I am getting sick. I don't feel well." Mary said as she approached the sofa to lie down. She closed her eyes and a short nap took her into its protective stress-escaping custody. There she found a few moments of peace, as long as the nap lasted.

She slept for what seemed to her to be only a few minutes, but was actually a little more than one hour. She was awakened by a bright light that invaded her domain and she was hearing several different voices.

She awoke quickly this time, sensing an emergency. She guessed that EMS had arrived to take her to the hospital and that her passing out was the result of some severe episode such as a heart attack or a stroke or God knows what!

However, to her surprise there were no EMS personnel present. What she saw, as her eyes became accustomed to the bright light, was a circular field of illumination as in the screen of a large television monitor except that there was no monitor. In that field of light she saw Jack Henigson, and his pet cat or dog or whatever the six-legged creature was. Jack spoke in a very soft, low voice. It was as though he did not want to disturb someone.

Mary sat up and looked at what she thought was some kind of miraculous vision. She was very awake now. Adrenalin was running in her veins, but not to a severe extent. It was just enough to be the start of a "fright, or fight" reaction, but did not reach the point of "flight".

Mary yelled, "What is this? What is happening? What is this?" she repeated in an anxious and urgent mode. Much to her surprise, she was not so fearful that she would run away from what was going on in her house.

When she said that, Jack Henigson, the man in the "vision" spoke directly to her. "Mary, this is Jack. Please do not be frightened but stay seated where you are on that sofa. I have a lot of explaining to do. I have some very special information for you and DESE. You will find it very beneficial and very interesting as well! Here goes!"

Jack started to explain. "Mary, do you recall my days at Area 51, quite a few years ago?"

Mary answered, "Yes, Jack, how could I forget it? That is when you came back with that weird animal, cat or dog, now sitting by your side. You also gave me my cat, Guiness, who has been my companion. I could not forget that, could I?"

"Well, Mary, I need to let you know that there is a little more to the story that I now need to bring to your attention."

"Such as?" Mary asked.

"Well, how about the "vision" you think you are now having? You are talking to it. Don't you think that it is rather strange?" Jack went on. "Do you really think it is a "vision" or is it real? This is not a Memorex commercial, you know."

"I really am afraid to answer that question. Jack, you tell me. Which is it?" Mary requested.

"Mary, it is very real. It is not Memorex" answered Jack.

"Really?" remarked Mary.

"Really." Answered Jack.

"Please explain to me what is going on. What is this that I am seeing anyway? I am somewhat confused at this point, and I need you to enlighten me" pleaded Mary.

"Mary, I thought that perhaps it might be better if we spoke in person, but on second thought, this is just as well. Time is limited and you need to know what the facts are, and you need to know it all before the DESE meeting" answered Jack.

Mary said, "Please continue Jack."

"Very well. It is now time for introductions. These introductions will be a bit of a surprise, Mary, so expect it. Mary, allow me to introduce you to my good friend here beside me, Mr. Xilx" Jack continued.

"Mr. Xilx?" Mary queried.

"Yes. Mr. Xilx. Mr. Xilx is the six-legged creature I found years ago while scraping around Area 51. It turns out that Mr. Xilx is not a cat or a dog. Mr. Xilx is an extraterrestrial and a Starship Captain from the planet Ida. Ida is a planet beyond our solar system. The Starship crash landed near Area 51. I found him and thought he was a mutant cat, or dog, that was injured by an object entering our atmosphere from outer space. Jack continued, "I was very wrong."

Mary was now beyond being shocked. She was now curious instead. She asked, "You say he is a Starship Captain. How do you know this? Please explain yourself."

Jack answered, "Mary, suppose I stop doing the talking. I am going to let Mr. Xilx speak with you directly."

Mary was again lost for words. She could not understand how a creature that looked like a six legged cross between a dog and a cat could speak to her. However, she kept an open mind. She said, "Go right ahead. I am ready for anything at this point!"

Mr. Xilx stood at attention, as much as a six-legged dog-cat ever could and began, "Mary, I am very pleased to meet you."

Mary's mouth opened wide as did her eyes. Not only was this creature actually speaking to her, but he spoke in a Cockney English accent to boot! It was almost more than she could bear and still shocking for her. Although she was sitting on the sofa, she still almost fell over. That this could even conceivably be a possibility was still a shock.

Mr. Xilx continued, "Many earth years ago my Starship, the IIS PIP, left our home, the planet Ida. We were searching for another planet in the universe that contained living and intelligent life. We were attracted to earth because of electrical radiation and radio beams which earth sent out into space. We approached earth, but we incorrectly estimated the strong gravitational pull of the earth and as a result, we lost our ability to recover our orbit around the planet. We had lost the power of our engines and the lack of light on the dark side of the earth failed us. Our engines are supplementally powered by the energy emitted from the stars. In your case, that star is called your "sun". We did our best not to crash. Our ship is still somewhat intact and is still buried under a sand deposit near what you earthlings call Area 51." Mr. Xilx paused a second and asked, "Do you follow me so far Mary?"

Mary had just about fully recovered from her shock at this point. She objectively answered, "Yes, I do. Tell me more, Mr. Xilx."

"There is not much more to tell at this point. Jack found me quite by accident. I managed to get out of the ship with my companion but I was unconscious and still under the sand to some degree. Jack found me and rescued me. He did not know who I was, but he was a good EMS worker." Mr. Xilx continued.

Mary asked, "Is there more?"

"Yes Mary. There is a bit more. I told you that I exited the ship with my companion, my helmsman, Agent 8575. Agent 8575 looks something like me, but he has four legs instead of my six. You see, I outrank him." Mr. Xilx continued.

"Where is this Agent 8575 now?" asked Mary.

Mr. Xilx continued his answer, "Mary, get ready for still another surprise. Agent 8575 was taken to a shelter at Area 51. It was determined that he was just a feral cat, and after testing to see that he bore no contamination, he was released."

Mary was curious. She had to ask, "Where did he go? What ever happened to him?

Mr. Xilx went on, "Mary it is very good that you have regained your scientific open-mindedness and objectivity because you are going to need it. Agent 8575 we also know as "Black Lightning". You know him as Guiness. He is sitting right in front of you. Mary, please say hello to Agent 8575!"

"What?" exclaimed Mary. "This day is too much. I am going to go back to sleep and wake up from this dream. This cannot be real," she exclaimed in indignant protest.

Jack intervened to save the day for Mary. "Mary, I know that this is a surprise and a shock. I rescued BL from the veterinarian at Area 51. They were just going to let him loose. I felt that he would not survive in the wilderness and so I took him home. I did not want to need to care for two such creatures, so I gifted him to you. I only found out later that he was the helmsman from the Ida Interplanetary Ship, the IIS PIP."

Mary remarked, "Do you mean to tell me that I have been living with an extraterrestrial all this time? Do you mean that you knew all about this and never told me? Do you really think that it was right to keep me in the dark, especially in my line of work? Do you really think that it was a fair thing for you to do?" Mary was very much perturbed to say the least.

Jack answered sheepishly, "You are quite right Mary. We felt that you had enough on your plate. You did not need to have another career problem to deal with. We needed to have a secure place for BL to live and to be protected. Now, however, everything has changed. We have knowledge of the threats against our country and all that we know has to be brought out into the open in order to deal with it."

Jack continued, "Mary let me introduce you to your very good friend, Black Lightning."

Black Lightning smartly stood up at quick attention, as well any four-legged cat could, and actually saluted and smiled. If that were not enough, he said in perfectly sophisticated British English, "Mary, I apologize for the deception. I am very relieved that the need for hiding the truth is now in the past." Black Lightning went on, "You are not fully surprised that I am not just an ordinary cat. You have had your suspicions in the past that I was not just a "normal" dumb animal. I had tried to communicate with you with subliminal mental transference and to influence your thoughts with regard as to my real nature. I have only partially succeeded up to this point. Since the time for the DESE meeting is close, it was necessary for us to place this revelation process at high speed. That is why I had to call on Mr. Xilx and Jack to lend a hand."

Mary continued to be surprised, but she could no longer express her emotions. She was all "expressed" out. There was just about a complete desensitization of the process whereby a body shows emotion or shock. Mary could just simply have been in a catatonic trance-like state. She did not move, but appeared frozen in time and space. There was no longer a reserve of any feelings for more shock or surprise left in her.

She said, "Why are you revealing all this to me now? Is there a reason?

"Mary", said Jack, "the reason is that you need to know that we are all part of your team. We are either official members of DESE or unsolicited volunteers on your side. We have powers and abilities that can help you to combat the evil influences that are currently threatening our country. These strengths and abilities will be used when needed. They are widely varied." Jack went on, "You do recall that I am a member of DESE as well, do you not? I know that you do trust me. You must also continue to trust me, Mary, on my "sub-agent" selections as well. They will be of great help to us in the days to come."

"Yes, Jack. You are a well known member of DESE, especially those of us in administrative office. I most certainly do trust you. Is there more for me to know?" Mary asked hesitantly, trying to be ready for any surprise that Jack might spring on her.

Jack continued responding to this invitation, "Mary, there is more. Guiness has been cared for by our paperboy, Henry . You know him. He is your paper boy as well as mine."

"Yes, I know Henry. He is a very fine lad. He is both reliable and responsible and becoming more mature every day. Traits such as his are hard to find these days in both the young and old of our society, unfortunately." Mary said in both gratitude for Henry's good character and in despair at the fact that so few youths had the same attributes.

Jack went on, "Mary, Henry Wilson is a very specially gifted individual. He is not only gifted, he is so outstanding that he is literally one in a million."

"Oh my God!" Mary exclaimed. "Don't tell me he is from outer space also. Is he an extraterrestrial also?" Mary was almost afraid to hear the answer to that question.

"No, Mary, he is not an extraterrestrial." Jack continued, "He is empowered enough to be one of us though."

"Thank goodness! What exactly do you mean by "one of us" Jack?" Mary asked, unable to hide her concern and curiosity for the boy's welfare.

Jack went on. "Henry's abilities are similar to those of Mr. Xilx's and Guiness's and mine as well. We have various powers, including telepathy, teleportation, transmutation, telecommunication and the ability to not only read minds, but to place thoughts into minds which can make individuals change both their decision making, but also their mood as well. This touches on only a few of our powers."

Mary said still in surprise, "Are you trying to tell me that my young Henry has all those powers?"

Jack assented, "Yes, he does. He has those and more. However, he is still in his infancy in developing them, but he is becoming increasingly quite aware of his growing power day by day. Not even his parents know of his abilities. With a bit of luck, they never will need to know. They probably would be frightened by them and we do not need to have that happen."

Mary said, "I agree. If it is not necessary, then they should be protected from that knowledge. It would shock them too. It certainly has shocked me. It would shock his parents even more!"

Jack went on, "Mary, we have enlisted Henry and hopefully some of his friends as well. They are not a gifted, but they do have some hope. We need the powerful amulet of youth on our side to counteract the evil doers which are trying to destroy and upset our nation. Ultimately, Henry's friends can join yet unknown powers to help defeat the vengeful enemies of our country."

Guiness popped up saying, "Mary, you know that Henry has been taking care of me. You can guess by now that I really did not need to have him take care of me. I only permitted it because I was under cover. Henry became suspicious when he found opened cans of cat food that he did not open. They were delicious by the way. My compliments are to be given to the chef. He knew you were not around and he wondered who opened those cans! It was very funny looking at his puzzlement! I slowly clued him in via thought implantation, similar to what I did with you, Mary. He knows that Guiness is an extraordinary animal. Henry has renamed me "Black Lightning" and I like it. Henry will never be the same again. First he is rapidly growing in his abilities and he now knows that creatures like me and Mr. Xilx exist in his world. He knows that we are extraterrestrials. It does not frighten him and he welcomes us."

"All right, now!" said Mary. "All right. I have it. Now what do we do? By the way, how did you get into my living room anyway? This is not television. What in the world is it anyway? What is happening here?"

Guiness, or Agent 8575, also known as Black Lightning, spoke up. "Mary that is a very special and advanced communication device. It has many functions, even beyond that."

Mary looked puzzled. "What has many functions? What kind of device is it and where is it?

"Why Mary it is right in front of you. Do you not see it?" asked Guiness in his most perfect British English.

Mary responded, "No, I do not see anything beyond the bright vision before me. What is this "it" you are talking about?"

"Mary it is my Rubber Band. It is what you think is my collar. It looks more like one of those "Hair Scrunchies" of today. It is really a very secret recorder and communicator. It keeps and records all data of what goes on every day and is also both a visual projection device and vocal recorder as well."

Black Lightning Continued, "It is on the floor and in front of the "screen". It projects images and sound behind the collar."

"How do you keep it working? Does it work on nuclear energy or what? You have been here a while now. I would expect that there must be some deterioration in its workability by now." Said Mary.

"It is really very simple. There is a chip, or device, within it which breaks down cerumen into its atomic basics and provides a virtually inexhaustible supply of power for its operation", explained Black Lightning.

"Oh", said Mary. "It's powered on atomic cerumen, is it? Is that what you are really saying to me? Are you serious?"

Black Lightning said, "Oh, I most certainly am. It is a rather very curious chemistry and its atomic configuration is unique. Cerumen is cerumen, you know."

Mary responded in almost a sarcastic disdain, "I most certainly do know, Guiness. I most certainly do know. I do not even want to know where you get it either! Nevertheless it is really a bit hard to believe, you know. After all, cerumen is ear-wax!"

Black Lightning answered, "Not really, once you know your chemistry and physics the way us Idians do."

"Idians?" Mary asked. "You mean Indians do you not?"

"No, I mean Idians!" responded Black Lightning, this time with emphasis.

"Are Idians a type of idiot or what?" said Mary.

"Mary, how little you know. I am an Idaian. Mr. Xilx and I come from the planet Ida which is outside your solar system. Was this not already explained to you? Nevertheless, that is how we are named. We are named from the planet from whence we came." Black Lightning spoke in perfect English. His accent was as impeccable as was his patience.

"Oh!" said Mary. "I understand now. No, I do not recall having it explained to me that way. Thank you very much." Mary reflected a little bit and then followed up her conversation with, "You know, Guiness, up to now you were just my cat. Now I'm not sure of what you really are."

Jack perked up, "Mary, Guiness is unique. You now know that he is more than just a cat. He is an extraterrestrial starship helmsman. You now know his history. Please do not be uncomfortable around him. You can still consider him just your cat, but I really would like it if you would view him as a protector, as a friend, as a confidant and as a fellow DESE agent, which he is under my enlistment. You can count on his undying loyalty."

Mary retorted, "Very well. I acquiesce. He can stay here. He has been here long enough so I am sure that it feels quite like home to him by now."

Jack responded, "Great. I am happy to have this loose end settled."

"Jack, are there any more surprises that you would like to spring on me? Have I been through your entire gauntlet now? If there are more, please let me know now. I like to have this entire trauma behind me. I do not need to be in pain, you know!" Mary said plaintively.

Jack answered, "Not that I remember. No, nothing more for now. If there is more, I will let you know very gently."

"Great!" said Mary. "Then I can relax at least for a moment or two. Right?"

"Right." Jack answered. "And with that, Mr. Xilx and I will say au revoir until tomorrow. If you should need to contact us, simply have Black Lightning throw his Rubber Band down and we will be in immediate communication, in stereo sound and in three dimensional, digital high resolution color!"

Mary answered, "Very good."

Jack and Mr. Xilx then shut down the CC, descriptively known as a Collar Communicator.

Mary then turned to her newly revealed house guest. "I suppose that now you want a bed of your own."

"No", replied Guiness. "I will be fine sleeping near the kitchen where I have been in the past. That cat bed is very comfortable. It is better than the bunks aboard the IDA. It is nice, soft, and comfortable. I could use a little blanket though."

"Great." Mary said. "We can continue as though nothing has happened. To the outside world you will still just be my pet cat. We alone, along with Jack and Mr. Xilx, will be the only ones who know the real facts."

"Not true, Mary", said Guiness. "You have forgotten Henry. He also knows.

"Right." Mary said. "Henry. I need to have a discussion with Henry, do I not?"

BL said, "I would not be surprised. I think you do. Henry may be equally enlightened as you in learning the new circumstances life has presented to you both. Both of you would probably benefit greatly from a discourse relating to current events nationally and within DESE. Henry will be a part of DESE through Jack Henigson's membership, will he not?" BL looked directly into Mary's eyes as he said this.

Mary expressed a bit of wonderment at this. Her mind was virtually declaring a bit of disbelief. She answered, "You are quite right, Guiness.

Henry should be by today to make his collection for his newspaper route. I will make it a point to have him engage me in an informational exchange! I expect that it will be very interesting indeed."

Mary went on, "Guiness, do you know if Henry is aware of my position in DESE?"

"Oh, yes. Definitely. He was told by Jack a short time ago. Henry is aware of what your office is. He most certainly does know." Guiness responded.

"Good." Mary said. "Good. That means I will not need to explain that part of my life!"

"I am not so sure, Mary. He really does not know much more than just that you work for the government and that you are the head of a secret department." Guiness went on, "You will most likely need to fill in some details for him."

"Will do, but those details will be cursory at this time until the DESE meeting when everything will be laid out in detail." Mary answered.

"One more thing, Mary", interjected Guiness.

"What is that, Guiness?" Mary asked.

"You recall that Jack said Henry is gifted and that his newly discovered powers are still developing?" Guiness said.

"Yes, I do. Why?" responded Mary.

"Well, you need to know that one of his "gifts" is the ability to read your mind. Eventually he will develop the supplemental ability to implant transferred thoughts as well." Guiness informed Mary.

"I'm glad you told me that." Mary said.

"Don't be shocked if he comes up with some facts you may be thinking about, but not yet revealed to him by you. Remember, that if you "think", he might be able to "read" that thought." Guiness said. "He may even tell you what you are thinking! Won't that astonish you!"

"It most certainly would." Mary said. "I will need to practice in making my mind a blank page. How do I do that?" Mary pleaded with Guiness for help.

"Good question." Guiness answered. "Good question. There are some exercises I can try to teach you, but you are an earthling, and I may not be able to instruct you adequately into the secret mind set to make it completely effective. However, we can try." Guiness went on, "I would hope that there would be some secrets you should be able to keep private. There is a mental switch, on and off, that I think would work very well for you."

"I hope so. I do not want all my thoughts read, only those that are not the most private, you know." Mary said.

"I do know, Mary. I've been here quite a while now and I know what goes on in your head!" Guiness responded.

Mary blushed a bit. "Yes. That is the kind of thing I want to keep to myself. After all a girl has her own fantasies and very private thoughts you know!"

"I most certainly do know, Mary. Let us not dwell upon the past, but let's deal with the future instead, since that is where we all will be going." Guiness said in philosophical wisdom.

"Agreed." Mary said.

CHAPTER FORTY-NINE
HENRY COLLECTS FROM MARY

As if almost on cue, the doorbell rings its melodic Big Ben sounds. Mary does not rush to answer the door. She prefers to be very careful these days, what with all the recent "extras" in her life. Instead, she is cautious. She walks to the window and sneaks a peek through the curtains at who is requesting an audience.

She is both surprised and pleased to see that it is Henry coming for his Thursday collection. Mary sees that he is alone. That makes Mary happy, because she has met enough persons of varied character in her recent past and does not really want to meet more, at least for a while.

Mary takes her time walking to the door.

Henry, meanwhile, is standing at the door and is eager to meet BL again. He was not sure that Mary was at home, although she usually is on Thursday afternoons. He expected to see both of his friends, BL and Mary.

"Oh, no, Mary. Don't tell me that you are not going to open the door", thought Henry as he saw the curtains rustle. He was used to that because his experience has been that when that happens, he has another deadbeat on his hands. "Mary, please open the door" thought Henry almost speaking that thought vocally. Once again, as if on cue, Henry heard the doorknob turning and the door opened.

Henry was surprised that there was no one behind the door and that no one really turned the knob. Mary was several feet away from the door when it opened. Mary was quite amazed that the door she was ready to open actually opened by itself! She said to herself out loud, "Am I developing powers I did not know I had? Have I been keeping company too long with all these people who have such abilities? What is going on?"

It was not Mary who had powers. It was Henry. Henry was not even slightly aware that he even had the power of telekinesis. It was a power just developing within himself. Henry never knew that such a power even existed and never expected such a power to grow within himself!

"Mary, did you open that door?" Henry asked because he saw Mary standing too far away from the door to have opened it.

"No, Henry, I did not!" Mary exclaimed.

"Well, neither did I!" said Henry.

"Then who did it, Henry? If it wasn't me and it wasn't you, who was it?" Mary said. Mary and Henry just stood in dumbfounded silence there for a second or two. They were staring at each other and then at the door and back again.

Suddenly the silence was broken, "I did it you two numbskulls! Me, your BL or your Guiness! I did it!", said BL in a beaming and smiling glee. "I did it", he repeated for apparent emphasis. "I knew that Henry was behind the door and that Mary wanted to see him, so I just opened the door and killed two birds with one stone!"

Both Mary and Henry just stood there a second, staring at this nervy black cat who was bragging and strutting his extraordinary abilities. It was still taking the two of them a bit to get used to the fact that Guiness was not just the loveable black cat they had known in the past, but an extraterrestrial instead!

Mary said, "Guiness, did you really cause that knob to rotate and open the door?"

Guiness answered, "Of course I did. I used the same powers to open the cat food cans. That most certainly mystified Henry!"

"Wow!" said Henry. "I had guessed that it was you, but I decided that perhaps Jack Henigson came over to feed you occasionally, but I was not one hundred percent certain."

"Sorry", said Guiness. "It was I. I am really quite self-sufficient, you know."

Henry answered, "I can see that. I know you; you know. We made our acquaintance when I was at Jack's house along with Mr. Xilx. I know quite a bit about you and Mr. Xilx."

"Right-on boy!" answered Guiness in mellow British tones. "I have just used that very same technique to communicate my existence and my talents to Mary a short while ago. It was quite effective. I had to have Jack and Mr. Xilx lend me a hand to make the shock of having one's cat change into an interplanetary starship helmsman! Jack and Mr. Xilx both acted as intermediaries to make the blow easier for her."

"I knew that it was quite a shock for me to know that. How are you taking it Mary? Are you alright?" asked Henry.

"Oh yes", said Mary acerbically. "I am quite used to having a meteor slamming into my life. I meet people from outer space every day, literally. How was I to know that I was living with one?" Mary let out a short "Ha, ha" and threw up her arms signifying helpless despair.

"Well, I am happy to hear that you are o.k.", responded Henry.

"Of course you are." Mary said somewhat caustically. "After all Henry, they need told me that you are one of them!"

Henry protested emphatically, "No, Mary, I am not one of them. Definitely not!"

"Please explain, Henry. Please." Mary repeated.

"Well, it seems that I have certain abilities that few of us on earth have." Henry started. "I seem to have had some "gifts" bestowed upon me when I came into this world. I did not ask for them and I did not seek them."

Mary answered, "Henry, I am sorry. Perhaps I was a little too hasty and unfair. I should really understand where you are coming from. I have had a few extraterrestrial experiences myself. I have had some that one could say are mythological as well. Now", reflected Mary, "Who in the world has ever had one of those!"

"Really", said Henry.

"Really!" exclaimed Mary. "Really, really, really!" Mary exclaimed in frustration. She went on. "Henry, I know that you are a young man, but you are very mature for your age. That is good, because maturity and intelligence are two things we need. You know by now that I work for our government."

Henry answered hesitatingly, "I have heard something about it. Yes I do know that, but I do not know too much about what you do or even what your office is."

"That is both good and bad. It is good that you know something, but it is bad that you don't know more. Let me explain. As Jack told you, everything we tell you is top secret. You are to tell no one about what I am going to reveal to you. Do you agree to that?

"Henry nodded a yes which was accompanied by a faint and timid vocal, "Yes."

"Henry, I am head of a very top-secret agency within our government. My department is called the "Department of Extraordinary and Supernatural Events", usually abbreviated as "DESE." Mary informed Henry.

"Tell me more", said Henry.

"There is more, much more, Henry", said Mary. "I Think that I will let it all unfold with the passage of time. I understand that one of your "gifts" is reading other's thoughts, but that you are young and inexperienced in using that "gift", as it were."

"That is true, Mary," said Henry. "I do not mean to pry, but other people's thoughts just pop into my head without my trying. In fact, I am trying to control that feature. It is not easy, because it is a. subconscious."

"Well, Henry, we are going to have a DESE meeting of all our agents from around the country. The meeting is very secret because our organization is very secret. I need you to be there, Henry. There you will learn what our country is up against, and we will need to develop a plan to protect our country and ourselves.

"Mary, I know that I am quite young. I know that you have doubts about me as part of your DESE. I can assure you that I am up to whatever comes my way." Henry said.

"You are quite right, Henry. I need to question the fact that you are so young." Mary said and went on. "Nevertheless, you come highly recommended. Jack and Mr. Xilx, with whom I need a more personal interview, have informed me that you are developing certain gifts. Thought reading and input are only one of those gifts. Henry, this is quite extraordinary in our society. The "extraordinary" undoubtedly places you in the Department of Extraordinary Situations and Events without question. You will be an agent instead of an investigated phenomenon. We need people like you."

"Mary, which sounds like an invitation. I will accept. I love my country and will protect it with whatever means I have. If I am "gifted" then I will use those gifts in that direction. You do need to know that the "gifts" are many and they are developing exponentially without my even trying. Mary, it is almost frightening." Henry said.

"I do not think you need to be frightened, Henry", said Mary. "If you do have fears, get in touch with Jack. I am sure that he will be able to help and reassure you. I know that Jack thinks very highly of you and that he counts on your help very much. I also know that you will not disappoint him either."

"Agreed", said Henry. "Agreed. I could not disappoint Jack, especially now, after all that has happened to me and after all that I have learned about the world and myself. I am sure that you know a bit more than me. What I know is enough for me to probably make a career out of working for DESE in the defense of our nation and the world!"

"Excellent," said Mary. "I hope to have the DESE meeting by the end of next week, probably over the weekend. That would be most convenient for just about all our agents." Mary continued, "Travel arrangements are at the government's expense and facilities normally used by our government."

"Mary, that would be most convenient for me, also, since I am still a student in high school. I am eager to see and meet the different agents and hear all about them, what they do and most of all, what they need to say about our national trouble." Henry responded.

"Henry, I am glad to have you aboard and to have our new relationship out in the open. I would never have believed that the boy who delivers my papers would ever be an agent for me in DESE. I'll see you next Thursday and next weekend. I'll let you know when and where the meeting will be. Thanks, Henry."

With that Henry and Mary parted company. Henry went on to continue his paper route. The paper route was beginning to dim in relation to the new happenings in his life. Dealing with extraterrestrials and the development of extraordinary powers and abilities are most certainly more exciting. Nevertheless, Henry decided to keep the route as "cover" so as not to alert his friends and parents that his life has changed.

CHAPTER FIFTY

HENRY, JACK AND MR. XILX CONFER

Jack continued on his route, making his routine collections and missing those patrons who wanted to put off payment to another day. Henry knew that he would get them sooner or later. The routine of paper delivery and collection and even school was starting to get a little boring. Henry's life changed a lot. He found that he knew almost everything his school classes were to teach him. He did not know how it happened, but Henry's schooling abilities to learn, with no study, had his head reeling with knowledge far beyond that of his classmates and even his teachers. However, he knew that it would be necessary for him to continue what was a charade so as not to raise any suspicions of his changed psychic and mental powers as well as unrealized additional abilities, whatever they might turn out to be.

Henry continued his route to Jack Henigson's house. That is where he really wanted to be. He wanted to talk with Jack and Mr. Xilx about his meeting with Mary and the upcoming DESE conference. He needed to talk with them. He was happy to continue the newspaper front. It kept him in contact with Mary, Black Lightning, Jack Henigson and Mr. Xilx and all without raising any suspicions!

Jack's house was just ahead, and Henry now wasted no time getting to his front door. He was not surprised, this time, to see that the door was opening as he was approaching. There was no one at the door or even near it. It was Henry's desire to enter the house to discuss events with Jack that triggered his powers of telekinesis which unlocked Jack's door, turned the knob, and swung the door open. Henry knew he opened the door. He felt the power emanate from him as a laser beam to the door. It was a power of will. It was one he could not deny, or even control, in his youthful psychic development.

Henry also was not surprised to see Jack and Mr. Xilx waiting for him. They already knew that he was approaching and what was on his mind.

"Henry!" they both exclaimed at the very same time in choral unison. It was as though the two separate bodies acted as one as the word exited their mouths since their lip movements also were identical and in unison.

"How nice it is to see you!" said Jack. "I do not need to ask what this visit is about, besides the usual Thursday paper collection, because Mr. Xilx and I already know. However, let me hear it from your lips. Mental transference is nice but when you are in our presence it is always preferable to get the idea directly from its source. You are the source so let us hear exactly what you have in your mind!"

"Well," started Henry, I have just had a very nice visit with Mary. She told me all about herself and DESE. I know that she did not tell me everything because I was able to absorb some of unspoken thoughts. I know that she has her reasons. For instance, she wants me to experience meeting the different agents of DESE and hear their reports directly. I understood that she felt the impact upon me would be greater than if she simply explained what she knew. In any case, I also gathered that she, herself, is waiting to gather the full details of each report directly from each agent as well. She is not fully cognizant of the complete story each agent has to reveal. She is waiting as well for a full, detailed and comprehensive report from each of her various agents. In short, she realizes that she does not know everything either."

"Neither do we, Henry," said Jack. "We all will need to wait for the DESE meeting which will be scheduled for next weekend."

"How do you know that?" said an amazed Henry.

"Easy." Jack said. "First of all, it is in front of us and both on and in your mind, Henry. Second, we have already received a mental image from Mary. We know most of her deep thoughts just about as soon as she does. That is a necessity because of her position and in order to protect her from any harm as well."

"Oh", said Henry. "I understand. Does that mean that Mary has no secrets at all? Is that not a risk to her as well? I mean that if you can read her mind from so far away, can her enemies do the same?"

"Not really," said Jack. "I have taught her how to keep some of her most private thoughts to herself without allowing revelation to the outside world. She still needs to work on its improvement though. It is very astute of you to realize the liability of randomly broadcast thought. I can see that you also need to have some lessons in keeping some of your thoughts private as well. Unfiltered and widely broadcast random thought can endanger all of us. Since you will be a part of our team, it will be a requirement that you learn to control thought emanation as well, Henry. That will help to protect us and our missions."

"I am both excited and apprehensive at the same time in regard to this DESE meeting. Will it be something that I will need to be on guard about? I have no idea about why I would need to be there at all. Can you give me a clue?" Henry asked quite concerned.

"Actually, Henry," Jack continued, "I do have some ideas about why you should be there. Mary wants you to become fully informed and involved in what DESE is all about and how we protect our country against evil and harm. More so, we all do. We all want you to be there. That includes Mr. Xilx, your good friend, Black Lightning and I. There is much to learn there, Henry, and you need a lot of learning."

"You are probably right. I have learned a lot in the last few weeks. I guess that shows me there is most likely more for me to learn," answered Henry.

"Do not be too worried about the DESE meeting, Henry, you will be among friends. It is just a natural fear of the unknown that is bothering you and nothing more. I assure you that it will pass and when it does, you will be quite a changed and more confident individual," reassured Jack.

Mr. Xilx, who had been silent up to now, spoke up. "Henry, I know that you are full of fear. Henry, you see me here. I am not from your world. You know that. Henry, it is a big world and an even bigger universe. You will meet more people like me at the DESE meeting. Do you not think that would be interesting? Even more, you will meet creatures from your world that you never would have believed really existed. Henry, even more, all of the people that you will meet are your friends. There is nothing to fear, so be at ease."

"I do find your presence inspiring. To think that you have come from so far away to earth is amazing. It does show that we are not alone and that we need to keep our minds open." Henry answered.

Jack intervened with "Henry, let us keep our heads. The meeting will answer many questions and will give us a direction to go in."

"Agreed", said Henry. "You owe four dollars and fifty cents for the paper this week." Henry had more than enough of that conversational topic and changed it abruptly and without warning. Jack and Mr. Xilx both were surprised and returned Henry's change of topic with a second of stunned silence and rapidly followed with raucous laughter and delight.

Both Jack and Mr. Xilx once again, in unison, loudly said, "Agreed!" They were happy to have survived the gauntlet of Henry's fears. Once again, Jack paid his paper bill and added his usual generous tip. Then they said their goodbyes and Henry left.

CHAPTER FIFTY-ONE

THE DESE CONFERENCE

Mary awoke bright eyed and very excited this morning. She was full of unlimited energy and performing all her morning functions and duties with virtual lightning speed. This is the day that DESE has made for Mary's exhilaration. She had worked towards this day for quite a while. All her trips, all her consultations with agents in different parts of the country, all her planning and all her arranging have come down to this day. It could not be more important.

Mary studied her exercises in thought control that Jack Henigson taught her. The last thing she wanted was to have the "gifted" agents at the meeting know her thoughts before she could put them either in the order or in the context in which she wished to present them.

She showered, had herself a very good breakfast and a cup of the Asheville Fresh Foods' Café Angelica coffee. Her appetite returned in ravenous fashion and breakfast was quickly devoured.

The day was gorgeous. It was sunny and mild. The sky was a crystal-clear deep blue and almost cloudless. There was only a mild, caressing but occasional breeze and nothing more. Mary hopped into her car and made her way to the local DESE offices. She was eager to see Wyatt, Frank, and Matt from the California area, Seemore and Hepseva from the Fairbanks area, H. Brad Gaunt and Larry Carl from the Palm Beach area as well as Jim Barrett from the Cos Cob, Connecticut area. He is the GAO liaison who arranges payment for the meeting expenses including accommodations. His services were needed to provide for the expenses of this meeting.

The agents from across the USA were all staying at the same Hotel. That made it easier to transport them to the secure meeting room. The room was something like a dining hall. However, there was a big screen in the middle along with a podium and multiple loudspeakers so that no one would miss anything.

A midafternoon social hour preceded the actual meeting, and it was there that their earlier feeling of "old home week" developed. All the agents were feeling very much at home with people with like-minded goals and interests. It was also nice for them to meet agents they had not seen for a while.

When it came to agents Seemore and Hepseva, the usual, "All-American" appearing agents were a bit cautious since not many of them ever really met a real Gnome. They were not sure if what they were looking at was a gnome or a regular human midget. Most of them dismissed the Gnome idea, relaxed their apprehensions, and thought of them as midgets. It was a bit difficult for the Gnomes to overcome their timidity and to socialize, but they overcame their basic need for privacy for the greater good.

Mr. Xilx and Black Lightning would also have had a tough time fitting in except that they realized that "normal" humans might have difficulty in conversing with agents appearing as a cat and a six-legged "cat-dog". They simply adapted to the situation by corporeal transformation. Black Lightning turned back into that beautiful girl Henry met some time ago and Mr. Xilx turned himself into a rather very well dressed and dashing, well-educated older gentleman of the Sean Connery sort, but one who spoke with a Cockney accent! He was easy to spot! His appearance was outstanding, but the accent identified him immediately. They found the change easily made.

Jack arrived with Henry. He really was Henry's mentor. He was the person who inducted Henry to this extra-normal world. Henry relied on Jack to help him navigate his way among the different "agents" with both introductions and conversation. Henry had the feeling that he was walking on hot coals and was extra careful to neither be hurt nor offend anyone. Jack was his very able guide.

Larry Carl and HB Gaunt from sunny Florida came into the room. It was as though the sunshine delegation arrived at once. The Frank German and Matt Ovlas team from southern California followed them shortly after the Floridian entrance.

Mary was most interested in the entrance of Eddy Erp, who has been better known at DESE as Wyatt. Eddy is her main man, her investigatory contact from agent to agent, at least some of them anyway. Mary did her share of inter-agent communications and exceeded the number of contacts of any other agent. After all, it was her responsibility to watch over all her agents. However, she never thought of it that way. She felt it was just part of her job to make certain that each agent was productive and secure.

The meeting's social hour was quite delightful, but the time was coming when the meeting would be called to order. That time is now.

Mary left the reception floor and made her way to the podium where she announced, "This year's special Department of Extraordinary Situations and Events' meeting will now come to order. May I have your attention please?" She pounded the gavel three times and repeated both announcement and gavel once more.

The room slowly became silent. The agents all sat at their respective tables and ceased conversation. All eyes were on Mary.

"We have much to discuss and coordinate." Mary started. "You all have a Schedule of Presentations. Our group, while not small, is just about the right size to permit detailed reporting and deep discussion about each report. In other words, each agent will give his detailed report, holding back nothing. It is necessary to tell all, no matter how minor or embarrassing. That report may be followed up with questions and discussion. When all the reports are given, we will split up into three or four committees. Those committees will be assigned several different reports which will be summarized for a final analysis. Each committee will then recommend a means to deal with the problems and threats the contents a the particular report presents."

The room remained silent. Mary asked, "Are there any questions?"

The room remained silent. There were no questions. Mary was thankful about that. Mary said, "We will start with the first report. That report will be given by the Palm Beach team of Larry Carl and HB Gaunt."

The slight hum in the room ceased as the audience gave full attention to the two men at the podium.

HB started, "First I need to admit that my reluctant enlistment to DESE proved to be a pleasure. I have enjoyed each day of investigation into the strange events which have occurred in the Southeastern United States. I have learned much about my environment, but most of all and most importantly, I have learned about unseen and unannounced threats to our nation and our environment.

There is a group called the Veneficum that has vengeance and destruction of our economy and environment as its goal and wants to hurt us all, both as a people and as a nation. They have created the shaking of the earth in Southern Florida and freezing temperatures which have resulted in the partial destruction of Florida's crops and has killed some of the tropical birds and animals which are sensitive to that temperature drop. It was extensive in some areas, but not all over. The cold was sudden and lasted a day or two, which was enough to develop the destruction the Veneficum sought. The earthquake was minor. Many buildings in Florida are not that tall. The taller buildings in Miami, especially near Southpointe, suffered minor damage but the potential still exists for major destruction."

Larry Carl took over, "HB and I found and recorded a Veneficum meetup west of Juno Beach in the Indiantown area. We both overheard their plans directly via the "Cogito-Lector". HB and I recorded the entire meet on the TCC camera. Their plans included a peach blight for Georgia that would be certain to keep "Georgia on Your Mind". They also planned a watermelon and cantaloupe mold disease to further destroy the crops. If that were not enough, they also were planning a drought to be followed up with a grass and shrub fire which would create a longer lasting destruction and further economic and environmental loss throughout the entire southeastern states. Of course, this would include the loss of houses, other buildings, and an inadvertent loss of life as well. These people are very dangerous and are enemies of our nation."

HB again took over the podium, "When we get to our subcommittee meeting some of the committee members will take a peek inside the TCC photograph. They can only have a short and distant glance because entering that photograph could be perilous."

The two men left the lectern. Mary again took the podium.

"Thank you for that report gentlemen. The next report will be from Frank German and Matt Ovlas from southern California."

Matt and Frank went up to the podium. Matt started, "Fellow agents of DESE, I, Matt Ovlas, am also a reluctant recruit to DESE. I must admit that I was not actually that unwilling an enlistee. My friend Eddy Erp, or Wyatt as you know him, came to visit me at my humble abode in Huntington Beach. While he was there, we experienced a very unusual meteorological event. It was a very heavy snowstorm with over six inches of snow and ice accumulation. The snow alone was an extreme freak of nature if that is what it was. However, there had to be more than just nature involved. There had to be some kind of spell or curse on the entire southern California area because there was not even one cloud in the sky. The sun was shining all the time although the temperature dropped to below freezing in a matter of minutes from seventy-five degrees warm!

Wyatt and I were taking in the sights at the Huntington Beach Pier and had just finished a snack at Ruby's Restaurant at the end of the pier. We were enjoying the warmth and the sunshine when suddenly there was a snowflake and then another and another. By the time we got to our car, which was parked near the western end of Main Street and close to the pier, there was at least four to five inches of snow on the ground and the temperature was freezing! We barely made it home. Most Californians do not drive in snow so there were accidents all over the place! It was then that Wyatt asked my help and enlisted me in DESE. While I regret the snowstorm, I am happy that the event prompted Wyatt's offer of DESE recruitment."

Frank German then took over the podium from Matt.

"Hello. My name is Frank German. I have had an interest in strange and extraordinary events ever since the crash landing of extra-terrestrials at Area Fifty-one in New Mexico. I was a much younger man then who wrote about the crash site. I was one of those who never believed the story that all that they found was the remains of weather balloons. I still have an interest in the matter. That is why Mary Kent enlisted me in DESE.

The event that Matt just described to you certainly fills that bill regarding extraordinary events. The lack of clouds as a source of moisture for snowmaking is not a natural event. Snow is natural, but the time, place and circumstances of snow creation from a cloudless sky is not. The event was one caused by a regional division of the Veneficum. They caused destruction in southern California as they did in the southeastern part of the United States. You all know that California tends to be dry as far as moisture is concerned. As a result, we have had not only unexplainable snow, but also major fires destroying hundreds of acres and some houses. Fortunately, the loss of life has been low.

I used DESE equipment to record a meetup of the Veneficum in my area. My DESE TCC recording also can be seen by subcommittee members when we gather later in this meeting."

Matt took the podium again, "Wyatt and I did a little research at Huntington Beach. We located a place where a local coven was reported to gather in the Fountain Valley area. While neither of us cannot be certain, one of them certainly ran the bar we entered. It seems that a woman who tends the place can transform into a different creature. In this case, it was a parakeet. It was a talking parakeet as well. I know that you will say that parakeets talk and that it is not unusual, but this one can also think like a human being. In any case, it could think as an intelligent being. Neither Wyatt nor I can be sure that whatever it was, is human! We did not find a connection at the bar about the environmental changes, but the DESE recording does make the connection."

Mary reentered the stage and took the lectern. "Thank you for your report, Matt and Frank. The next report on the agenda is from agents Seemore and Hepseva from Alaska. Seemore and Hepseva come to us from the mountain chain between Norway & Sweden and we are incredibly happy to have them on our team." The room broke out in applause and whistles. The Seemores were very welcome indeed. However, the Seemores were not certain as to what all the commotion meant. They thought that they were not liked at all. The two were hesitant to approach the lectern. However, encouragement from the ever-present Mary prodded them on.

Seemore and Hepseva slowly, and cautiously, approached the lectern. Although they had met most of the people at the meeting, public appearances and public speaking was not their forte'. It is well known among Gnomes that associating with humans is bad enough, but speaking and partying with a bunch of them is unconscionable!

Seemore, being the head agent, took the bench, which was adjacent to the lectern and stood up on it. Fortunately, it was of the exact height he needed to reach the top of the podium and place his meager notes on it. Hepseva stood by his side for encouragement and goading him on. That was Hepseva's favorite thing to do, and she did it with delight. She enjoyed every second of it. Much to her surprise, she found greater pleasure when she could do it without fear of reprimand from Seemore and before a crowd! It was so delightful!

Seemore began, "I am not from your country, but I have learned to love it and I care for its welfare. Where I live, in the northwestern wilderness, I have noticed strange things happening. In Norway and Sweden, where we come from, we see the Northern Lights to our north. Here in the United States, the northern lights are to our south. This was reported to DESE. They told me that northern lights in southern Alaska is not the way it is supposed to be. It is an aberration. They, the DESE researchers, did not know it, but they were very right. It was not just an aberration, but an aberration of morality."

Hepseva tugged strongly at Seemore's jacket practically pulling him down off his bench. Seemore bent down to hear what was bothering his wife so much. He put his ear close to her so that he could listen to what she was saying. He nodded and returned back to his podium and stood back up on his bench.

"My wife, Hepseva, wants me to relate to you the events that Mary and I both witnessed in one of the DESE photographs we entered," said Seemore. "The DESE photographs are interactive. That means that we can physically enter and manipulate the live happenings within that photograph. The danger is that beings or events within that photograph can physically injure us, but only while we are present inside it. The beings within the photograph are captured in the picture and cannot exit. We can, on the other hand, both enter and exit the photograph."

Seemore continued. Hepseva was silent. "Mary and I both entered one of these pictures and we saw both witches and demons in it. We overheard how they control the northern lights as an exercise in magical power over the elements of nature. They were only testing their capabilities to affect our natural environment. One should recall that witches originally were guardians of the earth and its ecosystem. These witches have betrayed their country and now seek vengeance on man by disloyalty to those entrusted duties, mainly environmental protection and harming no one. "

Seemore paused and searched out the people in his audience, looking left to right. "I cannot tell you how frightening and risky it is to be in a situation where you are in danger of being discovered and harmed by demons or evil witches." Seemore added emphatically, "You need to understand that by injuring or destroying us, even though the picture is one which occurred in the past, those witches or demons can affect us in the present. Once we are maimed, or even killed, that injury will carry forth into our present. Our present would be their future. If we are injured in that past picture we are also injured in the present. We most certainly do not want to be killed either in the past or in the present. In short, we do not want to expose ourselves to that risk any longer than necessary. The DESE photographs, while they record historical events, can be very dangerous because of the interactivity attribute which can affect the present."

The small man standing on a bench at the podium created a quasi-comical sight, with his reddish nose and white beard bobbing up and down as he spoke. Nevertheless, his audience was very quite, very attentive and above all, very respectful. Here was a person who was almost a mythical creature himself relating some unpleasant and risky experiences. There was not one person in the audience who moved. It was almost as though no one was even breathing as they remained there entranced and frozen in time.

Seemore went on. He found himself to be a bit of a ham in front of an audience and he surprised himself. However, Seemore could not help himself. He had all these words and stories to relate that he had kept pent up within his mind and heart for decades. Hepseva was aware of what was happening to Seemore. Seemore was being afflicted with what Gnomes call the "Gnome Traveler Flu". It is like a cold that affects only Gnomes. Their nose gets redder and redder. They tend to release all their pent-up emotions and thoughts. Hepseva stepped in to save Seemore from himself. She again tugged at his jacket.

Seemore looked down at Hepseva. He knew what was happening to him and he appreciated Hepseva's intervention. He whispered to her, "I know. I know. I will stop right away. Just one more story, please. Kick the bench out from under me when I finish that one. All right? Seemore asked plaintively.

"All right." said his loving Hepseva and threw him a hidden kiss, which Seemore appreciated.

"Now these witches have their evil friends with their evil powers." Seemore continued with an authoritarian index finger waving in the air like a musician conducting an orchestra. "We, Hepseva and I, as well as DESE, have our own, almost blessed, powers and friends. I can only tell you that mythology is not all make believe. Some of it is real and most of it is on our side: the side of good over evil."

Seemore had to stop because somehow the bench fell out from under him. That "somehow" was Hepseva. Instead of being angry with her, he hugged and thanked her for her rescue. He did not want to reveal Gnome secrets, such as his friendship with Peganni, to any crowd. He was heading that way. Hepseva's running interference saved him.

Mary, the DESE meeting organizer once again took the podium. "Thank you, Mr. Manlein for that very informative report." Mary did not dwell on the Manlein report particulars and seemed not to want the audience become too afraid of what Seemore said, so she rapidly moved on the next speaker.

Mary looked around for that speaker. There were about four more. Mary said, "Jack Henigson, are you here?"

The response came from the back of the room, "Yes, Mary, I, and my entourage are here!" Jack called out.

"Very well, Jack could we have you come up to the podium for a short presentation?" Mary asked.

"Of course, Mary; May I bring my associates up as well?" asked Jack.

"Certainly, Jack. The audience will be very happy to meet them and it would be very nice if they had a proper introduction to the DESE organization." Mary answered pleasantly.

There was commotion at the far end of the audience as Jack and his following made their way to the podium. Chairs had to be moved this way and that in order to accommodate the wheel chair's width and the three people who were with Jack. One could hear the apologies from Jack and his associates as they bumped and displaced people on their way up to the stage along with the expressions of discomfort the disturbed audience members experienced.

Finally, Jack's chair made it to the stage and Jack approached the podium. He lowered the microphone to his chair and said, "My dear fellow DESE members, it is a pleasure to be here this afternoon both to meet and become acquainted with you all. It is very necessary that we meet because we have a grave threat against our country and us. It is a threat that is not fully developed at this time. I want you to know that it is real and will manifest itself unless we meet and challenge it right away. There is no more time left."

Jack paused, both for effect and to check if the audience was receptive to what he was reporting. He wanted to be certain that he had their full attention. The audience was becoming genuinely concerned as to what was being reported between Seemore Manlein and Jack Henigson. They all were starting to develop the thought that not only their country was in danger but also they themselves. The audience stirred and murmured.

Jack went on, "You all here present know of the different types of equipment DESE owns and which we have in our armamentarium. You have some of it in your closets and in use in the field. You are to get it all out of the closet and out of mothballs and put it to use. This is not a war where conventional weapons are used. This war is not even yet declared, either against us or by us against our recently discovered enemies. It is truly a battle belonging solely to the Department of Extraordinary Situations and Events. What is happening, as you have heard in the reports given here today, is that we are being assaulted on environmental, agricultural and financial fronts. It is a battle where magic and malevolent spirits are involved."

Jack paused to take a sip of water. He continued, "There is need for the joining of each of us, in unison, to function as one body. We are that body, but we need to have an intelligent, coordinated plan to deal with these forces in full strength. We have many different peoples on our side who have joined our need to preserve our country, our society and our way of life, as we know it. Not all these people are necessarily from our world or our culture. In that diversity we have even greater strength."

Jack took another sip of water. "I have with me some friends who are and are not from our world. We are blessed with their modesty and their wish to join in defending our country against those who wish us harm. The time has come for you to meet them."

The three people standing alongside Jack straightened themselves up and smoothed their clothing, preparing themselves to be formally introduced to their DESE associates.

"I first want to introduce someone whom each one of you would never think could be a DESE member. This person is gifted in many ways and mature beyond his years. He is a young man I have known for quite a while now. I have watched him grow. He is my paperboy. I would like to have Henry come to the microphone and say a few words." Jack said as he turned towards the reluctant Henry. Henry was being physically pushed to the podium by his extraterrestrial friends, Mr. Xilx and Black Lightning who will be known at this meeting simply as Elizabeth Sam.

A spectator who was seated near the podium could overhear Henry saying, "O.K., O.K. I am going! All right!"

Henry was headed toward the lectern, but it was under visible protest. He was not eager to give any type of talk. He did not see himself as an extroverted and chatty type of being. Getting to the lectern was not his choicest thing to do. Nevertheless, he saw it as a duty and, despite his wishes to the contrary, he would see it through.

Jack shook Henry's hand as he approached the podium. "Ladies and gentlemen, I present Henry to you."

Henry was now at the podium. He looked out at his fellow DESE members and received the surprise of his life! He could hear their thoughts very clearly. If he wanted to focus on one thought over the many others, all he had to do was to face the direction that thought was coming from just as if he were facing a source of light. That would permit him to have an increased focus on that one thought and amplify it to the exclusion of the many other thoughts in that room, even though they were generated at the same moment.

Henry began, "I want to thank Jack for that very nice introduction. I have found my new membership in DESE to be very enlightening."

Henry noted a thought projection about his youth and the inappropriateness of his being a member of DESE. Another thought projected towards him was that he would probably make an error which could cause DESE to lose its special relationship with the government and the direct control of the President, both in the reporting and control of the organization as highly secret one.

Henry went on pointedly towards the critics. "To those of you who think that I am too young for this group I need to admit to my age. However, you do know that I have several additional gifts, which are not yet known to me. I also have been told by my mentors that these gifts will manifest themselves as time goes on and as I mature. For instance, I hear right now from Valerie Ovlas, sister of Matt Ovlas of Huntington Beach, California, who reported earlier to you, that I could make an error which might endanger DESE's relationship with the executive branch of our government."

There was an "Oh my goodness!" low-level cry from the middle of the seated group of delegates. It was from Valerie Ovlas. As far as man named Alex Rekrap goes, you do not need to think that my youth is inappropriate for DESE membership. I think I have proven my point. I know what all of you are thinking immediately as you think it!"

There was a minor commotion happening in the middle of the other side of the aisle as Alex Rekrap nervously shuffled about in his chair. He doubled the commotion as his chair tipped over, spilling him out on the floor and onto the laps of some unfortunates sitting behind him. He was very apologetic and embarrassed as well.

The audience was quite hushed now. Each one of them had to be afraid to even to think now because Henry would know their thoughts. That this person, this man who was really just a high school boy, could have such abilities was frightening. They were all afraid, and that combined thought reached Henry. He said reassuringly, "You do not have anything to fear. Most of your thoughts are ignored. Only evil thoughts are remembered, and for good cause. That cause is for the protection of each one of us and our nation."

Henry was pleasantly surprised as some very nice thoughts now came his way. He went on, "I have enjoyed meeting all of you. I know that we will all work together for the betterment of our country, our planet and our society. I thank those of you who are sending me nice thoughts and for your attention."

With that, Henry left the podium to the small roar of a thunderous and appreciative applause.

Mary, the default master of ceremonies, went back up to the podium. "I think you can now understand why Henry is an asset to DESE personnel. Despite his youth, we can recognize that his potential is just developing. Henry will be more of an asset as time goes on and his abilities are multiplied."

Mary continued, "It is my pleasure to now have you meet the next remarkable agent who is really out of this world. Elizabeth Sam came to our team a short time ago. She is a very attractive young lady. However, do not let that deceive you. She has abilities and attributes beyond comprehension. She is quite complex and mysterious in many ways. Elizabeth, would you please come to the podium?

With that introduction, a slim, tall woman in a nicely fitting black sheath dress came up to the lectern. She smiled a winning smile. When she smiled, ample lips separated showing beautifully shaped and even, white teeth. As she took the stand, her orientally shaped yellowish eyes joined the smile. Her face glowed with the glamour of youth.

She addressed her audience, "Good afternoon. I am very happy to be with you and DESE. We all have a major and very serious task before us. DESE has excellent instruments in its armory to deal with the problems we are facing right now. Only about half of you are aware that any problems exist. You will learn something about them now and in your reference committees when they meet. We face an attempt to destroy our country from within. It is not by direct attack on our cities and our people. It is an indirect attack, which will hurt us financially, agriculturally and environmentally. Some of our citizens may be hurt physically or even killed."

Elizabeth went on after a short pause and a sip of water, "We know that the army that is making the attack is a result of the evil within some of our own fellow citizens. They use a force beyond nature and are controlling its destructive forces. This means no weapons, guns, bombs or anything of that kind will attack us. The attack is more insidious than that. Things will happen that are outside the realm of normal. For instance, we may suffer extreme heat, a very long dry spell, a rash of tornadoes and hurricanes. Tsunamis, forest fires, windstorms, snow, hail, excessive rain and flooding are the kinds of weapons that will be used to hurt us. I do not want to leave out volcanoes and earthquakes as well. The actions will not be overt. We need to determine which calamities of nature are caused by these evil forces and which are not."

Elizabeth went on, "In any case, DESE and our innate abilities will provide us with whatever is needed to confront these problems and defeat them. It will not be an easy battle because of the stealth of our enemy. It will not be easy because the enemy is within. We will need to identify our enemy in order to counteract their evil."

Elizabeth closed her talk with, "I hope to meet and work with each one of you and consult with each reference committee as we develop a mode of confrontation to deal with this problem. Thank you."

Mary thanked Elizabeth and then turned to the final DESE agent and Jack's companion. "I would now like to introduce the next remarkable agent. He is Mrazy Xilx. His abilities and capabilities are enormous. We still are not fully aware of all his abilities. We only know that he is on our team, and we are grateful for that. Mr. Xilx, would you please come up and address our agents?"

This time there was no pushing or shoving. Mr. Xilx was pleased to address his fellow agents. He took his suave and dashing self to the podium. He is not a very young man, but mature with graying hair at the edges of a widow's peak hairline. His dress is very neat and in the latest fashion. His three-piece tweed suit with a buttoned vest sported a golden chain, which went to a pocket watch he kept in a vest pocket. He cleared his throat and followed that up with a "Harrumph". Then he began to speak in his Cockney accent.

"Good afternoon, my fellow DESE agents" he began, "It is with great pleasure that I am here today. I have come a very long way to be here, but that is a story for another day. Our country is in danger from within. We have elements within our borders, which seek to destroy a lot of what we know. There can be no limit as to what their capabilities may be. We do know that they are conspiring with demons and other evil spirits. Mortal man may not have sufficient powers against these supernatural beings. Of course, with DESE agents such as Seemore, Henry, Jack, Elizabeth, and I, DESE has excellent capabilities to destroy the evil they wish to impose on our nation and probably eventually the entire planet. The intelligence that the four of us have gathered from the mental emissions around the world is that our nation, in particular, is at the highest level of danger and most likely to be attacked.

I am receiving brain wave broadcasts from this audience. The basic question is "What do we have in our possession to deal with the evil at hand and what do you need to offer in our defense?"

Mrazy Xilx went on, "I think that you all are aware of the different devices DESE has. If you are not familiar with them, then it is your duty and obligation in this virtual emergency to know your equipment.

Another question being mentally broadcast to me is "What do the four of you need to offer in the defense of our country? Further, there is a demand that I prove myself. Very well, I shall."

Mr. Xilx continued, "As a showing of what abilities I have, I would like to first apologize for the disarray we caused in your seating arrangements as we all approached the stage from the rear. Second, I would like to correct the seating, not to where you were earlier, but to a more organized, orderly seating arrangement accommodating all of us, and with a decent center aisle for wheelchair use included, be made."

The audience murmured in questioning tones. Mr. Xilx continued, "Before I do that, I need to have those of you who have seats take those seats and hold firmly onto the arms. Those of you, who have no seats, please go to the back of the room now and stay close to the wall. He then asked rhetorically: "Is that done?"

The audience again answered with a buzz and signified that they had.

"Good", said the speaker. "Please hold on."

With those words, the chairs, including the people seated in them moved slowly at the start. Soon they moved at a faster pace. They rearranged themselves as in an auditorium with a wide center aisle, big enough to accommodate Jack's wheelchair. Some of the chairs elevated themselves, including their occupants, and flew into the air above other chairs when they were in the way. Multiple chairs were flying about with their occupants tightly holding on fearing for their safety. The audience was spellbound, silent and in awe.

Mr. Xilx continued, "Is everybody all right? Now, this is the arrangement your chairs should have been in at the beginning. Is this a sufficient display of our abilities?" the speaker asked in earnest.

The audience murmured again in a definite yes.

"This has been only a modest showing of our abilities. We will use whatever powers we need to deal with the threat from the Veneficum."

The audience spoke among themselves, but the only intelligible sound at the podium was just a buzz, buzz, buzz. However, the mental broadcasting by the spectators showed a positive response.

"Very good", came the response from Mrazy Xilx. "I thank you for your attention. Now Mary has something to say."

Another round of applause ensued. Mary approached the lectern with a business-like walk. She was definitely pleased. The demonstrations of supernatural abilities was unexpected but welcomed. It showed that all the powers were not just the province of the evil witches. DESE has its share of gifted people as well and witchcraft or magic had nothing to do with it at all.

Mary started, "My fellow DESE agents, I would think that the abilities just demonstrated is more than just adequate proof that we are able to deal with the evil powers at hand. What is more amazing is that this is not the end of all the powers these very special agents possess."

Mary paused. "It is now time to have our reference committees deal with each of the several topics at hand as well as those brought up at this presentation. You will arrange yourselves into groups and find space in each of the rooms which are adjacent to this meeting room. We will meet here again in one hour when each of the groups will make separate recommendations sought to solve each problem. One of each of our field experienced agents will either be with your group or will visit while you deliberate."

With that, the audience shuffled about, arranging with their peers to develop their groups and get off to their reference meeting rooms.

CHAPTER FIFTY-TWO
REFERENCE COMMITTEES

The first committee reheard the stories of Frank German and Matt Ovlas about the snow and cold in southern California. Matt told of the sudden Huntington Beach snow storm and Frank spoke of the cold around San Diego, the destroyed crops, the mixed up traffic lights, and the switched one way signs. Both of these incidents caused numerous accidents and injuries.

The reference committee members found all that very curious. They all wanted to know the "why". Why would something like this happen? Why would DESE agents be involved with these matters? They were supposing that the entire events, both in Huntington Beach and San Diego were just a freak of nature and that is all there is to that!

An agent in the front row stood up and said, "Frank and Matt, strange things can happen in nature. Why do you think that there is and extraordinary situation here? Do you not feel that all this is just one of those freaky things? Are you not making too much of this?"

Matt rose and answered saying, "It is true that there are weird happenings in nature. However, snow always comes from clouds. There is usually a dark and dismally cloudy sky. We had only sunshine and a warm day beforehand. There were no clouds at all. That is more than just a freak of nature!

Frank interjected his defense as well, "It has never been that cold in San Diego. That is the place where the finest climate in the United States resides! Anyway, south of us in Tijuana and north of Los Angeles, it was seventy-eight degrees warm! In Imperial Valley to our east, it was close to one hundred degrees warm! Cold to freezing temperatures simply do not occur in spots like that. It covers much larger areas and weather forecasters have some idea of its coming and its going. There was no warning and the meteorologists are all in defense mode. They have no explanation of what happened at all!

Matt then took over for a quick second with, "We know that it has gone beyond nature. We know that the cause is by malevolent beings, human and otherwise. We know that they are mean and vindictive and without mercy. Frank has the proof you need. We need your help."

Frank introduced the topic of the TCC photographs. "I have the proof right here in these thick cardboard tubes. You will note that these tubes are well sealed and locked. The DESE Extraordinary Clampers guard them. These Clampers are a combination of a Engineering breakthrough and Magickal spells. We must treat them with care. Otherwise, they will clamp onto whoever is unauthorized to open them. It would be more than just a severe "bite" because they also bark. Furthermore, they will chase the unauthorized person until they catch him."

The audience murmured and backed into their seats and increased the distance between them and the possibly hazardous clamps on the tubes.

"Henry and Frank both asked in unison, "Would anyone like to view the photographs?"

A snarly-nosed middle aged man with graying hair and a receding forehead, in a widow's peak, stood up and questioned the veracity of the two presenting agents. "How can we believe what you are saying? You say that the so-called proof is in those cardboard tubes. What kind of proof could that be? Are there snowstorms in those tubes? Is there arctic cold and wind in those tubes? I need to see that before I can believe anything. Supernatural effects, witches and evil spirits! Nonsense! Ha! Bah! I want to see what you have in those tubes, now!"

The snarly-nosed man's mouth also snarled. He was obnoxious and as nasty as nasty could be. He was New England, especially Massachusetts nasty. The two agents, Matt and Frank were taken aback by the apparent antagonism of this man. He did not seem to be the cooperative type at all, but adversarial instead.

Matt responded. "Certainly. We will be very happy to show you any photograph you wish. You need to know that there need to be rules. You must agree to them before we can even start. Since either Frank or I need to accompany you, should you wish to enter the picture, you must know that you need to follow our direction or else you cannot enter the picture, This is for the safety of both of us. Do you agree?"

The hook-nosed man uttered a reluctant, sneering and contemptuous, "Very well. I agree."

"All right. The audience must stand back as I open the tube and give me a lot of space. When I open the tube, the photograph in it will expand rapidly, something like the air bag in a car and almost that fast. It will be between ten and fifteen feet long and between eight to ten feet high, depending on the height of this room's ceiling. Furthermore, only one other person is permitted to enter the picture with the accompanying agent for safety's sake. This is something like entering a tiger's cage, but different. In some ways, it is more dangerous. In both cases, it is possible to lose your life. Do you all understand?" Frank asked authoritatively.

The audience answered in unanimity with a loud and uninhibited, "Yes!" Then they all moved their chairs towards the rear wall, but keeping the same seating pattern.

Frank then stepped towards the tubes and chose one at random along with the still sneering man. Frank asked, "What is your name?"

The man answered, "I am Harum Holgash."

"Do you have a next of kin?" asked Frank.

The man became a bit uneasy and hesitatingly asked, "Why? Why do you ask that kind of question? Are you trying to intimidate me?"

Frank responded, "No intimidation intended. You need to know that what we will be doing shortly is very dangerous. If we are killed when we are in that photograph, we will not be returning here. Ever. We will be permanently dead. We need to know who to contact in your family. Do you understand?"

"Wait a minute. This is very serious. I am having second thoughts about this." Harum said.

Frank answered, "Harum, you have raised the question of proof. It is a valid and a good question. If you follow my instructions while we are in the picture, we should be all right. We will not be there very long. If it starts to appear that it will become dangerous, we will just step out of the picture. The evil ones in the picture are not able to follow us but you must stay close to me at all times, just in case we need to leave quickly. Again, do you understand?"

This time Harum answered a more subdued "Yes. I understand and I will follow your lead."

"Very good", Frank answered. "Let us get started. As Frank said those words, he spun the combination on the clamp and whispered some words to it in a low tone so that no one could hear them. The clamp opened and dropped to the floor where it lay quietly. Frank then reached into the three-foot long container and withdrew the photograph. It immediately grew to its fifteen-foot length and raised itself to the ten-foot ceiling.

One could see the details of the photograph. No figures, or other elements, were in motion. It was just a plain, but enchanted, photograph or so it appeared. The saying goes that appearances can be deceiving and that is the case here. The photograph is similar to a video placed on "pause". The uniqueness of it is that in order to get that "video" running, it has to come to life. It does that when you enter the picture. On the lower left of each photograph is an unmarked entry point known only to DESE operatives. Frank takes Harum by the hand and leads him to that point and into the photograph.

Harum is shocked. He loudly says, "Wow!"

Frank is now shocked and quickly places his open hand over Harum's mouth. Frank says in a firm, low measured tone, "Quiet. You are placing us in danger. We are in live enemy territory! Just be silent, make no sound. Follow me and you will have all the proof you need."

With that Frank and his companion, Harum, made their way around several trees and bushes until they came to a spot near the protected crest of a hill where they could look down on a gathering. In the middle of the group of fifty or so people was a low wood fire. The people attending are adorned in all kinds and colors of robes. Some wore strange, pointed hats with broad brims. Some of the vestments looked new while others were very worn and even patched. The center of attention was the five persons who lined themselves at the tips of a five-pointed star drawn in scraped markings on the ground. The fire formed the center of the star. Each of the five persons was staring outwardly from the fire and appeared as though they were the guardians of the fire. The remaining forty-five or so participants arranged themselves in groups of nine and each approached the "guardian" stationed at the tip of the pentagram. Owls and vultures were flying directly over them apparently for protection and as lookouts. Occasionally, a newly visiting witch would fly in on the latest model broomstick and some others would leave the same way. The majority of them stayed at the meetup.

Frank and Harum could hear the words clearly. Frank had the Cogito-Lector pen with him and he pointed it at the speakers. Now they not only could easily and clearly hear what they spoke, but also what they were really thinking.

The witches at the points of the stars spoke in a chant. "Master of our needs, master of our desires, master of our powers, master of darkness we ask you to appear to us and give us guidance and increase our powers. We beg your help."

These witches repeated these words again and again in a monotonous chant. Harum and Frank just kept their covert position. They were frozen in awe at the sight. Their awe was only increased when, in a flash of light, as if an explosion and out of the middle of the star and the center of the fire, arose a figure. It was an unearthly, bright red and scaly creature in the form of a very tall man over seven feet high. It had a short, pointed tail, squinty eyes, and a pointed, bearded chin and a sharp, long, pointed mustache. The creature grinned a broad, toothy grin and stepped out of the fire.

When the creature stepped out of the now low burning flames, those surrounding the fire cheered loudly. The guardians of the pointed star reassembled themselves in a grouping with one witch at their head and the remaining four paired behind him. The head witch was the spokesman.

The five witches, neatly dressed in their finest outfits, bowed down in unison and said, "Welcome, master to those who are your servants. We ask your counsel and assistance."

The creature grunted his acknowledgement of their welcome and waived his left hand.

The five then led the creature to a glowing red, throne-like chair, which appeared out of nowhere, in the middle of the pentagram star where the now disappeared fire had been located. The creature took his seat.

"It is with great pleasure and satisfaction that I visit you. I will provide as much help as you request." The creature spoke echoing a deep, raspy, almost guttural voice. The witches were silent, and their attention was fully on the creature. The flying witches, vultures and owls took to landing and were attentive to the creature and his words. They understood who he was.

"Master", said the head witch, "It is our desire to right the wrongs this country has befallen upon us. The pain and unjust and unfair justice given to our brothers and sisters Martha Corey, Rebecca Nurse, Sarah Good and others accused and tried in Salem, Massachusetts on March 1, 1692 is to be avenged, even at this late date. The world, especially this country, has to know that there are consequences to be paid for the wrongful and irreversible treatment of persons our persuasion, no matter that it happened so long ago. We simply seek justice."

The creature responded, "Justice indeed. Justice is not what you are seeking. However, it is a sort of justice that you seek. You are looking towards the settling of scores in an extreme solution. I can see your thoughts, and I can see deep into your hearts. I know what lies there; it is vengeance."

The head witch answered, "Yes Master, this is ultimately what we are seeking. The ruin of what this country holds dear, its resources, its produce, its centers of government and its people. The lack of respect for what we, the multiple covens around this country, hold dear and our rejected beliefs and desires is what we want to avenge."

The creature responded, "It will be as you request. Your need is my need. I will provide you with the power to amplify your own spells as high as your need may be."

The head witch said, "Thank you master. Thank you." Then the five central witches again bowed down.

The creature announced, "This visit is completed." Those words and a wave of his left hand resulted in the flash disappearance of the throne and of the creature himself. The fire did not return. Its remains were just low smoldering and coals emitting the blackest smoke. The owls and vultures returned to their flight. The witches wished each other a "Merry Meet" and started to leave.

Suddenly, a vulture called out, "We have spies. We are being spied upon. Two non-believers are searching us out. They are spies! Warning! Warning! Warning!"

That was all that Frank needed to hear. He rapidly and roughly grabbed Harum by the hand and forced their retreat towards the exit. A bolt of lightning struck the earth near them, and where they were standing, raising up a cloud of fire and dust. The witches were on them! Harum and Frank ran for their lives! Then Harum tripped on a protruding root. Frank, panicking, pulled Harum up and they continued their run. They could see the shadows of one of the witches on the hill's crest and several witches on brooms, flying overhead and virtually dive-bombing towards them. There was not a moment to spare. The witches were almost on them. Then Frank even more firmly grasped Harum's hand and did not let go. Harum returned the firm grasp, not wanting to be left behind. The risks now became quite obvious to him. Frank jumped out of the picture and the nearly dragged Harum followed, both covered in sweat and breathing heavily.

"Wow!" exclaimed Harum, struggling to catch his breath, but gasping and speaking at the same moment, "That was an experience I do not want to repeat."

Frank asked, "Now you can say your "wow" out loud. We are safe."

Harum looked at Frank earnestly and responded, "I think I have all the proof I will ever need. Thank you."

Harum addressed the reference hall. "My fellow DESE agents, it is all true and then some more. We are in very great danger, even now. I have seen the proof and it is very real. Frank and I were almost caught by witches and evil creatures. We are up against black magic, evil itself in the most demonic forms and even demons themselves. We must do all we can to win this effort. Our country is in danger as are we all."

The crowd acknowledged Harum's report and gave a positive response via their usual murmur.

CHAPTER FIFTY-THREE
REFERENCE COMMITTEE TWO

Reference committee two met right next door to reference committee one. Each of the committees met in numerical order along the side of the main meeting room.

HB Gaunt and Larry Carl were the main attraction. They took steps to organize the meeting and get it started.

Larry Carl called the reference committee to order. "Attention please. Would you all be seated so that we can get started?" said Larry in a firm, authoritative tone. "The matters before us are serious and we need to examine the facts and come up with some kind of conclusion when the main meeting resumes in about a half hour or so."

The dozen or so people in the meeting room turned their attention to the podium and then they turned again and found their seats.

Larry Carl began, "It is with great pleasure that I have met all of you. We have much in common, especially now. HB and I are located in the southern Florida region. We monitor northerly into the Smoky Mountains in the North Carolina-Tennessee area. Together we have experienced powers that are not natural. In any case, the environmental events we have witnessed have never been seen or noted in the area HB and I monitor. These events simply never happen. They are totally abnormal to the point of being unnatural."

HB took over the stand, "Abnormal and unnatural are simply words!" HB urgently and loudly exclaimed to a shout, "The experience of an earthquake in Florida and freezing cold are more than just freaky events. Environmental experts cannot explain any of the happenings in any way. They all say that what happened is not possible. However, these events did happen! They did! It does not matter whether it is possible or not. The happenings we have experienced first-hand are so spooky that they had to have been caused by powerful, paranormal controlling forces."

Larry Carl now pushes HB aside, as HB had done earlier to him, to gain the stand. "That is what we first thought!" Larry exclaimed. "That is until we found actual proof of unnatural influences on our environment. We have seen those who are causing our southeastern climatological problems. They are not all human, and those that were, are not the most savory type of person you would trust to watch your baby sister! We have seen them. They are witches and warlocks! There may have even been some short and strangely deformed non-human creatures, goblins and such, among them."

Larry continued, "They have targeted certain areas as test points. For instance, they took the canalled area near fifty-sixth court in Fort Lauderdale opposite the Presbyterian church on Federal Highway, as a test case. Not all the canals except that one near fifty-sixth court were affected. HB and I watched and listened as the witches chanted, "Idushka, Idushka Macht Ihre Haus Unterwasser, Unterwasser Sein." They repeated it again and again, at least several dozen times in a dull, monotonous chant.

As they chanted, the fire in the center glowed brighter and brighter, as each emphasized word was intoned, although the flames were no higher. It pulsated and pulsated, brighter and brighter with each risen vocal tone as each word was spoken. It was as though it were a transmitting beacon of power! Eventually we came to realize that was exactly what it was.

The pulsating fire was actually a transmitter. It was a transmitter of evil. One could see emanations of convection-like currents of air radiating out of its center. The exception was that these currents, when you looked at them closer, revealed miniscule spirits of what appeared as thousands of fiery demons with pointed chins, pointed noses, and tiny horns on sharply sloped-back foreheads. They were smaller than snowflakes and their tiny faces wore a gleefully mischievous smile as they flew up and away from the fire. From far away, they looked like sparks. Closer up or with a powerful spyglass, it was different. The nearly microscopic demons flew up from the fire and scattered in all directions up into the darkness of the night air. They were well on their way to do the witches' bidding.

We later learned that rising waters flooded all the houses at the northern branch at fifty-sixth court. The water rose about twenty-five feet above flood stage, but fortunately only caused minor damage. The remarkable thing about it was that this was the only canal that rose way above flood level. The adjacent canals were left without experiencing any effect at all. It was only one canal that was affected out of all of the ten or so canals!"

This was just another one of their Florida test cases. The witches only needed to make certain that all their powers were powerful, intact and working. They were. This was only a test.

Cindy Park, a stickler for details, rose in the center of the audience and said in a firm, strong and almost a scolding tone, "All right. Now that we have knowledge of what is going on, what are we to do about it? How can we combat such supernatural powers? Do we have the ability to deal with these people? "

She went on, "The word "people" brings up the question of identification. Sure, it is easy to know who they are when we can see them at one of their so-called "meetups" and dressed in their witchery outfits. However, when they are not at these meetings, they live among us and for all we know they could be our neighbors. How will we know them?"

Mr. Carl answered, "Cindy that is an excellent question. Identification of individuals is neither completely difficult nor is completely easy. We have the means to read thoughts and moods of populations en masse. Our instruments focus down to specific areas and then to specific individuals. The technique is sort of like a microscope, going from low to higher powers.

In any case, you can see them all around you. Some are actively causing unrest. That is one of their goals: to disrupt the organized society we have developed over the several hundred years our country has been growing. When you see people who do not respect the outcome of a properly performed election or legal trial and they are protesting in violence and in groups, someplace in the midst of those people will be one of the evil ones, betraying what is good and just in our society."

Larry went on, "The same thing goes for those who do not respect the law and the courts the judges and the police officers who are entrusted to enforce the law for the benefit of all of us. When the president comes to town and there are those who allegedly are angry with his guidance and his decisions. Their malicious signs and booing and sometimes violent behavior belies an evil one in their midst. Their disrespect for the man overcomes their respect for the office. They display their contempt in pathetic, violent, or nearly violent, and unfairly insulting protest. There will be at least one of the evil ones in their midst, perhaps several, each one of them goading the unruly mob on and encouraging their disrespect and lack of civility and encouraging the basic destruction of society. These otherwise innocent individuals become the unwitting instruments of societal devastation and they now do not respect the fact that a majority of voting fellow citizens respects the man. Otherwise, he would not be in office. Such events tear down our civilization bit by bit insidiously. We eventually can become so accustomed to these means of violent protest so much so that we may all consider such protest as being a normal and permissible event, which it is not."

Larry went on with his lecture, "Sure, it is all right to protest, but people do not need to be crass, crude and lack dignity both for themselves and those they gripe against. People of limited intelligence resort to this form of demonstration that borders on anarchy. That is the limit of their personal resources. To call another person vile names destructs civility and our social structure. There are other ways that intelligent, civilized persons express their disapproval. Their vituperative expression is influenced by the evil beings that are hidden in our midst. You can just sense the unreasoning, evil hatred if you are ever in the middle of one of those demonstrations. You develop an eerie, creepy feeling which can be frightening. You fear for your safety in those demonstrations because the raw emotion they develop is guided by the evil-motivated ones. It is truly dangerous. Can you imagine someone in their midst who has a contrary opinion? So much for freedom of speech. They would irrationally and physically destroy him!"

Cindy, now apparently the spokesperson for the group, once again rose and said, "I can appreciate what you say. I have personally witnessed such events and we see them on television all the time. What is our country coming to? Mr. Carl, you need to equip us properly and we will all cooperate in arresting this malevolent action. I mean all of us, Mr. Carl. We are defending our country and ourselves and that is our duty, not only as citizens but also as members of the DESE organization. That is what we are here to do. That is exactly why we are active participants in this organization. Thank you, Mr. Carl."

HB took to the podium, "We all have seen the results of riots. We have seen the opinions of people that are contrary to adjudicated law. We have seen innocent people jailed and later freed after a number of years as a result of vindicating DNA evidence. Many of these people were imprisoned based on public opinion. It is even worse in politics where there is no DNA at all, only gossip and prejudging. Much is to be said about mob rule, to say nothing of slanted news reporters and newspapers who tailor reporting to suit their own goals."

HB went on, "Where do you think that this unfairness comes from? It does not come from a thinking man's honest opinion. If the statement they make is destructive to the good of our society, it comes from an evil influence on our society. Whenever you see or hear this kind of happening, look for "evil ones" in the crowd. You will find it easy to identify them with the DESE equipment in your supply packs. Use that equipment well and wisely."

Larry Carl then asked the group, "Does anyone have any questions?"

"Yes, I have a query," said reference committee member Daniel Pip.

"Yes, Mr. Pip. What is your question?" asked HB.

"I have heard about these photographs DESE is taking of events which actually exhibit weird happenings which endanger our world, and in which DESE has interest. Of course, the interest DESE has in these pictures is regarding how these actual events affect us. All that I want to know is if this is true?" Mr. Pip asked politely.

He continued, "If so, do you have any of those pictures here and if so, can we see them?"

HB answered, "What? You do not think that the photographs are real? You do not believe that they even exist? Of course they do. Of course they do." HB repeated in moderate, but easily visible, indignation. He went on. "So you want to see one, do you? That is no problem. HB went to one of the several three-foot long tubes he had alongside, but to the rear of the lectern. He announced, "All you committee members, please stand to the rear of the room and against the wall. What I am about to do can be dangerous if not performed properly. I do not want anyone to get hurt."

Mr. Pip asked, now becoming a little concerned, "What do you mean by "get hurt". How can looking at a picture in a three-foot long tube ever hurt?

HB answered, bending over towards Mr. Pip's ear and raising his right hand just as though he were telling a secret in a low voice, "Oh Mr. Pip." He said in a sing-song teasing voice." These are not just any kind of photograph that you might be used to. These photographs are not just "Kodak" pictures and the recordings they contain are not just "Memorex", oh no. These are very special and very secret photos. One might even say that they are magically enchanted, and they are. Even more so, these "enchanted" photographs involve a magic of their own. The magic they contain can directly affect you in the present, even though the pictures can be as much as several decades, centuries, or millennia old."

"Oh", said Mr. Pip skeptically. "How could that be?"

"These are "living" pictures. They are alive. We can affect history. Conversely, the history they contain can affect us." Said HB, waiting for a reaction from the committee members.

That waited-for-reaction again came from Mr. Pip who said, "But history does affect us, Mr. Gaunt. It affects all that we do and all that we are today."

"That is true", said HB. "That is most certainly true. However, perhaps I should have explained that if we change an event happening in the photograph we could change the course of history. In reverse, the events in the photograph could change us. Characters in the photograph could attack, hurt or even kill us. In that case, we will not be returning out of the picture. As I said, these pictures could be dangerous indeed. That is something you need to know and understand."

"So what do you suggest, Mr. Gaunt?" asked Mr. Pip.

"I do not suggest anything. I just want you to know that when you first see the picture, it appears as an ordinary photograph. However, it is an interactive and living photograph. That makes it unique. In some sense, it is a captured time capsule. In another sense it is a time-travel device in the form of a document. That makes it very exceptional. The fact that it is living makes it very valuable. The fact that these particular photographs contain active enemy activities makes it dangerous for us" said HB.

"I understand," said Mr. Pip. "Then what does one need to do to ever experience the photograph? I mean, if you cannot use the picture in its full capacities, then what good is it?"

HB answered, "You can use the picture in its full capacities. Any agent is permitted its use. However, whoever uses it takes a risk only because our enemies may catch us while we are vulnerable inside the photographs and do us harm. If you are willing to take that risk, we most certainly enter the picture and learn more about our enemies' intentions and plans."

"I would like to see what any one of these photographs contains. It should be the experience of a lifetime. I am very eager to do that." Mr. Pip answered.

"Fine," said HB. The rules are that only one other person can enter and an experienced agent must accompany that person. That agent is either Larry or I. Additionally, we must always be close together. There can be no separation between the two persons and you must agree to follow orders. This is for safety's sake."

"Very good," responded Mr. Pip. "Let us do it!"

"Right," said HB and proceeded to unlock one of the tubes which he picked at random. He dialed a combination and whispered softly into the lock. The lock opened its jaws and fell with a clang to the floor where it lay still. HB reached into the tube and pulled out the photograph. It immediately expanded to fifteen feet long and ten feet high. One felt that the photograph was life size and so realistic that you could almost feel that you were a part of it. Nevertheless, you knew that you were not. Everything in the photograph was still and unmoving. There were birds caught in mid-flight. There were no people visible though. It was just a nice, quiet Florida scene. Only birds were frozen in their action of flying. Nothing else was visible.

"Now," HB said to Mr. Pip, "You must take my hand and come with me. We must stay close and be ready to run if necessary."

Mr. Pip did as he was told. Suddenly, HB increased his grip's pressure on Mr. Pip's right hand to the point where it produced some pain. Then he yanked on it and in that one moment they had both jumped into the photograph. Immediately, Mr. Pip was awed. So was HB. He had been in this picture before but the sudden change in environment was always a humbling event, especially when one knows what is happening. HB found that it is always an exciting experience. It is always a very exciting moment.

Mr. Pip was amazed. The stationary bird was no long still. It fluttered off to be followed by a half dozen or more of its kind, stirring up leaves and creating a soft breeze as they made a hasty departure away from the intruders. HB and Mr. Pip continued entering deeper into the picture and were no longer visible to those outside the photograph. This was especially true after they traversed behind trees and bushes and out of the originally viewed site. The adventurous pair eventually came upon a rise and positioned themselves behind some bushes immediately upon spotting a group of people just ahead of them. The people arranged themselves in a circle barely one hundred feet away. If they had walked only a few more steps they would have exposed themselves and placed themselves in harm's way. Fortunately, the pair dropped to the earth in a near crash dive. The people ahead of them were arranged in a circle within a circle, only two rows deep. In their center was a moderately blazing wood fire. Their dress identified them as witches and warlocks. Among the witches were persons short in stature, intermingling with their associates. The black robed, peak hatted witches gathered around a very tall witch who was one and one-half times taller than the average participant. This bearded witch was not only very tall, but he was also very large framed and very muscular, just as a football linebacker might be. All the other witches and other creatures gave obvious respect and deference to this person.

HB and Mr. Pip could easily hear the tall speaker as he said, "My brothers and sisters. I am quite aware of your deepest, darkest desires and goals. We are an oppressed group that has been tortured and even killed since the beginning of so-called civilization, and despised over the centuries because we were not understood. The National Organization of Witches, Warlocks and Wizards have discovered a means to amplify the power of any of our spells to create an astounding powerful effect."

The witches murmured.

"Let there be a tribulation event which cannot be ignored by the public. There must be an event that is such a freak of nature that the entire nation, from east to west and north to south, cannot ignore or deny it.

The dark mass of witches and warlocks cheered a witches' cheer consisting of a roar, a growl and a cough, in that order. This signified agreement with the head witch Speaker of the House.

The Speaker of the House then said, "I would like your harshest, most wicked ideas to create that tribulation. Spells must be one which can induce an almost immediate effect."

A small, mole-like appearing witch with a long, pointed nose with laterally extended bushy whiskers stood up. He was dirty, raggedly attired and shouted out so loud that it seemed as though he used a megaphone: "Fire and Ice! Earthquake and Wave Quake! Birds in the air! Droppings here, there and everywhere!"

The coven cheered again with a roar, a growl and a cough.

"Then so be it" said the speaker of the house. We will cast a spell for the creation of an Earthquake and Ice event."

The coven again responded with a roar, a growl and a cough.

"Let us begin," said the speaker who suddenly disappeared in a flash and a puff of smoke. He went instantly from where he was standing and reappeared in the middle of the fire, which was now in low flame with none of it affecting him or his clothing. The bearded speaker slowly raised and waving his arms began a chant. He started his chant soft and low and increased its growth into almost a shout. The coven members joined in with the speaker mimicking the chant but with a slight lag. This lag created an eerie, echo-like chant, which filled the swamp. Remaining birds scattered in all directions and dashed away in panic, snakes, even those unseen, rapidly slithered away and hidden crocodiles splashed into the swamp in order to escape the threatening witches' fest. They knew these witches were a danger even to them.

Mr. Pip became uneasy and, as a result, was becoming careless. He started to stand up, but HB yanked him down. HB then said, "That is it. You cannot stand up. You will expose us to the wrath of these evil witches.

Let us get out of here while we are still all right and undiscovered. This is dangerous. We have both heard and seen enough."

Mr. Pip agreed and they joined together in the departure that the birds, snakes and crocodiles earlier initiated. They both popped out of the picture shortly thereafter but were surprised at the distance they had traveled.

Mr. Pip said upon leaving the photograph, "I am sorry, HB, that I almost put us both in danger. I had no idea of what we are against until this moment. It is truly frightening."

HB explained to Mr. Pip, "It is really frightening. We are dealing with people who are human beings, but some of them are not human. Their form and appearance may be human, but in reality, they all are not. There are some very evil creatures among them."

Mr. Pip announced to the members of reference committee, "It was an adventure all right. It was one I do not care to repeat. It was as dangerous as warfare. In fact, it is warfare. We are at war. It is a war like one we have never known. We are at war against the forces of evil. These forces call upon the underworld to increase their earthly powers. The Evil One below has placed his powers at their feet. They can call on him at any time. They did so when I was in the picture. I could not wait to get out of there and some place safe. It seemed like forever in there."

Miss Valerie Emilia spoke up, "You were only in there for a minute. It was not long at all."

Mr. Pip responded indignantly, "A minute! You say that I was just in there for a minute? Look, I know time. HB and I were in there for a half hour at the least!"

Valerie Emilia said, "Sorry. It was only about one minute at this end. Do you mean to tell me that you thought a half hour had passed by?"

"Yes," responded Mr. Pip. "One half hour at minimum."

"Sorry," said Valerie Emilia. "It was not just one-half hour. Perhaps it was one half minute instead. Really, you both were not in there long at all."

HB entered the conversation, "You are both right." He further explained, "Entry into the photograph also distorts time. Outside the photo, time passes normally. Inside the photo time passes quickly so when one exits the photo what seems like an hour to the photo traveler is only a fraction of that in reality. Things are moving much faster in the picture since it all was pre-recorded."

Larry Carl interjected, "All right now. Mr. Pip has witnessed the problem and has proven the content of our report and presentation here today. We did have an earthquake in Florida. We also had extreme, unusual freezing cold. Our current task, however, is to produce a solution to present to the general conference. Let us put our heads together and develop a presentation at the main meeting.

The Reference committee members unanimously agreed. Hearing agreement from the group, Larry Carl and Frank German left the podium and mingled with their partners to develop a prospective solution to the threat facing the nation.

CHAPTER FIFTY-FOUR
REFERENCE COMMITTEE THREE

The meeting in the next room had Jack Henigson presenting the DESE and the witch project.

Jack started out addressing his committee, "I was happy to greet you earlier as part of the entire DESE organization. Now, however, it is time for us to get down to brass tacks. We need to address the problem before us. It is up to us to review our report and to come up with a solution to present to the main meeting. We will then vote on what each reference committee has come up with and try to integrate all the different reports into one. We will then have a direction to follow and resolve the current dilemma.

Each one of you has special characteristics that we used in recruiting for your inclusion into DESE. Some of you have abilities that go beyond extrasensory. In any case, DESE has equipment that can enhance supposedly "normal" capabilities. That does not apply to most of you in the audience."

The audience gave a mixed reaction to that statement. Some thought it was humorous and laughed loudly while others just mumbled, not being sure if the statement was a complement or an insult. Eventually, they all saw the humor in it and the entire audience laughed and applauded Jack's observation.

Jack continued, "We are faced with a very extraordinary problem. That is one of magic, spells and malicious witchcraft being used to hurt us all. It is a major dilemma. Our problem is to develop a plan to resolve it. We need to come up with a solution."

"Part of our solution will come from you, our members. The rest will need to come from extremely gifted persons in our midst. I know that most of you have gifts and powers, but some of you are exceptional. One such person was recently discovered in the person of Henry . Henry will now take over for a short discussion and information session.

"Thank you", said Henry to Jack Henigson. "I do appreciate that introduction. It does put a bit of pressure on me to justify what you say and I hope not to disappoint." Henry continued, "I realize that I am not only a newcomer to the DESE company, but also quite young. Do not let my youth deceive you. However, all that is only a matter of interest and has nothing to do with the dilemma which faces us."

The audience murmured agreement.

Henry continued, "I have only recently been apprised of the situation dealing with malevolent beings seeking to do harm. Obviously, we cannot let them succeed. The question is how to do it. What do we use to counteract the malicious and destructive actions these individuals want to impose upon us. I cannot call them "people" because there are other beings among them. The other beings are not from our earth as we know it but from a darker part of our existence. I will try to avoid the word "demonic", but there is evidence that this word applies. The calling of these dark forces to affect our world and to hurt us is beyond the pale. We need to have forces equally as powerful and as anti-evil on our side. The question is "what are those forces?". That is the only way we can counteract this evil. "

Henry could not let go of his "bully pulpit" and went on, "In my case, my very young age can help me to dispel evil. It is my youth and the innocence of that youth. That innocence is what the evil ones do not have. They have the opposite of innocence. They have guilt. Their guilt is the betrayal of their kind. Witches, historically were to be guardians of the earth, its creatures and natural resources. Unfortunately, in every bushel there is at least one rotten apple. Not all the witches are evil. Most witches are still guardians of the world's natural treasures. We must find those witches because they are not evil, but instead are beneficial and contrary to everything the evil ones stand for. These witches will be our allies in this war."

Henry continued, "I also have several very special young friends I can call upon to help. Their innocence and pure youth will help them discover the evil in those who are enemies of good. When they meet them, their senses will warn them that such a person is the dangerous sort of person, both to them and to those around them. We can use their help in the search for evil. The only drawback is that these young friends of mine have limited time to devote to the cause because of school work, family duties, et cetera."

Henry then said, "I have said enough, for now, that is. I reserve my right to return and continue, however, if the need arises."

Jack returned to the lectern. "We have reports from the other agents where they have actually witnessed coven meetings with spirits from the dark kingdom. They have actually seen these meetings, witches and wicked spirits. They have not only heard their planning of destruction and all types of malevolence. They have actually recorded such sessions. Also, the data from field equipment demonstrate the actual destructive events that have already occurred. You are all free to look over the information and recordings. "

Jack then told the audience, "Now, let us all think together as to how we can be proactive in combating this threat."

Both Jack and Henry left the podium and mingled with their fellows and began deliberation in several small groups.

CHAPTER FIFTY-FIVE

REFERENCE COMMITTEE FOUR

Reference committee four was just about ready to begin. The three head members were discussing who was to be the first speaker. It was finally decided that it had to be Mary because she was more of a "normal" size compared to the Gnomes. She should be the first speaker. She could introduce the Gnomes and provide an explanation of why Gnomes were a part of DESE.

The audience was already agog regarding the odd-looking couple. An explanation was definitely in order. Mary is most well qualified to do so. She certainly would be the one to provide all sorts of information regarding the Gnomes and more.

"Hello", I am Mary Kent," Mary formally introduced herself. "I am very pleased to see all of you here in this reference room. Several years ago, I went on a DESE agent recruitment tour. I even went outside the USA. I met some very interesting people, some on purpose and others by accident. Accidents do happen, you know, and in this case, it led me to the recruitment of unique people. Namely, the two agents, who are standing by my side right now, are very special people. They happen to be husband and wife and come all the way from the Norway-Sweden mountain area. It was a fortunate accidental meeting for me and DESE and a very unusual one. Hepseva and Seemore Manlein are persons that usually avoid any human contact. They tend to keep to themselves, but I have encouraged them to join our group for the betterment of the world."

Mary went on, "As Gnomes, they have the ability to discern and sense the conditions and changes in our environment. They also have the distinctive ability to communicate with nature and animals wherever they make their home in any part of the world. Beyond that, they also have the special gift of meeting and enlisting the help of creatures we formerly thought of as being mythical and ethereal. Their friends include faeries and elves!"

The reference room group mumbled and some even snickered. Mary continued, "Yes, it is very true!" Mary quickly added firmly. "I know that it is true because I have been there, and I have actually witnessed this and affirm that the existence of their legendary and woodland friends is indeed a fact. The reason most of us do not ever see these folks is that we are dangerous to them and part of that danger is our disbelief that they even exist. I have personally seen them, and that includes the mythological as well!"

Mary was on a roll. She did not stop there. She went on, "Well, feast your eyes on these two very real persons. They are right here before your eyes. You can speak with them and shake their hands. That will need to wait, however, until after their presentation."

The audience shifted out of both curiosity and some uneasiness. They were no longer snickering and there was attentive silence. Their incredulousness turned itself over to actuality. The reality was that they were actually going to meet personally with these "creatures". The reality fully captured their attention. They were going nowhere.

Mary closed her introduction. "I would now like to introduce both Seemore and Hepseva Manlein."

There was a short commotion at the podium as Seemore and Hepseva were still undecided as to who would take the podium first. The struggle did not become physical, but it was quite animated with arms and all gesturing. Finally, Seemore, being a gentleman, let his wife have the first word, although he realized that she probably would also want the last word as well!

Hepseva took the stand. She had to wait a bit for a stool to be brought to the podium so she could see over its top and look out at the audience. She was not tall.

"Hello", Hepseva spoke in a melodious tone, the sort only women can produce.

"Hello", the audience responded in delight.

"My name is Hepseva Manlein. It is a pleasure to meet with you. We usually do not get to meet very many people and I am very happy to see that all the people here are so nice and so friendly. You need to know that as Gnomes, we do not associate with humans, at least not on a regular basis. It seems that this was a mistake. I find that all of you are simply terrific people."

The audience applauded in agreement.

Hepseva continued, "It was not an easy start for me to become involved in DESE. It was very accidental indeed. It seems that my husband met this woman one day and brought her home to meet me."

The audience gave a commentary laugh.

"Yes, it does sound funny. I was not happy to meet her at first. However, Seemore and I both saw the turquoise she had on her walking stick. It captivated us. We Gnomes just love gems. I understand that this is also a favorite pastime of American women. We have a lot in common! However, one thing led to another and before I knew it, we were here in the very beautiful USA!"

The audience again applauded and laughed at the "American women" part.

"I have found Mary to be a very good friend. She is a delight and we share the same interests in regard to our environment and our adopted country as well as gems." Hepseva became very serious at this point. "Our country is in grave danger. There is evil afoot. There are those, both from this world and from the dark part of our world, which lies beneath us, who will most certainly do us harm unless we stop them. They will harm our environment and each one of us as well. Not all of those who wish to hurt us are human. There are also dark spirits involved. We cannot let them win.

So far what destruction they have done has had only a minor effect. They are planning more. I will let Seemore tell you the rest." She then turned to Seemore who was already chomping impatiently at the bit and anxious for his turn to speak with the humans he formerly had tried to avoid.

Hepseva introduced Seemore, "Now here is my husband."

Seemore took the podium from Hepseva stool and all with relish. Unlike Hepseva, who was a bit apprehensive at first, Seemore was all smiles and happy to finally have his chance. One would think he was a publicity hound! He wasted no time replacing Hepseva at the lectern.

"Hello", Seemore said without the melodious sounds Hepseva intoned at her greeting the group. "I am Seemore Manlein. I am formerly from the Sweden-Norway part of the world. I am now from Alaska. It is nice. It is different from my former home, but I love it even more. The USA is now my country. I will protect it to the best of my ability from the wicked ones. Hepseva has already told you something about the problem we face. We, in the USA, have allies who are the very antithesis of those called up by the wicked ones who fight against us. The wicked ones and their dark friends have no chance against our forces and us."

The audience respectfully applauded. The tone turned serious. There were no smiles and each one had somber expressions on their faces. The words they were hearing left no doubt that what they were facing was malevolence personified. They were fully unified into a single force and behind Seemore. They had heard more than enough.

However, Seemore went on, "There is much more. We do have the photographs that are interactive time-captured events. Each one of these photographs can be entered. That is why they are "interactive". They can be entered at any time, but always with an experienced guide because the pictures we take are fraught with danger. They are surveillance pictures of our enemies."

Seemore added candidly, "You need to be told that we do have DESE armamentaria, but we have armamentaria that DESE has no part in.

It is the armamentaria of the Gnomes. We have friends in the areas of mythology and fantasy. I will reveal to you that some of our acquaintances and helpers you will find to be unbelievable. Nevertheless, you need to know that they are real. We know many of them and they will only reveal themselves to us because we are their very special friends. Mary did meet some of our friends as a special favor to Hepseva and me. It was because Mary and us share the same respect for nature and for all living things in our forest and in our world. Together Hepseva, Mary and myself have met many different creatures. These magical and almost magical beings will help us in our fight against the evil spirits in our country. I have no question whatsoever that we will prevail."

"We will all go over the reports and data from the DESE equipment and we will all come up with a common thought for action to win against our enemies, the wicked ones, the dark ones and their demon agents." Seemore terminated his talk with, "Now let us all collaborate and cooperate to develop a mode of action, with direction and a victorious conclusion."

With that Mary, Hepseva and Seemore left the podium and mingled with the group, discussing and answering as they delved into the crowd, which rapidly engulfed them.

CHAPTER FIFTY-SIX
REFERENCE COMMITTEE FIVE

Reference committee number five's prospective meeting would prove to be most interesting. The characters, Wyatt, Xilx and Elizabeth were out of this world two to one, except that the audience did not know that.

Wyatt, being the only real human in the hosting group, took the stand before the gathering. Unlike Hepseva and Seemore, there was no bickering and no deciding who would be first. It was already in quasi-military order, Wyatt would be first, then the Starship Admiral Xilx and lastly Yeoman Elizabeth.

Wyatt took the stand and started his presentation. "Fellow DESE agents, I am very happy to meet with you all. Our job here is to have the three of us up here to present what we know to you and to develop a joint strategy with your help. The strategy we develop will help our organization. We will address the problems you have already heard about. Unfortunately, what you know is only a small part of what is happening. We will describe additional facts to you. We will assimilate all the facts, conclude and deal with the problem at hand."

He continued, "When I went to San Diego recently, I took a side trip to Huntington Beach which is not too far north of it. The climate there is generally mild and there is almost never any atmospheric disturbance at any time. I experienced severe cold to freezing and a snowstorm in a city where it never snows. It never snowed there in the past. This was more than just a freak storm. It was one without clouds!"

The group listening to Wyatt went into a dithering murmur. Some were shaking their heads to say "no" while others were saying "yes". In any case, they all agreed that snow in Huntington Beach was not normal, especially without clouds.

"While I was there, I was made aware of a witches' meeting place. My friend, Matt and I, went to investigate the place in Fountain Valley. We are certain that we were entertained by a corporeal transforming witch, both in the form of a well-spoken parakeet and a very beautiful waitress. However, the facts never were easily visible, but our belief, that the parakeet and the witch were the same, goes beyond question," Wyatt continued.

Mr. Xilx took the stand next. "I want you to know that I am from out of this world." That grabbed the audience's attention immediately. All faces froze in a stare towards the suave speaker. "I suppose you think that I speak out of conceit. I do not. Nevertheless, you will think your own thoughts no matter what I say. In any case, you do need to know that this earth is in trouble. Specifically, the USA is in great danger from both worldly and unworldly forces. These forces have as their goal the destruction of our country and they have no concern whatever for the welfare and safety of any of our citizens. If we are killed, these people will have no misgivings whatsoever.

These enemy forces are evil in the very darkest sense of the word. I said that I am out of this world. That is very true. It is also very true that the demons who help these evil witches are also out of this world. We all know where demons come from, do we not? What we may not know is that they can be the nicest and most beautiful people you have ever met when they are in human form. They have the ability to snare you with their beauty and delightful conversation.

They may bring you gifts and even do "nice" things for you. Beware because the things they do are simply to cultivate you to their sympathies. You will know who and what they are when they reveal those sympathies and seek your assistance in completing their goals. They can deceive you into thinking that you are doing good, beneficial acts while the opposite is true. Since you cannot always tell them by what they look like, it is by their deeds and their thoughts that you will know them. DESE members also happen to have a sixth sense which enables us to feel the evil in those who are the wicked ones. One of the criteria DESE used to recruit each one of us was your ability to sense evil."

"In this box I have a Krumbishilx. You see that it is no bigger than a medium sized cooler you might take on a picnic. However, locked inside this box is one of the most evil of all spirits." Mr. Xilx continued. "I do not think that it is necessary for me to open this container-imprisoned creature. Its evil permeates the immediate area around the box but not very far. I want each one of you to come up here and see how close you must be in order to sense the evil in this container. Since there are only about fifteen of you, it should not take you very long."

Mr. Xilx goaded the first row towards the box. "Come on now. Let's go. You first." With that prodding the first row started to move towards the box. As the first DESE agent came within a foot of the box, he stumbled and started to shake. He mumbled and stuttered in his speech. He was afraid and fear showed itself as a painful grimace on his face. He withdrew much more quickly than he advanced, bent over in retreat.

The next agent came close to the box. This agent sensed the evil within when the distance away was three feet. This continued until all the agents passed through what seemed like a gauntlet of recognition of what evil felt like. Some agents did not even need to get within ten feet of the box to develop a reaction. In all cases, every agent proved that the recruitment requirement was successful and sensitivity to evil was in full effect. Each agent was sensitive to the presence of evil and that it was reinforced to a higher level by this exercise. It was like a booster injection for immunity purposes.

Mr. Xilx said after all had passed through, "This is what evil feels like. What each of you felt is different from the other, but the commonality of sensation is the same. It makes you cringe both in pain and in fear. You sense it as a danger, which it is of course. You want to get as far away from it as you can and as quick as you can. What you sense is really a self defense mechanism that very few people have."

The box rattled on the table as though the creature within wanted to get out. Of course it did. It could not fulfill its function because it was imprisoned in that escape proof container. Everyone panicked when the rattling box fell to the floor. Fortunately, the box remained sealed and sound. The audience was quite relieved.

Mr. Xilx then said, "This is a small part of the evil we are fighting. The box you see before you is not very large, but the creature within can poison the hearts and souls of thousands of people with minimal effort. This being will never leave the box and it will eventually be destroyed by happiness, beautiful music, joy and reverence for the higher power we all respect. We do not need to kill it, but we can destroy its functionality with kindness and love. However, all has to be performed with care because until the creature is changed it is very dangerous indeed."

The audience let out a unanimously loud sigh of relief and applause upon hearing those words from Mr. Xilx.

Elizabeth Sam took the opportunity for the break during the applause to take her turn at the lectern. The audience, which was quite keyed up at this time by the run through with the box of evil, were eager for a change. They quickly quieted down and gave Elizabeth their rapt attention.

Elizabeth started, "I also am happy to meet with each of my fellow DESE agents. Like Mr. Xilx, I am also from out of this world, but I am down to earth enough to know what the score is in relation to the danger we face. It is a danger that is like no other we face. However, some of these beings have been around since before the Garden of Eden. As they tempted human beings then, their associates are tempting us all now. Unfortunately some humans are being fooled into the thought that they have powers and spells which come from their own beings. This is not completely true. That is part of the evil one's modus operandi. You all must be careful. Luckily, we are armed with a natural self-defense mechanism which will go a very long way towards protecting us individually from the evil ones, as you all just witnessed."

"These creatures are a part of the entire universe. They are interplanetary. They are as old as time itself. They are both spiritual and physical beings, not necessarily human but they can take human form, and they can switch from one to the other in an instant. It is hard to realize that this is a fact. Believe. It is true. Some of the interactive time-captured photographs reveal some of these evil beings from beneath the earth. Sometimes these beings can take the form of animals, snakes, spiders, scorpions. I am sorry to say that the "familiars" witches like to keep around them are in the form of black cats. I hasten to say, however, that there are many innocent black cats around which have no connection to witches or black magic. I personally have a black cat of which I am very fond and I know for a fact that my black cat is honorable and definitely not a witches "familiar"." Elizabeth stated this fact in near protest because in her non-human form, she is the cat known as "Black Lightning".

Elizabeth went on, "Now let us all gather in small groups, say three or four each, and discuss what means we may have at our disposal to combat the evil menace which has come to us. We need to come to a consensus on our approach to present at the main meeting which is going to resume shortly."

The reference committee then came together, and with much animated discussion, reached their final remedy to the threat facing the country.

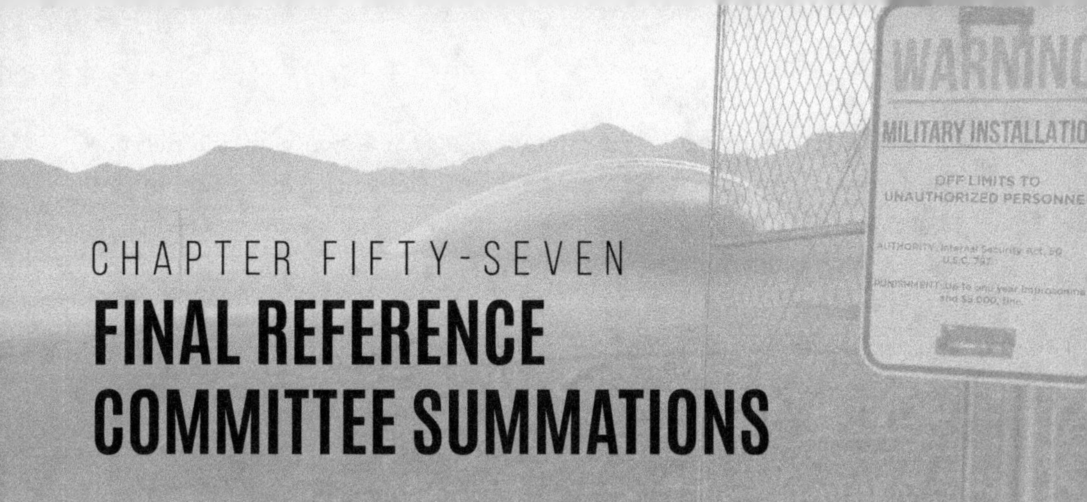

CHAPTER FIFTY-SEVEN
FINAL REFERENCE COMMITTEE SUMMATIONS

The main meeting hall was full of excitement as each reference committee reentered and took their places. Each committee sat together and did not mingle with the other committee members. The animated discussions were between committee members, as though they did not have enough occasion to deal with each other's ideas in their separate committee rooms. The task before the full house will be to develop a unified resolution to deal with DESE's function and solutions to the upcoming crisis. The hubbub took to silence as the head of DESE, Mary Kent, approached the podium.

Mary started with, "This meeting will come to order. Please be seated."

The members readily cooperated without any commotion. The room was quite and the mood was somber. The reference committees opened the eyes of the members to the seriousness of the situation facing the country.

Mary went on, "We have the final reports from each of our five reference committees, do we not?"

There was silence for several minutes. No one knew how to answer that question. Mary then continued.

"It seems that no one group wants to start their reports first. Perhaps I should rather call on the leaders of each committee for a report. That seems to be the better way to go. Therefore, I am going to call on the "civilian" head, and not the hosts, of each committee." Mary went on,

"The first one to make its recommendations for action will be Reference Committee Number One leader. That would be the Reference Committee hosted by Matt Ovlas and Frank German. Will that leader please come to the podium and let us have your results? "

The room was silent again. All eyes were on the table where Committee Number One had gathered themselves together. A bearded, older man stood up and went to the podium.

"Hello, fellow agents. My name is Glen Kohen.

I have been a DESE member since its inception. Our committee deliberated on the problem and we have come up with certain decisions regarding a solution. We decided it is obvious that these persons cannot have their way in destroying our society, our country, and our people. We can affect their attacks both directly and indirectly.

First, we can use DESE equipment to investigate their mindsets, their intentions, plans and immediate actions before they actually start any encounter.

Second, we can enter each of the time-captured pictures DESE agents already have on file. Since those are interactive, we can use the mind and sentiment reading equipment to assess their attitude. When we have determined that their position is destructive, we can use the DESE mind-changing, mood changing equipment to influence and induce a different, less destructive direction for these witches to go. Since these photographs were taken in the past, it will affect what they do in their future.

Their future is our present. In short, we will have stopped their mindset regarding revenge and destruction on our country before they even would have started. The only problem is that we do not have historic photographs of every coven meeting so we would not be one hundred percent efficient in affecting all the evil witches' plans.

Third, DESE has generalized mood-sensing equipment that we can use to survey the entire country. Those areas we cannot reach on land we can reach by air. We can search out, by constant over flights, areas where covens are meeting and eventually pinpoint the location and persons involved in the planning of our destruction. Fourth, we do have friends in mythological places who are not evil, but good. Such friends are those of Hepseva and Seemore.

Lastly, not all witches are evil. There are witches who are still true to their initial calling of protecting and benefiting the natural environment and its inhabitants. Those "inhabitants" include us. We can enlist their aid. Going beyond the good witches, we can pray for divine intervention as well.

The Angels of Fatima, which protected the appearance of Mary and the sign in the sky she caused, from the evil ones who did not want the event to happen, may also be able to help us. We can only hope for their help. The good witches, as witnessed by Seemore at the time, helped to keep the evil ones at bay then, if you recall Seemore's report. In short, we are not alone. There are Good Witches and Evil Witches. Our resources are many and widely varied. Our main problem then will be how to integrate and implement each of the tools we have at our disposal."

Mr. Kohen ended with, "This is the essence of the final report from Reference Committee Number One. Thank you."

Mary Kent took the stand and said, "Thank you for your report Mr. Kohen. May we now hear from the leader of Reference Committee Number Two? HB Gaunt and Larry Carl hosted that committee. Will that Committee Leader please come to the podium?"

The Reference Committee Two's chairman stood up and went to the lectern. He said, "My name is Brad Barker. I need to agree with Glenn Kohen. The options he proposes are the most reasonable and really cover all the bases DESE has. The only addition I would like to make to Glenn's report is that where we can, we should enlist more "gifted" human help. We need a bigger "army". I propose that we have our eyes and ears open to the opportunity to recruit these persons when we encounter them."

He went on. "The events directly witnessed by Larry Carl and HB Gaunt show us that the way to counter evil intents is with the "mind changer and sentiment changer". That is right in the area suggested by Glenn and it is our suggestion too. Reference Committee Two recommends that we actively intervene in each of the recorded memory capture photographs and simply change their minds before they act at all! Those covens where sentiment is evil will need to be searched out by more broadcasting means. Different areas of the country need to be examined en masse. Thank you." With those words, Brad Barker left the podium and resumed his seating with his reference group.

"Well, thank you Mr. Brad Barker, that was a short, sweet and efficient report and we all are appreciative of the time we have saved. May I please have the leader of Reference Committee Three, hosted by Henry and Jack Henigson, come to the podium and report?" Mary asked plaintively.

There was no movement in the hall. Finally, a scholarly looking gentleman rose and slowly and purposefully meandered his way and took his time in stepping up to the lectern. He started with "G'day. I am Hercules Canue. By day, I am a barrister and by night, I am a husband and a father. In between, I am a member of DESE, always on the lookout for its interests and its developmental prospects.

Reference Committee Three has come to the same conclusions as Glenn Kohen did and for the same reasons. We also need to agree with Mr. Brad Barker's assessment that we require additional agents as well. We do have a force, which is efficient for its size, but we need to have more people in the field and over a wider area. The only other way to increase our functionality would be to use means that would allow us to have survey over a greater region or territory. We recognize that we have limitations in our ability to locate active coven meets and limited ability to time-capture photograph details of a meet, but it would be advisable to increase the use of such photography and train more of our present members in the use of that equipment."

Mr. Canue went on, "When one considers that it is actually possible to enter an event, which occurred in the past, and affect our present for the better, one cannot come to any other conclusion than this would be the very thing to do. We do not have weapons of destruction, we do not kill, hurt or maim. What we do have are the intelligent weapons of mind and sentiment changing. We have the desirable weapons of gentle persuasion. This is a much wiser, kinder and more humane way to treat the problem. We can do it secretly, silently and unnoticeably. We have the ability to change history by entering the past and undoing errors! What a gift that is! It has to be a top-secret weapon. The cautionary note here is that although we recommend an increase in the use of the time-capture photography, it cannot be indiscriminately supplied. Its distribution has to be limited to a few trained and fully trusted people to minimize its loss to the wrong hands."

"I therefore suggest a limited production but a wider distribution of, say not more than twelve such instruments to be in the care, custody and use of only long term trusted and mature members of DESE in collaboration with at least one other similarly entrusted member. Thus the care and responsibility will not accrue to only one DESE member, but will be shared. In that way security, care, responsibility and use will be improved." Mr. Canue appeared to be waiting for a reaction, but none came.

He continued, "In any case, we agree with Glenn Kohen's assessment, but we also think that increased use of the DESE photography system is in order. Thank you."

With that, Mr. Canue left the podium and took his seat with his reference committee.

Mary Kent once again took to the stand and said, "May the leader of the Committee Number Four hosted by Seemore and Hepseva and myself please come to the podium and let us know what you need to report?"

There was another pause as the members of Committee Number Four had their chosen leader go to the stand. Hepseva was pushing Seemore to go up to the podium and he resisted and pushed Hepseva back so that she would go up. It proved somewhat hilarious if the reasons for the meeting were not so serious. Despite that, the audience laughed at the sight of these two short, and somewhat comical, people pushing each other towards the limelight, but only for a very short time. The laughter died down and one member of the Fourth Committee stood up, encouraged by the other members of that Committee, not Hepseva nor Seemore, and approached the podium.

"Hello, fellow members of DESE. I am Peter Swain. I have been a DESE member since its start. We have, in our committee, the personages of Seemore and Hepseva Manlein. They have both been instrumental in my coming to the podium."

The audience let out another bit of laughter because they all witnessed the real reason why Swain arrived at the podium.

Peter Swain went on, "Our committee is in full agreement with Glenn Kohen. Glenn has enumerated the armamentaria at DESE's disposal. We must first identify where and when all the nations' covens meet. Then, after we have located them, we must determine their mindset. That is are they witches that only seek to benefit the world and our environment or are they witches that seek to do the opposite. In other words, are they the witches associated with evil or not? That is the major question. If we determine that they are not associated with destruction, then there is nothing for us to do. However, if they are the ones we seek, then we must attempt to change their mindset using the DESE equipment for that purpose. Should we fail, we can additionally use the very difficult mind and mood changing devices in the few DESE time-capture photographs we have on hand and attempt to reset the evil witches' future to something harmless. We may even be able to change their thoughts to beneficial ones regarding the future, which would be our present."

Peter Swain then paused briefly and let out a sigh. He continued. "However, should we fail in that effort to change the mindset of the evil witches and their demonic friends in the present, I am afraid as to what we might need to do to counteract their evil intentions. We will need to decide on that if and when all other efforts fail."

The house murmured and made all kinds of almost inaudible comments at that last statement.

"In any case, we fully concur with Glenn Kohen's approach to the problem, as well as the other Committee members comments on the matter. Thank you for your attention and the opportunity to present my Committee's conclusions." Peter Swain then turned and left the lectern.

Mary Kent once again took to the stand and asked, "Will the representative of the Committee Number Five, the last Committee, hosted by Wyatt, Mr. Xilx and Elizabeth Sam please come to the podium and let us know what you need to tell us?"

The whole room turned to face the seating area of Committee Five. With a little fuss and bother, the representative of the committee followed the suit of the other four committees. She stood up, gathered some notes, and made her way to the lectern.

Upon arriving at the podium, the young woman introduced herself. "As all the other committee reps have said, I am also very happy to be here and have the opportunity to address my fellow DESE members and report for my committee. My name is Kathy Lewiesle Scott. I am a relatively new recruit to DESE. Nevertheless, I have been well trained and indoctrinated by DESE staff."

"Our Committee is in complete accord with every remark each Committee Speaker has said. We are in full agreement. We are very much concerned with failure of our efforts. Although we feel that with all the abilities, both ordinary and extraordinary, of our regular and very specially gifted DESE members and the very highly secret and specialized environmental and psychological equipment we have in our supply, that success is inevitable. However, contingencies must be planned in the event our efforts do not achieve one hundred percent success."

Ms. Scott continued, "This takes up where Peter Swain left off. What will we do if we fail in our efforts to change some of the more resistant covens and mindsets of the most violent and the most evil individuals or even entire coven organizations? What will we do in the event these covens become overtly hostile? What will our actions need to be? What is the most constructive, and conversely the least destructive, approach to rid ourselves of this evil in the midst of our country and our neighborhoods? All these, my fellow agents, each and every comment we have made as Committee Reps need to be integrated. All has to be integrated now into a plan of correction and even a plan of attack should either psychological, emotional and even physical involvement become necessary. In short, what is the worst-case scenario? All the comments we have heard today, and all the suggestions need to be integrated and put into action. We have no idea how much time we have before a really serious disaster strikes us. "

Ms. Scott went on. "We at Committee Number Five have come to the conclusion that the solution has to be a combination of all our opinions, simply workable, easy to put into operation ASAP and above all, successful. We must now develop that formulation. I thank you for your attention." Kathy Lewiesle Scott turned and left the podium.

Mary Kent immediately arrived at the lectern. She said, "Thank you Ms. Scott. I feel that these last words really summarize what we need to do. We will have all the leaders of each Committee come together and develop an integration of all the answers each Committee has presented to address this problem. Our final, integrated approach will be announced, and everyone will know what it is. More importantly they will know how their participation in it will develop."

What Mary said was to be expected. There could be not other way to go. She then announced, "You may retire to your residences for now. You will be sent information regarding our common approach to the situation."

The audience then moved out of the auditorium, except for the Leaders. The hosts also remained behind. They knew more about the problems facing the country first hand, and thus they would act to guide and inform the Committee Leaders to a workable and efficient mode of operation because of their experiences.

CHAPTER FIFTY-EIGHT
MODUS OPERANDI

The Committee Hosts and Leaders went to the front of the auditorium where they gathered at a long table capable of seating at least twenty people. The final members of the audience left the hall. The group leaders and their hosts found it easier to settle in with the house empty, the leaders and their particular hosts sat together.

Mary, being the head of DESE, took command of the small group. She began. "Well, here we are. Opinions and plans will be melded into a workable plan. The plan and direction we take must work in the hands of just about the least capable of our members. Whatever we do agree on does not need to be just one plan, but it must definitely be an effective plan. It needs to be plan which fully eradicates that which threatens us. We have already suffered destruction and mayhem in different parts of our country. We know that greater devastation is being planned. We do not know how, where or when, however."

"Some may call what we are hoping to do a "pre-emptive" strike, but that is not so. We have already been struck in several places around our nation. I call what we plan to do a defensive counterattack, and a reaction to the damage we already have suffered. Our goal is to prevent more attacks which have the potential to be even worse." A satisfied Mary then took a seat, not at the head of the table, but in the middle.

She continued, quite serious and authoritatively. "We seem to have a concurrence of opinion centering on the First Committee's report given by Glenn Kobren. We do not disagree on anything Mr. Kobren has offered but we desire to make his plans somewhat more comprehensive by the addition of various items. Those items vary with each additional committee leader's report."

Ever the authority figure, which is both her right and her duty, Mary continued. "The second leader, Brad Barker's report asked for a bigger "army", intervention in time photographs and use of the mind and sentiment changer. He also asked, in his very short presentation for possibly an aeronautical "search" for all undiscovered covens of evil sentiment across the entire country. This latter would most certainly be a very large but not a mission impossible."

"The third leader, Hercules Canue's opinion is also in agreement with the Kobren report, but he advocates the judicious distribution of additional DESE time capture photographic equipment to enter more malicious and evil covens and then to use our specialized DESE equipment." Mary said and takes a sip of water.

"Mr. Swain, the fourth leader, wishes us to add the extensive use of the time-capture photographs and mind changing equipment. However, more seriously, he wants us to develop plans in the event of a possible failure. A very good cautionary thought, Mr. Swain. A very good thought indeed!" Mary's statement acknowledges Mr. Swain's contribution.

Mr. Swain rises on that note and takes a bow and gives a wide toothy smile accompanied by a short, but wide and flamboyant, wave.

"The fifth leader, Kathy Lewiesle Scott, also shows agreement and wants us to take advantage of our extraordinally-gifted members, is also concerned regarding the possible failure to change mind-sets, the intermingling of all of the DESE advantages, between equipment and personnel powers and special "gifts" as well as consideration of a "worst case" outcome." Mary continued.

"All these are excellent suggestions, and each will be integrated in our plans of action. I say plans, in the plural, because it is obvious that we certainly should consider the possibility of failure of a first plan. As the head of DESE, it is my responsibility to conjoin all these thoughts into a working plan, or plans, in this case. I frankly agree also with all the ideas brought forth. We shall incorporate all the thoughts into one plan." Mary went on non-stop.

Pointing a pencil in the air to emphasize enumeration Mary said, "First, we will need to increase our numbers and more effectively use the members we already have. We will distribute time-capture photographic devices only to the heads of each committee as well as keeping those of us who already have them in service. Their distribution will be limited, however, because of the secret nature of the devices as well as to guard against any harm, they have the potential to produce. Each camera will be fully accounted for at all times.

She continued. "We will have daily reports on national coven activities and meetings. We will deal to change the mindsets of the evil ones. We have the benefit of using the US Air Force to help us search out hidden covens and general population mind-sets. The examination of wide land mass areas where evil is being brewed will be exposed. We then can narrow down where such goings on are located and once again send agents into the area with the TCC, time capture cameras."

Mary then added, "The nice thing about the time capture cameras is that one can change the minds of evil creatures wishing to do harm, at their past meetings from the luxury of our homes or offices. It makes no difference when or where the picture was taken. History can be changed retroactively. All you need is to have a time capture picture taken. We determine when we want to enter the picture and effect a change. We can enter the picture anytime and do it at our leisure, or better yet, after consultation with this DESE office. A joint effort could produce some very desirable results. I repeat that this modality is a most effective and major approach to the problem."

Apologetically she added, "Unfortunately we are limited because we do not have such photographs taken of every one of the past coven meetings where evil existed. Therefore, unless we can uncover them and take a current picture we cannot use mind reading and mindset changing equipment with complete effect. In short, if we do not have a picture of the past event, we cannot change their moods, mindsets or their future plans to do our society harm."

Mary went on. "Our major weapon against these beings is our ability to read and change minds. We have some other resources, which I cannot reveal, and which must remain top secret except to the most aged, secured and screened agents. DESE agents do not know all there is to know. DESE has some secrets which will be kept that way.'

A concerned look crossed Mary's face. Her eyes squinted and her mouth pursed up. She then said, "A major problem could be one of fierce resistance or our inability to change our enemies' sentiment before we can stop them from doing damage. The real question is : How can we force them to cease and desist? Do we have any such weapons within DESE? I guess we can always call on the police or even the military, but they most likely will not act until the damage and destruction has occurred. Then it will be too late. In any case, we still want DESE to remain the secret part of our government it has always been. If we need police or military action before the fact, we would need to reveal ourselves and we would no longer be the secret organization we are. That is something we do not want to have happen."

Mary had a look of despair about her. She asked, "Does anyone here have any ideas on how we can meet a confrontation or how we can force the evil ones from completing their act? I can use all the help I can get."

Everyone at the table appeared to be at a loss to give Mary a solution. Mary went on, "Just about all of DESE's equipment had to do with peaceful means of creating mind and sentiment changing. It was never a matter of force. DESE has been an information gathering office and not a military or paramilitary one. DESE mostly deals with the science of information and has never done anything forceful and certainly never anything warlike or a police action. This thing may be different if we cannot change the direction of destruction the evil ones wish to force on us. I am looking for ideas. Can anyone give me anything workable?"

The table was silent, but only for a very short moment. A small man who stood up and then stood up further on his chair broke the silence. It was Seemore. He was excited and noisy. "I do! I do!" he said loudly while even jumping up and down on his chair and waving his arms, just like a child would do in having a tantrum.

Mary was taken aback, put her right hand flat against her chest and said, "Oh, my! I think Seemore has something to add. Seemore go right ahead. I am sure that we all are as eager to hear what you need to offer as you are to say it!"

Seemore stopped jumping. He now had the floor, or in his case, literally the chair! Of course, since he was short, standing on the chair brought him up to a conventional normal human height, so standing on a chair was not out of order. The jumping was, however.

"Mary and fellow DESE leaders and hosts, you all know that I am different than all of you. However, I have dealt with these people and their evil creature "friends" in the past. I am quite old. My people live past several of your lifetimes. We have that "gift" if you can call it that. As a result, I have long time friends in literally "high" places. I also have friends in low places as well. I have friends throughout the forests of the world. We Gnomes have the ability to communicate with those friends and I can call on them for assistance."

The audience was incredulous. They were not sure if Seemore was pulling their collective legs or if he was telling the truth. Nonetheless, they were fully attentive and the fantasy side of what Seemore was relating raptured some. All eyes were upon him and some mouths were wide open in near surprise. Some eyebrows were elevated.

Seemore continued to enthrall the crowd. "I would be able to surpass all of your conventional military air searches in half the time or less. The combination of DESE relocation equipment and the ability us Gnomes need to communicate cooperatively with my different friends, makes it "easy" for me to learn about all evil coven meetings in a matter of only a few days. It might take the air force a week to factually uncover that which

I can learn in a few hours' time and more reliably because my different friends would be able to differentiate and know the evil coven meetings from those which are innocuous."

The audience was impressed. They still found all that Seemore was relating as almost unbelievable, but they all kept an open mind to his proposals.

"You see even after the air force search, and whatever other means of discovery of both ongoing and new coven meetings you employ, you would still need to sort out the harmless ones from the harmful. My agents, the birds in the air, the squirrels on the ground, the deer, the antelope, the ground squirrels, all domesticated animals and the like would be more able to cover our country in detail and let me know exactly where those covens, creating or planning evil destruction and harm to us all, are actually meeting. We do not need to waste time in the sorting out of one from the other."

The hall was silent. Everyone, both hosts and leaders, were fully attentive and actually hung onto every incredible word Seemore uttered. Everyone did wonder how DESE could possibly employ the country's animal creatures, both wild and domesticated, as information sources. However, they all did recognize that Seemore was unique and one who had a different relationship with animals than "normal" humans.

He continued, "It is then that DESE can dispatch agents experienced in the use of the DESE time-capture photography can be dispatched, make the recording and then immediately return to base. The recordings will be reviewed here at the main offices and if we need to change minds and sentiment, we can do it on an integrated basis. We will place all the different time-capture recordings from all around our country into analysis and affect only those that we deem most harmful by having experienced DESE agents walk into the photograph and using the appropriate DESE equipment at that time but at our convenience. The hard work is in the searching out, taking and returning with the time-capture photographs and the analysis which follows."

The entire hall burst into applause and a standing ovation. Seemore had stolen the show. All recognized him as a master planner. Here was a system that would fully deal with the entire national problem quickly and efficiently. In the least, Seemore's plan would be a major easing of logistics and tasks. This was just about what Mary was seeking to accomplish.

Mary then called for the audience to settle down and promptly took control. She, the ever pensive one, said, "Seemore that is an excellent plan. It is a plan that seems to have the overwhelming support of all our members."

Mary went on, "However, it does not address all the issues. The major question left unanswered is: What do we do in those cases where there is resistance to mind and sentiment changing? I know that DESE equipment can effectively work ninety-nine percent of the time, but what about that remaining one percent or so which will not change its mind and proceeds with national destruction? How can we deal with that? To me that is the major remaining question. One or several malevolent covens can cause major destruction throughout our country. We still would need to deal with those remaining. The question is how to do it."

She said, "I think that we are all in agreement. I will take it upon myself to develop the most inclusive plans of all our joint opinions to combat our enemy. I will then send each of you a copy of the plans and you may distribute them only to your own, long serving and very trusted agents."

Mary continued, "Although we feel that with all the abilities, both ordinary and extraordinary, of our regular and very specially gifted DESE members and the very highly secret and specialized environmental and psychological equipment we have in our supply, that success is expected to be inevitable. However, contingencies must be planned in the event our efforts do not achieve one hundred percent success."

Seemore, pleased with the table's favored reaction to his presentation, now took a more aggressive and in and open public action, quite unnatural for a Gnome, asked, "Mary, when do you think you will have the plans written up and handed out?"

Mary responded, "I will have the plans for our action prepared within twenty-four hours or less. You will have them in your hands in short order and you all should start acting on those plans immediately. If any of you have a problem with the final plan you are to contact me personally and right away. Does everyone understand that?"

The small group responded with a positive mumble and an occasional weak sounding "Yes". Although there is enthusiasm for the project there is also some trepidation. Not all were as brave as the next one. They knew, from what they already have heard, that there is possible life threatening danger involved and some were not so eager to face that outcome. So the "Yes" was somewhat muted, but acknowledged by all in the select group.

Mary then told the group, "This meeting is ended. We have accomplished our task. The rest is now up to me. I will be back to you virtually right away with the finished plan which will incorporate all the stipulations we have discussed."

The meeting ended.

CHAPTER FIFTY-NINE
THE PLAN INITIATES

Mary went back to her office and immediately started to meld all the suggestions into two different plans. The first plan was for a peaceful approach to the problem and the second a more forceful plan in the event the first one failed.

There was no doubt that all the DESE instruments and devices will need to be used. The same certainty went into the use of the time capture photographs. Mary decided that she will follow the plan that Seemore laid out because it was the most sensible and reasonable direction in which to start.

Selected pairs of agents will seek out covens, which DESE research uncovered, and then stealthily enter the area where an event was occurring. They will be equipped with the mind reading/sentiment feeling apparatus and the time capture camera. They will then record the event, bring it back to HQ and then seek the next coven's meeting. The agents receive their data from aerial research, and by Seemore's friends as relayed by Seemore. Then there is Henry, Jack, Mr. Xilx and Black Lightning. Their special talents and their concomitant use of DESE equipment would make them invaluable.

The mood of an entire region will be detected by air surveys and wherever they found evil sentiment, mood and thought, they will narrow the target down to the exact center of the originating problem. Then they will descend upon that area, exactly locate the precise source and view the meeting or whatever was causing the situation. They would then take their time-capture recording. This way the agents would be able to cover wide areas quickly and record many events. Mary will give the agents one week to cover the nation, record events and report to HQ.

222All the agents would be involved in some way or another. Only the heads of each group and the long time, experienced agents, and their cohorts will be allowed to take the time capture photographs with a later entry. The number of such agents will be equal to the number of such cameras that DESE would allow out into the world. Equipment that allows one to enter the past to change the future is both very special and very dangerous indeed.

DESE will keep a very, very strict tabulation of who has them and where they are. Unknown to the average DESE agent, the cameras contain a remotely controlled tracing device as well. Wherever the cameras are, DESE will always know. The remote tracing device has along with it a self-destruction mechanism that will render the device inoperative in the wrong hands. The instruments will be tagged to the DNA of the authorized persons who use it. It will be caused to either explode or melt down into nothing depending on the severity of the situation in which the time capture camera finds itself. If the device is in an impossibly hostile, life-threatening situation, it will create a violent and extensive explosion. Should it locate itself in a less threatening situation it will simply melt down. Which ever it does will be under the control of DESE central or under mind control based on the stresses which the operators are sensing should their very lives actually be in danger, providing it is no longer in their hands, but in the hands of the enemy. In a sense, the device is booby-trapped. Woe unto the unwary enemy!

The hosts of each reference committee, being most familiar with what is going on within the evil covens' meetings, will be fully trained in the use of the DESE time capture cameras, safe entry to the meeting areas, and eventually their re-entry to the photographs they are taking. Some hosts will be paired while the more experienced hosts will be able to take a willing, highly rated and long-standing uninitiated DESE member with them to experience the routine.

That is to say, the routine of recording the DESE time capture and the re-entry of the photograph at a later time. The advantage of the DESE time-capture photos being that one does not need to be there for the full coven, or other, event. One can stop recording at a certain point but still have the ability of actually going beyond that particular stop point. It is like have a "wedge" or a "key" into entering history at a certain point but then having to go through the entire time at what seems to the individual to be passing at a "normal" speed. One would need to spend that actual initial amount of time within the photograph in order to learn the happenings after the photograph has passed its actual "stop" point. Therefore, it is possible to have history actually repeat itself and look into the future beyond that "stop" point on the recording!

Mary, speaking to herself all alone in her office said, "I will decide the pairing up of hosts and decide which hosts can survey the actual covens. I will publish a list of paired agents. I will not post it, but hand deliver it to the senior member of the pair. I want to avoid having the list and its intentions possibly become a spread of information that is wider than intended. Only the principals involved need know their own individual pairing. Other pairs will not be informed as to who is paired up with whom. The general mass of agents will simply get a notice that selections have been made and are to be kept secret for security's sake and the safety of the paired agents."

Mary then thought, "What will we do with the covens or individuals that do not want peaceful change and who are resistant to correction? What do we do with those who become violent, loose tempers and actually threaten our agents and our society? Easy, she thought, we will need to use our heavy armor and, depending on the level of danger, we will need to eliminate them. They need to either reform or fight, because we cannot take chances on truly evil and destructively effective witchcraft, spells and life threats. The evil ones, either witches or actual demons or whatever creature they might be, may actually eliminate some of our agents. I will not permit my agents or any innocents in our nation to be harmed, disfigured, maimed or killed. It will need to be an all-out police action without the actual police. Fortunately, DESE has federal police powers, so that is no problem. Should deadly force be needed it will be available."

Mary's thoughts were not hers own alone. Jack, Henry, Mr. Xilx and Black Lightning all of whom were "tuned" into her mind's emanations, read all her thoughts completely unknown to her. Unknown to her, they also were in mental contact with each other and fully agreed with Mary's planning. It was as though Mary was on a conference call with the parties, and although she was not a part of the conversation, but merely a contributor to the thought "party-line". Her thoughts came through to each of the "gifted" agents just as though she were speaking to them in her very presence. Although they were far apart from each other as well as from Mary, they had a lightning-speed mental discussion. However, they would not let Mary know that they sort of "eavesdropped" on her mind! They did not think that Mary would be too keen on that! Mary knew that their power existed, but she still had not developed the strength of "double-thought". That is the ability to think two different thoughts at the same moment with the more secret one being a bit less prominent. It was thinking on two levels. This technique in thought control development takes time to master and experience. The technique, once mastered and put into action, confuses any "eavesdroppers"! It is an art Mary was trying to develop but had not succeeded in accomplishing fully at this time.

Mary would consult first with Seemore who had an "in" with all animals, feral and domestic, as well as mythological creatures. Seemore himself was a mythological being. It had to be no wonder that his rapport with his friends was reliable and secure. Secondly, Mary expected to seek the counsel of Jack, Mr. Xilx, Black Lightning, and Henry. The reality of the matter is that these last people already had her counsel. All that they would be able to provide her with was the actual "doing" of the tasks before them all.

CHAPTER SIXTY
PAIRING UP

Mary now had to decide how to assign the selected agents. She thought that she would first place the names of the hosts on separate slips of paper and pair them up that way. It was sort of like playing solitaire. She was the only one in her office. She also toyed with the idea that perhaps an uninitiated agent together with an experienced one would be a good way to expand the photographers' ranks but had not yet made that decision. She would wait to see how the "pairing up" would go and then decide.

Slips were for Kathy Lewiesle Scott, Wyatt, Mr. Xilx, Elizabeth Sam, Peter Swain, Mary, Seemore, Hepseva, Hercules Canue, Henry , Jack Henigson, Brad Barker, HB Gaunt, Larry Carl, Glenn Kohen and Matt Ovlas .

Mary shuffled the slips on her desk to come up with what she felt would be the best combination of agents. While she still was not fully happy with the combinations, she started out having Wyatt paired with Mr. Xilx, Elizabeth Sam paired with Henry, Jack Henigson paired with HB Gaunt, Larry Carl paired up with Frank German, and Seemore paired up with Matt Ovlas. That was the number she came up with: five pairs which match up exactly with the number of available DESE cameras.

She felt that Hepseva could join the team of Seemore, her husband, and Matt. Wyatt and Mr. Xilx would make an interesting combination, especially when joined by Brad Barker. Larry Carl and Frank German could have Hercules Canue join their team and make a happy threesome. Hercules could bring along the Merlot. Glenn Kohen paired with Kathy Lewiesle Scott and supplemented with Peter Swain. Glenn Kohen was the master planner anyway and should be directly involved in his own plan.

Mary posted the list of names and pairs immediately and included the names of the supplemented agents and their group assignment. She sent the information to the involved agents via secure internet e-mail and then, in addition, she called the head host of each group to make certain that they knew about the e-mail and the arrangements. The head host will then contact those in his group and give them the news. Mary then added the bombshell: training and practice would start the next morning at six A.M. All selected agents and their added agent were to present themselves at the DESE headquarters at that time.

Mary was on a roll. She then contacted James Barrett to see to it that all the necessary DESE equipment would be on hand in the morning.

Her next step was to make flight, room and board arrangements for the members of each surveillance group. It was like a combination of going on vacation and going into battle and doing both at the very same moment. She contacted the military transportation facilities and made full arrangements for all within an hour's time.

When all that was completed, Mary took a break, went home, and took a nap, only to wake up to need supper, a short review of the next day's schedule and then to bed. Morning would come soon enough, and it promised to be full of action of unpredictable sorts.

The next day came, sunny and cheerful with a bright blue sky that was sparsely cumulous clouded. The air was clear, and humidity was light. Mary rose, showered, had a light but nutritious breakfast and enough coffee. Smartly dressed, she hopped into her car and landed herself at DESE headquarters, passing through check points with quick ease. She entered DESE headquarters and found that a little more than half of the agents assigned were present.

James Barrett had all the required equipment on hand and was quite ready to review and re-train the experienced agents and do initial training of those agents that never really received any training at all. By the time the day is finished, every one of these agents will be well trained to complete expertise level in equipment use. James Barrett would see to it.

Additional DESE agents were coming into the main hall in DESE where the gathering was taking place. Barrett took them into his control and started reviewing and training. The third wheels, as Barrett called the third addition to the pairings Mary developed, would also be trained to expert level before the day was through. The scene could be described as controlled chaos but in a strangely orderly fashion.

Mary took attendance and checked off each expected agent's arrival as they entered the hall. When all arrived, Mary checked the entire group in and sent them off to James Barrett's training sessions.

James Barrett took them all after they fully assembled themselves in their groups to a different area off the big hall. In one area, he instructed the group in the use of the Extrasensory Perceptor. When he completed that to his satisfaction, he continued with the Percipio-accipio and then the Premonition-Mood-Emotion devices. The Cor-Cordis device was the best accepted at this time.

James stressed the use of the Thought Reader and Inducer because that is the one piece of equipment that the agents would most rely upon, along with the Cogito-Lector.

Distant transport too far away places could be accomplished without military airplanes or other modes of transport, real or mythical, by the use of the improved landing converted Confugio conveyer. With this device, transcontinental travel could occur in the matter of seconds or a fraction thereof. In testing the device while James Barrett was training the un-initiated, one of the female agents had to make an emergency bathroom visit. She thought that the Confugio device would be an ideal way for her to get there quickly. She was right. She did manage to get the Confugio to work very well indeed. However, she did not fully set her mind to where she really wanted to go and wound up in the Men's Bathroom instead. It was a minor problem here, but one which needed immediate rectification. That was accomplished very quickly under the circumstances!

This was an embarrassing moment for the young woman, Elizabeth Sam, and one that she could not easily forget. She will never make that kind of mistake ever again. She will henceforth always make fully correct settings on the Confugio and in her mind.

Even with the trip-making Confugio, the agents needed to know where to go. The Confugio could only be of use after identification of the destination.

Mary stated to the group, "Now that you all have completed DESE's basic training, we need to determine where you need to go. I will need to have agents board the military airplanes we will use to scour the country for enemy meetings and gatherings. The use of the Premonition-Mood-Emotion device, which we will call the PME from now on, will be aboard each airplane with a qualified agent. We have enough of these devices so we can use every agent who was trained here today aboard each aircraft and handling the device alone. That way, with the use of every agent, we can use many more aircraft and cover a much wider area quickly."

With those words, the group, although attentive, began to confer among themselves. They did not want to be alone and separate. They wanted to have at least one other trained agent with them. Mary overheard the discontent and relented.

"Very well, it will take a bit longer, but I still want every agent involved, including the newly assigned third party. You will need to pair two agents together and you can go that way. I must insist that at least one of the two need to be a field experienced agent, otherwise it is a no go."

This made the agents happy, and they agreed wholeheartedly to the proposal. However, Seemore was not so sure. He raised his hand and caught Mary's attention.

"Yes, Seemore?" Mary asked.

Seemore did not respond but went up to where Mary was and whispered in her ear.

Mary immediately dropped everything she had in her hands and put all her papers and documents aside. She motioned to Seemore to follow her. Seemore did so.

"Seemore, what did you say you could do?" Mary asked.

"I said that I could cover the whole country and Alaska inside of twelve hours and bring you back the reports you need in fifteen hours from the time I start." Seemore answered.

"What? What did you say?" asked an incredulous Mary.

"You heard me. I said that I could cover our entire country and Alaska in twelve hours and have your report in your hands in fifteen." Seemore answered smugly.

"Really? How do you plan to do that? That's almost an impossible feat." Mary said.

"Easy. Remember Peganni?" responded Seemore.

"Yes, of course I do. How could I ever forget that?" Mary answered.

"Peganni, myself, and one other small person could cover the entire country in a matter of hours. We could fly without sound and invisibly. You remember that when one flies on Peganni that you are invisible. Think of it: silence, invisibility, and speed. That should be a winning combination. Do you not agree?" said a still very smug and assured Seemore.

Mary's eyes lit up. A big smile crossed her face. "Do you think that Peganni would agree to something like that?"

"Of course. Mary, do you not remember that Peganni told you that he would be happy to help us in our cause against the evil ones?" asked Seemore.

"Yes, I do" answered Mary. "How could you do it so fast, Seemore", asked Mary still incredulous.

"Easy. We do not have an "Easy Button". We very simply fly far beyond the speed of sound and also faster than the speed of light. We fly at the *Speed of Spirit!* This is something you do not know about Mary, but I do!" said the now authoritative Seemore. He repeated it once more for emphasis: "The Speed of Spirit!"

"Then so be it!" exclaimed Mary. "So be it, whatever the *Speed of Spirit is!*"

Seemore's expression changed. He looked a bit concerned. He said, "Mary, you cannot discourage the agents that have just now been trained. They are now looking forward to an exciting adventure on Air Force jets. How will you handle this? They will not need to use the PME to discover locations. I hate to see them disappointed."

"You are right, Seemore," responded Mary. "I will announce that there have been some changes in plans and that they will have use of not only the PME, but also the Confugio device as well."

"Please explain," asked Seemore.

Mary explained as Seemore requested, "Simply inform them that we have a secret way, faster than the speed of light that will fully survey the nation from coast to coast in a matter of a few hours. After we have determined the "trouble" spots, we shall send them to specific coordinates.

When our paired agents arrive, via the Confugio, at the indicated spot, we will have them locate the areas more specifically using the PME at areas designated by you and Peganni. After an investigation as to the validity of their search results, they will need to report to us. If we all agree that their search is valid, we will have agents make a Time Capture Camera, that is a TCC, available to them. Experienced TCC agents will enter the sensitive area and take a photograph." Mary was very excited at the prospect of having the data DESE needs to make necessary changes."

"We can have all the data we need in the matter of days instead of weeks!" Mary said excitedly. "We can enter those photographs and intervene in the conquering of evil at our convenience and in DESE offices perhaps thousands of miles away from where the photograph was originally taken."

"Interesting," responded Seemore. "Very interesting indeed!"

"Yes, it is. Is it not?" quipped Mary.

"The real question is what we do after we have done all the intervening and mood and mind changing there is to do?" quizzed Seemore.

"Easy", said Mary. "We sit a while and wait. We wait to see if our efforts have borne any fruit. We wait and see if there are any mood changes in the specific areas we have photographed, say after about a couple of weeks. If there are changes for the better, we will continue to wait and observe again. If there are changes for the worse, we will send in our agents and seek once again to change their minds and moods from evil to good. In accomplishing that, we will protect our people, nation, and environment."

"That is very good, very wise and very patient." Seemore said approvingly. "A tincture of time and a tincture of DESE magic in mind changing." Seemore paused pensively and asked, "Mary, what happens if all fails in any circle of evil? What happens if they go forward with destructive activity? How will we stop that? How can we protect our country then?"

"Those are very good questions, Seemore", Mary answered. I think we will need to come up with a solution to that in the future. There is no sense in planning about what probably will not happen. Our DESE agents and our equipment are more than just an even match against the forces of evil. Seemore, you alone know enough in the way of magic. You can call on your very special friends, both mythological and those who are biologically natural wonders in our world, to deal with the forces of evil. These forces have no chance whatsoever against DESE and the forces of Seemore." Mary responded with an appreciative smile.

"Perhaps", said Seemore sounding doubtful. "It will remain to be seen. We will learn in time what the results will be."

"Agreed", said Mary. "We will wait only a short time because we cannot chance that the evil in these areas will develop into a greater force to the detriment and destruction of our environment, our people, our society, our nation. I think that perhaps three weeks' time will be an adequate indicator of where we are going with this. After three or so weeks of expending our effort to change the evil mindset nationally, we will know what direction we need to take to deal with these agencies, these evil covens. We will not just sit and wait forever and be at their mercy. We will not wait for them to produce destruction and hurt, maim or kill our people. We will need to see what comes, then we will decide what goes!"

Mary was grim and dead serious. There was no humor in what she was doing or what she was thinking. Seemore had an idea of what was on her mind, but Jack Henigson, Mr. Xilx, Black Lightning, and Henry, "heard" every word, both spoken and unspoken. They knew what was on her mind although Mary never ever could realize that her mind's thoughts were not just her own. As far as these four were concerned, Mary's thoughts were a blaring, flashing billboard. There were no secrets at all.

CHAPTER SIXTY-ONE
THE EXECUTION

The time to act had arrived. Mary summoned all the "paired" agents and their third wheels to a short meeting. The agents all thought that Mary was getting ready to send them off on their military jet aircraft and to do their job as was originally planned, but she had a major revision for them.

When they were all assembled and settled, Mary began, "My dear fellow agents. I need to let you know that the means of transportation we had originally designed for you is changed. You will all be transported by the Confugio device each of you have as your basic equipment and not military jets. You have just received full training in its use and some of you have used it already and have experience with it. The settings must be specific to avoid finding yourselves in places you do not want to be. There is an emergency "return" button on the device each of you needs to be familiar with its use, just in case you have created a major error."

Mary went on, "We have found a more efficient means of locating the "hot" spots in our nation. Instead of taking perhaps more than one week to locate these spots, we will be able to discover them in a matter of hours. You will be sent to each hot spot in an assignment to evaluate it for evil and malicious coven activity. We are aware that all covens are not evil, but the few that are will need to be corrected. We will do that together."

Continuing, Mary said, "What I am going to say now is very important. Please take notes. There cannot be any errors. Now please pay full attention. After you arrive at an identified "hot" spot which you evaluate as malicious, you will report that fact to headquarters immediately. A TCC will be supplied, along with a trained and experienced TCC operator on the spot.

The TCC operator and one of you will go along and document, by TCC photograph and your own visual witnessing, the goings-on at the malicious covens or other evil sources. You will then immediately return that TCC photograph to DESE HQ. After we have gathered all TCC photographs from the different parts of our country, we shall examine and evaluate each one separately. Our attention will not be divided. We shall examine only one at a time and we will get one evaluation and report on each."

The group of agents mumbled as usual and then they quieted down to hear more from Mary.

"Right now, the country is being surveyed for the "hot" spots." Mary continued, "We will know where evil is sensed, and you will dispatch yourselves to those identified areas. We will assign those exact areas to you. You will use the Confugio as directed and instructed, and you will arrive at the specific location in seconds. That is faster than jet aircraft, by the way."

Mary instructed further, "A word of caution. You must be properly dressed for the location to which you go. For instance, if it is a cold and snowy place, you do not want to be dressed in shorts and a "T" shirt. On the other hand, if where you are going is hot and humid, you do not want to present yourself in a down jacket and thermal underwear! So please know where you are going and dress appropriately. Remember that there is no lag time. You will arrive at the area specified almost immediately."

Mary went on, "You will quickly check out the specific "hot" spot and then you will follow the instructions I just gave you. In short, you will notify DESE immediately. To delay could prove dangerous to you to the point of losing lives. This is serious business, and we are not dealing with merciful and moral people. Some of them would just as soon kill you as to say "hello". They will kill you and then say their hello in a celebration of your death."

The grouping of agents was changed souls. There was no mumbling this time. They were very quiet and somber instead, as well as being fully attentive. There was a heavy, palpable feeling of foreboding apprehension in the air. The agents were very aware that they were going into battle in a very special way and with very special equipment, some of which had never been seen or used anywhere in the world.

Mary continued, "It is estimated that the so-called "hot" spots will be fully identified in less than twenty-four hours. This is a marked improvement over military jet flight. Your Confugio device will transport you to specific locations in seconds. The speed at which you travel is almost instantaneous. That means you can do what needs doing and return here in short order. You can be home in time for dinner!"

Mary's audience was still very attentive and hanging onto every word. Mary went on, "There is a "however" though. That "however" is that, depending on the number of sites discovered, you may be required to do more than just one "surveillance" in a day. In any case, DESE's equipment will let you do several of these exercises and still have you back home in time for dinner! I just want to make you aware that this is a possibility."

After this last statement of Mary's, Elizabeth Sam asked, "How many sites do you think will be uncovered? Are there many such things happening in our country? Will we all need to make more than one or two "surveillances"?"

Mary was very understanding. She responded, "We have no idea of how many malevolent covens or other sources of evil are out there. I cannot answer that question because we really do not know. We do know there are at least four different areas that need investigation. I base this conclusion on reports we received earlier from agents in the field. We already have some TCC photographs on file, but we are looking not only for photos that are more current but also for TCC photos of newly noticed sites. We will simply need to wait and see. We will know in less than twenty-four hours."

Elizabeth Sam acknowledged the answer, "Thank you", she said and then sat back onto her chair.

Mary concluded, "I will notify you all at about ten o'clock tomorrow. I will make assignments then. In the meanwhile, have a good evening and get plenty of rest. Tomorrow will be a new adventure for all of us!"

Mary dismissed the group with those words and wished all of them good luck. She also asked them not to discuss anything said at DESE with anyone other than DESE members and agents. Lastly, she encouraged them not to be too concerned over the next day's task because much of DESE's operations have security features attached to them. Mary told them that there was very little to be concerned about and that they should relax and have a good evening and a good rest before the exercise began.

CHAPTER SIXTY-TWO
THE FLY-OVER

Seemore was busy contacting Peganni and getting Hepseva and the PME equipment ready for the national "fly over" survey. Hepseva was cooperative, but not very eager to once more join Seemore on the mythological flying animal across the entire USA and their home in Alaska. Nevertheless, she did resign herself to it.

Seemore said, "Hepseva, my dearest, it will not take very long, and it should be very interesting. We will get to see the entire United States from a flying front-row seat. We will be quite comfortable. I have prepared a saddle built for two, something like the bicycle built for two, but in this instance, it will be on a horse-like creature. The magic of mythology and the specifics of flying on Peganni is that no matter how high we go, we will not be chilled at all. That is part of the magic. In any case, we will not be flying very high at all. We want to survey the country in detail so we will fly no more than about two to three thousand feet above the ground."

Seemore went on jabbering like a child with a new toy, "The PME will record all the data we need and fix coordinates on the locations of malevolent meetings and covens or whatever is evil and whatever is seeking to do evil work. At the same time, it will also seek out the good covens and the Wicca who seek to benefit their environment and the world."

All this excitement stimulated Seemore's appetite. He always wanted to munch whenever he became excited. He called out, "Hepseva, bring us a nice snack box and lunch. Perhaps a bit of clover mead, honey and crackers and cheese and…"

Hepseva interrupted his asking with "Eat, eat, and eat! Is that all you think of? You get a new play toy and food, food, food. It is a wonder that you are not fatter and heavier than you are even now. Poor Peganni, who has to carry you in the air for a twenty-thousand-mile ride. I feel sorry for him."

Hepseva chided, "Seemore, do not worry about food. I already had a premonition that it would be needed. Didn't your PME tell you that? Ha! I know you, Seemore. I have already prepared enough food to last us several in-flight meals."

Seemore laughed and asked, "Will there be a stewardess aboard too?"

Hepseva, good naturedly replied, "You bet. You are speaking to her now, you lummox!" Then she gave the much bigger Seemore a short, fast pounding on his shoulder that sent him flying.

Then they both had a good, hearty laugh.

Seemore finally made mental contact with Peganni.

"Peganni !" Seemore shouted in delight. I am delighted to hear from you. I need to see you. We have need of your services. How soon can you get here?"

"Very soon", said Peganni. Very soon indeed!"

As the last word was mentally transmitted to Seemore, a loud "swoosh" was heard outside Seemore's residence. It was Peganni. Seemore did not seem the least bit surprised.

"Peganni, old friend! I am surprised to see that it took you so long to get here!" exclaimed Seemore.

"That is true. Although I travel at the "Speed of Spirit", there was a lot of traffic on the turnpike, and I got slowed down." Peganni answered humorously.

They both laughed. Seemore gave the more human laugh and Peganni gave a cross between a human laugh and a horse whinny.

"How can I help you, Seemore?" asked Peganni.

"Peganni", Seemore began, "It has been determined that there is a major threat to create chaos and destruction of various sections of our natural environment in the USA. The sources of evil and malevolence are presently located in different parts of our country. We, at DESE, need to know where those places area are as precisely as we can."

Peganni acknowledged Seemore's statement with, "I already know about that. Tell me more."

Seemore continued, "DESE has supplied me with a device which can detect Premonition-Mood and Emotion accurately in different parts of the country and from a distance. It is basically a mood and intention detector. We need to identify the "hot" spots where malevolent emotion and evil are located. At the very same time, we want to identify those places where covens are still providing benevolence toward our country and our environment. In short, we want to know where the "good" witches are as well."

Peganni responded with, "Go ahead. Tell me even more."

Seemore went on. "We need to get this completed as soon as possible. DESE is concerned that these persons can hurt, and perhaps even kill, some of the humans who get caught in their planned environmental destruction either directly or indirectly."

"And?" Peganni asked.

"And so, we need you to help us survey the country at the "Speed of Spirit". We might be able to get this done in the matter of a day or two. Don't you agree?" Seemore conned Peganni with this question.

Peganni became indignant. "A day or two! A day or two! Definitely not!"

Seemore asked in quizzical humor, "What do you mean by "definitely not"?

Peganni answered, "Don't tease, Seemore. It is not nice. You know very well that when I go at the "Speed of Spirit" that I travel almost instantly. You already know that."

"Sorry", Seemore answered apologetically. "I just wanted to get a rise out of you. It was said in jest."

"Your apology is accepted. However, many a truth is said in jest, so be careful." Peganni responded.

"What do you think we can do?" a bashed Seemore asked timidly.

"I think that, depending on the range of coverage and the speed of recording on your PME device, that we can accomplish my flight over the country in the matter of several hours. That means three or four hours on a leisurely "Speed of Spirit" flight. That is without even trying hard", bragged Peganni.

"Excellent!" exclaimed Seemore. "I have created a saddle to use if you do not mind. Hepseva will hold and manipulate the PME device. She will also handle and manage the munchies and lunch."

"Lunch?" exclaimed Peganni. "Great! Are you bringing something for me? I'd like to make this duty a bit of fun for me too!"

"Of course, what would you like?" asked a solicitous Seemore.

"My favorite munchies are Rose Hips and Lilies of the Valley, either separately or as chips. As far as drinks go, either pure water from the Poland Springs or Nectar from the Melody Plant will be just fine. The only problem with the latter is that one has to hum for a minute or so after having a drink. However, I am not a bad hummer." Peganni said.

"Good to know" said Seemore. "I thought that a Hummer did not give a lot of miles per gallon!" Seemore quipped laughingly.

"Oh Seemore!," Peganni exclaimed. "One more corny joke like that and I'm off and away!"

Seemore said, "This is not my day. I apologize for the corn. Let's get to work."

"Right" responded Peganni.

Peganni stood quietly as Seemore fitted the saddle onto his back and placed it just behind his wings. Hepseva had been silent up to now.

"Am I going to have the front or the back seat?" Hepseva asked.

"I don't know," answered Seemore. "Do you want to be a back seat driver?"

"It is my right to do so if I wish" answered Hepseva.

"Actually, Hepseva, there is no driver on this trip. The driver is the car itself, in this case it is Peganni, the latest model too!" responded Seemore.

"Why, thank you Seemore. I am happy that I am the so-called "latest model"!" Peganni interjected.

"Well, you are, and the best too" flattered Seemore in response.

"Well, where do I sit?" asked Hepseva.

"Why my darling, you will sit in front and get the best view. I have set in the saddle fittings for our snacks and our lunch", responded Seemore.

"Very good," said Hepseva. "Are you not forgetting something else?

"You mean the drinks?" questioned Seemore.

"No silly. I mean the reason for the trip to begin with. Do you remember what it was?" Hepseva said with some sarcasm.

"Oh yes, I do. Are you trying to ask me where the PME is going to fit?" said Seemore.

"Exactly" answered Hepseva triumphantly.

"Hepseva, darling, it is already on board. I have incorporated it into the saddle so that you do not need to hold on to it." Seemore answered lovingly.

"Oh!" said Hepseva. "That is great. Thank you, my love. You always think of me, don't you, my honey?"

Peganni added, "Please, please stop that mushy stuff. Please. You are changing my complexion from white to blushing pink!"

"It's all right Peganni. We are married. She will hold onto the PME, and I will hold onto her with my loving arms", responded Seemore.

"Oh, my Unicorn!" exclaimed Peganni in despair. "I guess there is no hope, is there, for me to escape this loving duo!"

"None at all", said Seemore, "None at all. By the way, Peganni, we both love you too!"

The pure, bright white Peganni did actually change his colors to a light pink at these words. He actually blushed. That is hard to do when covered in horse-like fur. Nevertheless, he did!

"Why Peganni, are you really blushing? Please do not. We will not embarrass you any further. You are held in the highest esteem, and we respect you. Please do not be embarrassed by us!" Seemore added apologetically.

"All right," said Peganni, "Let's get going!"

"You are right on." Seemore said. "Hepseva, you get on first. Let me help you up".

Seemore helped shove Hepseva in place on the Peganni saddle, and then strapped her in. Since Seemore was the hero in this adventure with Hepseva, he felt he had to impress her. He suddenly "leaped up", not just figuratively speaking, but actually. Hepseva was amazed. Seemore sought this reaction.

"Not too old yet!" he exclaimed to the now very respectful Hepseva.

Peganni let out a groan in despair. He said, "I guess it is hopeless."

"You bet," answered Seemore smartly. "Now let us get this show on the road,"

No sooner had the last word escape from his lips, Peganni was airborne with the power of a Concord jet takeoff.

"Now," said Peganni, "Where do we go? Where do we start?"

Seemore said, "We will start about five hundred miles from the Canadian-US border. The PME has a range of about five hundred miles in any direction. We will fly at about three thousand feet above ground level, and we will overlap the southern one hundred miles on each subsequent pass."

"Very good, Seemore, are you certain that you never were a pilot before?" asked Peganni.

Not waiting for an answer Peganni added, "We shall start monitoring at Bangor, Maine and then travel south five hundred or so miles and then head west towards the Pacific coast. Upon our return, we will start eastwardly at the southern border of Oregon and California and keep moving. We will then head back westerly over Washington, DC and back to California. Then we shall return at about the San Diego latitude and head back east ending our tour over Florida. It should be fun. Hold onto your hats!"

Hepseva was a bit timid about flying on a horse's saddle, although its shape was more like an upright-backed chair. She was busy manipulating and tuning in the PME and recording its readings. She noted the "hot" spots in red and made an adjustment to mark the coven meetings that were not evil, or malevolent in blue. She exclaimed, "I'm holding on tight! Peganni, is this a fast as you can go?"

Hepseva was being a bit sarcastic and kidding Peganni. However, Peganni was not sure that she was not serious, and he piled on the speed. He asked, "Hepseva is this better?"

Hepseva was holding her breath and did not want to answer. "It most certainly is! You do not need to go this fast, but it is all right. Thank you," answered a tamed Hepseva.

Peganni asked, "Will your device accurately mark the places you need to know about?

"Most definitely. At this low altitude, we are right on. If we need to, we can magnify the readings at the lab. It will be something like Google Earth, but the spots we are most interested in will be separately marked and identified," explained Hepseva. "They will be very easy to pick out."

Seemore entered the conversation. "At this rate, we can cover the entire country in three or so passes. We are traveling at the "Speed of Spirit" which is faster than science lists the speed of light. We can do this in less than an hour!"

"True", said Peganni. He then added, "Do not forget that we also should survey, Hawaii, Alaska and Puerto Rico as well!"

"That is right", Seemore acknowledged. "We will add another half hour to do that. It will be a snap!"

With those words, Peganni swooped up to Maine to start the journey. Faster than the speed of light they flew, sometimes at only three thousand feet above ground level and then occasionally five thousand feet. They flew at the lower level often. The lower altitude allowed closer, more defined readings than did the higher altitude. Nevertheless, both altitudes were more than sufficient to gain the needed information.

Hepseva proved to be a whiz at managing the PME, which was clicking and flashing away while working and storing all the information gathered. All the data was digitized and would be easy to work with when they returned to DESE headquarters.

They started as planned at Bangor, ME and looking down they spotted the thirty-five-foot-tall Paul Bunyan statue dedicated to his birthplace. It was just a flash, lasting less than a second, but saw it they did. It did not look very big at three thousand feet, but seeing it was a thrill for the Manleins.

They then scooted over Vermont and New Hampshire without incident. They then went down to the latitude of Buffalo, NY and they paralleled the Canada-USA border across to the West Coast, moving North at Portland, OR to cover all of Alaska. They duplicated some of their data on Washington and Oregon on their return to the contiguous states to make the easterly return run starting at Eureka, CA and maintaining their paralleling of the Canada border to end their easterly run at Norfolk, VA. They then jumped south to make their reciprocal west coast run beginning at Charleston, SC and ending at Los Angeles, CA.

Their return trip east saw them heading toward Houston, TX from LA to cover all of Florida and then, for the sake of convenience, they went south to cover Puerto Rico. That completed the southern branch of their survey. Their mission was now complete, and they returned to base. Nevertheless, Hepseva kept the PME recording closely. She knew that, upon entering any data, the eventual photo capture would permit the use of other DESE TCC equipment and create a "time warp" by changing minds and past mood and sentiment and thus subsequent events.

Hepseva said, and with some truth, "You cannot need too much data. If we find some of our data to be repetitious, we can edit it out. However, if we newly discover something additional, we will need to repeat examining that piece of data. It can only be of benefit, so if you don't mind, I will continue recording the mood below us."

It is an amazing thing. No one ever saw Peganni and his "crew" as they zipped across the nation even at their lowest altitudes, some of which were at twenty-five hundred feet. They were not recorded on any radar. Their speed was faster than the speed of light of 186,000 miles per second. Such speed supposedly changed them into pure energy exactly as the Einstein theory states. Amazingly, however, they retained their corporeal integrity and the integrity of all their instruments and possessions in flight. This was despite exceeding light's speed of travel. They were not physically affected because they flew under conditions unknown to Einstein and under the unique physical laws of nature that are peculiar to transport at the "Speed of Spirit".

CHAPTER SIXTY-THREE
RETURN AND AGENT DEPLOYMENT

Peganni approached Seemore's residence and slowed down. He was below radar detection, as he was when he initially arrived. They were in a private and very secluded area at Seemore's place and Peganni said, "That was a real trip, was it not? Now I think we all deserve some of the goodies Hepseva packed."

Hepseva, now off of Peganni's saddle, said in surprise, "Oh, my goodness! I was so interested in our journey and my manipulating the PME that I completely forgot all the food I packed."

"Well, I did not forget it! Flying with two passengers is not what I usually do, you know. I could surely use some refreshment! We creatures of the so-called "mythological world" also enjoy a nice repast. A soothing drink of Melody Plant Nectar and a spring water chaser is just what I need!" chided Peganni.

Hepseva retorted, "Is that all you know. I thought that Seemore was the "eat, eat, eat" person in this group. I should have known that his friends are just as ravenous!"

"Is that so?" asked Seemore good-naturedly. "Is that so indeed! Last I heard this woman named "Hepseva" also likes a good feed as well!"

Hepseva blushed as reality came to the forefront. Seemore, she knew, was quite right. Hepseva was not shy when it came to eating either. Hepseva set a delightful meal for all of them, herself included, from their picnic container.

"Enough talking." Hepseva commanded. "Let us enjoy what we took on our over twenty-thousand-mile trip!"

She then added, "Mr. Peganni, you do not think that all I brought for you was only Melody Nectar and Spring Water, do you?"

"Really?" responded Peganni. "What are you saying? Did you bring a special delight just for me?"

Hepseva responded with a gnome-like, rosy-faced smile, "But of course! I brought Camellia Infusion, Frakatiny-Mapivalley Styled Rose Hips, Watercress Greens, spiced with Ethereal Radishes, Celestial Berries and lateral rooted, Stout Red Carrots to go with the Melody Nectar. I also want you to know that I have several servings, just for you!"

"No kidding! You really do! Look at that." Peganni said with a Unicorn-Pegasus kind of smile and unabashedly showed his full, "unbridled", appreciation. Hepseva spread out a feast fit for a Pegasus-Unicorn King.

While all this was going on, Seemore stood quietly, with his mouth open in amazement and hoping for some nice surprises for himself. He was famished and waiting for his turn. After all, travel at the Speed of Spirit is not an easy thing to do, you know. However, where were his deserts anyway? Seemore appeared next to unmistakable pouting.

Hepseva, turned toward Seemore and said, with her hands on hips and in no soft tones, "Well, Seemore, what are you thinking?"

"Oh, come on, Hepseva", begged the now impatient Seemore. "You know that I am starving. I might not be able to stand up even another five minutes unless I get something to eat and just about right away! What do WE need to eat? Quick, before I pass out and lie on the ground not only in exhaustion but also in starvation!"

Hepseva gave a cheerful, gnome-like laugh. "Oh, don't be silly, Seemore. I would not have my husband starving and lying on the ground because of exhaustion and starvation. No way!"

That cheered Seemore up a bit. His hopes and expectations rose, and it showed in his face! The rosy-faced, red-buttoned nose and churlish lips separated in a gnome's smile, revealing not-too-pretty teeth. Nonetheless, he was still waiting.

"Well, what do we have? What do we have, Hepseva?' implored the impatient Seemore.

"Well, I did bring exactly what you asked for. I brought a supply of Clover Mead, Chocolate Bear Bee's Honey, Whole Wheat-Grained Crackers, Swedish Cheeses from our homeland in the Kjolene Mountains and several cheese varieties from Wisconsin in our own USA. An additional surprise, since we are back at home, is the fact that I will complement your feast with Walnut-Almond Ice Cream for desert." Hepseva answered the now very impatient Seemore, who was feinting that he was collapsing, humorously of course.

"Let me at it!" Seemore exclaimed as Hepseva put out the spread before him. Hepseva's self-protective instinct made her instantly move out of Seemore's way to let him attack the food.

"My goodness gracious!" exclaimed Hepseva. "One would think that you really are starving. From the looks of you, that is very hard to believe!" Then she let out a good-humored laugh.

Seemore just ignored her and dug in with ravenous delight. Peganni was doing the same. Hepseva delighted in their enjoyment of her preparations but took her time in joining them. Of course, she did eventually, much to her own satisfaction and enjoyment.

The meal was soon devoured. Seemore sincerely thanked Peganni for his help, "Thank you so very much, Peganni. What we accomplished in the few hours we were gone would have taken weeks, or perhaps even more than a month, to accomplish using the usual means of transportation. Military jet aircraft are just too slow." Seemore tried to stretch his arms about Peganni's neck, but the neck was bigger and Seemore's arms were shorter than the task of giving Peganni a hug. It could never have been accomplished given the disparity between the two.

"It is always my pleasure to be of service to you and the cause of good against evil", said Peganni proudly. "Any time Hepseva wants to put out such a good meal she is free to call me. I will arrive promptly", Peganni responded to Seemore.

Turning to Hepseva, Peganni said, "Hepseva, I want to thank you for that very delicious meal. I do not remember having such a good banquet in a very long time. I truly appreciate it. Thank you."

Hepseva replied, "No, no, Peganni. It is I who thank you. You have provided all of us an invaluable service. Thank you, Peganni. I will most certainly be inviting you to another feast when things are settled. It will be my pleasure to have you."

Peganni said, "That is very kind of you, my dear. Thank you."

Then facing both Seemore and Hepseva, he said, "I will be seeing you. Right now, I need to take off. Goodbye for now, I shall return!"

Peganni took off in a "swoosh". This was just the reverse of his initial arrival. He disappeared when he was less than one hundred feet in the air. He was apparently again traveling at the Speed of Spirit.

Seemore and Hepseva stood there waving at Peganni almost up to the instant of his disappearance, then they just looked at each other for a second. Seemore spoke first, "Well that is done. We have almost the entire afternoon left to get this data over to DESE and Mary Kent for analysis and the next step of our project. She will be more than just surprised. She will be shocked. Getting this data so quickly is beyond even our expectations!"

Seemore went to the telephone and called Mary. "Mary, this is your erstwhile buddy, Seemore. Guess what I have!" Seemore was obviously boasting, and Mary knew it.

"I guess you are going to tell me that you are in San Francisco enjoying a Starbuck's Cappuccino at Pier Thirty-Nine where all the seals are laying out. Please let me know what you are talking about", Mary said pleadingly.

"I have what we need", said Seemore matter-of-factly.

"Pray tell what is that? We need a lot!" replied Mary.

"Very simple. I have the entire country's PME survey as requested", Seemore informed Mary nonchalantly.

"What!" Mary exclaimed. "What did you say? Please tell me again. I think that I am hearing unreal things. Say that again."

"I said that I have the entire country's PME scan as you directed." Seemore understood Mary's incredulity, but he was a bit tired from the trip and contented by Hepseva's meal, nevertheless, he was only slightly annoyed at having to repeat himself.

"How were you able to get it so fast?" Mary asked.

"Peganni, that's how. Peganni flies faster than the speed of light. We did it all in the matter of a few hours. That is how we did it." Seemore explained patiently.

"Oh!" Mary said. "That is fantastic! Incredible! Would it be possible for you to bring the PME machine and all the data over to DESE as soon as possible? We still have most of the afternoon to peruse the data and make some decisions as to what we need to do. The sooner we make our decisions, the faster we will be able to deal with the problem."

"You bet", Seemore answered. "I'll be right over. Just give me about a half hour to recover from my twenty-thousand-mile trip."

"Oh", Mary said. "I most certainly can understand. That would be just fine. I'll see you in about forty-five minutes then, all right?"

Seemore answered, "That is just about perfect. I'll see you shortly."

One hour later, Seemore arrives at DESE headquarters. He runs up to Mary's office and places the PME machine with all its data on her desk. "Here it is Mary. A few hours' worth of work, travel and touring. It needs to be analyzed as soon as possible. We need to run it now."

Seemore is re-energized by the excitement of the moment. The prospect of discovering exactly what the PME contains is at hand and he cannot wait a moment longer.

Mary said, "I cannot believe that you toured and surveyed the entire country in such a short time. But then again who could believe that Peganni really exists anyway? I believe it because I was privileged to meet him in person. I am glad that he is on the side of good and that he is our friend."

"Agreed", said Seemore. "Your amazement is noted, but do not forget that we have also surveyed all of Alaska, Hawaii and Puerto Rico." Seemore said proudly.

"Peganni's friendship is a blessing indeed." Once again and impatiently, Seemore almost pleads, "Can we please get started with the analysis? Please?" he begged.

"Fine", said Mary. "Bring the PME over here to the lab bench and I'll hook it up to the big screen. "

After a little fussing and dealing with contraptions and wiring, Mary said a short time later, "There we are. The PME is all hooked up. We will be able to check the entire US and its territories for the presence of evil mood, premonitions, and emotions. Everything we see will be recorded and archived, just as we watch it."

Mary explained, "The screen will display a map of the USA and wherever serious data is located will be marked in red. Neutral data will be marked in blue and favorable data will be marked in orange. We can magnify a suspicious area to just about pinpoint any event within fifteen feet."

Mary turned the machine on along with the projector. Immediately the image showed up on the five by seven-foot screen. It was a topographic map, which is changeable into a political map with cities, rivers, and such, labeled. Structures on the screen could be "Google-ized" into actual physical pictures of the location, but in better detail, at the flick of a switch. Details and locations were all easily visible with minimal effort. It was as though one was right there, on the actual scene. Of course, Mary is also able to obtain current, up to the minute details of any scene by accessing the US Government military satellites. She first preferred to use Google Maps because accessing the military satellites would generate a record which could possibly expose her secretly organized DESE. That is something she would only do as a last resort in emergencies.

The PME recording first started up in Maine and went on from there and continued the entire routing and back to base.

The PME produced its first blip near Wells, ME. It showed up on Mary's large screen orange in color which indicates a favorable location and not a threat. The observation took only one second and the screen spotted another blip in the next second at Salem, MA. Everyone in the room, of course only Mary and Seemore, expected that. It would have been more surprising had there not been a "blip" there. That blip showed up in blue, meaning neither harmless nor harmful, but somewhere in the middle. The common thought is that such a place would be kept under surveillance. Perhaps a future on the ground inspection would be needed, but at this moment, DESE was looking for bigger fish to fry.

The next blip happened over Middlebury, VT and over Lebanon, NH. The colors here were also in the blue-brown range meaning that the covens there were neutral to favorable. "Favorable" indicates a possible ally in confronting evil witches and their demonic associates. This is well noted and the PME would finally print out a listing describing where these different areas were. It would print out in color and blends of color, depending on the PME reading as to what was going on down below. The printout would indicate possible allies in the changing of the more evil covens to helpers in the battle against their wayward colleagues.

The word "battle" most certainly applies because demons mixed in their meetings have influenced formerly good witches. Demons are dedicated evil because they come from evil. One cannot expect good from evil. They are contrary terms. These demons do not give up because they cannot. It is not in their nature. Evil in the world and its installment into living beings is their only cause and their only goal.

However, one needs to realize and know that these witches were good in the past and formerly cared for their environment, its creatures, both flora and fauna, as well as for man himself. When the evil witches betray the "Rede" and produce harm and destruction to more than just the environment they risk, not only neutralization by DESE, but also the consequences of their "Threefold Law". The witches' "Rede" proclaims that they can do what harms no one. The "Rule of the Threefold Law and its Return", is a return that could do three times the damage to the very same evil witches who promulgate destruction upon those attacked and harmed. They therefore may cause their own destruction even without DESE's intervention. The demons delight in the destruction of both the innocent and the wicked. They happily collect the spirits of the wicked to their dark lair.

The good covens that are aware of what their now evil compatriot covens are doing are deeply concerned. They want to protect the members of the ill-directed covens from the "three times multiplied return vengeance" because of the "Threefold Law". In a sense, the beneficent covens are desirous of protecting their demon-infected fellows from the creation of their own destruction, simply based on their outward attacks on the environment, people, animals and things. Therefore, if such an evil coven creates evil destruction, such destruction will be visited upon the evil doers at a three time more damaging rate. This is something from which their beneficent brethren would like to protect their evil leaning fellows who apparently have either ignored or forgotten the consequences of the three-fold law.

The next "blip" on the screen developed in the Albany, NY area close to Scotia in the Collins Park area. The color was red. This was noted. The survey continued westward over Ohio and Pennsylvania and the next "blip" occurred in Ann Arbor near the Forest Hill Cemetery on Geddes Ave. It was also red.

From Ann Arbor, and only a second later, they were over Chicago and they received another blip over the Cicero, Illinois area. They were clear of red blips until they reached the Gifford Pinchot National Forest area in Washington State between Mt. Rainier and Mt. St. Helens. There they developed a high intensity flashing red blip. They also developed a red blip near the Manlein homestead as well. This piqued Seemore's interest quite a bit. The flash return trip took them between San Francisco and Los Angeles. They received several areas of orange that meant that these areas held beneficial covens or senses of mood.

All along their route over California, they received multiple readings of blue but not as many reds as they expected. They did anticipate a red blip over Huntington Beach, but there was none. That changed when they approached Las Vegas and then there were no additional reds until they reached the city of Amarillo but went off the scale again at New Orleans. There were blue and orange blips all over the place. The next red blip occurred in the Asheville, NC mountain area, although not in the city itself, but the environs.

They then dropped down through the Florida peninsula and picked up several red blips at South Beach and the Singer Island area of West Palm Beach. Fort Lauderdale came in with several red flashing blips. The Fort Lauderdale area near Fifty-Sixth Court blipped rapidly and was especially bright near where it intersected with Federal Highway, or US Route 1. It was as though the whole Fort Lauderdale police department was there and their patrol cars were flashing brightly and in supernormal fashion. Thereafter they noted that there was nothing as they approached Puerto Rico, neither red, blue nor orange. "Probably a normal area without evil or much of an opinion on environmental events and perhaps anything else", remarked Mary.

Seemore quipped, "Yes, especially since much of the trip from Key West south was over water and there would be very few fish witches around!"

Mary laughed in agreement, "Yes. You are right! Even the flying fishes don't have brooms, do they?" Then Mary laughed again.

"Not as far as I know," retorted Seemore good-naturedly.

Puerto Rico itself flashed mostly orange. Occasionally blue blips would pop up, but no more than three throughout the whole Puerto Rican Island. Even the area where the Bacardi bats had inhabited the buildings blipped orange. Puerto Rico was definitely a friendly neighborhood.

The survey was finished. Mary and Seemore mutually agreed that the red-blipped areas need further investigation. The matter of agent assignment to investigate is the next hurdle.

Jack Henigson, Henry , Elizabeth Sam, Mr. Xilx, and all the leaders of the reference committees would be major players in leading investigations. The leaders are to pick only two of their best sub agents to accompany them on their mission. Only one of the sub agents could enter the immediate area to be photographed while the second agent stood sentry. This is no longer fun and games. This is now the real thing. There is no chance for on the job training. Lives are at stake.

Only the experienced DESE agents will enter each of the red-blipped areas, investigate and photograph any meetup events they found for as long and as much as they could using the TCC camera. They then need to bring back their detailed photographs to headquarters for analysis and decision-making. A plan to confront, deter and even battle against evil forces will be placed in the works. The plan deemed most effective will then be immediately enacted.

Confrontation, battle of spirits, battle of wits and morality, and even perhaps, physical battle would take place. This is a war of a different kind. It is one which never happened before, but one which is as old as mankind. This encounter continues man's facing the choices between good and evil. It is the battle of all time because it changes what had been a usually spiritual combat into the tangibly physical. The physical battle over a spiritual one makes this tangible confrontation truly unique. The fate of the earth and its creatures as well as humanity lies in the ultimate outcome.

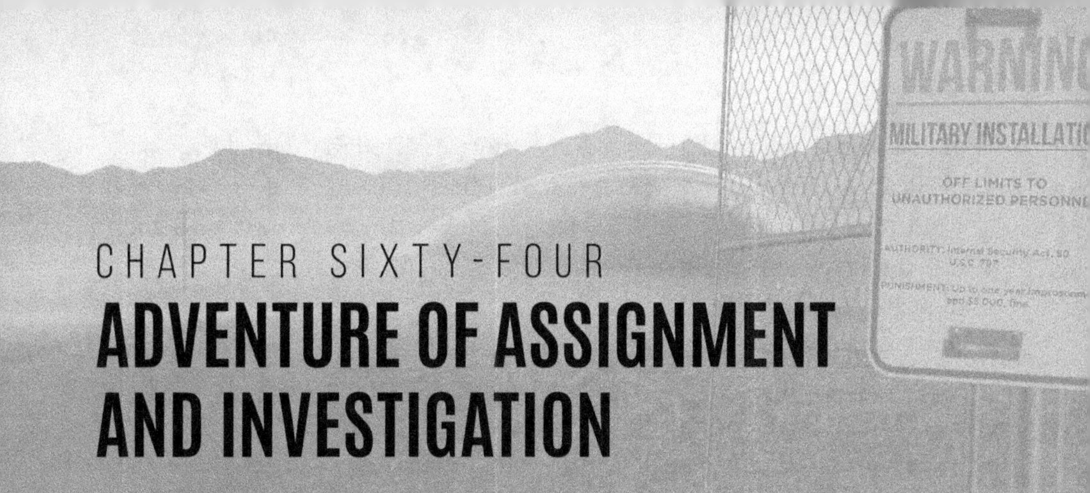

CHAPTER SIXTY-FOUR
ADVENTURE OF ASSIGNMENT AND INVESTIGATION

Mary and Seemore summoned the reference committee leaders to an impromptu meeting the day after they fully analyzed the aeronautical survey. The mood was one of tense excitement. The sense that there was something tremendous about to happen was in the air. Some of the "gifted" committee leaders already knew what was yet to be spoken. The minds of Seemore and Mary were an open book to them and very easily read. Henry, Jack Henigson, Black Lightning, and Mr. Xilx had no problem knowing what was to come. Mary still had virtually no ability to hide or disguise her thoughts. The four gifted minds were as one. What one knew, the others knew, and they conversed, without spoken words, between themselves.

Mary began, "Welcome. We call you here to begin action in countering the evil beings who want to harm us and they even want to destroy those who have been manipulated to create our havoc and destruction. You are all aware that we are fighting creatures of the underworld. Unfortunately, not all our enemies are underworld characters. Some of them were our friends and our brethren in the past and, with good fortune, will return to the fold of friendship once this is over. Demonic forces have invaded and influenced the lives of these friends."

Mary continued, "Witches are humans who believe in the protection of the earth, its flora and fauna. They are as human as we are. Regrettably, they have been led astray even unknown to themselves. Witches who create destruction will have that same destruction reflected to themselves. That is the goal of demonic possession. It is to collect the souls and spirits of man and to take them back into the darkness beneath the earth. The demons see it as a victory. While the demons persuade these witches to destroy us, they are seeking the destruction of these very same witches. They must collect their souls and spirits and bring them to the netherworld. We see it as a loss to humanity. In a sense, you are on a rescue mission to save these mal-influence humans from their own self-destruction. We want to save them from themselves and from the demons and at the same time we will protect our country."

Mary went on, "Demons are not easily denied their victory. They are powerful creations of an evil spirit. There is no good within them. They are full and only evil by definition. This makes your venture one that will take you into the world of the supernatural and the unknown. A United States government agency has never fought evil spirits. If congress only knew what we are up against, they could never believe it. Most likely would deny us funds and government support. Some of them are influenced by demons of their own. Such a conclusion was suspect in the past and may be true. The rescuing of congressional members is not our task at present. That can be for another day."

Continuing, Mary added, "Our challenge lies before us. We have collected sufficient evidence to proceed. The President has been informed. He agrees that we must do what we need to protect our people and our country. We have his permission to continue our mission."

The small group before her applauded softly.

Mary said, "Very good. I want to get on with the final steps to our survey. That is when you are assigned to a direct and close up visual and sensory investigation of only the highly suspected areas. These are the areas where the PME has revealed the greatest affection of evil, including evil witches, other underworld creatures and even demons, I am sorry to say."

The small grouping became uneasy at these words and stirred and mumbled their concern.

Mary noted their concern. She said, "I can see that you are worried about this assignment. However, there is really nothing to be anxious about. The less experienced of you will be led by an experienced agent. That agent knows the rules of behavior. He will not take risks. Caution is the by word and caution will always prevail. It must. The safety of our agents and the retrieval of pertinent data are our goals. We will not shrink from that."

Continuing, Mary added "Seemore and I have come up with a listing and pairing of agents. Our final pairing is as follows:

Mr. Xilx will pair up with Kathy Lewiesle Scott.

Seemore will pair up with Hercules Canue.

Elizabeth Sam will pair up with Henry.

Jack Henigson will pair up with HB Gaunt.

Larry Carl will pair up with Glenn Kohen.

Frank German will pair up with Matt Ovlas.

When she had completed the reading of this list, she added. "You will all receive directions regarding your destinations and its particulars, as far as can be determined from satellite imaging, of the places to which you will be going. You will place the coordinates into your Confugio Devices. You will then join hands and press "start". You will then be instantly transported to the location you programmed in the Confugio. Are there any questions?"

Kathy Lewiesle Scott piped up, "My favorite question in the past, and one which has little to do with this excursion, has been "Are there vitamins in sea water?" but this time I am going to ask a much more serious question. That question is what do we do if we have trouble and need to escape a dangerous situation?"

"That is a very good question. Who knows the answer?" Mary spent a few seconds looking around the room eagerly seeking a respondent. There was none. Then suddenly, Matt Ovlas raised his hand and said, "I know the answer." Matt was very serious.

Mary asked, "Well, what is the answer?"

Matt answered, "Do you mean to tell me that you do not know the answer either?"

Mary did a slow burn and wondered where this wise guy came from, "No, Matt, I know the answer. The real question is "Do you know the answer or do you not?"

"Yes, I do" Retorted Matt, continuing his toying, antagonist attitude.

"Well, Matt if you really do, will you please let the rest of your agents know as well? Do you mind?" Mary asked.

"All right, I shall do that. I was just funning anyway. We are all too serious. This is not a funeral, you know. It does not need to become one either. All us agents need to do is follow instructions and we will return safely," Matt answered.

"That is all very true, Matt. However, that is not an answer, is it?" goaded Mary.

"No, it is not. The answer to the question is that you push the "reverse" or the button labeled "escape" on the Confugio. You will then be returned to your point of origination just as immediately as you were earlier transported to your originally dialed destination."

Mary said, "Thank you Matt. However, there is more to know and for you to explain to the rest of your fellow agents. Can you tell me how the "return" or "escape" button works differently?"

"Yes, I can." Matt's attitude was now much more serious, and he stopped fooling around. "The difference is that you do not need to hold hands on the return trip. Whoever was with you will return with you even if they are not near you. It is a safety feature of the Confugio." Matt answered proudly.

"Excellent!" Mary exclaimed. "That is exactly right." Turning her attention to the other agents, Mary said, "Now all of you will examine and become familiar with your team's Confugio Device. Each team member will become familiar with its operation to the grade of "expert" before you ever are allowed by DESE to use it. James Barrett most likely instructed you in its use. If so, then consider this a refresher."

She continued, "You can see that its use is very important to your safety. If you enter the wrong coordinates, there is no telling where you will end up. If you end up in the wrong location, you could possibly be hurt or even killed. That is something no one wants to see happen. You could wind up in the middle of the ocean or in the middle of a volcanic lava flow. Anything like that could be disastrous. Your coordinate entries need to be exact and without error. Do you all understand that?"

The agents all responded with a definite "yes". That pleased Mary and she went on, "Then please do a little review with your partners. When you are fully certain that you will properly use the device, you are to come up here with your partners for final instructions for your "adventure" into the unknown."

There were now several moments of silence and then some scurrying as the agents joined with their assigned partners with whom they exchanged greetings and examined their Confugios. Another five or ten minutes passed when the first pair of agents presented themselves at the lectern where Mary was.

The first pair was Elizabeth Sam and Henry. These two had a long history with much in common. Mary was now fully aware of their history. She was somewhat shocked when she learned that Elizabeth Sam was really her home companion, Black Lightning the cat, now transformed into this beautiful young woman now standing before her. Henry was fully aware of Elizabeth's real identity, after all he had seen her transform. He thought she was beautiful then and still did feel the same even now. Then there was the thought melding. They could communicate with each other without words, and they did so regularly. Elizabeth knew Henry's thoughts and vice versa. They smiled at each other as they approached Mary.

Behind Mary's lectern was a table on which were multiple pads of paper. Behind that table was still another table and a large rack on which hung coats and jackets. There were backpacks on the first table alongside one which held paper pads. The sheets on the pads were not blank. On each pad and each page of the pad contained printed instructions on what the paired agents needed to do upon their arrival at their assigned coordinates.

Mary said, "Well, congratulations. You are the first to go on an incredible journey. Your experience with DESE and DESE equipment will be a great asset to you." Mary then walked to the table and picked up one of the pads. She read several and replaced them as though she was searching for one in particular. When she found what she was looking for, she returned to where Elizabeth and Henry were standing by the lectern. They had not moved. They were waiting for Mary to get whatever it was she was seeking and get back to them.

Mary looked from one to the other and said, "I am sending you two on a very special mission." Then addressing all the selected DESE members she added, "All of you are going on special missions, but this one is extra special. It is as special as are the two of you. Your destination will be probably the most dangerous of all. This particular area has presented with recent activity and, as a result may be one where malevolent activity is continuing right now. I want both of you to be extra careful."

With those words, Mary handed the pad to the two agents. They immediately and eagerly read the contents.

Elizabeth Sam and Henry turned and looked at each other. They did not need to say a word aloud because their minds were like one. What one thought, the other knew without sound. Their assignment was to be in the Las Vegas area.

Mary then called on the next pairing. "Will HB Gaunt and Jack Henigson come up to the podium?" The two agents almost immediately arrived at the podium and stood before Mary. Mary again went back to the table loaded with assignment pads and after a shorter minute or two came up with a pad designed for the two agents.

Mary said, "HB and Jack, you are also a very special pair of individuals. You each have special talents and abilities that are different from each other, but those characteristics complement each other and make your pairing into a very special, and even a "super", one. You also have a very special assignment. It is also one that is fraught with danger and current evil activity."

Mary handed them the assignment pad. They readily and ravenously opened it. The pair read the words excitedly and then HB Gaunt and Jack Henigson turned and looked at each other. They did not need to say a word aloud because their minds were like one. What one thought, the other knew without sound. Their assignment to the South Florida area involving South Beach, Singer Island and Fort Lauderdale in particular were all HB's home stomping grounds and Jack Henigson's wintering grounds.

Mary then took her place at the podium and loudly ordered the attention of all the agents. She then announced to the entire group, "I want you all to be aware that the places we assign you are places that have been identified by the PME detector for current or recent areas of evil doings, most likely malevolent witchcraft. In some of these areas, there may be covens where demons are influencing unsuspecting witches. In short, you may come up against demons, or other type of demonic spirits bent on collecting the souls. These demons have that as their goal. They do not seek to be of help to the otherwise environment protecting witches. They seek to pervert and corrupt a good witch's innate desire to protect nature and the environment."

Mary continued in a very serious didactic mode, "You also need to know that they do not seek only the souls of witches. When you finally locate them and are in their proximity, you are also subject to them. You cannot let them know that you are nearby. All we want you to do is to take their pictures with the DESE Time Capture Cameras, then turn around and leave quickly. The longer the Time Capture picture you take, the better our chances are to analyze exactly what is going on at any particular coven meeting. When you return with the photographs, we can enter into them much more safely here at headquarters at any time and at our convenience."

"You are warned; never try to change a demon's mindset. When you are dealing with demons, you need to know that their minds do not change. They are made of cunning and evil only. There is no good within them. They are ruled by a lower and stronger power than you have available to you. If you do try, you will fail and you will expose your presence and your own selves to extreme danger. You are not invincible. If the demons take you and your souls we, and your loved ones, may never see you again. Once more, please do not intervene at all for our own sakes and the sakes of those you love and those who love you. Please. I cannot stress that enough. Please beware. Each place is fraught with extreme danger for you all." Mary ended her short harangue.

Mary went on, "Now that this has been said, I will announce the next pairing. Will Mr. Xilx and Kathy Lewiesle Scott come up?"

Mr. Xilx and Kathy quickly made their way to the front as requested. Once again, Mary turned to the pad-ladened table and quickly retrieved the one designed for Mr. Xilx and Kathy. Of course, Mr. Xilx already knew the contents because Mary could not keep a mental secret from his mind reading ability.

Kathy rapidly opened the pad and read its contents. They were to go to the Cicero, Illinois area.

Mr. Xilx and Kathy Lewiesle Scott turned and looked at each other. Kathy did not need to say a word aloud because she knew of Mr. Xilx's ability for mind reading. Whatever Kathy thought, Mr. Xilx already knew, and Kathy was fully aware of Mr. Xilx's abilities. It was a conversation from Kathy to Mr. Xilx and not the reverse.

Their assignment is to be the Chicago area and Cicero, IL in particular. Cicero, IL had been the headquarters away from the city for Al Capone's distancing himself from the Chicago Police. Mary continued, "Apparently the PME has once again pointed it out as a location where unholy goings on were happening. Kathy and Mr. Xilx willinvestigate."

Mary went on, "Now that this has been said, I will announce the next pairing. Will Larry Carl and Glen Kohen come up next?"

Larry Carl and Glenn Kohen both approached Mary. Mary told them, "Your pad is on the table behind me. Please retrieve it and let us all look at your assignment."

The pair went up to the table, where only a few pads remained and quickly and easily found theirs. They then turned and went back to Mary.

Mary said, "All right. Let us all know where you are going. Please open your pack and let us all know your assignment."

Glenn Kohen and Larry Carl impatiently opened their prize. Then they both seemed to be pleased. They were to go to the University of Michigan area in Ann Arbor. Larry Carl had attended Michigan a decade or two ago and was quite familiar with the area.

Continuing her assignments, Mary announced, "Will Seemore Manlein and Hercules Canue approach the podium?"

Seemore and Hercules quickly made their way to the podium. Mary once again turned towards the pads and almost immediately picked up the pad designed for the pair. She then turned to the two of them and then said, "Seemore, I know that you know what this assignment is because you helped to develop it. We both did. Nevertheless, I would appreciate it if you both would open your pad and read it together." She then handed the pad to Hercules Canue, the newer member of the pair.

Hercules turned over the top page of the pad and began reading. The text told of the high red reading of the PME over the area they were to examine. That area was the one near New Orleans. That was the place where Katrina sought vengeance, as the agent of evil, against the US Government for complaints, real or imagined, which took many innocent American lives, including children.

Hercules Canue and Seemore Manlein turned and looked at each other. They did not need to say a word aloud because their minds were like one. However, in this case, what one thought, the other could only suspect. They did not have mutual mind reading and thought transfer abilities. This was the status of things even though DESE used special techniques to aid dual mental thought transfer development for all its agents.

Mary continued, "At this time I would like to have Frank German and Matt Ovlas come up front."

Frank and Matt wasted no time whatsoever in responding to the call. Each of them was up front in a split second.

Mary continued with her now familiar distribution of pads. She told the pair, "This is the final assignment for now. Once again, I want you to open it here and read the contents together." She then handed the pad to Matt, although Frank's hand was there at almost the same eager instant.

Matt started reading the text. It announced that they were to investigate the area south of LA to San Diego. The text cited their familiarity with the area and the recent snowfall incident at Huntington Beach as well as the freezing weather in the southern part of California. It was an assignment that they were both pleased to have because it was like going back home. Their interest in protecting what was close to home was ideal for each of them.

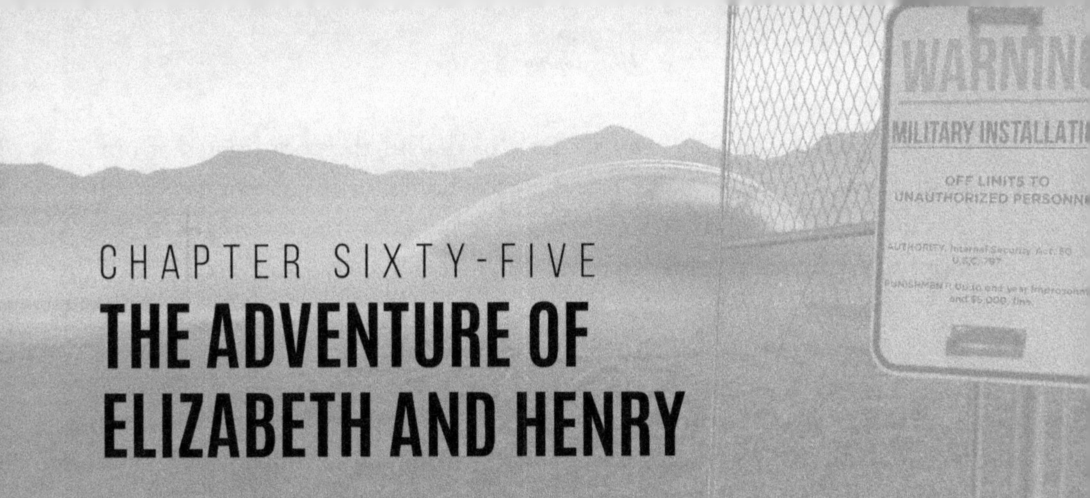

CHAPTER SIXTY-FIVE

THE ADVENTURE OF ELIZABETH AND HENRY

One morning at the very crack of sunrise when the air was crisp and the just setting moon was still visible, Henry met Black Lightning outside Mary's house. They decided that their journey was to begin at this early hour, and they were on their way. They had their assignments and were quite eager to get an early start.

Their concomitant mind melding decreased any need for vocal speech. Their wordless conversation went as follows:

"Henry, are you all packed for this trip? It will most likely be hot in the daytime desert climate, but cold at night. We need to be ready for both extremes, even though those extremes remain unknown to us," asked a concerned Elizabeth Sam.

Henry responded, "I am ready for anything. You name it and I have it!" he bragged his answer.

"Do you have the Confugio Device so that we can get there quickly? Do you know how to use it?" asked Elizabeth.

"Of course I do. What do you think? I was not sleeping during the instruction lecture, you know," replied an offended Henry.

"Really?" retorted a supercilious Elizabeth, implying that Henry's abilities were questionable.

"Of course. All you need to do is to dial in the coordinates of our destination and press "go". To come back home, or in an emergency all you need to do is press "return". The starting coordinates remain in the Confugio's memory. It is a safety valve in an emergency," answered Henry.

"Correct. Absolutely correct," repeated Elizabeth.

Henry beamed with delight at his more than satisfactory response to Elizabeth's questions. However, his gloating smile did not last long. Elizabeth came out with a block buster of an announcement.

"Henry, I have news for you," she said firmly.

"What kind of news?" Henry asked, now concerned.

"We are not going to use the Confugio. We'll take it but only as a backup," she announced.

Henry was perturbed but hid his feelings well. Nevertheless, Elizabeth could read his thoughts, even those he did not want to transmit, so she knew all. She knew that Henry was disgruntled.

She telepathed, "Don't be too concerned, Henry. I have a different and better means of transport. "

Henry was now even more concerned instead. Whatever she had in her mind worried Henry even more. He asked, "What do you ever mean, Elizabeth?"

"I mean that we can use my necklace which you see as a rubber band. It has many more features, it records, transports, is a weapon if needed and easy to carry and easy to use." Elizabeth answered.

"Really?" Henry asked incredulously.

"Really." Elizabeth answered. "most assuredly."

"Demonstrate. Explain." Henry asked.

That was the cue Elizabeth, or Black Lightning, was waiting for. She took the collar, which she always wore, and removed it from her neck. She adjusted the dials it contained and then threw the device on the ground. Immediately it ballooned, in a flash of light, creating a spatial opening to another place in a poorly defined, but definite, shimmering doorway. The place beyond was Las Vegas. The coordinates placed them at the location the PME reported as being the one where the readings were highest.

"Stay where you are Henry! Do not enter that frame!" Elizabeth exclaimed vocally. She did not want Henry anywhere near the entrance to Las Vegas. "I need to go over the ground rules with you about using my "collar," she said laughingly.

It did not take a lot for Henry to obey. He was very much amazed at what he saw. Here he was right at home, but there, through a virtually magic doorway stood the City of Las Vegas! He wondered, "How did she do that?"

The answer was quite easy. She is not from our world. She is not Elizabeth Sam. She is a Starship Yeoman. She was from outer space and had knowledge and exotic equipment about which Henry did not know a thing. It was not for him to know. Elizabeth would only reveal to him that which he was ready to understand and needed, and nothing more.

She began, "This is a part of my so called "collar". To humans it appears as a "rubber band", however it is really a very advanced and sophisticated instrument. It has the ability to multi-task and many other features that do not require your concern.

Continuing she added, "Henry, when the "door" is opened, one does not just enter it. Any person on the other side of the door cannot see us. They cannot see "in" the door. It is very important that those of us who have opened the "door" look through that door and determine the safety of entrance. "

Elizabeth went on, "For instance, you may be entering at the edge of a cliff or in the middle of traffic. Even worse, you could possibly enter the center of a war or other kind of battle. There are worse things also. You could enter in the middle of a fire or even a volcano. These are not things which are recommended."

It did not take much for Henry to see the point she was making. Henry had an "allergy" to fatal adventure. He could only say, "Wow"!

Henry answered, "I fully agree. I do enjoy staying alive indeed! So let us look into the doorway and we both can determine the safety of entrance at this location."

Elizabeth responded, "Right. So let us take the next step which is first to look out on the scene from within the safety of "home".

They both paused and looked out together at what appeared to be a very quiet scene.

Elizabeth then added, "Now we stick our heads into the scene and check it out one more time."

They both placed their heads into the scene and looked about.

Henry said, "What do you think?" he asked Elizabeth.

"It looks safe and quiet. I think we can enter the "doorway" as it were. We should be all right", responded Elizabeth.

Still not fully certain as to what they were really entering, both cautiously left the safety of "home" and placed their feet into the Las Vegas scene.

Elizabeth turned and placed her hand into the doorway. Henry became alarmed that she would desert him. He said, "What are you doing? Where are you going? Don't leave me here alone!"

Elizabeth answered, "Relax. Take it easy. I am just going to retrieve my "collar" or "necklace" as it is now disguised."

With those words, Elizabeth bent down to the bottom perimeter of the doorway and snatched up her necklace. The doorway disappeared. They were now somewhere in the Las Vegas region. The return door was closed and, in its place, just off the distant horizon, was the city of Las Vegas. The lights of the city could be seen and the greenish lighting on the MGM Grand hotel was clearly visible just past Las Vegas airport.

Henry asked, "Now what do we do?"

Elizabeth answered, "That is a very good question. The sun is just starting to rise in this part of the country. I think that we should scout around very carefully. This is a desert area. I am glad I brought my jacket. It is a bit chilly right now."

Henry agreed as he put on his jacket as well. He said, "We should keep together and search the area very slowly and carefully."

Elizabeth agreed.

Together, they scouted the immediate area, appearing to be lost explorers, just wandering around in circles. Just circling and circling, again and again. However, unlike explorers, their circles were ever expanding, covering, and surveilling a wider and wider area. The idea is to seek out anything extraordinary. They were doing this for about an hour and one half. They were feeling a bit bored and hopeless about finding anything. However, they were ever the optimists and ultimately their optimism and enthusiasm were rewarded.

Henry was the first to spot it. The rising sun accentuated a letter shadowing effect and what was there showed up easily, almost emblazoned. It revealed itself as scratches into the earth. There it was as an encircled pentacle. It was very large, almost seventy-five feet across. In the center were the remains of a wood fire, encircled by many footprints of all sizes. Elizabeth and Sam were astonished to see that there were also animals involved, probably sheep or goats and cattle, they assumed. After all this is the far West and such animals were reared here. Thus, it was no surprise that they were present.

The question actually was "What in the world were sheep, goats and cattle really doing walking around a campfire with people. Was this an exhibition or what? There were no animal droppings of any kind. Elizabeth and Henry remarked on the oddity of the exposition but did not think much about it.

In the center of the pentacle, where the charred remnants of an earlier fire were located an clear area was present in the center of that fire-encircled area was an old chair. It was exactly in the center of the pentacle. The place in front of the chair where feet would have been placed was only the shape of cloven hoof prints. There was no sign of naked human feet or even shoe prints.

The sun had risen only a bit more now and it was starting to get warm. Elizabeth suggested to Henry, "This should be documented. Do you not agree?"

Henry answered, "You bet."

He removed the time capture camera from his knapsack and began to create a panoramic photograph of the entire area. He stepped back to get the entire pentacle in the picture, including the central chair. He took detailed photographs of the footprints and the hoof prints as well.

Henry just finished his photographic documentation of the site but left the TCC running to make a record of any events that might occur during their exploration. They both heard a soft, rustling sound behind them. They had enough knowledge of Western movies to know that what they heard was the pulsating rattle of a snake. They turned to see the rattler, who, instead of assuming the usual coiled pose prior to creating a strike, took on a "standing" stance more like that of a King Cobra.

Henry and Elizabeth both stood transfixed and frozen in their boots, as the phrase goes. They did not move at all. Henry broke the instant silence that fell upon the scene.

"Elizabeth, if you hold still the snake will most likely go away. If you move, it may strike", said Henry.

Elizabeth nodded in agreement. She telepathed back to Henry that vocal speech was not necessary and not desirable under the circumstances. She feared that any vibrations could adversely excite the snake.

Suddenly a third voice entered the conversation. It was a strange voice full of "s" sounds and was a cross between guttural tones and a hissing whisper. It was a vocal, strangely pleasant, and reassuring voice. It was seductive. However, it also connoted an ill-defined danger.

The voice said, "You humans are not here on a beneficial mission, are you?"

Henry and Elizabeth, still frozen, telepathed to each other, "What is this? Who is speaking?"

"It is I, the third person in your party, the uninvited guest."

"Who are you?" asked Elizabeth.

"I am your host."

"Who are you? What is your name?"

"I stand before you, in all my glory. My name is Legion, but you can call me "Friend"," said the strange voice, telepathing his thoughts directly into the minds of the two DESE agents.

Henry asked, "Friend, do you have any knowledge about what has happened here? We see all these strange footprints and hoof prints, appearing to have circled a chair placed in the center of a fire. All the prints appear to have moved in the same direction. What is all that about?"

Henry added as a reflective afterthought, "Listen to me. Here I am speaking mentally to someone who is not there!" He then added, "Am I delirious or am I speaking to a snake "standing" before me?"

"It is true. It is I, the no-legged creature "standing" right in front of you. I am the one you see as a snake, but you have called me "Friend". I appreciate that," the snake responded, ignoring the fact that such were the instructions he gave to the two agents at the beginning of their curious conversation.

"Well, Friend, can you give us any information as to what has been happening here?" Elizabeth asked.

"Yes, I can," answered the snake. "It was a party. My party. It was a meetup. Those here met with their friends from the immediate area and beyond."

"Beyond. Beyond what?" asked an impatient Henry.

"Beyond the beyond. Beyond the Great Beyond," responded the snake.

"The Great Beyond?" asked a very puzzled Henry. "What is and where is this "Great Beyond"?

The snake did not move closer or further away but remained in its original location and continued to sway in a pendulum motion. Side to side and side to side again and again, all the while keeping its eyes fixed on those of the two strangers, one set of eyes at a time. It was almost mesmerizing. Perhaps that was his intention. Snakes do that, you know.

"The Great Beyond is a world beyond this one. People and creatures that are no longer alive make their home there. It is a nice place for me, but not for everyone. I can survive very well in both your world and the world of the Great Beyond," the snake continued.

Henry, ever seeking the final point of a discussion, queried, "I won't go there," he commented. "Pray tell, what is a meetup meeting?"

"It is a meeting of Friends from both worlds: those Friends from the world above and those from beneath the earth's crust. You call it the "nether" world. I call it home," telepathed the snake who was now changing both color, shape and size.

The creature before them was now no longer a snake, but changed into all manner of mammalian animals, going from mouse to rat to rabbit, to dog, to goat to cow, to deer to satyr to the final stage, that of a hoofed horned red man with a pointed chin, goatee and a long handlebar like mustache. This all happened with flashes of light, like lightning, with one change occurring each a few seconds after the other.

Henry and Elizabeth now had no question about who their conversational partner was. Nevertheless, Henry pursued, in all innocence, "What was the meetup about anyway? What did we miss?"

The demon laughed, "You missed a lot! You missed how the wronged Wicca of the past will now return to take their vengeance upon those agents' descendants in the world of man who unjustly tortured and destroyed them and whatever they loved. They are returning to "even the score", as it were. They read aloud references to passages out of the "Witches Hammer" literature to reinforce their need for vengeance, only partly because of the unfairness of the churches and the so-called religious, holier than thou, clergy for three hundred years, and more, of torture and unfair persecution including burning at the stake of millions of innocent women. Vengeance, hatred, retaliation, and destruction are my forte. I, and others like me, thrive on the energy of such emotions. Such feelings are in my favor and make those who call me "Friend" truly my friends indeed!"

The two agents, Henry and Elizabeth, were once again frozen in place. They were shocked as to with whom they were speaking and his classical demonic appearance, but also about what he was reporting.

"I know what you are doing. You are seeking evidence to bring back to your headquarters. Go ahead, take my picture, and show it to your leaders. I do not consider it a threat to me or to my already deceased members, all of whom I call "friend," the demon stated.

The encouragement reminded Henry that he never turned off the time capture camera. It had recorded everything.

The demon then asked the pair, "Would you, my new "Friends", like to visit my home? Would you like to come to the earth beneath the crust with me? You are most welcome indeed!"

The demon uttered a horribly guttural and animal-like laugh that terrified them both. The quasi-triumphant laughter motivated the frightened Elizabeth to cast down her collar and resulted in their immediate departure from the scene. They left the Las Vegas area in a flash and were now back home at their starting point.

Henry and Elizabeth just stood upon the spot where they returned without moving for several minutes. The shock was so great. They were both relieved to have escaped safely from the demon's invitation.

Elizabeth was the first to speak, "Holy Willikers!" she exclaimed. In my world, one would say "Holy Whiskers!" but I am in your world, so the first will pertain. "What was that? Is that the kind of creature which exists in your world?"

Henry replied, "Such has been rumored, but I never met up with one before. Nonetheless, that creature is not just a creation of my world but of the universe, including your world and beyond!"

"Don't use that "beyond" word, please. I have heard enough of it, thank you, for one day." Elizabeth responded.

"Are we safe?" asked a wary Henry.

"We are safe," responded Elizabeth matter-of -factly. The door will only admit the people who went on its merry trip to return. It does not accept those who were not present at time of departure. The demon was not at departure with us, therefore, he is not here at all."

She added once again, "We are safe. Do not worry, Henry. We are safe." She repeated again for emphasis.

"Now what do we do?" Henry asked, as though lost.

"Very simple. We bring our camera and its recording back to Mary Kent. It is now in her domain. We have done our work," answered Elizabeth quite succinctly.

"But we did not see anything happen. We did not see any witches or any meeting at all. What will Mary say?" Henry asked, still lost and puzzled to boot.

"Mary will be very pleased, Henry. We saw what perhaps no one in our survey group would ever see. We saw a snake who is a demon and who gave us a full report on what was going on. We did very well indeed, Henry." Elizabeth spoke with confidence.

Henry started, "But…."

He trailed off. Elizabeth raised her hand indicating, "stop". She then supplemented that sign with, "Henry, don't you see? She can reverse the timed events to BEFORE we arrived there. The camera has the power not to just reveal what we saw and when we saw it, but also it can show you the preceding history. We can see the meeting we never attended. We can attend it as a "playback" feature of the camera. We cannot see the future, but we can see into the past. It will be as though we were there when whatever occurred happened. We can enter that photo and become a part of the past. We can see what happened in greater safety and with almost no risk." She then added with pride in her voice, "Henry, we are golden!"

Henry smiled a very satisfied smile and raised both thumbs upward.

With the ending of those words, the pair turned and scooted off to present Mary with the fruits of their labor, the DESE time capture camera and its recordings.

NOTE:

The Witch's Hammer introduced the world to 'the dangers of freethinking women' and instructed the clergy how to locate, torture, and destroy them. Those deemed 'Witches' by the church included all female scholars, priestesses, gypsies, mystics, nature lovers, herb gatherers, and any women 'suspiciously attuned to the natural world. Midwives were also killed for their heretical practice of using medical knowledge to ease the pain of childbirth—a suffering, the church claimed, that was god's rightful punishment for Eve's partaking of the Apple of Knowledge, thus giving birth to the idea of Original Sin. During three hundred years of witch hunts, the church burned at the stake an astounding five million women". This may be information overload for many readers, but it finally puts substance into the reality the world has suffered through. However, the book goes onto wrongfully assuming that there are no Pagans left in the world. That is where we come in. We must show the world that we are here, even after all this bloodshed.

Author's Comment:

The most sacred matter after God is the human heart, and its spirit, its needs, its hurts and wounds, its joys, and its sorrows. The needs of the human heart should be universally met.

We all make errors in our lifetime, and if we are lucky, we have that lifetime to correct them.

CHAPTER SIXTY-SIX

THE ADVENTURE OF HB GAUNT AND JACK HENIGSON

HB Gaunt and Jack Henigson were also ready to begin their adventure into the unknown. It seems that HB was all thumbs when it came to using the Confugio piece of equipment, although apprehensive. It was all due to nervousness and apprehension over the prospect of a potentially dangerous escapade. The setting dials were too delicate and tiny when it came to entering their destination coordinates and HB's large and calloused fingers could not do it, at least not right away. After fumbling with the dials for twenty minutes, HB managed to enter both the going and returning coordinates satisfactorily. The return coordinates are automatically set with GPS confirmation. Jack was quite patient, but still doing a slow burn just waiting for the manipulation impaired HB took to complete his task of setting the Confugio.

It was time for the pair to start their journey into the unknown. The area was more unknown to Jack than to HB. HB made that area his home and was quite familiar with the "normality's" of the region. It was the region he was in charge of monitoring. He would be able to pick up any out -of-the-ordinary changes right away whereas Jack would need to learn what was normal or use his extrasensory and intuitive powers to know the difference.

HB asked Jack, "Everything is all set. Are you ready?"

Jack nodded and said, "I'm ready. Let it rip."

Jack and HB held each other's hands and HB activated the "go" button. Upon activation, they started to disappear from the bottom up. First the feet, then legs, then torso and lastly their heads dissolved into thin air. Suddenly there was no one to be seen. The whole process took less than two seconds.

The pair experienced dizzying, twisting and turning, ups and downs and backs and forth motions. Suddenly that motion took on a direction and rapidly zipped off at incredible speeds. The speed was unfathomable. Lights and lightning-like discharges were sparking everything about them as the traveled revolving in an ethereal tunnel. All the pair could later report was that it was very, very fast.

The "tunnel" opened and let the two out at Phil Foster Memorial Park in Riviera Beach. Fortunately, no one witnessed their entry which was behind the boat locker. They both needed a few minutes to recover from the not-to-comfortable trip.

"Wow!" exclaimed Jack. That was quite a ride, but here we are in mid Florida in the matter of less than forty seconds. It is a two and one-half hour trip otherwise by jet plane!"

"You better believe it," said HB. He continued, "There is a good side to this though. We are near my home on Ocean Drive."

"I fail to see how that is a good thing. The Confugio is to have been keyed in with the coordinates produced by the PEM scanner. The coordinates are to have been where the strongest signs of evil and discontent were received," said Jack.

"That's right." Answered HB. "Sure as shootin'."

"HB don't tell me that you entered different coordinates in the Confugio just to get let us off closer to your home!" asked an indignant Jack.

"No, of course not. I wouldn't do something like that, would I?" HB responded with a wink.

Jack was now a bit perturbed. He was not certain if the coordinates placed in the Confugio were those the PEM device read or if HB changed the coordinates for personal reasons.

"I can see that you are upset," said HB. Do not worry. I did not change the settings from those of the PEM device readings. What you see before you now is what you get."

Jack responded, "Good. I would hate to think that you would have altered the settings we need for our investigation, but what are we doing here anyway? This is almost the center of activity for Riviera Beach, just off Blue Heron Boulevard. That is a main road connector to Singer Island. There is too much public activity here. There could be no way that any "evil" or wicked "witch" activity could go on here. It would be noticed by everyone."

"That does seem to be an obvious truth, but that is what the PEM read. There are three buildings there. Any meeting could take place behind any one of them," said HB. He then continued, "What I find upsetting is that this is so close to where I live. The DESE detecting devices I placed in the area did pick up some abnormal readings which I sent back to headquarters, but I had no idea that any meeting of malevolence would take place at what is virtually my back yard!" HB replied.

It was still early morning. The reports taken from PEM detector are not that old, perhaps close to only twenty-four hours old.

Realization that the newness of the PEM report was virtually "current" Jack said, "HB, the reports are not that old. Let's search out the area and see what we can come up with."

"Right, let's do that, but we need to stay together," answered HB.

"All right," answered Jack. "That would be a very good idea, for safety's sake. Whatever went on here happened only a few hours ago."

The pair first circled the building towards the front and center of the island and then the one next to it on the east side. They then circled the building on the northwest side of the island. That is the building furthest away from the busy Blue Heron Boulevard.

As they reached the rear of the building, they noticed the remnants of a fire. It was not warm, but it was not cold either. They both said, at the very same instant, "This is it!" Then they both looked at each other because of the unanimity of the conclusion they both reached at the very same moment and let out a short laugh. HB took out the DESE time capture camera and began recording what they were seeing.

Jack said, "This is it. Look at this place. There is a circled pentacle drawn on the ground and the fire placed at the center. There are signs of cloven animal hoof prints as well as human prints, both with and without shoes, going counterclockwise in a circle around the chair."

HB remarked, "It did not seem to have been a very large fire, but a low campfire instead. Look at that!"

Immediately behind the campfire was an old, gold paint peeling, and brown rusted card table type folding chair.

Jack and HB both stared at the chair which, although rusted and in disrepair, appeared to have a weird semblance to a poorly designed throne. They both came to the same interest in closer examination, so they entered the pentacle area and headed towards the chair.

As they entered the pentacle, and approached the chair, it appeared to change its form. It was changing into a well-designed throne instead of the derelict they first laid eyes upon. That was not enough. There was more.

HB and Jack hesitated a moment, both mystified by the changes they had just witnessed. Then they hesitantly and warily continued a slow, step-by-step advance toward the chair for a closer inspection. As they did so, there began to form a figure of a man seated on the chair. This was a bit much for the two, and they stopped in their tracks about ten feet short of their destination.

The chair now contained a fully formed man who was as handsome as any movie star one ever knew. He had deep black hair and a very long and fancy mustache of the handlebar type. He was dressed, inappropriately for this climate, in a black suit with a black shirt, but a very red tie. He gave the pair a winning smile and said, "Welcome to you both, Jack Henigson and HB Gaunt!"

Jack and HB were now not only unmoving in their tracks but also frightened nearly to death. They both realized that they had stumbled onto one of the great evils the world knew in all its history.

The handsome man rose from the throne and stood before them. The throne changed to brilliant gold and was fully bedecked with glittering precious gems and bore the words chiseled in solid gold, "The Throne at Pergamos". The man held a pointed black, but very fancy, cane with a horned, gold metal head at the DESE agents. He was very tall. He was taller than any basketball player they had ever heard of by at least one foot. The two agents strained to look up to see the man's face. The man looked down on them as though they were bugs.

He then said in a very assuring tone, "Do not be afraid. I will do you no harm. You are late comers to the meeting, are you not? Then again, you have missed a great part of the meeting. That is unfortunate. However, you are not a part of my "Friends" group, are you? You can call me "Friend" anyway. That is my preference, if you do not mind."

HB was the first to speak. "Friend, what happened here? How could there be a fire on this island. It is not permitted. I know because I live nearby. The Fire Department should have been here within minutes of its being started. How could a fire not be noticed? What is this all about anyway?"

The "Friend" answered, "Very simple. You see the way I showed up in that "chair". You see it now. It is not just a "chair", is it? It is part of my life, you see. That is a very special chair. It is really a throne and a very nice one at that."

"Go on," said an impatient HB, as is his nature. "Tell me more."

"Do not be so impatient my Friend. You will get to know all, in due time, that is. The public never saw, heard, or smelled anything. There was nothing for them to smell, see or hear. It was all magic, you see. Now that the meet is over, there is no need to hide anything, and it is now available for public inspection and notice."

The strange man kept pointing his cane at the two in a jabbing motion. It made them quite nervous indeed. At times, either HB or Jack would duck to avoid contact with the cane's tip, but it never came to that.

The man went on, "You see, I am not from your world, but then again, I am. I am here, there, and everywhere, sometimes simultaneously. It is in my power to do such things. You may think of me as a collector. I collect garbage mostly but sometimes there is a brilliant gem among the refuse. I use those "gems" to decorate my throne. I place them into the chair's frame and my cane, one at a time. Foolish mortals indeed! You can see that I have no shortage of gems, do I?"

The man now paused in his talk, giving Jack a chance to speak. "Jack naively asked, "What kind of gems are they?"

"Oh, they are only the most special gems one can ever get. They are neither diamonds nor rubies, nor tanzanite nor emeralds. Look at those in my cane's handle. You can see the luster and clarity of the gem. It is just about as perfect as one can obtain." The man turned his cane around so that the pair could check the beauty of the stone.

Jack and HB both looked at the stone carefully. It was not held close to them although the man was advancing slowly. It was apparent that the man wanted to touch them with his cane. As the man and came ever closer, they both could see that inside each of the gems were faces peering out. It gave them fearful goose bumps. They saw that hands were placed on the inside walls of each of the stones. The mouths were moving in apparent shouts, which could not be heard, although the gifted Jack did sense the most horrible feelings and thoughts of despair. He heard, via his second sense, "Lasciate ogni Esperanza Voi Que Entrate......" and that was all.

The hands inside the gem were moving frantically. Whatever was inside the stone wanted to escape its prison.

That was all the pair needed to see. Without another word, thought or advance warning HB pressed the "Return" on his Confugio, and the pair immediately vanished, quite unlike their departure earlier, when they did a slow "dissolve" into nothingness. This was an emergency if there ever was one. HB was not waiting for any discussion. For all they knew they were the "gems" the so-called "Friend" was seeking. They would have made a nice addition to his chair, but they vanished into nothingness, leaving only a flash of light like a photographer's bulb, and just as fast, the light faded. It was a though the tall man had his picture taken. Although his picture was not taken at the moment of the flash, the time capture camera was running all the time and recorded everything. It was never turned off in all the excitement. All was recorded.

The man and all his accoutrements also disappeared, but the pair could not know that. He had done his job. He did manage to collect some gems at the last "meetup". He was happy for the moment, but only slightly perplexed at the sudden disappearance of his hoped-for quarry. Nevertheless, there will be a next time. He satisfied himself with the thought that there will always be a "next time". He laughed at the idea, just before he also disappeared and went back home.

Meanwhile, HB and Jack were recovering from their fright. They knew their mission was dangerous and looked about themselves to make certain that the "man" was not with them. The Confugio programming would not allow that anyway. Two left and only the same two were permitted to return. They were satisfied that they were now safe.

Jack said to HB, "Ohmygosh!" he exclaimed. I have seen many strange things in my lifetime, but I never expected to see something that was like that! It was supernatural. Do you know who that was?" he asked the equally frightened HB.

"Unfortunately, I think I do. I think I do know who he is. He is the opposite end of good. He is what we came to discover. He is the source of all the evil in the world. Do you have any idea of how lucky we were to escape?" said HB.

"I do," answered Jack. "Let us get the camera back to Mary Kent right away. I do not even want to be near whatever the image it contains! It is better in Mary's hands. She, and her staff of experts, can do with it what they will. I have had enough for a day or two at this point and I could use some R & R!"

HB nodded in agreement and they both went off to headquarters without wasting a moment.

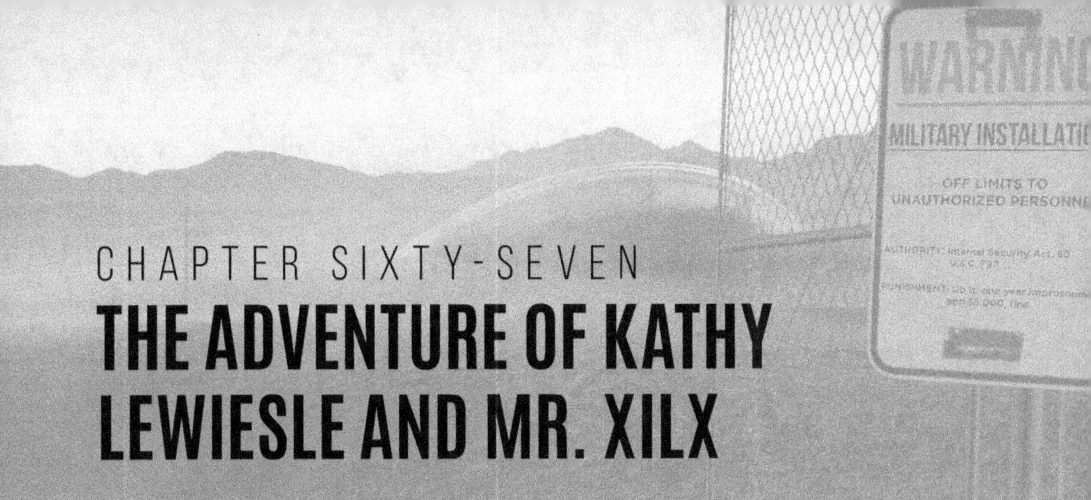

CHAPTER SIXTY-SEVEN

THE ADVENTURE OF KATHY LEWIESLE AND MR. XILX

The team of Kathy Lewiesle and Mr. Xilx was nearly ready to leave on their assignment, the Cicero, Illinois area near Chicago, the former headquarters of Al Capone. Mr. Xilx did not have use of the "Rubber Band" as did Black Lightning, but he did have use of the Confugio Device which acted similarly. However, it was less easily portable. Carrying the "Rubber Band" as a disguised necklace is more convenient and easier.

The Confugio Device was almost as portable but did not have any of the extraordinary features of the "Rubber Band". The Confugio was only a transportation device and worn as either a belt buckle or a wristwatch. In these modalities, it was somewhat disguised and would not attract attention.

Kathy, as the less experienced agent, is under the command of Mr. Xilx. This suited Kathy just fine because she would freely admit to her inexperience and appreciated the much greater and more extensive skills Mr. Xilx could access. She saw his abilities as a kind of "protection" and appreciated that fact.

Mr. Xilx could read Kathy's thoughts. However, the reverse was not a possibility, at least not yet in Kathy's DESE training.

He asked solicitously, "Kathy, are we ready to go to Cicero?"

Kathy answered, "I think that I am. What about you? Have we forgotten anything?"

Mr. Xilx replied in authoritative certainty, "I am all set, ready and raring to travel!"

"In that case, what are we waiting for? Let's roll!" answered an eager, though cautious, Kathy Lewiesle.

Mr. Xilx pushed the "go" button, which sped them toward the coordinates programmed in the Confugio. At the very start, Kathy closed her eyes tightly and grasped Xilx's hand with great force.

She shortly opened her eyes to see the two of them spin and twirl with flashes and streaks of light going in a circle and gyrating all about. They experienced all kinds of motion including the feeling of rapidly alternating rising and falling.

They exited their spinning journey at the junction of South Central Avenue and 25th Street, at West Morton Park, essentially the only park near the center of Cicero, Il.. Kathy looked at all about her, as did Mr. Xilx. They were both very surprised when they realized that, although in the center of a park, they were in a densely populated, urban area. They both assumed that Cicero would be in the suburbs of Chicago. They were very wrong indeed. It was a suburb, but more urban than they expected. They immediately looked about themselves once again and were very amazed that no one witnessed their unconventional arrival out of thin air. Perhaps people arriving that way were a normal occurrence in this Chicago suburb of about 100,000 people, but they both doubted that.

However, they were surprised by a red and green horned gremlin sitting at the edge of a swimming pool within the park just staring at them sporting a mischievous smile. The creature was motionless and, apparently, the only witness to their arrival. It showed no surprise or emotion, but simply took their sudden appearance in stride.

The PEM detector provided this arrival point as the location of an evil and destructive planning witches' meetup with malevolent vibes. Mr. Xilx started the time capsule recorder and scanned the area immediately upon their arrival. He felt that whatever unknown event that could happen might start unexpectedly at any moment. He wanted to be ready. The unusual and very surprising presence of a real Gremlin proved him right. Every move and every sound and every attribute of the area was being recorded. The presence of a real Gremlin was now recorded history.

Kathy and Mr. Xilx sensed that the appearance of a Gremlin could not be a good omen. The multi-colored Gremlin was about the size of a small middle school boy, say about four and one-half feet tall, even. The smile continued, but the jaw moved in a "chatter", somewhat like that of a scolding squirrel. The sounds were not words anyone could understand, at least not immediately.

Mr. Xilx's otherworldly experiences across the parts of the universe he traveled were kicking in. Slowly, but surely, he was beginning to understand the Gremlin's speech. It was speaking English. The only reason it sounded like "chatter" was because the words were coming so fast. It was more like a tape recorder playback at high speed.

Kathy, on the other hand, did not have Xilx's abilities. All she heard was chatter. The multi-tasking Xilx was not only able to interpret the speech of the Gremlin, but also the confusion in Kathy's mind.

Mr. Xilx did not only have the ability to read minds, but also had the capacity to transmit thoughts to those he chose. This fact also applied to those not gifted as him. It applied to Kathy. Mr. Xilx mentally transmitted the interpreted speech of the Gremlin to Kathy's mind so that she would think that she was hearing intelligible words directly from the Gremlin's mouth.

They heard the Gremlin's words, "Welcome, my Strange Friends, to the Home City of Al Capone. Welcome to the City that contains 2122 North Clark Street. The site of Al Capone's St. Valentine's Day party. The S-M-C Cartage Company building is now gone, but the "song" lingers on." The Gremlin uttered a short, guttural laugh in an apparent and fond reflective reminiscence.

Kathy, now understanding what the Gremlin was saying, shuddered in fear. The legend of the mobster, Al Capone, is well known. She knew that Chicago was his base of operations. The Valentine's Day party was no party. It was a day made infamously known as the "St. Valentine's Day Massacre". That was a message from Al Capone to George "Bugsy" Moran in rival gang warfare. The building, though gone and now replaced by a fenced-in park with five trees, the center tree marking the location where the massacre occurred, carries a negative effect on those who just walk by it to this very day. The bullet-pocked bricks from the destructed building apparently carry a curse and malevolence. Anyone who possesses one supposedly encounters misfortune, illness, or tragedy in short order.

Kathy knew all this because she did a quick investigation into Cicero and Chicago when she learned that this was her destination. That she now met a "greeter" who spouted this information did not make her comfortable.

Mr. Xilx was the first to speak. "Good morning, my friend. May I ask who you are?"

"Well, Mr. Xilx, I am an emissary from a world within a world. I am here, there, and everywhere. At the same moment, I am not here, there or anywhere, confusing, isn't it? Sometimes I feel like Alice's Cheshire Cat!"

The Gremlin paused, and then continued, still smiling, and showing multi-colored, but not-to-pretty, saw-toothed teeth, "I know the unknown and the known. The here and now. The now and what was now. The "was" and the "is". However", the Gremlin now began to speak slower and with a very distinguished British accent, "the real question is: How can I help you and Kathy?"

The twosome was again mutually surprised. This creature somehow knew their names. Fearing the worse, Mr. Xilx did not pursue how the creature knew their names, but rather sought to gain information regarding the results the PME indicated and the reason for negative readings. After all, that was why they were there!

Mr. Xilx answered, "We understand that a very special event took place here recently. It was a gathering of some sort. Could you possible tell us anything about it?"

The Gremlin said, "I could if I would, and I would if I could. As a matter of fact I could, but would I?", he asked himself giving the sarcastic smile of the Cheshire Cat. Then he raised his head and perked up and raised his right index finger and said, "I could, and I would!"

"Yes?" asked an eager Mr. Xilx with Kathy hanging onto every breath and every word.

"Look at the wall," commanded the Gremlin.

Kathy and Mr. Xilx looked for the wall. There was no wall. This was a park. This was a pool, but not too far away was a building and there was a wall. They both stared at it. The Gremlin pointed his gnarled, long and twisted index finger at it.

Suddenly, it was as though his finger was a camera projector of some strange sort. The tip of his finger glowed, and images began to form on the building's wall. The images were not initially clear, but slowly came into focus.

The projected scene showed people in long, black, flowing robes standing about a moderate fire and a cauldron. The hair on several of them was in the disarray of unkempt dreadlocks. Others sported hair of many colors. Some heads were orange, chartreuse, shocking pink, green or orange. Others had hair incorporating all the colors, while some of the weirder ones sported the historical Iroquois spike-bladed haircut along with myriads of ugly tattoos.

These had to be witches. There could be no doubt. This was a witches' coven meetup with "Merry Meet" spoken aloud and all around.

The witches gathered about the cauldron from which wafted streams of putrescent and iridescent purple-, green-, red- and orange-colored vapors as it boiled and bubbled.

There it was, shining, phosphorescent multi-green streaked lines including varying shades of red, orange, and purple-colored, and a stinking, thick flowing liquid. The apparent head witches, who announced themselves as Juday DuMealyworm and Miguel Barberry to the group, then ordered some lesser demons and goblins to bring in an old crate which appeared as a dilapidated, patch-covered old pirates' treasure chest, with a broken lock just hanging loose thereon to the proximity of the cauldron. They opened it and took out several dozen flattened and rolled up plastic looking sheets that appeared as witch cutouts. The forms were on a rusted steel cylindrical roll containing at least fifty such molds each. The roll was something like fruit rollups, or those rolled plastic bags at the fruit counter at some grocery stores, but much larger. As they unrolled the forms, they detached each from the remainder of the roll when another separate form came to its perforated end. They then picked the first one up, turned it upside down so that the feet end was at the top. While they were chanting a monotonous, unintelligible mantra, they used a large ladle filled with the mysterious liquid and poured it into the empty part of the plastic form.

When the form had been filled to the top, they stopped and each waved their multiple wands over it, in unison, and continued their chant. Within a few short moments thereafter, they turned the filled mold upside down so that the foot end was now on the ground. Suddenly, upon the placement of the mold's feet on the ground, the cast witch image came to life, dressed in a multi-colored witches' outfit, broad-brimmed peaked hat and all. The newly created witch happily greeted the community members, and each was well received. The witches repeated the procedure a dozen times and almost doubled the number of witches attending their merry meet. "Is that helpful?" asked the accommodating Gremlin who now ended the exhibit.

"Yes!" said Kathy and Mr. Xilx at the very same moment. Very helpful indeed," continued Mr. Xilx. Mr. Xilx added, "Out of curiosity, how did you know our names? We never told you who we were. How did you know?"

The Gremlin laughed his guttural laugh, "Easy," he pointed someplace over the heads of each of them. "It is the labels."

Mr. Xilx and Kathy looked at each other, puzzled. "What labels?" they both asked.

They then looked at their chests to see if they had taken off the "HELLO" labels from their meeting at DESE. They did. There were none on them. They both felt that this was a real mystery unless the Gremlin had other powers.

"The labels over your heads," explained the Gremlin as he pointed a crooked finger at them.

"There are no labels over our heads," said Kathy indignantly.

"Oh, but there are," the Gremlin continued. "These are labels which follow you all your life. You do not see them, but you are who you are, and you are so labeled. One would say "for all to see", but that is not completely true. It is a gift that only us Gremlins use, or so it is said. You see that way there are no disguises. You may try to hide from yourself, but in the final analysis, you really cannot hide from the world. You certainly cannot hide from us Gremlins. That is certain. It is our power. We have powers you know, more than you would ever imagine!"

"Thank you", said Mr. Xilx and Kathy nodded an assent.

"No problem", said the Gremlin. "Now I am neither here nor elsewhere and that is where I must go. See you again."

With those words, the Gremlin faded into thin air and dissolved away.

Mr. Xilx, satisfied with the visit, pushed the "Return" button on his Confugio and he and Kathy dissolved into nothingness.

A drunken vagrant who was bedded down under a nearby bush, but a bit away from all the action, witnessed everything. After he saw the strange Gremlin creature and the two visitors disappear, he said very much aloud, shouting towards the place where the three just disappeared, "That's enough! I have had it! I am never going to drink again!", and threw down his paper bagged bottle, then rolled over and went back to sleep.

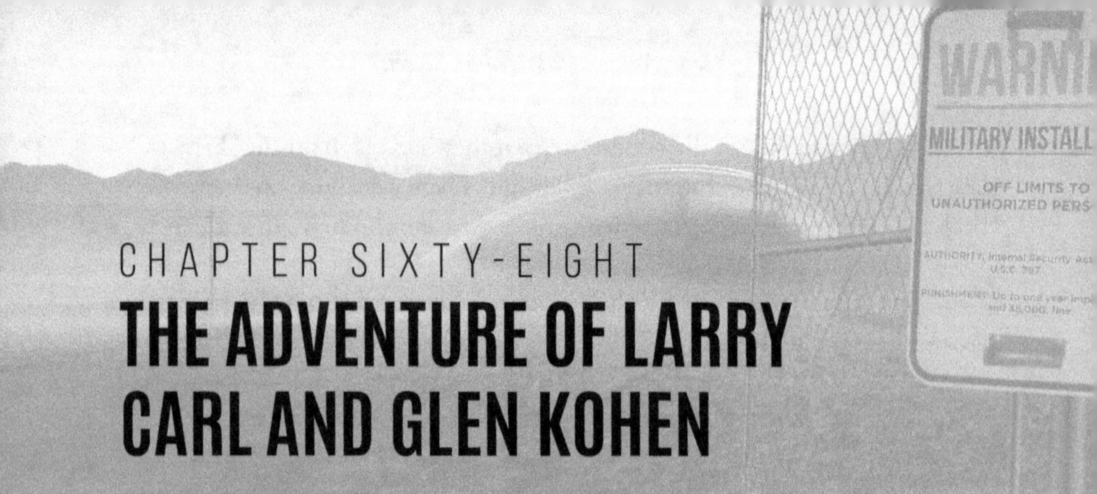

THE ADVENTURE OF LARRY CARL AND GLEN KOHEN

Larry Carl was quite ready to make the return visit to his Alma Mater. He always looked upon the years he spent at the University of Michigan in very fond memory. Artes, Scientia, Veritas. Art, Science and Truth. These are the words on the Michigan Shield. He recalled his days at the Michigan campus, his classes at Angell Hall, the Science Building and the passing of time at the East Quadrangle, where he lived for several years. He recalled the mysterious fall nights when he would hear distant tom-tom drumbeats as the "Michigauma", an honors group that dressed in Indian costume with war paint, tapped yet another member. He remembered a lot, considering the passage of years.

Soon, he and Glenn Kobren will make a sudden arrival some place in Ann Arbor. In some ways, he was very eager to be there, and, in another way, he was more anxious about the reason for his journey. Seeking a source of evil was not exactly what he considered a pleasure trip at all.

Glenn Kobren was suitably dressed for the trip, as he was. It was now time to push the "Go" button on the Confugio.

"Glenn", asked a concerned Larry Carl, "are you ready to take off?"

Glenn responded, "I am. Let us move." Larry had no apprehension whatsoever. In fact, Glenn wondered if Larry ever knew fear. He doubted it.

Larry checked the Confugio to ascertain that the settings were as the PEM dictated. They were. There was no need to delay their "adventure" any longer. A less eager Glenn held onto Larry's hand and then he pushed the "Go" button and off they went. They simply dissolved away uniformly from bottom up, and not too quickly. In the matter of three seconds, they were gone.

They took the wild ride, up, down, in, out. Lights were flashing and twirling everything about them. Larry closed his eyes to gain some equilibrium. It worked. He quieted down emotionally and enjoyed the rest of the trip. It was a trip of less than twenty, or so, seconds. The Confugio unceremoniously "dumped" them out almost in front of the Stockwell and Mosher-Jordan Halls, the girls' dormitories.

The two were not that fortunate. Perhaps, however, they were. They were "dumped" behind the entrance to Forest Hill Cemetery, which is located across the street from the dormitories. They were inside the walls of that cemetery. Glenn Kohen was not pleased about where he was, but Larry Carl could have cared less. We are here again at the University of Michigan campus.

Larry Carl found it curious that a place of malevolence as indicated by the PEM could be so close to a college girls' dormitory complex, but this is where the PEM placed them. The coordinates were accurate.

Larry and Glenn looked around searching for any kind of evidence that would point to some type of event that happened within the last few days. Those days would be concurrent with the flight of the PEM over the area. The PEM would not lie. Something happened here a few days ago. The problem was to locate where it happened and to film it with the Time Capture Camera. A cautious Larry Carl had set the Time Capture Camera in operation almost immediately upon arrival.

The graveyard was not small and encompassed several acres. The TCC, though capable, but not designed to be survey equipment. It was a camera, although a very special one. Taping the entire cemetery would be out of the question.

Larry was happy that it was daylight. He recalled that when he dated Maggie Quick many years ago, he was invited to enter the cemetery with her. The problem was that it was nighttime. Darkness and cemeteries did not agree with Larry's superstitious yellow streak. Larry declined the invitation. He was easily spooked. There was no way that he would enter any cemetery in the darkness of night, even with a flashlight and a girl friend. At that period in his life Larry was not as fearless as he is now.

The Confugio was designed to place arrivals in the approximate area dictated by PEM coordinates, but within a safe distance from where the action took place. It would be up to them to search out the area for signs and indications of malevolence or any form of depressed mood or emotions.

Larry and Glenn decided that they would not separate. The reason being that if one did encounter some type of evil the other should be immediately on hand to help with whatever problems might arise from whatever confrontation event.

They were in the center of the cemetery when they heard a creaking, groaning sound behind them in an area they had just passed. They both turned around at reflex speed only to see what appeared to be an open grave. They were alarmed. The "grave" was not there a moment ago. At least, that is what it appeared to be at first glance. The two drew closer to the grave only to find that it was not a grave at all, but a descending stairway instead.

They wisely took caution and stopped in their tracks. They peered into the opening. It was quite dark despite the fact that it was daylight and the sun had risen to about fifty degrees above the horizon. It was about eleven o'clock and the sky was bright and cloudless. Even so, the interior of the staircase-crypt combination was blacker than the blackest night. The end of the staircase was not visible. The base just trailed off in darkness.

Larry and Glenn knew that they had found what they were seeking. A cemetery does not usually contain down-into-the-earth staircases.

Glenn asked Larry, "Now what do we do?"

Glenn was fearful of what Larry would say and even more fearful of what Larry might want to do.

"Simple. We photograph the staircase going down into the earth. This is obviously an entrance to the underworld and the source of the PEM's diagnostic readings. It is a source of evil. Can you not just feel it? My skin feels "crawly" with invisible insects. Don't you just feel the evil here?"

"Right", responded a worried Glenn. "Then we can go home. Is that right?"

"Well, since this is a Time Capture Camera that can read the past, perhaps we can," reflected a more thoughtful Larry. "Perhaps we should leave. All we need to do is to present the recording to Mary and she can read its past history. We can learn what happened here several nights ago."

A much-relieved Glenn gratefully responded, "Terrific. You are already recording the staircase. Let us go now!"

"On the other hand,", Larry went on, "We can go down the staircase and learn where it leads. That is also a good idea."

"No, we do not need to do that." Glenn responded peremptorily. "It is not a good idea. It is a very bad idea. Besides, I thought you were braver than I! I am not as brave as you. I want to go. " retaliated Glenn.

"Think Glenn. We have the Confugio. If we get into trouble, all we need to do is to push the "Return" button. Then we would be safe. There is no problem."

"I know. I also know that sometimes things do not work. We have never tested the "Return" button, have we now?" asked a very worried Glenn. "What if it doesn't work when we need it most? Huh? What then?"

"I guess the other side would be having roast chicken. Our gooses would be cooked, but in this case it would be chicken especially where you are concerned!", replied a joking but more conciliatory Larry after considering what Glenn had said.

"Great," answered a very anxious Glenn. "Now let's get out of here right now! This is too spooky."

"All right," said a conciliatory Larry. "Just let me go closer and get a better look inside. I will only take a second."

Upon saying those words, Larry did not wait for Glenn to answer. He stepped forward towards the opening and put one foot on the first step. Suddenly, the interior of the crypt lit up brightly. The walls of the crypt alongside the staircase were embedded an array of human skulls along side which were additional small alcoves containing canary bird cages.

Inside each birdcage was a fully fleshed human head, not a skull. The disembodied heads were alive and as Larry took the first step, their eyes turned to look at Larry. Blue eyes, brown eyes, hazel and green eyes all turned to see Larry. Larry saw eye upon eye. The living heads all started speaking to him in unison, warning him of what lay below. Larry stopped.

"Do not enter. Halt. Verboten. Kein Eintritt. Alto. Ferme'," they were all saying in a cacophony of sound.

Larry recognized that phrase from Dante's Inferno and written over the entrance gates of hell, *"Lasciate Ogni Esperanza, Voi Que Entrate"*, "Abandon All Hope Oh Ye That Enter". Larry did not expect to see that phrase etched in red over the transom at the base of this staircase.

Larry knew that he already saw more than he wanted to see. He had his finger on the "Return" button.

The already brightly lit interior of the crypt, almost brighter than sunlight, exploded to an even brighter light at the foot of the staircase. Larry saw the creature at the staircase's base and began to retreat off the first step.

"Where do you think you are going, Larry Carl?" said the creature.

Larry was shocked that the demon knew his name but continued to back off.

"You are going nowhere. You now belong to me!" the creature at the stair base said, spewing fire and smoke at each word coming from his mouth.

The creature was a great, glowing red, six-horned demonic Dragon, wings and all, sitting in a pool of flaming lava. The creature started to make its way up the stairs towards Larry, much faster than one would expect in relation to its size. Larry was now in a well-deserved panic. The creature was now reaching for his foot, almost touching it. In a virtual reflex action, Larry pressed the "Return" button.

The two instantly dissolved into nothingness just as the demon was about to complete his grasp of Larry's foot. The demon had lost.

The reverse Confugio trip was similar but easier than the departure since the routing was already set in the device. There was not as much light, bumps, twisting or flashes on the way back.

However, the "dump" was still an unceremonious one. The Confugio placed them exactly at their point of departure. There was no gentleness to their "dumping", despite alleged Confugio improvements. They were both flattened on their buttocks with a stinging, moderately hard force. Both travelers were breathing hard. Larry had beads of sweat all over his forehead. His fear factor was breached.

"Well, I told you so," said a scolding Glenn. "I told you it was not safe. Do you know how lucky we are?"

They both looked around, fearful of hitchhikers. They were relieved that none was there.

"You were right," conceded Larry. "You were right. Let's get this film over to Mary right away."

It was barely three Eastern Standard Time in the afternoon. Their day of thrills was over for now.

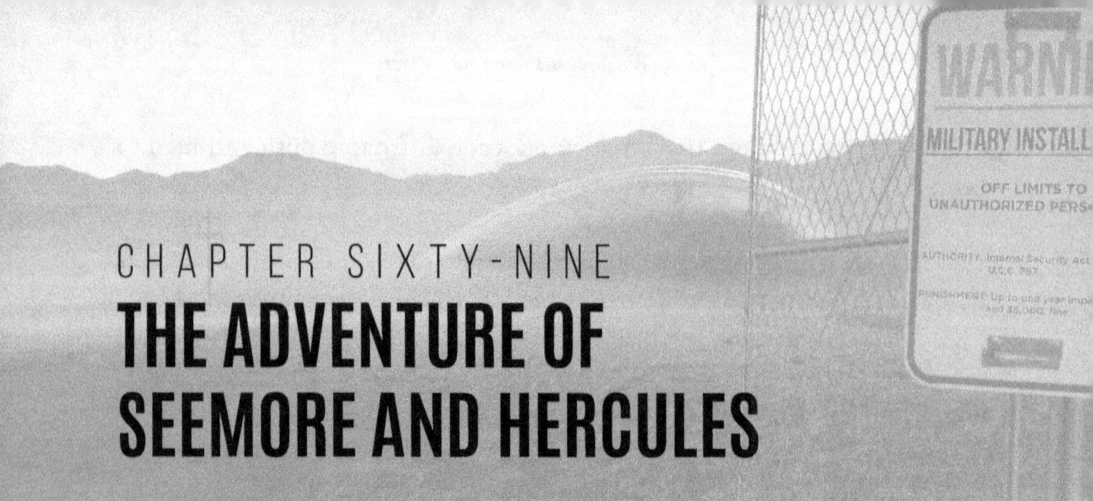

CHAPTER SIXTY-NINE
THE ADVENTURE OF SEEMORE AND HERCULES

Seemore Manlein and Hercules Canue were soon to depart for their New Orleans destination. Seemore followed the same protocol as the other agents. That protocol was the way they learned to use the Confugio and the TCC. The instructions are to start recording immediately upon arrival and keep the Confugio controls handy, just in case.

The hardest part of departure was that they had to hold hands upon initiation of the trip. Hercules was totally repulsed having to hold a Gnome's hand, but that is the only way they could make the trip. They had to be together upon departure in order to escape danger at their destination in the event of an emergency. Hercules knew that Seemore was a naturalist. He did not know if Seemore ever washed his hands and so he was reluctant to hold them. Hercules could not help but show his reluctance to hold Seemore's hand. Seemore never noticed that Hercules was repulsed in the slightest.

The Confugio dropped them out of their labyrinthine journey in the middle of Jackson Square, located just about in the middle of New Orleans. They found themselves in the center of the circular designed plantings and walkways around it.

They were only a block away from "Sulies' Magic Shoppe" on Royal Street, open for official business from Thursdays through Sundays from 9:00 AM to 12:00 Midnight, except when the moon is full. Then the store remains closed at night, although it is open during the daylight hours. There it is known to vend various kinds of elixirs, Voodoo spells, and dolls as well as ritual magic items. Witchcraft and magical items from all around the world can be bought here. Nevertheless, it is known that "Sulie" himself is one of the good witches and would not hurt a fly. He would hurt mosquitoes, yes, especially if they bite. He would not hurt one. After all, they might be someone's reincarnated relative, perhaps even his own!

The PME device, however, pointed out that here was the point of highest discontent and malevolence. That is what they were here to uncover and discover. Hercules and Seemore looked about the park very carefully and cautiously. They knew why they were here. Their task was to learn what caused the PME to create its recording of evil, discontent, and wickedness at this location. They knew that danger was waiting for them at this location, but they could not know what it would be.

The two searched out the concentric circles by moving out from the center and systematically seeking clues to what the PME uncovered as evil. They did not see anything and were about to simply give up the search when immediately in front of them was an old, rusted wrought iron gate with a broken latch and a broken, rusted padlock which simply and suddenly manifested itself only one foot before them.

Hercules said, "What in the world is that?"

Seemore answered, "It is a gate. That is what it is. That is all."

Seemore's response was quite a matter of fact statement. There was no emotion or fear involved.

"That's all?" retorted Hercules. "A gate appears suddenly before you and you barely avoid colliding with it and you only can say, "That is all"? Seemore, you are too much" added an incredulous Hercules.

"That is all it is", replied Seemore. "One does not get as old as I am by getting excited over such minor things. There are greater dangers in the world than just an old, rusted gate in your path, believe me. Look behind the gate. There is nothing out of "normal" there. Do you not agree?"

"Perhaps", answered Hercules. "I guess that if we are continuing our investigation we must go through that gate. Do you agree?"

Seemore immediately responded, "Yes. I do agree indeed."

Hercules carefully reached for the gate. He was making extremely cautious contact with the rusted metal. He touched it with one finger.

Nothing happened.

Hercules now felt assured that nothing would happen should he open the gate.

He did. Nothing happened. Seemore and Hercules, thus assured, entered through the gate.

When Hercules and Seemore stepped through the gateway, a surprise greeted them. They turned around and looked back through the gate. There they saw Jackson Square, but ahead of them was a different location. They did not see the finery of a park. They were no longer in Jackson Square. There were tombstones and religious statues all about them. There was a mist hovering over the entire cemetery which cut through their clothing and chilled them so that they both shivered from cold, even though the sun was up and even though before they entered the gate, the weather was warm. They noted the contrast readily, and did not appreciate the cold.

They found themselves instead in Lafayette Cemetery. Across the street was St. Joseph's Orphan Asylum Cemetery. They were in an area of almost three square blocks of cemetery. They did not consider the change of location to be one they found desirable, although they did find it exciting but dangerous. There was no explanation.

They followed their routine, although they could not know what it was. They just knew that the situation was not "normal". They did not even know what their route was to be, but they knew they had to follow it. It was their duty.

The cemetery was quite a common one. Tombstones and semi-raised graves lined both sides of a central pathway. This is nothing out of the ordinary for connoisseurs of cemeteries. This is just another graveyard.

The pair stayed close to each other as they toured the cemetery.

Hercules reflected aloud, "This is not my idea of a tour or a recreational outing. That is for certain."

Seemore noted "The most unusual thing about this cemetery is that it has an abundance of crows, more than they ever saw in any cemetery or even any town. They sat alight atop wires strung between poles. Look at that. These birds are sitting lined upon wires up and down the street between two cemeteries."

Hercules admitted, "That is very interesting." He added in even greater amazement, "There need to be at least three hundred crows sitting on the different wires."

Seemore added, "Look there. Other kinds of birds are there as well."

"Yes, that is so." Hercules agreed and then added, "However, the dark crows stay on one wire and group themselves together. The more brightly colored birds have arranged themselves separately on adjacent wires."

"I see that", said Seemore. "It is as though they were on rival teams of some sort."Seemore went on, "The number of birds is very unusual. Look at that!" he exclaimed excitedly. "Birds of all kinds have spaced themselves from each other, using even spacing between them, out on a light boom, a ridged roof top, an electrical telephone line, a video cable wire, a clothesline. There must be hundreds of them!"

Hercules said, "The even spacing between them is not unusual. I see that all the time when traveling up and down I-95 on the lamppost light extensions over the highway. It is obvious only to those who are observant. They also do that on wires, long tree branches and the like. I need to admit that it is a bit curious, is it not? There must be a reason why they evenly space themselves out like that and are not bunched together." Seemore, being the animal liaison connection between wildlife and humanity went closer to the birds, as they would permit. He communicated with one of the more colorful birds, a cardinal, to the tune of an extensive and highly animated conversation. The cardinal flew down and sat on a tombstone and apparently developed a conversation with Seemore.

While they conversed, Seemore was pointing and occasionally waved his hands while the bird flew up and down and spreading his wings as though pointing this way and that. All the while Hercules waited impatiently some distance away, completely taken by the scene before him.

Seemore managed to enlist the cardinal's aid in that he and his group agree to become agents for the good causes of DESE. The cardinal explained that the black crows were creatures acting in agency for the nether world.

Seemore learned that the reason the birds were spaced had to do with Marconi and his radio inventions. The birds were spaced according to transmission of interspecies neural vibration, electro-magnetic radio type signals to each other as well as to agents who were far, far away. This trait also belonged to Seemore, the animal-human DESE agents' connection.

The cardinal told Seemore "The spacing between us varies depending on whether we are transmitting or receiving signals. The spacing out for the varied respective linear configurations actually tunes in a certain neuron-mental-radio vibration frequencies for transmission or reception of signals going to and from each group and now, since meeting with you, to and from DESE as well."

The cardinal went on, "The closer together we align ourselves, the higher the frequency both of transmission and reception. The further apart we sit, the lower the frequency. We transmit or receive as a group. When we use our joined power, it acts as an amplifier in both directions." The bird then did the equivalent of striking his own chest in praise of his virtues and added, "This is truly an ingenious arrangement and discovery, do you not agree?"

Seemore told the bird that he most certainly did agree. The entire conversation and communication with a bird was not believable. Hercules, who witnessed the event, however, did most certainly believe. It was unlike anything he had ever seen before in his entire lifetime!

Suddenly the bird's excited movements ceased. It went into the human equivalent of depression. The bird related to Seemore "Regrettably, the same holds true for transmission and reception for the evil ones." The now somber cardinal explained, "Some Wicca do advocate a vengeful, hateful, destructive, and harmful Wicca way of life. Seagulls, crows, ravens and even pigeons can be the agents for both sides, with the black colored birds mostly in consort with the evil Wicca, not the good ones."

The now "serious" cardinal said to Seemore in confidence, "The dual agents can be receptors and disseminators of information either to the Wicca or to DESE. It is hard to tell who the turncoat will be."

Usually, but not always, the darker birds such as the crows or ravens, call out messages to each other with their raspy "caw, caw, caw" and transmit signals to the Wicca. That is what it appears innocently to the human, non-discriminating public.

The cardinal continued, "Seldom do these dark toned bird agents work for DESE. However, this is not always true. Some of the dark colored birds work for the betterment of their environment and of humanity. Some of these black birds are dual agents. They rarely give the Wicca valuable information that they instead destine for DESE only. They report to the Wicca just enough non-important information to maintain their cover and nothing more."

Seemore was most impressed with the sophistication of this cardinal who was apparently an intelligent and thinking being.

The cardinal continued, "Unfortunately, when these dual agents are found out, they are usually killed by the Wicca. The favorite agent the evil Wicca use in destroying the newly discovered dual-agent birds is the employment of the West Nile Virus. The birds die and then are located by man's ecologic environmental agents and the fact that West Nile Virus has reached a certain area of the country is trumpeted in the news."

The cardinal let out a short but sarcastic bird version of a laugh, "Man is sometimes so naïve and simple minded. Man can be fooled into believing almost anything. It is the evil witches who mercilessly aim the West Nile Virus at the newly discovered dual agent crow, and thus they are eliminated."

Seemore was fully intent on the words and information the cardinal divulged. The cardinal continued his treatise, "The evil Wicca rejoices and decent human society despairs. Man has no idea as to the real cause or reason for the death of the magnificent dual-agency birds. The disguised assassination agent is successful. The humans blame the bird deaths on the spread of the West Nile Virus instead of the real cause: Infection via an evil Wicca curse and magic. Fortunately, for DESE, only a very few bird agents are ever discovered."

Seemore noted that Hercules was becoming impatient and relayed that to the cardinal informant. He thanked the cardinal for his counsel. The cardinal appreciated his almost unilateral conversation with Seemore and said his goodbye. Then he flapped his colorful wings and flew back up to his "post" on the wire above.

Seemore went back to Hercules and related the information he gleaned from the cardinal. Hercules was amazed. Here was a "man" who could converse with birds!

"That is truly amazing Seemore. Truly amazing indeed!" said Hercules.

"It is nothing," replied Seemore, obviously proudly receiving Hercules' praise.

"But we have not yet found the reason why the PME sent us to this place," continued Hercules.

"We need to keep looking. The strange gate entrance that sent us here has to be an indicator that we this is going in the right direction. We just need to continue our search," replied Seemore.

"Right", agreed Hercules. "Let us continue."

Seemore and Hercules went on searching the graveyard for clues. They went up one aisle and down another. All they found was tombstone after tombstone and grave after grave. They eventually came upon a large rock which seemed out of place in a level field of graves. It was large enough for one to sit on, but certainly not one that a person would trip over. The granite mass was at the base of a maple tree and the shadow of the tree fell over the rock like a dark blanket.

This attracted the attention of both agents, and they walked over more particularly to inspect it. Both agents stopped suddenly in their steps. There was a sizable something or someone that suddenly moved under the tree. The movement continued. The pair stood frozen and simply observed the moving article, whatever it might be.

They were finally much relieved when the shadow rose from under the tree and showed itself to be a slightly crippled old man using a cane to steady himself and not anything weird or other-worldly, simply resting there.

"Hello," the man said. "Can I help you?"

"Please, if you will," replied Hercules. "First let me ask where this place is?"

"Oh, that is an easy question," the old man answered confidently. "You are in the Lafayette Cemetery and across the street", the man pointed using his cane and nearly falling over, "is the St. Joseph Orphans Asylum Cemetery. I come here to monitor the peace and quiet and to get away from city noise."

"I see", replied Hercules. It certainly has to be peaceful here since everyone here is not alive. Who are you? What is your name?"

"Oh my, yes. It is usually very quiet here, except for the birds. Sometimes they make a lot of noise and soil the area under their roosts" he responded.

"But what is your name?" Hercules repeated.

My name is Francis Loa. I was a priest in my younger years and fought off the evil Zobop influenced people. I now try to watch this place for my friend Joe German who opened it many years ago. The birds are a nuisance though, but they only show up after these weird black robed people show up. Then they are gone within a few days. I think that is a strange coincidence, but that is what happens every so often. I never know when they are coming, but the birds always make a mess.

"I'll bet they do." Seemore answered. "Why are they here anyway? Do they like this place or are they migrating or something?"

The man replied offhandedly, "Oh, I guess that they do like this place, but they are here only once in a while, and not every day."

"Tell me more", prodded Seemore.

"Well, believe it, the other day some people held a party of some sort here. Strange group they were too." He paused pensively. "Imagine having a party in a cemetery! That is certainly strange, but they did not seem to have a very happy party of joy and happiness, but then again it was not a sad party either. It was just strange, as strange as they were."

"Why do you say they were "strange"?" asked Hercules.

"They appeared to be wearing uniforms of some kind, with pointed hats and judges' black robes. I do not think that there was any drinking or eating. There is nothing one could associate with a party. There never is any laughing or singing, just weird, monotonous chanting. They never have cake, coffee or even beer or wine. There was not even any hors d'ouvres!" said an apparently very disappointed old man.

"Is that a fact?" answered Seemore.

"That is a fact indeed. I would have crashed the party if there were hors d'oeuvres, believe me! I just love them," the rickety old man answered emphatically although barely able to stand. He almost fell over because of the strong, vocal emphasis in his own speech.

"Can you tell me more?" continued Seemore. "Was there anything unusual besides what they wore?"

"Yes, that is when the birds come, especially the crows and ravens. They come first and later the other birds show up. That is also a strange coincidence. There must be at least three hundred or more birds all over the place. I cannot relax at all", the man said. He was apparently exasperated over the periodic return of the partygoers.

"Yes, that is all very interesting, and probably the kind of information we are seeking. Do they do anything unusual or strange in any way?" Hercules butted in.

"Well, I guess you mean the fire?" asked the old Mr. Loa.

"Very good. Yes. Tell us about the fire" a now eager Hercules asked.

"Very interesting fire indeed! I never find any ashes when they leave. It is as though they were never here at all! The place where they party and wherever they make their fire is always clean. In any case, you would never ever know that they were ever here!" responded a quizzical Francis Loa.

"Great!" exclaimed Hercules. "Please show us the place where they created their fire."

Francis Loa made his way a short distance from where he was sitting and pointed with his cane, "There. That is the spot. Go check it out. See if you can see any ashes or anything at all!" Francis exclaimed.

Hercules and Seemore went to inspect the location of the "fire" and the witches' meeting place. There was nothing to be seen at all. The nearly exhausted, hard breathing Francis Loa made his way back under his tree and rock while the two continued to survey the meetup scene. Francis once again made himself comfortable sitting on his rock, under the shade of the old maple tree. The pair of agents was too busy filming the meeting site to notice that Francis had left them.

Their filming was over, and they turned to seek Francis Loa and to thank him for his help. He was nowhere to be found. Then they saw that he was sitting comfortably and quietly back on his rock and in the shade of the maple tree. They went over to thank him but were surprised that he was not there at all.

Sitting on the rock under the shady maple was a solid stone statue of an old man with a cane. The rock had one glazed surface on which are written the words:

"HERE LIES FRANCIS LOA

GUARDIAN OF THIS CEMETERY

AND GOOD FRIEND OF

ST. JOSEPH GERMAN

FOUNDER OF THIS CEMETERY.

1875-1925

MAY HE REST IN PEACE"

Seemore and Hercules snapped their heads and just looked wordlessly at each other. Chills went up and down their entire bodies. This was unusual for a Gnome, but it happened.

Seemore said, "I have seen enough. Let us get out of here now!"

There was no argument coming from Hercules. He pressed the "Return" Confugio button and the two were immediately transported in less than "coach" style back to their point of origination.

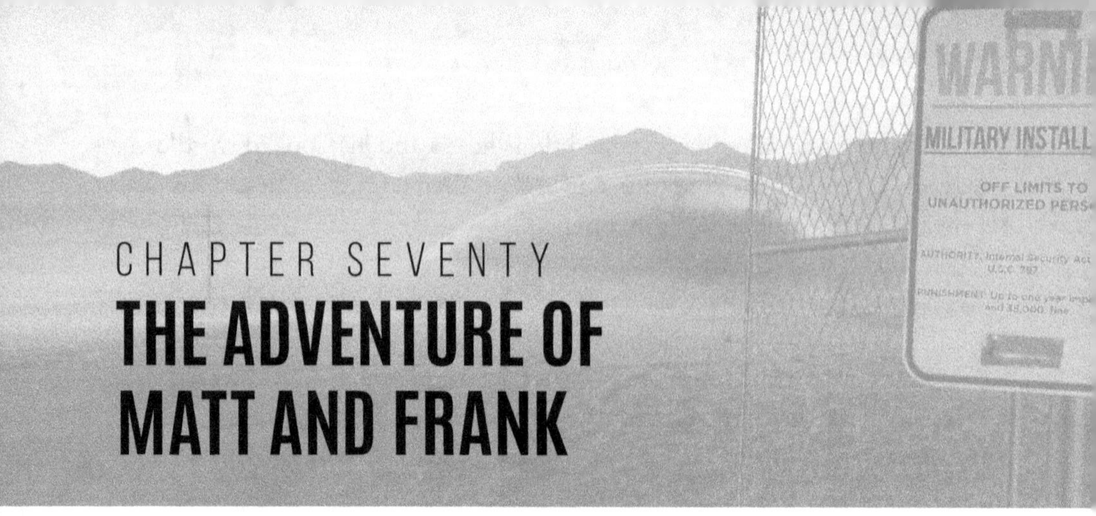

CHAPTER SEVENTY
THE ADVENTURE OF MATT AND FRANK

Matt Ovlas and Frank German were not quite ready to depart for their adventure to Southern California. Matt was not certain as to what he should wear. After all, his most recent experience out there with Wyatt was one of snow and cold. However, Southern California was usually mild or warm and very comfortable.

Matt spent time searching the web and the NOAA site for any warning of snow. There was none. Matt remembered that there was also no warning of snow on the day he virtually experienced a blizzard. However, how could the weather bureau predict a phenomenon of snow and cold without clouds in the sky or moving warm and cold fronts? It had to be impossible to make any prediction under such circumstances. "That snowstorm and the weather changes were not natural", he said aloud to himself.

Frank was extremely edgy, just waiting around for Matt to make up his mind. He overheard Matt's self-directed comment and said, "Matt, so it was not natural. That is the nature of our mission and the business of DESE. You remember that, do you not? Put something on that you could wear for any type of Huntington Beach climate and let us get on with our mission. The rest of the investigators are probably finished by now. I'll bet that we are the last ones to go. You are such a slow poke."

"You are right, Frank. "You are right," he repeated for emphasis. He then grabbed a thermal filled jacket and gloves and said, "All right. I am ready to go."

Frank looked at him and laughed. He said, "No you are not. You are so worried about the weather and its strange causes as well as what weather we might encounter that you forgot the most important things!"

"What?" answered Matt. "What do you mean? I have everything I need."

"No, you do not," Frank shot back.

"What am I missing anyway?" pleaded with an unsuspecting Matt.

"Think. What is the most important thing we need besides your clothing dilemma?" quizzed Frank.

"Oh, What?" asked Matt.

"You are forgetting the Confugio and the TCC. You know that we need to get there and that we most certainly need to get back here. Don't you remember that?" asked Frank now becoming worried that the stress of this mission might be too much for Matt to manage.

"Oh really; Do you really think that I have forgotten the things that can possibly save our lives?" replied Matt.

"I do not see them anywhere near you. Are you hiding them under the bed or in the closet or even the refrigerator?" Frank asked in near desperate sarcasm.

"Frank, they are right there behind you," retorted a frustrated Matt. "All you had to do was to turn around and look!"

"Oh", said Frank, sheepishly. "Sorry about that!"

Matt continued, "You are probably right. We should get started. Do you remember how to get this Confugio running in case something happens to me?"

"Of course I do. I was there when we both received our instruction on the Confugio and the TCC. You do remember that too, do you not?" Frank was still goading Matt sarcastically, but in jest also.

"Then, let us be on our way." Matt announced. "You do remember that we need to hold hands?"

Frank answered, "Yes I do, but you are not my type."

"Cut out the baloney. Come on and let us go." returned Matt.

Upon the completion of those words and the clasping of hands, Matt triggered the Confugio "GO" button. The trip began. They were on their way to adventure.

The Confugio travel was just as though they were on an old Western wooden wagon without springs and driving on a bumpy, unpaved road. It was not comfortable. Varied, mesmerizing and magnificent, glowing and flashing colors of every shade in the rainbow swirled about them. They felt themselves going up, down and all around. Matt remembered his experiences on a merry-go-round and that he almost vomited after becoming very dizzy and much disoriented. He hoped that it would not repeat again, but he felt that he was coming very close to it happening again.

This time the Confugio let them off gently at an inobtrusive corner of the Fountain Valley parking lot near Fitzhew's bar.

The two were ejected from the Confugio in a sitting position. The TCC was on automatic start and began its recording immediately upon their arrival. The sitting pose was probably the safest ejection position after a three-thousand-mile journey in the matter of a few minutes and an improved part of Confugio basic programming. They just sat there without moving for several minutes. They did not even say a word to each other. It was pure silence. Surrounding sounds and movements had yet to reach them. It is as though time lagged in the speed of sound and the speed of light. When the several minutes passed, the sounds of birds, traffic and people reached their ears, but they saw the birds, people and traffic moving beforehand. They assumed that the phenomenon was due to the differences in the speed of sound and the speed of light. They deduced that they had arrived ahead of those two energies and that it took that long for them to catch up. They were right.

It also took that long for people in the parking lot even to see them. They were invisible to all in that short time. People were amazed that these two showed up seemingly out of nowhere and sitting on the pavement! Such weirdoes were not uncommon in California and some other parts of the country as well, but it always garners attention, even if for just a short moment.

Matt and Frank became aware of the situation in an instant. They both scurried to their feet and straightened up their clothing. They hid their instruments as best and as quickly as they could. They tried to "blend in" as best they could and as quickly as they could. It was not fast enough to suit them. The last thing they needed was a curious crowd's stare much less involvement of local law enforcement as well.

They both ran from the immediate area of their arrival, hoping to be as inconspicuous as possible. The small group that had gathered to see the oddity dispersed. They were now in the "normal" range of being "Californians". That is what they hoped for in the least.

Frank said, "Did you know what just happened? Do you have any idea of how lucky we were? We could have been run over!"

Frank was visibly upset. The more he dwelled on what "could have happened" the more upset he made himself.

Matt said reassured, "Well nothing happened. It is true that we were very lucky. It is also true that we have no experience in making arrivals via Confugio. If you remember, there were a few seconds before things really began to happen. We were in advance of time and motion in that lot. If we had more experience, we would know enough to get out of dangerous situations before they had a chance to affect us."

Frank answered, "That is true. We needed more experience to know accurately what to do, but to tell you the truth, this one time is more than just enough for me. I do not need any more experiences like that one."

"Unfortunately, Frank, you will have one more such experience before this journey is over." Matt warned Frank.

"Oh, no. I will not volunteer for that. No way!" Frank said emphatically.

"You will volunteer for that one. When I tell you why, you will agree immediately." Matt said.

"No, I won't", said Frank.

"Well Frank, have you given any thought as to how we will get back?" Matt questioned.

"Oh, that." Frank said as all the fight suddenly left him. Reason had won out. Matt was right. "We need the Confugio to return, don't we?" asked Frank, defeated.

"Right" replied Matt.

Frank then asked a more pointed question. "What in the world are we doing here? This is a parking lot. What do you suppose our being here is about?"

Matt answered, "It is about discovering what evil or malevolent influences or individuals are here and what their goals might be. That is why we are here. Do you remember?"

"I remember. How do we start? Where do we start? Suggestions please, Matt?" Frank answered, but not too eagerly.

"I have no idea whatsoever. I have no idea at all." Matt replied.

"Well, let us not just stand about here or else we will get more attention than we need. Let us look around and search for clues regarding a reason for being here. There has to be one otherwise the Confugio PME coordinates would not have us land here." Frank explained.

"I agree" Matt said.

They stayed together as they investigated the parking lot and the stores surrounding the parking lot.

"Check out this place, Matt," said Frank.

"It looks like a good spot to meet people. Let's go in" answered Matt.

Inside Fitzhew's Pub were three pool tables, dartboards, and a large screen television on the back wall over a polished oak dance floor. In the rear, behind the dance floor and to the left of the elevated television screen was a beaded entrance doorway. Most likely this entrance went into the establishment's business office. This place definitely had a warm and a very friendly atmosphere. Fitzhew's is a great Irish Pub.

Matt and Frank were happy to find refuge from that unexpected parking lot episode. Although it was still in the forenoon California time, the two did feel the need for a cold beer, which they ordered.

The bartender greeted them with, "Good late morning gentlemen. How can I help you?

Frank answered, "Two of whatever you have cold on tap."

"Very good" answered the bartender. He followed that up with "We usually are not open at this hour, but we will be serving a sandwich lunch shortly. Can I get you a sandwich as well?'

Matt answered this time. "You most certainly can. Neither one of us had any breakfast before we left home this morning. We will be happy to indulge in a sandwich brunch!"

The pair ordered their sandwiches, which arrived shortly, cut diagonally, and placed on a triangular plate. The bartender placed napkins adjacent to the plates. The napkins had advertisements on them and were quite colorful.

Matt and Frank sat there contentedly munching away and refreshing themselves on their tall glasses of cold beer. They were approaching full recovery from their journey. The two did not forget that they were on a serious mission, but refreshment and recharging of their batteries was in order. They were soon eager to go.

While enjoying their food, Frank was reading the ads on the napkins. Matt was doing the same, while eating and drinking.

Matt was doing a déjà vu. "I remember this place. I have been here before."

"Really?" asked Frank. "When was that?"

"I was here with Wyatt. That was when Huntington Beach experienced that freak snowfall and cold weather. We traveled by car and took the road here. That is why I did not recognize the location right away. Between the trauma of the Confugio trip and the disorientation of directional ground routing, I did not associate this place with my earlier visit." Matt explained to Frank.

"Bartender", Matt called out.

"Yes sir, will there be more?" he asked.

Matt asked, "What happened to the parakeet? Do you still have the same waitress here that was here several months ago?"

The bartender answered, "I'm sorry sir. I never had a waitress working here. I have a waiter here when the place gets busy on the weekends. There has not ever been a waitress here as far as I know, and I've been working here several years."

Matt was now very confused. He now fully recalled his last visit here with Wyatt. The waitress and the parakeet were one and the same. Wyatt and he agreed on that. The place was bewitched. The fact that this bartender never had a waitress cinched it.

Frank directed Matt's attention to the printed napkin. On it was printed in bright Irish Green colors was "Fitzhew's Pub: A Great Place To Meet And Greet. A Great Place For Meetups!"

Matt and Frank did a double take. "Meetups" is a phrase used when Covens meet, although it can also be used for perfectly innocent meetings as well. Matt knew this because he checked out "Meetups" on his computer's search engines regularly.

Matt and Frank realized that they had "hit" on something, although they were not certain as to what it was. Matt wanted to have a private conversation with Frank but away from the bar. He asked the Barkeeper, "Where is the men's room?"

The Barkeep answered, "It is in the rear, through the beaded curtains and on your left."

The two rose up and went toward the rear and through the beaded curtain.

Matt recalled those multi-colored beaded curtains and the more opaque curtain behind them. He remembered the parakeet walking through them and then this waitress coming out.

Frank and Matt walked through the beaded barrier and parted the opaque curtain behind it on their way to the men's room. They were now out of sight of the main part of the tavern and almost in "privacy". Matt wanted to confide in Frank the facts of his earlier visit but did not wish to do so at the open area of the bar.

Matt was about to place his hand on the doorknob. He suddenly and unexpectedly felt a soft, tender hand upon his. He turned to see why Frank's hand would be upon his and even wondering more as to why his and felt so soft.

"Hello. Remember me?" said this soft, come-hither husky female voice. This definitely was not Frank voice nor his hand. It was Juday, the waitress Matt remembered.

Frank was amazed at the long-haired blonde beauty who interjected herself between them and appearing out of nowhere. He jumped back because there was virtually no space between him and Matt. The woman's beauty soothed Frank's apprehensions because he thought that he simply missed the woman's approach from behind. He did not realize that such was not the case.

"Juday!" exclaimed Matt. "Of course, I remember you. How could I forget?"

"Well, I remember you and your other friend." Juday replied. Then she added, "Have you found what you were seeking?"

Matt became a little uneasy because he never revealed what he was seeking. How could this person, or whatever she was, ever know that he was investigating anything?

"Well, what makes you think that I was seeking anything?' Matt replied.

"Simply put, I know." she said mysteriously.

With those words, she opened the men's room door. She bade them to enter. They did so, however, along with the appurtenances of a men's room were also the devices of a witch's domain, located behind a full-length mirror.

The witch said, "Welcome to my abode. This is where I stay, but not always. I travel a lot."

"The mirror opened outwardly and as it did, a doorway appeared. Inside the doorway was a very commodious "apartment". The wall creating the partition upon which the mirror hung was only eight inches thick, but the apartment within those eight inches contained consisted of several large rooms. The existence of this "apartment" was magical. The mirror opened the door to a magical world. It defied logic, as magic always does.

"The owner of this pub does not even know that this exists, and I want to keep it that way. It is my secret. My friends and I meet here upon occasion. It is an ideal spot. Should the owner try to enter my home, even by tearing down the walls, he could not because it exists out of ether. I create it and I can move it to any place I wish. The mirror does not open for anyone but me." Such was the explanation the witch divulged.

Matt and Frank were dumbstruck. They did not know what to say. They did not know what to make of the circumstances in which they found themselves. It was as though she had them in her power, but the real fact was that they were awed into silence and slow mental processing about what was happening. They did not know how to deal with the situation that, so far, did not appear threatening.

"Do you have any questions?" the witch asked solicitously.

"Yes, I do." Matt replied. "As long as we know who you are, the question is why you are and tell me about that weird snowstorm several months ago. Can you explain that?"

"Yes, I can. Very simply put, it was magic. More than that, it was a spell. It was cast all over Southern California. It was cast as a mega-force willed by many Covens in this area. In other words, most of the area's Covens came together and simply cast the spell by their own joined efforts to chant the spell in unison and then merely "willed" it to be created. It worked, did it not?" The witch gave a wicked smile. As she did so, her beauty faded and she changed into an old hag with moles and carbuncles over her face. Her beautiful long blonde hair changed into ragged long and unkempt coarse and grizzled hair. Her very attractive clothing changed into a long and tattered black robe. A tall pointed hat now sat on her head.

The agents were further awed, but this time fear entered into their minds and hearts. They apparently learned what they needed to learn and much more than they cared to discover.

The full blown and configured witch then said to Frank and Matt, "Come hither. You can be mine and I can be yours!" She reached out with both of her long-nailed and crooked, noduled arthritic ridden hands to grab each of agent.

"Boom", it happened. Matt's reflexes worked just fine. The Confugio "Return" button was pressed, and they escaped capture just in time. The witch's nails barely touched their clothing before they were gone. Poof! Just like that.

The witch was now standing there alone, her opened-wide eyes expressing that she was puzzled and astonished at their sudden disappearance. She thought, "They must have some kind of magic too! I wonder, could they have been witches too?"

Matt and Frank did not care for the return journey either. The colors were fine, but the spinning and unceremonious discomfort of ejection from the cornucopia like tunnel upon their return was not as easy. They were dropped on their derrieres in the roughest fashion.

They both looked at each other once again and said, "Time to see Mary." Off they went, realizing what they were up against. "Mary and her office need to deal with this. It is in her realm. Let's go." Matt said to Frank. They both agreed and went off to the main DESE offices.

CHAPTER SEVENTY-ONE
RETURN FROM ADVENTURE

Mary's DESE headquarters was abuzz with excitement and confusion both at the very same moment. All the agents have returned to report on their different adventures and to turn their TCC recordings over to Mary for further display and for deeper investigation.

Matt and Frank were the last agents to return, thus completing the missions.

Mary went to the head of the room and took up her microphone in order to be heard over the commotion, "Please, please may I have your attention."

The noise did not quiet down, although attention was beginning to turn towards Mary and recognition that she was there and had to be heard. Shortly, the full attention of the group was hers. The mood changed to that of a group of agents who recognized the importance of what was to be in their future. It was an unknown, but combating the evil they all experienced in their adventures and its threat to the USA and even worldwide humanity is necessary. The question that DESE had to deal with was how to create and employ solutions to the problem.

Mary said, "Welcome back my fellow DESE agents. I am happy to see that you all made it back safely. Is that right? Am I wrong or is there someone here who experienced injuries?"

There was no response. The entire group was silent although everyone was looking around for anyone who may have been hurt. There was no acknowledgement of any physical injuries.

HB Gaunt raised his hand and said, "We all could have been injured, Mary. The Confugio needs to have the landing improved upon. I think that we all, although not disabling, have experienced soreness on our backsides which has most likely not left us at this point."

The group burst out in laughter and applause. All agents earnestly agreed with HB's assessment of the Confugio's ejection modality.

Mary responded, "As long as no one is seriously damaged, we need to go on with the purpose of our meeting. The purpose is to take the TCC recordings and see what they contain. We may enter some of the recorded pictures. We may enter none of them, only observing from the outside. You have all followed instructions and record the events at your destinations immediately upon your arrival. Is that correct?"

All in the audience sounded out their agreement.

Mary acknowledged the positive response. "That is excellent. The important aspect of the TCC is not the recording you make at the time, but that your entry at locations where the PME sent you will allow us to go back in time. This means that we have the ability to learn why the PME made a positive identification of your destinations a day or two in the past."

"Will we need to be present when you review our recordings?" asked Glenn Kohen.

Mary responded, "No. That is not necessary. We will be able to see what each of you saw and experienced. The big thing, as I said, is that we can go back in time and see exactly what happened before you arrived. That will be the most revealing and most important. We need to know the "why" for your visit at a PME designated location. We need to know the reason for the PME designation.

Mary paused, "To again respond to your question, the answer is that we will have everything we need. We now need time to review and analyze what we see. When that is complete, we will be able to create a plan to deal with the problems they reveal."

Kathy Lewiesle asked, "What should we do now?"

Mary responded, "You all should go home, take a day off to relax and regain your sensibilities and equilibrium. There have been no environmental problems reported in the last week or so. There most likely is no need for emergency review of recordings. We will call you back for a next adventure or if we need you in relation to your recordings."

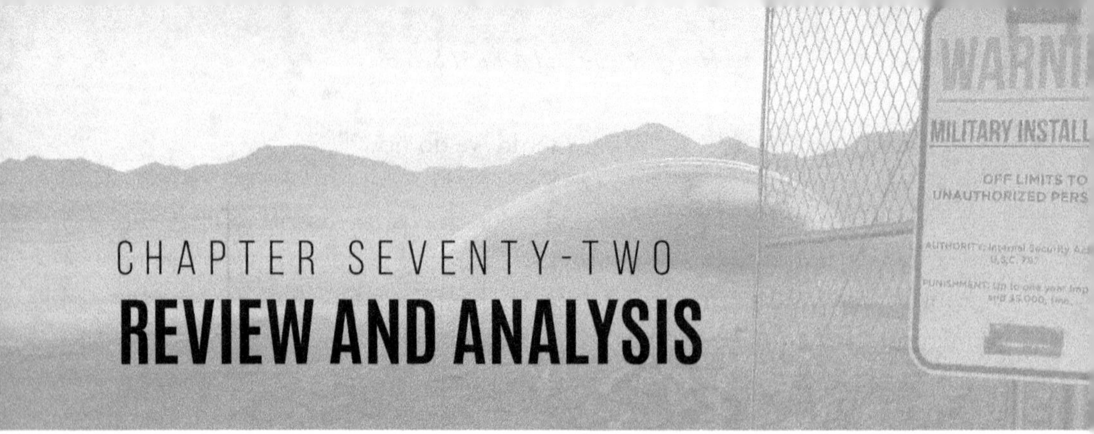

CHAPTER SEVENTY-TWO
REVIEW AND ANALYSIS

Mary Kent, Seemore Manlein and Jack Henigson were the masters of DESE technology and the officials dealing with TCC recordings. Jack and Seemore received mental image messages from both Henry and Black Lightning, now as Elizabeth Sam, also indicating their desire to be a part of the actual investigation of the recordings. There was real excitement because, although Henry and Elizabeth knew what they had experienced, their curiosity would not let them relax their interest in what the others had discovered. They simply just wanted to know, and, beyond that, they wanted to share the other agents' experiences. Such curiosity is definitely Black Lightning's forte'.

Reception of mental images by Seemore was nothing new. After all, he had communicated with Peganni that way for some time now. His reception from the relative strangers, Elizabeth Sam and Henry, however, was new for him. Up to this point in his relationships with DESE agents, he had only suspected that he had been "receiving" thoughts from somewhere, but he never suspected that DESE agents were that capable of mastering and using the technique. There was no mistaking the current slew of messages coming his way.

Jack Henigson had no surprise about message reception from the two agents. He knew of Henry's developing abilities and realized that they were now fully developed. Of course, Jack's relationship with Mr. Xilx extended as well to Xilx's friend, Black Lightning. Mental communication was not a new thing between the three, Jack, Mr. Xilx and Black Lightning who we now know as the attractive Elizabeth Sam.

It was a unanimous decision that Henry and Elizabeth should join the TCC investigatory group. The two were not only trustworthy, but also qualified by their extrasensory attributes. Getting Mary to agree would be a minor obstacle, as the mental images Seemore and Jack were receiving from her revealed that she wanted as much help as she could obtain without having a crowd at sessions of the TCC recordings exhibitions. Two more experienced and specially gifted agents are not a problem.

Upon being presented with the request from Jack and Seemore for the two added agents in reviewing TCC recordings Mary responded, "Most certainly. They are not only very welcome but sorely needed as well." Mary then added, "Jack, what about Mr. Xilx? I would like to have him present as well. Highly experienced and wise individuals are what we need at this time."

Jack answered, "Of course. Mr. Xilx would be very happy to be of assistance. He is very capable and wise. His experiences would provide ideal input. "

"Great", Mary answered. "Please get in touch with him so that we can get started right away. It will take some time to review these recordings."

"I will do it right away," Jack answered.

"Excellent", said Mary as she approached the exit on her way to the viewing section of DESE headquarters.

"Excuse me", she exclaimed as she began to step out of the doorway. She almost hit the person on the other side of the door with both the door and herself.

Mr. Xilx answered, "No harm done. I am quite all right." Then he asked solicitously of a shaken and slightly roughed up Mary, "Are you O.K.?"

Mary responded, "Yes, I will be all right. It is just that I did not expect that anyone would be at the door. I was quite shocked."

"I am sorry", answered Mr. Xilx. "I just received a message from Jack that you wanted me to help with viewing the TCC recordings, and so here I am!"

Mr. Xilx was quite happy about being included in the select group.

Mary was surprised, "But we just now spoke of having your help. How did you ever get that message?" Mary was bewildered. It shortly dawned on her that she had really "gifted" people on her staff. She realized how Mr. Xilx received the "message". She said, "Oh, how foolish of me. Of course, you knew, probably right away, that we would like to have your help. You both used that mental telepathy thing. Is that right?

"Absolutely" Mr. Xilx answered. He was still in a very cheery mood and smiling a broad, toothy smile. "I am most happy to be of assistance."

It was to no one's surprise that Henry and Elizabeth presented themselves only a few yards behind Mr. Xilx as well.

Mary remarked. "Mental telepathy must be a wonderful thing!" and let out an exhausted, but appreciative sigh.

"Well, now that we are all here, let us have at it!" Mary said in a recomposed and very positive attitude. She was inexplicably and happily reassured by the presence of so many "gifted" agents. With those words, the group went down the hall and up to the more secured area of DESE headquarters to start the viewing.

Mary continued, with her entourage, down the hall and up the stairs to the more secure part of DESE headquarters where the PME recordings were stored and viewed.

Mary entered the viewing room and the chosen agents followed. The room was something short of a medical school lecture amphitheater, with only three rows of seating arranged in a semi-circle about a pit forming a center stage. Above the pit was a very large screen. The screen was something like one in a full-sized movie theatre but had steps going up to a balcony-like platform located at the lower border with one at the right and left sides of the screen.

The agents sat in the front row with Mary, Jack and Seemore taking the center stage. Upon the stage was a large, elevated highly polished wooden table, which was about chest high to a standing individual. The table supported a computerized projection system and all the TCC recordings. Mary, Seemore and Jack were looking through and sorting the recordings. There was one for each investigating pair of agents.

Mary, being the chief of DESE was numbering and labelled the recordings. She announced, with agreement from Jack and Seemore, the order in which to review each tape. She added, "These tapes will be shown in what we, Jack, Seemore and I, feel to be most important first. We base our selection on the severity level of the PME readings. The most intense readings will be shown first.

The first recording will be of the team Gaunt and Henigson and their Florida experience. We may or may not enter the "picture" depending on whether the playback into what had occurred before the recording began reveals to us. Should the information we get from the past be either insufficient or hidden from the immediate area where the recording was made, then we shall enter the picture and venture into its depths to make a needed discovery. The PME does not make errors. I hope that we will not need to put ourselves at risk by entering any of the "pictures". The playback into the past will most likely reveal sufficient details to us to make such entry unnecessary.

The second tape will be from the team of Elizabeth and Henry.

The third projection will be from the Seemore and Canue team.

The fourth showing will be from the Ovlas and German squad.

The last will be from the Carl and Kohen pair.

All the agents quieted down as they took their seats along the front row of the amphitheater as the lights were dimmed only slightly to permit easy viewing of the screen and note taking.

Gaunt and Henigson were the featured stars. The scene started at their arrival with the unceremonious ejection from the Confugio "tunnel". The audience, experienced with Confugio landings, identified themselves with the comedy of landing. They quickly laughed at the scene and then just as quickly, silenced themselves. The display faithfully reproduced their conversation and their Phil Foster Memorial exploration. The audience was attentive, tolerant and quiet. Their interest was piqued at the discovery of fire ashes and intensified at the discovery of cloven hoof prints and the chair. The evolvement of the chair into a throne and the man sitting thereon created a tense and palpable build-up of collectively increased involvement. Almost all mouths were open in anticipation.

As the conversation between the man on the chair and the two agents wore on, if became apparent that what interested DESE was what happened before the pair arrived. Mary stopped the display. The audience moaned in disappointment. Each member of the audience was eager to see the entire display and did not appreciate the curtailing of an adventurous drama.

Mary saved the moment by saying, "That was very interesting indeed, HB and Jack. I want to see what happened earlier." She informed the audience, "We do not want to disappoint you. What you have seen so far is of great interest. What DESE really needs to know and what you really need to see is what went on before this display. I will play the TCC recording in "Past Mode" and run it as far as is necessary to learn what the man meant by "late comers to the meeting". That should be most revealing and is what the PME pinpointed. So, here goes!"

What then occurred on the screen was a rapid rewind movement to where the agents first arrived. It then went into dawn of the day of their arrival and into the night before their arrival and then into the day before their arrival and into the events of two nights before their arrival. The screen showed the existence of a lighted fire in the middle of the Park, but still the TCC rewound to where people were arriving on the scene and even before. It was at that point that Mary stopped the rewind.

Mary announced, "Please pay attention. We can now learn what went on the night of our PME survey."

Mary started to run the TCC in normal forward mode. Arriving individuals escaped from the blurred fast-reverse mode and took shape on the screen, being happily greeted by a group of what seemed to be "officials" of the event.

At least a dozen and one-half people were greeted which, in addition to the organizers, probably numbered twenty to twenty-two individuals. They arrived in a long black Mercedes limousine that made its turn into the park with difficulty because of its length.

The black limousine was quite appropriate because all the people who exited it were also dressed in long black gowns. Some of the gowns had hoods. These people were almost invisible in the darkness of night. It was black against black against black once again. The faces were visible only because they faced the flickering firelight. When they looked away from the fire, it was nearly impossible to see them at all. Some of the faces were attractive but most were unsightly and bordering on repulsive.

Seemore made the comment, "That is some party! Look! There are no refreshments and no Hors D'ouvres. Terrible!" He was summarily "Hushed" by the more attentive members and immediately fell silent. Mary gave him a "daggered" look and Seemore shrunk into silence.

The witches quickly gathered about the fire, and as they did so, they chanted a monotonous humming chant that varied in volume. Suddenly, there appeared in the middle of the fire the quintessential cauldron already bubbling and spewing forth its various colored steamy effluent. None of the colors were nice. There was black steam, brown steam, purple steam and even orange and chartreuse colored steam rising from the cauldron's bubbling and popping surface.

The mixture was poured into cocktail glasses and was their refreshment. When all had a glass in their hand, a chair appeared elevated over the fire's surface, but centered over it. A handsome occupant rose from the chair and mingled with the guests. The head witch hosts, Miguel Barberry and Juday DuMealyworm helped the demon off the throne and welcomed him into their midst.

The three huddled together in animated conversation. Mr. Legion was agreeing with the two head witches. They then addressed the group that gathered around the three.

DuMealyworm announced, "My brothers and sisters, we will create changes which will gather the attention of those who look down upon us and who tortured us over the centuries. The "Witches Hammer" tells the history of our wrongs and pains. We will demand our respect and we will demand change."

The attendees murmured in agreement and applauded.

Barberry went on, "We shall change the climate of this area and create an earthquake where none ever occurred. We shall hurt those who despise us by changing the climate and create physical and economic pain."

The group was gleeful in approval.

"Join me as we chant our spell and create with our joint effort the casting of it upon this part of the world", Barberry continued.

The assemblage gathered in a circle about the fire, and as Indians in a warlike dance, they began to prance about it, first thirteen steps in one direction and then thirteen in the other, all the while chanting their curse. This went on for about thirteen minutes, becoming intense and then less intense and once more they repeated the effort.

The group then once again entered fellowship and eventually disbanded about one and one-half hours after the event began. The demon said his farewell, walked through the fire, sat on his throne, and disappeared. The fire diminished and the limousine once again loaded its passengers, and the event was over. DuMealyworm and Barberry just simply disappeared, and the park once again became quiet and deserted. It was as though no one was ever there that evening.

Each of the DESE agents felt as though they were present at the event they had just witnessed. Mary fast-forwarded the recording to the next event.

The screen showed the darkness of night then turn into day and eventually once again showed the arrival of HB and Jack bouncing out of the Confugio and onto the Phil Foster Park pavement. Mary stopped the viewing.

Mary announced, "Fellow agents, you now can see how the TCC works. We can be there without ever having been there at all. The danger to each of us is minimal and although the visit is free, what we learn can be priceless."

We will now view the TCC projection of Elizabeth and Henry. Their trip took them to the Las Vegas resort area.

Henry and Elizabeth were sitting together in the front row. They shook hands and congratulated themselves.

The screen lit up and there they were, projected as big as life. Their initial entrance to Vegas elicited a frown from Mary who preferred her agents to use the conventional Confugio means of transportation. She felt it was more reliable than one which she had no knowledge or training. The use of Elizabeth's "collar" was not DESE equipment.

The projected screen showed their scouting of the area at which they arrived and revealed the circled pentacle and the chair in its center. The screen showed the snake which appeared and then changed itself into a demon. The demon's invitation for the pair to visit his "home" and sinister laugh, stimulated their immediate departure from Vegas and their return home, was also recorded.

The viewers were all silent and intent on what was happening on the screen and were disappointed at its ending. They were all intrigued that an actual "demon" was on the screen.

Mary interrupted the group's intensive concentration of the showing with, "That was very informative. However, once again, we need to go into "Past Rewind" mode to see what caused the PME to designate this location as one of evil, malevolence, and destructive mood. So get ready."

Mary pushed the "Past Rewind" control and set it back a full forty hours for almost two days' worth of history. Images on the screen flashed through time to the forty-hour mark. The screen showed a very serene scene. There was no fire, no chair, just desert, Joshua trees, cactus, and sand.

Mary then set the "Fast Forward" control to where the first new images would appear. The screen streaked through monotonous desert scenes until it reached a point where the scenes changed by the appearance of new images.

"This is the point where the action we need to know about occurs." Mary said.

Then Mary pushed the "Play" control and the viewing continued showing the events that happened before the DESE agents arrived. These would be the scenes in which DESE was interested.

The scene was reminiscent of the first showing. People of all shapes, sizes, colors, and dress arrived and greeted by several people. The greeters wore robes colored black, and slim and tall. Some were women. The women appeared to be six feet and taller. The male greeters were much taller and gave the impression of being not just taller than six feet but close to seven feet or more in height. Their slim figures and black robes made them appear even taller and their height implied their possession of overwhelming power.

The guests arrived out of nowhere. They simply materialized out of a green Miasma that occupied one area of the screen. They appeared one at a time and not several at once. Such was the yield of the fog.

"Welcome to our Merry Meet" said the leader of the greeting witches.

"It is my pleasure to meet you. I am Firewolf Noir," said the first entrant.

"Miguel Barberry here. You are most welcome."

The second greeter was another tall witch who welcomed the guest with "Merrymeet! You are so very welcome indeed." She then added, "I am Juday DuMealyworm and this is my colleague, Maggot Caprae. Please gather about the fire and the Cauldron of Spells. Our Guest of Honor will be with us soon. Make yourself at home!"

Although these witches were quite tall, not one was good to look at. Their smiling faces seemed to be covered in sores, pustules, and enormous, hairy moles. The female witches even appeared to have mustaches!

The arrival of guests and greetings went on for a good fifteen minutes. Mary was becoming a bit impatient and flashed the "Fast Forward" button now and then to scan to a next event. After a while, the constancy of introduction after introduction did not reveal much and was boring. No one objected to Mary's periodic "Fast Forwarding".

The next scene at which Mary allowed to run at "normal" speed showed the Cauldron spewing forth its bubbles and multi-colored steam and stench being served to the guests in rough and coarse ceramic cups. The guests drank heartily, and as they did so, their faces revealed a red-orange glow, where they were most difficult to discern before. Their complexions were not clear.

However, as they drank their brew, the moles, scars and pustules disappeared, and you could see that the women were now gorgeous and the men became very handsome.

There suddenly was a rumbling sound and in the center of the fire appeared a throne, much like that in the earlier recording, a chair appeared. The chair was vacant and elevated itself several feet above the fire.

The fire did not die, but the flames lowered, and a handsome man once again appeared as the chair's occupant. All the guests cheered and applauded as the occupant left the chair and joined the others. The flames in his path died down to only glowing coals. The coals did not bother the new arrival who was already red from the fire's heat.

The earlier guests immediately engulfed him. Miguel Barberry welcomed the newcomer with, "Friend, I am happy to see that you were able to make our Merrymeet event. We have need of your strengths."

"I am happy to help you achieve your goals", said the newly arrived Friend.

Miguel Barberry replied, "Centuries have passed, and we have suffered. We now want to return that suffering to those who caused us pain. We need acknowledgement as a force to be recognized. We need respect. Our kind has been persecuted for centuries and despised. We have wronged no one, as is our credo. We will no longer allow others to wrong us!"

The group applauded respectfully.

DuMealyworm continued, "We are in the middle of a desert. That means there is a shortage of water. I say that we create a flood in the middle of Las Vegas, such as has never been seen before. It will be a shock. It will most certainly be noticed."

The group mumbled and milled about. After some discussion, the group voiced their agreement with the Mealyworm. It was set. They would create a spell, with the help of their most recent guest, to flood Vegas.

The crimson man with the handlebar mustache, in the center of the group, raised his left hand in the air as a signal and began to create a monotonous chant and a dark gloom visibly covered the entire area. The rest of the witches joined in. The chanting went on for a full thirteen minutes. There were high tones and low tones. There were weird, guttural sounds and several goats and satyrs appeared in their midst as they circled the fire. The event slowly died down as the chanting faded.

Without warning, and as time wore on, one by one each of the guests faded into nothingness. It was a slow fade. Not all faded at once. Barberry, DuMealyworm and Caprae the Maggot Goat also faded away as did their fiery guest. Soon there was nothing there except for a smiling Gila Monster or two in their place.

The sun was soon to rise and as it did, the DESE agents arrived and then eventually greeted by a standing and talking transitional snake.

Mary recognized this as the point at which the Vegas episode began and stopped the playback. The audience was enthralled with the screening thus far and was once again disappointed in the stopping of a good "thriller".

Mary turned to the group and said, "You do know that we need to go through these and that we need to do it now. The welfare of our nation and us is at stake. Our country does not need any more terror from any source. I do know that you are also anxious to see us review not only your own experiences but those of others as well. We can learn from each projected visit as well as from each other.

The next screening will be that of Matt Ovlas and Frank German who covered the Southern California territories, excluding Las Vegas obviously.

Matt and Frank shifted in their seats and showed that they felt a bit self-conscious since they were the "stars" for the moment. The screen was turned on and there they were, sitting flat on their derrieres in the middle of a blacktopped parking lot looking very surprised. The recording went through the initial phases of getting away from the crowd that formed around them and their escape into Fitzhew's Tavern.

Mary now fast-forwarded the scene showing the initial conversation between the two and the bartender. That was when it became apparent that there was no threat there. Their passage and entrance behind the beaded curtain caused Mary to slow the fast forward control to frame-by-frame inspection. When the third person appeared between them, Mary allowed the full replay of the recording at regular speed for a more detailed inspection.

The conversation between the agents and the blonde Juday revealed that the two had reached their goal. This was a real witch. Mary did not need to continue the forward play. Instead, she did a moderate speed slow reverse which allowed the group to inspect the happenings before the two agents arrived. That would reveal the information DESE was seeking.

The screen showed the inhospitable arrival of the two agents, once again replayed, but this time in reverse. The reverse playback continued to disclose what happened before the moment of their arrival.

Shortly, the rewind revealed the presence of black robed individuals, but non-descript until Mary pressed the "play" button. The screen showed the now familiar presence of a group of witches standing and milling about a centrally placed fire in the middle of a circled pentacle located in the middle of the parking lot.

The "throne" was visible in the center of the fire. This time the fire formed itself into an almost perfect "protective ring" of moderate flames with a centrally clear area in the "throne" area of an approximate ten-foot diameter. Three very tall individuals once again led the witches. The three arranged themselves at the three points of an equilateral triangle. Each removed their differently made wands from under their robes and pointed them high into the air with their tips touching. They then, in a virtual snapping stroke downward, created a slit in the space between them. The slit, created out of nothingness, opened like an envelope. The DESE spectators were amazed when a black leathered high boot stuck itself out of the slit and onto the earth between the three witches. The body of a similarly robed witch slithered through the cut and followed the descending foot. This was followed by another witch and then another and another. Eventually there were at least twenty-five witches attending this "Merrymeet". The audience could clearly hear them introducing themselves to the witch attendees.

"Welcome and Merrymeet!" said the tall male witch. "We are so happy that you are here. I am Miguel Barberry. These are my most faithful colleagues, Juday DuMealyworm and Maggot Caprae."

The DESE audience were surprised once again when they heard the names of these same three witches. They knew that the source which designated these data points of malevolence in the USA, was the PEM. They knew that the speed of the PEM survey was very rapid and only took a matter of several hours across the entire USA as well as Alaska, Hawaii and Puerto Rico. They were incredulous that the very same witches could be in so many different places at the same time. They wondered at the powers these witches might have that either they could be in more than one place at the very same time or that they could equal or exceed the speed at which Peganni flew. That had to be impossible.

The two tall female witches nodded an acknowledgement and said in unison, "Merrymeet! You are most welcome indeed. Our traditional refreshment is currently brewing and will be ready very soon for your enjoyment and physical rejuvenation."

The newly arrived and newly manifested witches were quite happy with this greeting and the offer of Juice of Slug and Crushed Caterpillar's Gut, Dragon's Blood and Scorpion-Spider, Stinkbug beverage, which was brewing for them. They did acknowledge the greeting but moved aside so that the next witch could enter from the slitted nothingness.

They were here only to learn, create havoc and destruction and not to socialize, despite the Merrymeet greetings. There was nothing merry in this meet. Only hatred, a perversion of love, and vengeance, a supposed perversion of justice, were on their minds and in their hearts. Love and caring for others did not exist in these hearts. Indeed, it is questionable if they had hearts at all! These witches had a job to perform and that was where their interests lay.

The group, led by the three tall witches, then gathered around a central figure who acted as their mentor. The witches then knelt before the figure and, as they did so, the figure appeared to rise above them, both by a physical increase in tallness as well as an approximate four-foot elevation into the air before the group of witches.

The central figure raised both his hands towards the sky, as though praying or giving a blessing, but instead a bolt of lightning flashed from each hand, then split into smaller and smaller divisions, and flashed into the hearts of each of the kneeling witches.

Each of the attendees grasped their chests at the place where the bolts entered them and bent forward as though they were in pain. The contrary was true. They did bend over and grasped their chests but only in an act of gratitude and respect for the central figure who so "blessed" them. It was not pain that they experienced, but the infusion of a mysterious evil power instead.

The "blessed" witches then gathered around the central figure and raised both of their arms with wands of all sorts pointed toward the sky and they chanted their curse as they walked in a processional about the central figure. As the witches walked about and circled the thirteenth time, each returned to the slot created in empty space and returned to their place of origination. The host figures then simply did a slow fade and vanished away after the "guests" departed. It was shortly thereafter that the witches and their "honored" central figure disappeared that Las Vegas was flooded.

Mary then went on to the next recording, namely the scene in the New Orleans graveyard. This show would be of the adventure of Seemore and Hercules. It began where the pair landed in the park and Mary rapidly ran the recording to the presence of Reverend Loa and his return to his resting place on the rock.

Mary then reversed the recording to before Hercules and Seemore arrived at the park. It did not take long for the recording to reach DESE's point of interest.

The DESE spectators were astonished that in this new showing; the very same three witches were once again welcoming new arrivals to their Meetup in New Orleans. These three witches must have had extremely powerful magic at their command to be in different places at the same time!

Mary reasoned, "There had to be some sort of "time warp" which permitted them essentially to be in more than just one place at the same moment."

The DESE agents, including Mary and Seemore, were awed at this revelation. Seemore was not certain that even Peganni had such ability. Mr. Xilx, on the other hand, was not surprised at this at all. Elizabeth's Rubber Band and DESE's Confugio Device could most certainly approximate the feat.

Mr. Xilx said, "Without a doubt, this is no special "magic". Those of us who are from out of this world can approach this same act. Even you at DESE can do the same thing using the Confugio."

Mr. Xilx continued to explain, "It is without a doubt that when these witches appear at multiple locations, we are seeing the use of a tremendous power or device they have. These are possessed individuals, but they most certainly are not deities. We need to acknowledge that they are very much the opposite. It may be there, at a darker source, that they have this ability. There may be no device involved at all, but simply the supernatural power of a demon instead," Mr. Xilx continued.

Mary interjected, "It is also to be noted that these events only seem to happen at the same moment. Understand, this only means that it "appears" to happen that way. In actuality, this is not true. There is a time difference, however slight, between the different appearances. One also must recognize that the PEM device simply records the pinpointed location of some evil or malevolence or discontent in a particular area. These events may not be happening at the same time anyway. The Time Capture Camera's record is rewound. We reverse the recording to a past point from when our agents arrived to learn what caused the PEM to designate a distinct area. We really do not have a timeline on exactly when these seemingly duplicate appearances happen. All we can determine is that these same three witches are paramount in heading whatever happens at these so-called "Meetups". Each "Meetup" could be hours, and perhaps even days apart."

Jack Henigson cut in with, "What is important is not the powers these individuals possess but what they do at these "Meetups". The floods, the earthquakes, the changes in temperature and snow without clouds in warm climates may only be a warning of what these people can do. I say that what we need to do is to determine their purpose and cut off any destructive activity they might engage in or initiate. We need to remember our mission is to protect our country and its people and to intercept any destruction these persons initiate."

Mary then said, "Thank you Jack." Then turning towards the agents, she added, "Jack is right. We are not keeping our eye on the doughnut! It was just that the surprise of seeing the same three witches at different places in our country in a short time had us concerned about what powers they may possess. However, we must determine what they really intend in the future. We already know what they have done in the past. It is obvious that we cannot permit any more destruction."

Mary continued the playback of Seemore and Hercules' adventure in New Orleans. It was now getting boring. The showing was almost a duplicate of the other three. It started and ended just about the same way as in the earlier screenings. There was nothing new.

Mary announced, "We have one more left to show. The escapade of Larry Carl and Glenn Kohen and their visit to the University of Michigan at Ann Arbor is next."

Mary switched the recording and started the presentation. There was Glenn and Larry and their unceremonious dumping on their backsides just behind the columns at the entrance to the cemetery. The pair did not seem happy about the special derriere express delivery.

Larry said, "I am going to complain about this sort of transportation. It may be fast, but it should not be damaging. I am damaged! Just look at my shoes and my pants! They are all dirty and covered in earth and grass stains!"

Mary shrugged her shoulders and said laughingly and in a matter-of-fact tone, "I am sorry about that. It will need to be improved; definitely."

She continued the showing and rewound the record to an earlier point in time. The fast rewind button showed images passing in a smeary blur; however, when it was decipherable and when "people" started to appear, Mary stopped the rewind and pushed the "play" button. The showing began at an interesting point in the past as with the other earlier rewinds.

Larry and Glenn looked about themselves still bewildered and apparently trying to get their bearings. They were wary because they knew that where they were in hostile territory for DESE agents. Then it showed their searching around the cemetery and the staircase going down into the earth. It showed Larry placing his foot on the first step and the remnants of heads in various states of decomposition lining it, all the while speaking to him and warning.

The revelation of the demon at staircase's base created enough fear, not only at the time it occurred, but also now, at this showing. Mary quickly pushed the "rewind" and quickly reversed the recording.

Mary announced, "It is sufficient that we know the nature of what we are against" she said while pausing the rewind. "As frightening as that was, we really need to go back in time to determine what this demon and his cohorts and the witches we have been following are planning for us, for our society. Therefore, I will continue to reverse the TCC recording until we can see the involvement of humans interacting with these creatures. You need to remember that this demon is as old as the world and older than the existence of humanity. This is not new. His interaction with man is what concerns us. We need to be concerned with what he gets man to do. Let us continue to keep our eye on the doughnut and not the hole, as the saying goes."

Mary stopped the rewind at a point where the screen turned solid red. She said, "There must be something wrong with either the recording or the projector. I will need to slow this down."

Mary pushed the stop button. The TCC projector automatically went into "play" mode, which was not what Mary intended. She exclaimed, "I did not push the "play" button! The TCC projector just started on its own or else I slipped and hit the button by accident!"

The screen was still a solid red. However, as the TCC projector ran, the red tones flickered into orange and yellow tones. What they were seeing was fire. This was a very special fire indeed, because in the center of it was the very same "throne" the audience had witnessed in the other showings. The throne contained a creature of horrible appearance and who is the head of all demons.

The occupant rose from his seat, casually walked through the flames and approached his hosts. The hosts here were none other than the very same three witches that officiated at the other "Meetups". The DESE audience was awed once more at the constant reappearance of these witches who seemed to be everywhere, but no longer surprised.

The witches were happy to meet the "Master" of all kinds of evil. The tall witches let Miguel Barberry lead the conversation for their group. He said, "It is with pleasure that we meet you. We need to employ the use of one more of the basic elements.

Air[Earth]Water]Fire

We have used AIR in snowstorms. We have used EARTH in earthquakes. We have used WATER in floods. All we are missing is FIRE, the releasing of energy from matter."

The two sinister witches joined in. "We would like to have the fourth element, FIRE, consume the Southeast pine forests especially in Georgia. The District of Columbia would also deserve a nice burn, especially the White House and the Congressional buildings."

Caprae continued alone, "Almost no one likes these legislators, especially me. Most Americans vote for them and put them in office. There they almost never work in the interests of the common person. Their own self-serving interests and welfare are first. However, one must recognize that they do give raises. They raise their salaries and benefits and they then raise the public's taxes. The citizens do not have much of a choice. If that were not enough, they continually tax their people and work to invent ways to separate those who work hard and earn their bread by blood, sweat and tears daily from their earnings."

Mealyworm went on when Caprae stopped, "They tax and tax them while they are alive and then, when they die, they tax whatever they missed while they were alive. Obviously, the dead cannot protest, and their heirs are "under the gun" as it were, to obey the law. The dead and their heirs are defenseless."

Barberry brought the discourse away from politics and back to the witches' interests, "There is still poverty, illness and people starving in the USA. They continue pork barrel legislation for their districts; they betray the interests of other Americans in the remaining forty-nine states. That is selfish and greedy, and they see to it that all Americans pay through the nose for what they do and any errors they make."

He continued, "That alone is good cause, although burning it down would not change much, except to create notice. We want them to notice our cause and right the injustices we have suffered over the centuries to this very day. It is payback time. We will destroy Congress and attack the Mint. We will affect commercial and public interests as well as the monetary system with our attack on the Treasury. It will be terrific!"

Barberry was on a roll. He could not stop. Going on he said, "Even if we do not get the respect and recognition we demand, we will at least have the satisfaction of some measure of revenge for the centuries of wrong against us. We ask you to let us have the gift of Fire."

The Guest answered in a voice that is not of this earth. Its voice was not of man, nor of beast, but a low cross between a cat's purr, a lion's roar, an eighteen-wheeler's gearing down sound and a raspy man's voice. It was not a soothing or a nice voice in any sense. "You already have the gift. I did not give it to you. I am afflicted with it. It is both a blessing and a punishment. You have spells which can be used anywhere. Use it and use it well. Many of those in Congress are working with me and have been doing so for a very long time. I have many "friends" there if you can guess what I mean. They will continue to do so. Your fires will not harm my friends but go ahead. I always approve of destruction, disaster, pestilence, and death. It is my strength!"

The Guest ended his conversation with, "You have my counsel. I will be seeing you shortly. Adieu." The Guest then went back the way he arrived, and the fire and throne vanished.

Mary announced, "This is the end of the final record we have elected to show. It was not necessary for any one of us to enter the pictures. We were quite safe. The recordings were all self-explanatory. The enemy's cause is quite apparent. The question is: What are we going to do about it? We will now go into consultation with each other, in very small groups, and consider the evidence in the showings and conclude regarding our actions to deter and defeat the enemy."

The audience broke up into small groups and began their discourse.

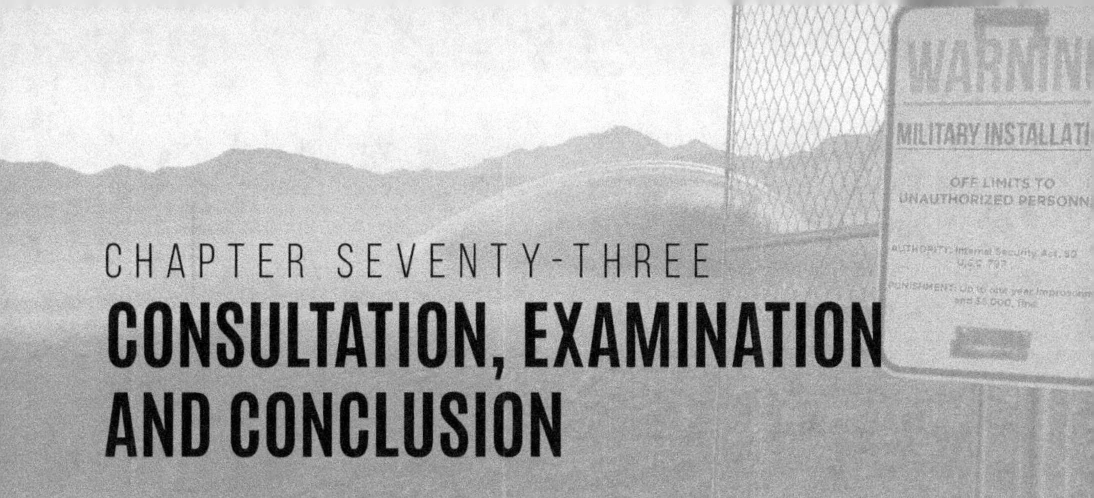

CHAPTER SEVENTY-THREE

CONSULTATION, EXAMINATION AND CONCLUSION

The groups were very small. This audience was very special. It consisted only of those agents who experienced, firsthand, the recordings on the screen. These agents may have arrived after each of the coven "enclaves" or other meetings, but it would be enough. The TCC permits sufficient retrospective information on rewinds into the past for our group to arrive at a final determination as to what was "out there" in very real fact.

Gaunt, Henigson and Henry comprised Group One; Elizabeth, Matt and Frank made up Group Two; Seemore, Carl and Glenn were in Group Three and so forth.

Mary stated, "These groups are to be small and exclusive. You, as participants, are now veterans. Your experiences and opinions are most valuable because you were actually "there". Some of our agents experienced direct confrontation with the evil one." Mary kept her position as mediator and went from group to group to get a sense of each discussion. She wanted to develop an overall opinion before the three groups wrote their report.

Henry was almost an outsider to HB Gaunt. He was, and still is, an old friend of Jack Henigson's. HB did not have the ability of thought transfer and mind read. Henry and Jack did have that special skill well developed at this moment in time. It was a skill most efficient especially between them. HB would be at a disadvantage.

It was laughable to see HB react to the conclusion of a mental conversation between the other two, which they eventually expressed verbally. HB thought the conclusion came out of thin air (which it did). He had no idea that these two already had a serious discussion, which would take ordinary, ungifted mind transferring persons fifteen minutes in vocal conversation to complete, but only one minute in non-verbal mental calisthenics. Ultimately, the two had mercy on HB and kept their conversation audible.

Elizabeth's outer space history remained unknown to Matt and Frank. Her mind reading abilities were limited to reading their thoughts, but conversation on a transference level between the three of them was out of the question. The other two had no inkling whatsoever that Elizabeth was able to read their minds. That is why they both were astonished to have her know what they were going to say before the words left their mouths. It appears Elizabeth, apparently because of a brilliant mind, would arrive at the very same conclusion each of them would. Then she would voice their thoughts using almost the very same words they were ready to employ. They both agreed that Elizabeth must be very brilliant to have the very same good ideas they would express. It was strange though, they thought, that those ideas were essentially simultaneous with their own!

Seemore, Larry, Glenn and Carl comprised the third group. The only super-gifted one there was Seemore. Seemore had attributes that far exceeded the abilities of the other three. The three cohorts would never know and could never comprehend Seemore's hidden gifts.

The collaborations went on for about forty-five minutes. That was a very short time for group discussions at DESE. Usually, such discussions went on for hours. Mary made the rounds and gathered some sense of where the different groups were going.

When it appeared that the three clusters of agents were no longer engaged in active discussion, Mary said, "My dear colleagues, if you are all finished consulting with each other, I am prepared to hear it all. I want you to come up with an analysis of the situation and what is required to combat the menace that is attacking us; I am quite prepared to hear your conclusions. When we have heard the different determinations from each group, we will develop a single plan of action that integrates the conclusions and thoughts of each grouping into one, concise and fully incorporated plan using all our ideas."

The three groups separated themselves from their immediate members, reassembled as the fully configured DESE agency, and quietly waited for Mary to make her request for reports.

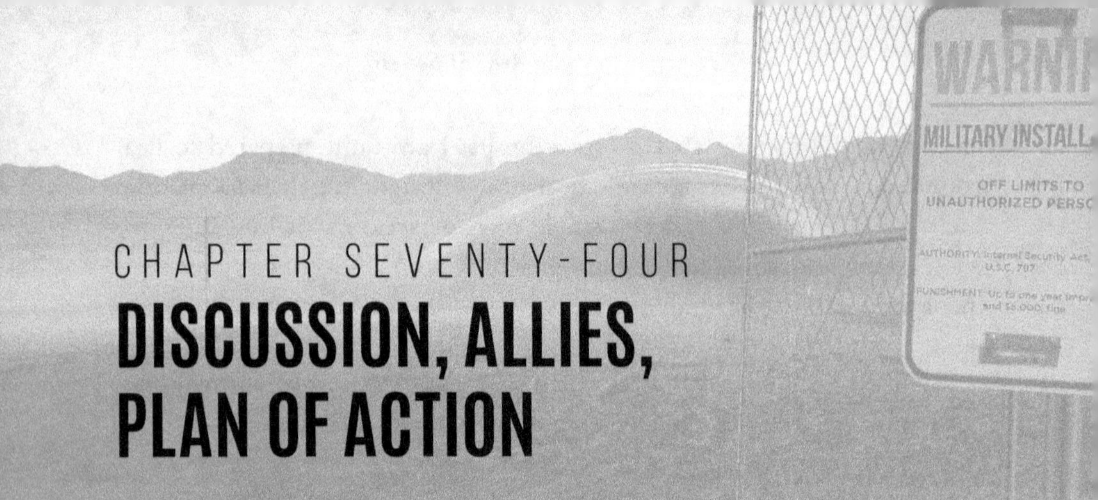

CHAPTER SEVENTY-FOUR

DISCUSSION, ALLIES, PLAN OF ACTION

Mary spoke after the constituency before her quieted down and gave her their full attention.

"The time is here for you to finalize our group thoughts and ideas, although I do not wish to belabor the point. Please, may I have the report from the Gaunt, Henigson team?

The named agents all stood up at the same time. The lead agent was Jack Henigson, who spoke for the group.

"Mary", he started, "This is not an easy matter to deal with. We know we are dealing with the supernatural and the spiritual as well as dark magic. However, the fact that living, flesh and blood human beings are also involved complicates the issue. We see the problem before us as requiring the division of these disparate entities into two main segments.

The first division is for us to deal with the human element. The second part we must deal with is to confront the supernatural element.

There can be no doubt that we have no choice but to intercede as a protagonist and prevent any further destruction of our nation's resources and our citizens' safety. These people are dangerous and as such, they must be stopped now.

We anticipate that dealing with the human element is simpler than the supernatural component. We can employ the DESE mind-changing equipment to rearrange the thoughts and feelings of the witches. We do, however, expect that some witches will have been so indoctrinated that their rescue might not be possible. We will need to deal with them differently.

Dealing with the supernatural portion is many times more difficult and we have not yet determined how to confront them. I am not aware of any DESE armamentaria being available and designed to counteract the supernatural. We need help with that one."

Jack, and his fellows, sat down at the end of his statement.

Mary responded, "Thank you, Jack. Your synopsis is short but to the point. I am hopeful that before our session here is over, we will fully deal with the entire dilemma." Mary paused and looked around. Her eyes rested on the next set of conferees. She then said, "May we now hear from Elizabeth, Matt and Frank?"

The team rose to their feet. However, they did not settle on a speaker to report for the group. There was a short, animated discussion with finger pointing, mumbling and hand waving. They quickly settled the matter and then selected Elizabeth, the girl from out of this world, as their speaker.

"Very interesting", she began, "We also have come to basically the very same conclusion as the previous agents. DESE has mind reading and mind changing devices such as the Cogito-Lector. With that device, we can read and change thoughts and minds. If we can change moods and mindsets with the Cogito-Lector, we can minimize conflict. Fewer people will be hurt, but hopefully no one at all. We are recommending that to approach the first part of the problem. The second part is much more difficult." Elizabeth paused.

"How does one deal with the greatest evil in the world and the universe? Indeed, how does one deal with an evil that has been afflicting man since time began? We cannot change the mind of evil, can we? Perhaps we could direct it elsewhere. Perhaps we could distract and misdirect evil so that we can turn it on itself. That would be most interesting; can one not agree with that?"

Elizabeth continued., "We need something or someone who could counter evil with good. It has to be a very, very special something or someone. If it is a person, should be one who is almost one hundred percent fearless and very brave. The mind of evil is not an easy thing to conquer. The face of evil is a terror to countenance. It is near impossible to bear looking into it. The evil one can turn reality into illusion. That illusion could be either wonderful or horrifying. We may find it impossible to tell reality from that illusion. Should we engage evil in the moral equivalent of "war", one must bet that the illusion the evil one would project would be illusions of horror and not beauty. Only evil can come from evil." Elizabeth's face belied the seriousness of the problem. It was a face of serious concern and deep involvement.

Continuing, "Does DESE have anything in its armamentarium to deal with evil directly? For that matter, what does it need to deal with evil even indirectly? Mary, can you answer that question?"

Mary kept mum for several minutes after that question was posed. She had to run her mind over the DESE inventory. She was deep in thought. After all, Mary was not one hundred percent certain on how to proceed either. However, Mary had absolutely no doubt whatsoever regarding the outcome of this problem.

"Good always wins", she thought to herself.

She answered hesitantly, "Elizabeth, we will wait for all opinions and conclusions to be reported. I believe that good always conquers and neutralizes evil. It may not be an easy thing to master, but I believe that it is possible. Let us now continue with the reports."

Continuing, quite sober because she found that last question difficult to answer, she asked, "Would the third group consisting of Seemore, Larry, Carl and Glen please rise and let us have your conclusions."

This last group already decided who in their group would speak. It was Seemore. Short, though he was in height, he was respected as a giant in his mind, his abilities and personal traits and values. He worked harder than anyone else in his group and his abilities were highly regarded and recognized by his group members.

The four-member group rose to make their report. Seemore stepped forward and said, "My dear DESE associates, the situation is quite bad, but it is not without hope." Seemore paused, placed his index finger on his chin, looked upward thoughtfully and said, "DESE has some fantastic equipment. It is as highly effective as it is highly secret. That is as it should be. DESE instruments have the power to change the world and its history as well. Its ability to enter the past and change minds makes these instruments more than just powerful; it makes them very dangerous. Such instruments cannot be in the public domain."

The audience and Mary were captured in hypnotic attention. Seemore went on, "However, DESE equipment is not all we need to use. We can also call on the good witches of the earth who have not betrayed their calling and their trust to protect and do no harm. They exist in greater numbers than evil ones. If that were not enough, we also have allies who are my friends. These will need to remain secret until they are called upon to help. Beyond that, we can also call upon spiritual sources for help."

Seemore, now fully aware that he was the center of a very captivated audience, experienced an ego boost. Seemore could strut, like a proud rooster. He did exactly that, before the small audience. He enjoyed the attention and the exclusivity his position gave him. Back and forth, he swaggered, spouting his conclusions as he paced.

Seemore explained further, "These entities have been on earth and occupy the entire universe since the beginning of time. They have no hope. They constantly battle to seize the spirits of the innocent and bring them into the fold of evil. They have succeeded only to a minor extent because there does exist counter forces for good, love, caring and protection since the beginning of time."

Continuing Seemore added, "Evil has no chance of winning. However, because of its very nature, it cannot stop itself. It is greedy and gluttonous. Evil never has enough and always wants more and more and still more. Evil wants it all, especially those of unsuspecting innocent human spirits. The unsuspecting ones can be easily swayed. They assume that all those around them are like themselves, innocent in thought, word and deed. Evil finds such spirits attractive bait and seeks them out. These innocents are at greatest risk."

"We suggest that all the counteracting devices of DESE be fully employed. We can enter the picture recordings we already have on file and influence the present and future retroactively. That might be the easiest way to go. We do not know of the future; we can only know of the past. We do not know where or when they will have evil meetups next. We do not know where they plan to afflict our citizens or our society next. We do not know any of their plans or where or how severely they will strike." Seemore said.

Adding to his speech, Seemore said, "I know that DESE has records of where witches of beneficial covens meet. We must enlist their aid against those witches that wish to betray their trusts and the REDE. The good witches will certainly help because it is part of their belief and their sense of duty. They will harm no one and they will help us to protect the environment."

Looking puzzled, Seemore thought aloud, "The problem, however, with entering the pictures to create change is that we will be working in the past. We also need to work in the present as well. We cannot call on my very special friends and their abilities to act against evil if we enter the pictures. They can only act in the present. Their capabilities to counter evil are perhaps greater than all of DESE's armamentaria."

"We need to consider how to deal against evil in the present. We need to know the where, the why and the now." Seemore thus ended his discourse.

Mary acknowledged the point in Seemore's speech and said, "Thank you, Seemore. All that you say is true. The task before us is difficult but we need to act and we need to act now."

"We will look up the meetups of the good covens and, using the Confugio, we will travel to their meets. We will then enlist the aid of those good witches to combat evil. We can once again go in pairs to these coven meetups and present what we know. We need to have them help us to help them protect the people, fauna, and preserve the environment and its contents as is their sworn faith and duty. This is the only way that part of it can be done." Mary said in agreement.

"It is done. This is exactly how we will proceed. We shall go into action, and we will win."

CHAPTER SEVENTY-FIVE

ACTION, CONFRONTATION, BATTLE

The good witches were easily enlisted in the service to change those witches that would produce destruction on the earth and its occupants. They eagerly volunteered. The number of witches that volunteered were so many only the most adept, experienced, and skilled could be accepted. The remaining "good" witches were put on a backup "second string". It would be possible to attack all the evil coven meetups at the same moment across the entire country.

The good witches were soaring high above the earth on their modern souped-up versions of the old-style broomsticks of a hundred years ago. There were chrome-plated and colored enamel broomsticks trimmed with flowing multi-colored streamers. Some of the broomsticks appeared to be jet propelled as they spewed forth a stream of star-like sparks in a "jet" trail behind them. Of course, they were not jet propelled, but they zipped along at high speed. The sky was full of them. There had to be several dozen flying witches dressed in the usual non-descript garb that witches have been always known to wear. The modern style broomsticks were the most modern and fancy thing about them.

The good witches made themselves invisible to those attending the evil coven meetup below. They created balls of water, each of which contained a powerful attitude, mind changing, and spirit healing spell. They hurled the water balls, each the size of a large softball at those below. As the balls of water fell, they split and split repeatedly into smaller and smaller droplets until they became mist-like. Those below barely noticed the falling mists and continued with their meetup, ignoring the mist.

Peganni and his father, Pegasus, flew in tandem. Peganni found it desirable to be on this special mission with his father. Peganni carried Seemore using the Cogito-Lector to read thoughts and induce thought change as needed. Pegasus carried Henry and Elizabeth. These last two worked well together. Since they both were able to read minds, they really only had to employ the Lector thought inducing section and not the mind reading Cogito because they did not need it.

They took turns in reading minds while the other directed the Lector beam to induce thought change and altered the minds of those below from malevolent thought to either a beneficial thought or a neutralization of the evil notions the subject witches possessed.

Both Pegasus and Peganni were able to fly at the Speed of Spirit. Peganni and Pegasus found it to be a simple matter to cover all the evil meetups across the nation in short order. Myriad good witches would already be hovering on their modern broomsticks overhead and hurling their multicolored goodness inducing beneficent spell containing water balls at different national meetups across the country which the PME designated as evil and malevolent. It would seem as though Peganni, Pegasus and their riders would appear in different places at the same time because of the speed of their flights. In any case, appearance would be difficult because of the invisibility shield both Pegasus and Peganni possessed when in flight. No one could see them anyway.

Laggards to mind improvement and change of evil thought found themselves treated to a DESE ground division only to lose to Confugio DESE agents with Cogito-Lector apparatus. The stragglers, those resistant to a resetting mind-change, always lose. The Cogito-Lector is that effective and powerful. These ground trooped DESE agents deal with the hard-core evil witches and develop their battle experience quickly and easily. The witches have no chance whatsoever. However, if they came upon a true demon, the DESE agents had to quickly use the Confugio and leave the scene. That was as ordered. The DESE agents had no protection from the power of true demons. The agents then call in troops more able to cope with and effectively decimate the unchangeable demons' evil nature and evil influence.

The more able troops were the angels, called in by Seemore. The angels were his very special friends he made at the Miracle of Fatima. He also had help from his friends of all kinds. The animals of the forests, the mythological creatures, Peganni, Pegasus and the kind, gentle and beneficent Unicorn mother, all begged the interaction of the heavenly hosts. The angels suddenly appeared out of nowhere, all in different places in the sky. They were already present, but unseen, everywhere as they always are in the battle between good and evil. All they had to do was to materialize and make their presence known.

These were creatures coming from good itself. The angels were heavenly messengers older than the earth itself and champions both in the past and in the present over the likes of demons. Demons knew that they were no match for angels from heaven. All an angel had to do was simply appear. Then each of the demons changed their form and split a million times into a swarm of black flying insects that flew around in large dark clouds eventually melding into the form of a larger demon who just stared at the attackers. The larger demon then again divided, returned to the form of a multitude of flying insects and faded away into holes in the earth and returned from whence they came.

The demons found the presence of immutable good impossible to countenance so they retreated into their holes in the earth. They found good repulsive. They began to develop a severe rash and had to scratch heavily. Those who resisted departing met with heavenly lightning and thunder, which the angels above cast down upon them. Each lightning bolt carried generous doses of goodness. The demons found themselves peppered with goodness.

The demons found all goodness repulsive. The very resistant demons were treated to even more powerful bolts of lightning from the sky, which contained a heavier static electric dose of virtue, kindness, consideration, love and purity. The true demons found this to be poisonous. They could not breathe and began to gasp, choke and had to rapidly retreat to their dark havens within the darkest caverns of the earth, deeper than those that man would ever discover.

It was as though they had an allergy to divine goodness. The angels saw the demons that did not change into insects below raise their thick and heavy claw-ladened leathery wings over their heads to protect themselves from the onslaughts of heavenly goodness. Finally, even these demons crouched low to the earth and disappeared from the scene.

The simultaneous battles across the entire country were magnificent. Each battle had the very same motif. Each was loaded with eclectic participants. The flying good witches on their multicolored broomsticks with flowing streamers and trailing sparks behind along with casting of colored balls of water downward upon the evil witches was much in contrast to the angels which flew above them. The angels spewing forth lightning one bolt after another while the speedy Pegasus and Peganni carried DESE agents using thought and mind changing equipment joined the scene in the creation of a cacophony of color, light and sound confined to the immediate area. However, much was neither heard nor seen by the public because of the participants' invisibility and the speed at which it all happened. All the public was aware of was an occasional thunder boom in the cloudless distance somewhere.

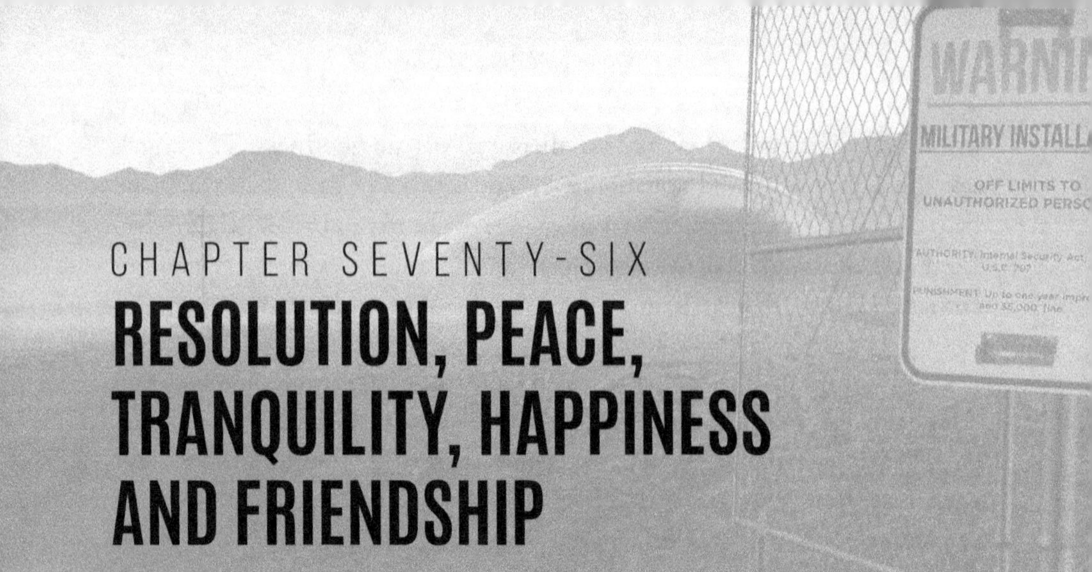

CHAPTER SEVENTY-SIX
RESOLUTION, PEACE, TRANQUILITY, HAPPINESS AND FRIENDSHIP

Defeat of evil has always been the way of the world. Certainly, the demons always try to be victorious in evil. They are most stubborn indeed because that is their programming. They have no choice. On the other hand, their adversaries also, since the beginning of time are programmed to do and create good. The head of demons lost a big battle to them at the beginning of time. That was long, long ago. However, the demons keep trying to get the better of the good angels, but to no avail. They can never win but they can never stop trying to do so. Such is the way it is.

The enemy was now defeated, and all was now well with the world, at least for the present. The DESE agents returned to Headquarters for a final meeting and winding up the loose ends, as they were.

Mary was waiting at headquarters like a mother waiting for her children to return from an outing and to welcome the returning victors. Although they returned over an eight-hour period Mary kept her watch. Near the end of the day, all agents returned exhausted, unharmed but wiser for the experience that made them veterans and also wiser in the ways of man and the spirits around us, both good and evil.

Slowly, HB Gaunt, Jack Henigson, Elizabeth Sam, Henry, Matt Ovlas, Glenn Kohen, Larry Carl, Frank German all returned. They were all tired from their different, but similar, adventures. The DESE staff and cooks amply supplied refreshments and food. The agents were all famished. They ate, and drank heartily. All were happy to have the threat over and to return home.

When the final pair of agents and all the Confugio equipment delivered ground agents was returned, Mary said, "I want to thank you all for what you have done. It is no small accomplishment. You have all done well and we have achieved protection from that threat for our nation. We have forged new alliances, and we are much better off than we were before this matter began."

Mary went on, "It is a fact that the forces of evil never sleep, but then neither do the forces of good. It is a constant battle from the beginning of time. It will not end in our lifetime, and we must always be on guard against evil."

"Thank you all once again. We all can return to our more normal lives at this time. However, you are always on call and will be contacted if needed." The group broke up after Mary said those words and went their different ways.

However, some things would never be the same again. For instance, where would Black Lightning live? Would she remain the pet, "Black Lightning" or would she remain "Elizabeth Sam"?

Then again, aside from being older, Henry would never be the same. He now knew that "Black Lightning" was more than just a cat. Canned pet food was no longer adequate for her tastes at this point. Henry's ability in mental telepathy is now perfect and Elizabeth and Henry were in constant communication with each other. They left the meeting room holding hands, looking into each other's eyes lovingly, and walking out the door.

Then there was Mr. Xilx. As with Elizabeth, who or what he really is no one knew. Was he a cat or a sophisticated world traveler or more? Was he man or extraterrestrial? Jack and Mr. Xilx were now closer friends.

There is also the matter of Mary's obituary notice. The question of whether or not it was real or a ruse to protect Mary from vengeful acts is questionable. Is it true or false?

In the beginning of this treatise, it was written that "it was a dark and stormy night. In addition, it stated that this is the way so many stories start, or at least the way the spooky ones are supposed to start."

That earlier statement now asks you for a definitive conclusion. Was this story spooky at all or do you consider it to be one involving you in a fantasy adventure? The answer to that question is yours alone. Meanwhile, be careful of whatever you think. You never know who is tuning you in!

These matters, and more, are the subject of yet another, probably never-ending story. Stay tuned!